SILENT

Sara Alva

Silent Copyright ©2013 Sara Alva

All rights reserved.

ISBN: 1493665901
ISBN-13: 978-1493665907

Published 2013.

Cover art by Dani Alexander

DEDICATION

For the people who inspired me and kept me writing
through a difficult year.

ACKNOWLEDGMENTS

Thank you to Tim, Dani, Jenn, Marleen, Daniel, Shayla, Luc, Jay, and Madison, without whom I'd still be staring at a Word document.

And thank you again to Dani for creating the perfect cover.

PART ONE

Chapter 1: New Shoes

I eyed my opponents warily, hoping they wouldn't be *too* tight today. If I could get in at just the right angle, and with just the right amount of force…

With one swift movement, I shoved my right foot into the dirty Converse sneaker. That was the best way to do it, but it didn't really make any more room for my big toe. A lump of nail pressed up against the fabric, where it was starting to tear the canvas away from the rubber sole.

Damn. Just when were my feet supposed to stop growing, anyway?

I'd outgrown my shoes enough times by fifteen to know I'd have that awkward, painful limp by the end of the day. For a second I considered trashing the sneakers and putting on flip-flops, but the teachers would probably throw a fit if they saw. No sense inviting trouble. It usually had an easy enough time finding me as it was.

Looked like I was just going to have to suffer through it. I sighed, beginning the torture of my left foot as well.

"Alex!" My mother's voice easily carried through the thin walls. "If that bitch PSA counselor calls here one more time about you cutting class, you won't be able to sit for a damn week!"

From the kitchen came the sounds of clinking beer bottles, which meant her boyfriend, Hector, was getting an early start on his day.

Or maybe not so early. Fuck, I'd be late if I didn't hurry.

I grabbed my backpack off the floor, ignoring the little cockroach that scurried away from its now-exposed hiding place. It quickly found somewhere to slip off to between the wall and floorboards, probably joining hordes of its kind. Gross as it was, it was my own fault—I'd left some tamarindo candy in my bag after Giselle's *quinceañera*.

The train blasting past the house gave me yet another reminder of my tardiness. It rattled the walls and kicked up dust through my open window, adding to the fine layer of soot that blanketed the lone piece of furniture in my room—an old white dresser I'd rescued off the curb a few years back. Of course, it wasn't exactly white anymore.

Taking off as fast as my too-tight shoes would allow, I scrambled down the short hallway and got all the way to the front door before Hector grabbed me and slammed me against the wall.

"Where the hell is my shit?" His stubbled face pressed close to mine, blowing foul beer-and-morning-breath up my nostrils.

I pushed back and easily freed myself from his grip. He wasn't going to be able to jerk me around like this much longer.

"Get the fuck off, man. I have school." Some of the paint chipped off the wall behind me and fell onto cracked linoleum as I stepped away.

"I know you took it, *hijo de puta*. You fucking touch my shit again, I don't care if you are your mami's son. You living in my fucking house. I can kick you out like I did your *puta* sister."

"Fuck off, Hector."

He raised his arm and struck my chest, making me bang my head into the wall. More paint—or maybe a bit of drywall from an already cracked surface—fell to the ground. Hector's rage-filled eyes darted over to observe the damage, and before he had a chance to regroup, I ducked, whirled, and burst out the front door.

I ran for a couple of blocks. I didn't really need to, because Hector was far too lazy to actually come after me, and probably too out of shape to catch me if he did. I was sure he'd just storm back to the fridge and pull out another beer, then crawl into bed next to my mother and—

I cut off the image before it went any further, distracting myself by pounding the pavement as fast as I could. People tended not to run through the streets in my neighborhood unless they were in trouble...and when you were in trouble, you weren't going to be running at no jogging pace. If fitting in meant dashing down the road like I had the cops on my tail, I was okay with that.

That is, I was okay with it until my toes started to feel like they were going to bruise black and blue from the pressure. I eventually limped to a stop, sensing a bit of cool air against my foot where it was not meant to be. One look down confirmed my fears—my sock was clearly poking through the front of my right shoe.

Fuck. Like I didn't already look ghetto enough.

I started hobbling at an awkward pace, trying to find the balance between the usual *I do as I please* saunter and the *I really should get to school* speed-walk. It was hard to look cool with my feet busting out of my shoes, but I still fought to maintain the image, giving my usual head-nod to the bums outside the local liquor store.

A stray mutt—with a lot of pit bull in its mix—bounded across the street in front of the little *tienda* where we bought groceries. Mr. Jimenez instantly appeared in the doorway with his broom, shaking it in front of his solid potbelly. When that failed to scare the pup, he resorted to shoving it away. He made the same shooing motion toward me as well, probably because I'd been known to lift a bag of hot Cheetos or two on occasion.

I gave him a sarcastic wave and decided to cut through the projects, keeping my head down, as always, when I passed anyone particularly shady-looking. Most of the prostitutes had hidden themselves away by this hour, but one strung-out druggie was still wandering down the littered sidewalk. She muttered loudly to herself about needing a goddamn pillow, scratching pointlessly at the lice that had already set up long-term residence on her scalp.

I used to look for Mimi around there, but deep down I knew she'd never be that close to home.

I barely made it into school by the second bell, when the principal's booming voice came over the loudspeaker to threaten us into heading to class.

"Ey, *cabrón*, where you been?" José appeared among the crowd of scattering students. He slapped my hand in greeting.

A short kid, and swarthy—like me, of course—José and his round cheeks hadn't quite grown out of that baby-fat stage, though I could tell from the new slicked-back hair routine he was desperately trying to look older.

"S'up."

"You keep this up, man, you gonna fail again, then you'll be the oldest kid in high school."

"Shut the fuck up." I shoved him into some nearby lockers, as was my right. Yes, I was old for a freshman, and yes, I'd been held back—in the fifth grade. But fuck if that wasn't a lousy year. I'd had other shit to worry about besides how many fucking words I could read per minute.

José pretended to be pissed, but one of the advantages to being older was being bigger, and I knew he wouldn't mess with me.

"Shit, man, what the fuck. I was just kidding. Besides, you gonna get tons of freshman pussy being all old and shit. The girls love that shit."

I mechanically bumped fists with José in agreement.

"Ey, what about that girl in pre-algebra…Blanca…she *fine*, and you can just tell she gonna be real easy. She's like dying to lose it. You should get with her this weekend."

My shoulders tensed but I rolled it off, shrugging. "Nah, man. I don't got no money to buy condoms right now…and ain't no way I'm gonna knock up some freshman."

"Yeah." José nodded, all serious-like. "No way."

I briefly wondered how many other guys had had this same conversation in the hallway, only to have their women become one more statistic.

I had high hopes I'd avoid that cliché.

~*~

I slipped into homeroom during the one-minute grace period, pulling out a book so I could pretend to be busy if Mrs. Elridge set her evil eye on me.

She looked pretty groggy this morning as she sipped her morning coffee. Hopefully she wouldn't be too strict on the "silent reading" bullshit. On the other hand, too little sleep made her cranky, which she damn well liked to take out on us.

"Edgar Alcazar," she droned from behind her computer, calling roll.

Edgar, the runt in the first row, raised his pipsqueak hand. "Here!"

"Alejandro Alvarez."

Bitch. No matter how many times I told her to call me Alex, she insisted on using my full name, adding an extra throaty rasp on the *j* like she wasn't the whitest lady I'd ever seen.

"Ey, ey, Alex."

Diego was trying to get my attention from a few desks away. He was too cool to pass a note or reach out to tap my shoulder—not that I would have minded the contact—so he just jerked his head at me until I looked over.

He wasn't my closest friend, and I did have weak moments when I wanted to change that. With his soft olive skin and Anglo features he could almost pass for a White, but I knew he'd much rather belong to the *barrio* instead...which was one of the reasons he was best kept at arm's length.

I leaned over to hear him once Ms. Elridge had taken my attendance.

"My sister said she saw your sister up at 68th the other day."

"Yeah?" I perked up.

"Yeah, they say she got a new boyfriend."

"A real boyfriend?" I stupidly asked, and damn it if I didn't let a little hope slip into my voice.

Diego gave me a look like *no seas tonto*. "Yeah, I'm sure he's Prince fucking Charming."

"Huh. Yeah."

"Silent reading!" Ms. Elridge ordered, and I slumped back into my chair. She passed down the aisle, eyes peeping out from over her tiny glasses. For a moment her gaze went to the floor, and I tried to hide the gaping hole in my shoe by covering it with my other foot.

Ms. Elridge pursed her lips and moved on.

The bell sounded a little while later, and I hopped up with the rest of the crowd, slinging my bag over my shoulder as I strode toward the door. I never rushed to class—only losers did that—but I was probably a little slower than usual thanks to my damn shoes.

"Alejandro?" Ms. Elridge's voice stopped me in my tracks.

Damn. Maybe there was something to be said for rushing.

"Yeah?"

"I couldn't help noticing your shoes," she began, fidgeting with a pen in her hand. "Are you planning on getting new ones anytime soon?"

I squinted in shame. "Nah, teacher. My mom, she don't...doesn't have no job, and I spent all my money on a new D.S. game before I realized my shoes had got so tight."

"On a D.S. game," she repeated, one eyebrow tilting up. "That might not have been the smartest choice, whether your shoes were tight or not. Where do you get your money from, by the way? Gift money? Allowance? Or do you work?"

"Uh, gift money," I stuttered.

And that would've been true, if Hector had gifted me his weed to resell.

"Well next time, consider saving it for something more valuable. Maybe you could start a college fund."

I gave her a blank stare, which was what she deserved. They could ram college-readiness down my throat all they wanted—didn't mean I was going anywhere.

"Right, teacher. Can I go to class?"

"All right, Alejandro." She sighed, and I knew she could tell she hadn't made much of an impression. "See you tomorrow."

~*~

Hector's pick-up wasn't in front of the house when I got home. I thanked God for small miracles and bounded inside, putting on my brightest face.

"Hey, Mom." I plopped down on the lumpy couch by her side and kissed her cheek.

She was all done up—false lashes, a ton of makeup, and fake blond hair hanging stiffly to her shoulders. I knew she felt like she had to work to keep Hector's interest, since he was only thirty-two, but I sometimes missed the soft halo of dark curls she'd had when I was younger.

"Hi, baby," she responded, her eyes barely shifting from the TV. She absentmindedly ran her freshly-manicured nails through a hole in the upholstery, plucking out some of the stuffing.

Her favorite telenovela was on, so I smartly waited till the commercial before interrupting again. "Mamá, do you think I could get some new shoes?"

She frowned. "I just bought you shoes the other day."

I rolled my eyes and worked on keeping my cool. The other day, the other year…who was counting?

"Please, Mami. The teachers at school are starting to notice."

"I don't have no money right now."

"You could ask Hector—"

"Hector's not gonna buy you nothing." She cut me off. "He's pissed at you."

I blinked, striving for the face of innocence. "Why, Mami?"

"You think I don't know?" She snorted. "I'm not stupid, Alex."

Damn.

"Besides," she continued, sighing, "you know he don't like that I can't give him a son, and you remind him of that."

I used to feel a twinge of guilt every time my mother brought up how having me caused that infection…until the day Mimi told me that was the best thing that could have happened to her. Having a kid with Hector would only have made a bad situation worse.

I wiggled a little closer, lacing my fingers with hers. "You don't have to say the money is for me."

She batted me away. "Ay, go get a job like other kids your age. You should already be in high school last year, you know. High school kids work."

"What job?" I asked, throwing up my arms in frustration. "What kind of job you want me to do while I'm going to school?"

The telenovela was back on, taking my mother's focus. "I don't know. Pick up cans with the immigrant children."

I resisted the urge to call my mother a bitch, even in my thoughts. She was more out-of-it than she was outright mean.

But I did need those shoes.

I left her and headed down the hallway, taking full advantage of her distraction. She didn't notice me slipping into her room—or *his* room, as he constantly reminded me.

I slid the dresser drawer open as quietly as I could. The last time I'd jacked some weed from this spot, I thought I'd left enough in the bag to keep him from noticing. But he had noticed, obviously, and there was none in there anymore. Time to check the other hiding places.

I rummaged through the remaining drawers, the closet, and underneath the mattress before I finally found some in the hollowed out bedpost. I took a decent handful, even though I knew I'd probably be in for an ass-kicking later. With any luck, I'd have new shoes to make the running away that much faster.

~*~

I exchanged the torn sneakers for my flip-flops and wandered over to the squat black and white buildings of the projects. We'd lived there once—just me, my sister, and my mom. Yeah, the places were crappy and some of the residents sketchy at best, but it wasn't like living a few streets away in an old crumbling house was all that much better. Besides, Hector's name was on the lease for the house, and that alone made it suck in my eyes.

Our old neighbor, Andre, was sitting in a lawn chair in front of his place, smoking and drinking a beer, as usual.

"Hey," I said as I approached. "What up, man?"

"Hey, Al. Whatcha up to today?"

After a quick glance around, I pulled the plastic baggy halfway out of my pocket. "You need?"

Andre grimaced and wiped his forehead with his arm before taking a long drag of his cigarette. "Nah, chico. Not today."

"What?" I blurted out. "But I only gave you a dime sack last time…you must be out by now. C'mon, Andre."

Damn, could I sound more desperate?

"Listen, listen." He put up his hands. "Don't flip, man, but I found me another supplier."

My left eye began twitching. Andre was one of the few people I knew well enough to feel comfortable dealing to. Without him, my moneymaking days were close to over.

"Someone else? Who?"

He looked away. "Franky."

Franky? That fucking gangbanger was moving in on my tiny turf?

"Franky? Jesus Christ, why?" I pressed, trying and probably failing to keep from sounding like a whining child. "Don't I always give you the good stuff…the best price?"

"You do, you do, little man…but it's about supply. Franky works for the big dogs—they always got stuff. You a kid stealing weed off your old man."

"Hector is not my old man!" My hands curled into fists. If Andre hadn't been twice my size, I probably would've taken a swing at him.

"Easy." He stood and pulled a box of cigarettes from his pocket to offer me one. I took it because I couldn't really think of anything else to do, and I obviously needed to calm down.

"Tell you what I'm gonna do," Andre said. He lit up my cigarette and waited till I'd drawn in a few times before throwing an arm over my shoulder. "I'll buy it off you today, 'cause I can see you really need it…but I can't keep it up. You gettin' too old to freelance…don't you wanna get jumped in? You'd make real money then."

I twisted away. "Nah, man. I'm cool. Lemme just sell this and go—I gotta go buy me some shoes."

Andre shrugged, pulling out a wad of cash from his pocket. "Suit yourself. But you're probably gonna have to make a decision about where your loyalties lie pretty damn soon. You ain't no baby no more. You sell to the wrong person…you could get yourself in real trouble, man."

We finished our transaction and said our goodbyes—possibly for the last time. There was no way I was joining a gang in these parts—and not for the reasons everyone thought. I wasn't too good for it, and I wasn't chicken…but I also wasn't stupid.

A gang in the ghetto wasn't no place for someone like me.

~*~

That night I shoved my new shoes into the bottom of my backpack before climbing into bed. I lay awake for about thirty minutes, staring up at the ceiling and thinking about the homework I hadn't done. Eventually I crawled out from the blankets and grabbed my shoes again, so I could pull them into the bed with me. They were shiny and white, and in the light of the street lamps streaming through my window they nearly glowed.

Mimi told me it was dumb to always buy white shoes, but she just didn't understand. Yeah, they got dirty faster, but there were those few glorious days where they were the brightest things I owned, and everybody who looked at me would know I'd just bought something new. You couldn't really get that effect with the more practical black shoes.

It was stupid, but I kept the sneakers next to me in the bed. I wrapped my arms around them like they were some kind of teddy bear, stroking the material between my thumb and forefinger until I fell asleep.

~*~

I awoke to a hand pressed over my mouth.

"Don't make a sound, *pendejo*."

Hector's speech was slurred, but he had a firm grip on my face, causing my lips to press painfully into my teeth.

In his other hand, he held my shoes.

"This what you buy after you steal from me, you little shit? This fucking shit?"

I tried to speak, but Hector tightened his hand, digging a nail into my cheek.

"You too fucking pussy to be a real man, so you think you can just take what you want, eh? Well you're wrong, little *maricón*. You never gonna take from me again."

He grabbed his lighter out of his pocket, releasing my mouth to do so.

"No, Hector, please!" Tears sprung to my eyes, not from the pain so much as the humiliation. It'd been stupid to think I could get away with taking so much from him...but I had *needed* those shoes!

And now they were about to go up in flames.

He lit the canvas and tossed them in my trash bin, where the crumpled wads of paper soon caught fire.

I knew it was a lost cause, but I jumped up from my bed anyway. "Hector, no!"

His hand flew across my mouth and I dropped to the floor, stunned, my lower lip stinging.

"Please," I begged. "I need them for school."

The tears escaping now, I crawled over to the trashcan as if there was something I could do to stop my shoes from becoming a pile of ashes.

"Cry all you want, pussy. Your mama's good and drunk and fucked to sleep."

A flame shot up over the rim of the can, licking at my face, and the heat ignited my fury. I charged to my feet and tried to ram Hector's body with everything I had in my five-foot-eight frame.

But through the anger and the tears, I wasn't thinking properly, and I just ended up in his grasp again. Except this time, he locked onto my wrist and flicked on his lighter, holding my arm against the flame.

I screamed and tried to pull away but he had me pinned, and it wasn't until spots of pain blocked my vision that he let me go.

I crumpled to the dirty hardwood, too exhausted to cry any more.

"Don't you forget," Hector said, and walked out.

Chapter 2: Up to No Good

I lay in a heap for a while, watching the fire. The flames danced with such energy, in complete control of their small world. I felt a bit like a fire sometimes...storming through life like I had shit all figured, when really any asshole could come along and put me out.

I managed to gather myself off the floor, ignoring the pain long enough to grab an old towel and smother the fire to death. When the room was dark again, I waited for my eyesight to adjust before examining my injury. The skin of my wrist was red and raw, and it was blistering slightly.

Staggering footsteps led me to the kitchen, where I took a bag of French fries out of the freezer. I held my breath, counted to five, and gingerly placed it on my arm.

A second later, I dropped the bag on the floor, intense pain rocketing through me and making me hiss out several half-formed curses. I shoved my good arm in my mouth to muffle the rest of what I wanted to scream. The last thing I needed was another confrontation with Hector.

Leaving the damn fries lying on the ground, I rifled through a kitchen drawer to find some aspirin. Then I dragged out a bottle of tequila and used it to knock back four pills, hoping the shot would make me woozy enough to fall asleep despite the pain.

I took the bottle back to bed with me, just in case I needed a little more help.

~*~

"Alejandro!"

My mother stood at my bedroom door in her glittery pink tank top and jean mini-skirt, a hand on her narrow hip. "What are you doing? Get your ass up and go to school!"

I tried to move and flinched when my arm touched the blanket. "Mami, I don't feel so good. Can't you call and say I'm sick?"

"You better get your ass up and go. Hector and I are going out of town for a few days. I don't have time to deal with you."

She stepped away then, leaving me to my pounding headache and fucked-up wrist.

When she and Hector had driven off, I got up and carefully dressed. My wrist had patchy, peeling red spots of skin from the burns, and I knew I'd have to cover it up before I left the house.

Feet shoved in flip-flops, I dug through the bathroom and the hallway closet in search of gauze. I didn't really think we'd have any, unless Mimi had bought it for some reason. My first instinct was right, however. We were not a first-aid-prepared household.

In the end, I grabbed some toilet paper and wrapped it loosely around my wrist. I taped it down and decided it looked close enough to a bandage. As close as I could get, anyhow.

José was waiting for me a block away from the school.

"Flip-flops?" He pointed a stubby finger at my feet, taunting me with his laughter. "Ooh, you gonna get in trouble."

"Fuck off," I grumbled. Obviously, I was in no mood for his stupidity.

He stopped. He could hear the tone in my voice, and he knew I'd back it up with a fist if I had to.

"What's the matter? Hector beating up on you again? Your lip looks a little fat. And what the fuck is that on your arm?"

I shot out the tip of my tongue, passing it over my lip and feeling the small cut there. "He's being a fucking asshole, but thank God he and my mom left town today. Probably going to Vegas or something."

"You have the house to yourself?" José's eyes lit up. "Fuck yeah, man! Let's have a party!"

I still had a headache, and the idea of loud noise and drunken partygoers making a mess of Hector's place didn't sound all that tempting.

"I dunno, man. I'm not sure when they gonna be back."

"We have to, Alex! I have some beer…you can take some of Hector's weed…"

My wrist throbbed.

"Nah, man. I can't do that no more."

"Fine." He rolled his eyes. "Then we get someone else to bring some. We can do it tonight…they ain't gonna be back in one day."

"But I can't cut class. The PSA counselor said she's gonna turn my mom in to the DA if I keep cutting. She'll kill me."

"Okay, so we end it early and go to school the next day. It'll be Friday—we can make it through one Friday with a little hangover, can't we?"

José blinked at me hopefully, his smile pushing out those round cheeks of his. As annoying as he was

16

sometimes, it was hard not to like him…the way you liked an ugly stray dog that came around begging for scraps.

"Fine. But you better stay and help me clean up so I don't catch shit."

If he had been a dog, he'd have been wagging his tail and jumping up and down with excitement when I finally gave in.

~*~

Blanca draped herself on me, purring into my ear. "You sexy, Alex, you know that?"

"Mhm," I replied absentmindedly. I'd been told I was fairly good-looking by several girls, so I had no reason to doubt her.

Music blared and smoke filled the house. With the lights dimmed and all the smiling people moving about, it almost didn't look like the shithole it was. Of course, the main reason it was such a shithole was because of Hector's parties—some asshole or another was always getting a little too high and breaking a chunk of wall or a piece of furniture.

Someone on my left passed me a blunt, and I took it gratefully.

"What's on your arm?" Blanca's tiny fingers danced along my chest, making their way toward the bandage. "You been wearing that all day."

"Nothing." I tried to shoo her away, but she persisted.

"You got jacked up by your stepdad again?"

Bitch.

"He ain't married to my mom, and you know that. He ain't never gonna marry her."

At least, not if I had anything to say about it.

Blanca stuck out her lower lip, tilting her head in a way she probably thought made her look cute. "Sorry, baby." Her hands kept rubbing my chest. "But why you let him beat up on you like that?"

"Shit, I didn't let him do nothing." I glared at her. "I popped him right in the face. If he didn't have that damn lighter, I woulda fucking messed him up."

She wiggled even further into my lap, and suddenly her lips were moving against my ear. "I know it, papi."

I jerked in my seat to stop her breath from tickling me. "Blanquita, you making my leg fall asleep. Can you move?"

Her nose curled up. "But Alex—"

Careful to keep my injured arm away from her, I stood, and she slid right to the floor. "You heavy, and I gotta take a leak."

"I am not heavy, *pendejo!*" she called after me as I stumbled down the hallway. "You'd best come back and let me sit on you to prove it!"

She probably weighed eighty pounds when wet, but I had no intention of letting her lay her grabby hands on me all night. José was right when he'd said she was a total slut-in-training—anyone could see it.

I found a ragged patch of grass and weeds in the corner of the backyard to finish off the blunt, away from all the cramped bodies. I needed the time alone to process the mess of feelings—the general happiness that so far, my life was still normal…and the growing fear that it was getting just a little bit harder to maintain every day.

Diego strode over to invade my solitude, and again, my emotions were split. I minded…but I didn't, really.

"Yo." His long, thin fingers tapped his cigarette. Ash fell to the ground, almost touching my bare toes. "What up, Alex?"

I instantly zoned in on his hands, unable to tear my eyes away. Weed did that to me, sometimes…made tiny things seem like they were the most interesting objects in all the world.

And Diego just happened to have really nice fingers.

I passed him the blunt—I'd obviously had enough—and our hands touched for just a moment.

ABCDEFG, HIJKLMN...

I screamed the alphabet in my head to keep my thoughts in check. It was an old trick, and not my best, but I wasn't at my smartest when high.

"You know, I saw Franky today. He wanted to talk to you," Diego said.

I stopped the alphabet. "Franky? Why?"

"Why do you think, *cabrón*? He knows you deal...you lucky he hasn't told nobody else yet. You lucky *I* haven't told nobody else yet. What the hell you fucking around for? Why the hell don't you want to get jumped in?"

Again with the fucking gang. My thoughts on Diego's fingers quickly faded into the background, and even high I knew this problem was only going to grow.

"Listen," Diego continued. "I might be able to talk to someone about getting you in. Not José, though. Don't tell that little fool."

I shrugged awkwardly—first one shoulder, then the other. Hopefully Diego would blame that on me being drunk and not me being so nervous I could feel my heartbeat in my throat. "I'm fine with what I got goin' on right now."

Diego rolled his eyes. "What you so scared of, man? They ain't gonna break your bones or nothing. You just cover your face, it's over in a few minutes, and you can be the fucking boss of this shit place."

He fake-jabbed at me, and I ducked. "Yeah...'cause I always wanted to be the boss of a shit place."

"Man, it's gotta be better than that dime shit you doin' by yourself."

I shook my head. "Nah, I'm not doing that no more."

"Why not?"

"Uh, I..."

Fuck, he had me against a wall. I couldn't tell him it was because of lack of supply—he'd have an obvious solution to that problem.

Diego inhaled from his cigarette, his long fingers twitching. "You either a fucking coward, or you think you better than us...which would be pretty fucking stupid, considering you a bastard kid living off your mama's deadbeat boyfriend."

My stomach twisted, dark thoughts flooding my head. And not the kind of thoughts I could keep back by screaming the alphabet. How long could I put it off? How long could I hold on to this life before I became the outcast, or the enemy?

Andre was right. I wasn't a kid anymore. I'd have to make a decision soon, but either way I had the sinking feeling I was damned.

"I gotta go back in. Blanca's waiting for me, man. I think I'm gonna get some tonight."

Out of the frying pan and into the fire.

~*~

Blanca rolled over, her skinny arm slapping my wrist and making me cringe. I needed to blink several times to get the room into focus, but once I had, I immediately wanted to shut my eyes again.

Beer cans lined the floor of my bedroom, along with cigarette butts and general filth. And, of course, there was a naked girl in my bed, which really just completed the whole fucked-up picture.

"Blanca." I nudged her. "Wake up."

The early-morning light streamed through my window, lighting up the dust and dirt particles in the air.

"Blanca, wake up. We gotta go to school."

She yawned delicately. "Mmm, why don't we just stay here? I hate school."

I made a frantic scan of the room and sighed in relief when I found the tied-off condom on the floor.

Blanca caught it and giggled. "You didn't think I was that drunk, did you? No way I'm letting you ruin this body."

She kicked off the covers and stood, flouncing her hair and thrusting out her tiny hip.

If she'd had a bit less breast, she almost could've passed for a boy. A little boy.

But I wasn't no pedophile.

"Get dressed and get moving."

~*~

Diego wasn't the only one with his head down on the desk in homeroom that morning. There were a few other people with bleary red eyes and greasy hair, as well as two empty seats. I'd downed a couple of aspirin before coming and replaced my makeshift toilet paper bandage with a paper towel one, figuring that would hold up a bit better to the daily wear and tear.

And it was Friday, after all. I only had one day left to survive until I could lock myself away for the weekend. With any luck, I'd be alone, too. I didn't need my mom or Hector around to screw up my privacy...and the time I needed to do some serious, not-high thinking.

"Psst." Diego waved a hand at me. "Did you fuck Blanca?"

I grinned. At least there was a bright side to that— bragging rights, and a little taste of normalcy. Maybe continuing to sleep with girls would be the answer to all my problems. "Yeah, man. She's a good lay."

Not that I remembered much of it.

"I bet. Jeremy...he a junior...he said she a tight little thing."

"Jeremy?" I frowned. "I thought Blanca was a virgin."

Diego burst out laughing. "Blanca a virgin? Yeah right, *idiota*!"

"Diego and Alejandro!" Ms. Elridge snapped. "Come to the front right now!"

Aw, fuck.

I slid up toward her desk, trying to keep the *thwack-thwack* of my flip-flops as quiet as possible. Diego walked over with his hands in his pockets, never dropping his cool-persona for a moment. I couldn't help but find his defiance impressive. And maybe a little attractive.

"A young lady's virginity is not open for discussion in this school at any time, silent reading or otherwise."

Her face was all pinched, making little lines appear on her lips.

"If I hear you discussing it again, you can go to the office and discuss it with the principal."

"Yes, Ms. Elridge," we said in near-unison, then shuffled back to our seats. Diego didn't look my way for the rest of the period.

Not really a good start to the morning...I should have known things would only go from bad to worse.

I tried to move a little faster to get out of the room when the bell sounded, since Ms. Elridge was already pissed at me. But one of my flip-flops ended up flopping right off my foot, and I stumbled like a fool, getting a laugh from more than a few classmates. They sobered quickly, though, when Ms. Elridge zeroed in on me.

"Alejandro, I need to speak with you."

Everyone else dashed out of the room, before she could find some offense they'd committed as well.

"Yes, teacher?"

"Flip-flops in class?" She raised her eyebrows menacingly. "You know that's not appropriate foot wear for school. If there were an emergency—an earthquake or something—you would not be able to move quickly and safely."

We'd had to rush for gun lockdowns much more than for earthquakes, but she'd never bring that up.

"Sorry, teacher. I know I need new shoes, but I haven't gotten them yet."

"And just what is that you've been wearing on your arm? Some kind of gang fashion statement?"

I glanced over at my paper-towel bandage and held back a snort of laughter. What kind of gang would be that stupid?

"No, ma'am. I just got a little...cut...and we ran out of Band-Aids."

Her eyes narrowed, like a predator picking up some kind of scent.

"Let me see. You might need to go to the nurse to get it cleaned up."

Fuck!

"No, teacher, it's okay. I promise."

"Alejandro." She tsked, opening her desk drawer to get out an office referral slip. "Take it off right now, and I'm writing you a pass to the nurse for a proper bandage."

Heaving a sigh, I carefully put my finger under the tape and ripped the paper away.

I heard her sharp intake of breath, and immediately knew I was in for trouble.

"That's a burn, Alejandro!"

"Oh, yeah."

"Well, how did you get it?"

Damn. Story time.

An image of Juanita Romero flashed into my mind. Everyone in second grade had called her *la monstrua* because of the strange, thickly puckered scars on her body. Turned out they were caused by burns, from when her *abuela* had spilled some boiling soup on her. I'd teased her that year, like all the rest, but at the moment, I might've called her *mi salvador*.

"Soup," I said with complete confidence. "I spilled some soup on myself."

But predator-Ms. Elridge one-upped me on that one right away. "What kind of soup?"

23

What kind of soup? Jesus, I didn't know. My mom didn't make soup. I didn't like to eat soup. What kind of soup would a normal family be making? Did different soups make different kinds of burns?

And why was I taking so damn long to answer?

"Um...ch-chicken soup."

Ms. Elridge's eyes were narrowing into slits, and her brows were so furrowed they were going to meet in the middle. "Alejandro...did someone in your family do this to you?"

And that was when I made my biggest mistake.

Both palms instinctively made fists, and the tension in my injured arm aggravated the wound once again, sending sparks of pain to cloud my thoughts. "Just because that fuck-up lives with my mom don't make him family!"

I did not get reprimanded for my outburst. Instead, Ms. Elridge's pen started scribbling furiously on her referral slip, and she stood seconds later.

"Go to the nurse," she ordered, and I didn't stick around to ask questions. I left immediately, crumpling up the referral and heading off to class instead.

But Ms. Elridge left the room right after me, her heels clip-clopping straight for the office...and I just knew the bitch was up to no good.

Chapter 3: Keep Your Mouth Shut

"Man!" José greeted me outside our last period. He had less gel in his hair than normal, and it made him look softer...more like the kid I'd known when we were younger instead of like a wannabe *cholo*. "Ey, you fucking scored last night!"

Suddenly longing for simpler times, I barely gave him a nod. "Mhm."

"You gotta give me some pointers or something. The girls are fuckin' all *over* you."

If I could have, I'd have happily turned over all the attention I received, but sadly the only real advice I could give him would be to grow a few inches taller.

"Yeah, man. You just gotta act cool about it...like you don't want 'em." At least that wasn't too far off base, in my experience.

We strutted in, and the moment I took my seat, Blanca whirled around to bat her dark lashes at me. I wondered when she'd had the chance to put on so much makeup— she must've had it in her backpack or something. I rarely saw her without the perfectly drawn eyebrows and glossy lips.

While Mr. Ricks droned on about x and its values, I offered Blanca a cocky half-smile, dredging up brief glimpses of the night before.

I remembered her pushing me down on the mattress, and then forcefully undressing me. I might've tried to do the same to her, but I'm pretty sure I needed some help. Beyond that, I recalled her inviting smile, and the way she'd rubbed my bare chest with those tiny but surprisingly strong hands—hard enough that it was almost painful.

She'd definitely been in control. Of course she wasn't a virgin.

Rosa—the girl who sat one row up and over—passed me a folded piece of paper. I didn't have to look at Blanca's wink to know it was from her.

Let's have fun this weekend.

I closed my eyes, slouching in my chair so Mr. Ricks wouldn't yell at me for sleeping in class.

What would it be like, if I really could have fun with her? Maybe I could learn to like her a little more…and maybe being sober would help. Of course, my first awkward attempts at sex had been sober ones, but maybe now that I had a clue about how things worked I wouldn't be such a fucking wreck.

I tried to imagine myself smiling up at her as she mounted me, and actually meaning it. Imagine her fingers sliding over my chest in slow, *gentle* circles…then gradually traveling downwards…

But damn it if those fingers didn't turn into Diego's the moment I let my guard down.

A loud knock collapsed my daydream. My hands instantly curled around the bottom of the plastic chair, heart pounding out a responsive rhythm…like I knew it was for me before the door even opened.

Mr. Ricks greeted a plump woman in a tired-looking gray suit and a cop, and the three of them spoke quickly in hushed voices.

"Alejandro Alvarez?"

My mouth went dry. A fucking *cop* needed to see me? Could someone have ratted me out for the occasional drug deal? Jesus...I was so small time I hardly deserved an arrest on school grounds, right?

"Alejandro?"

Stomach sinking, I stood and walked to the front of the class. "Yeah?"

"Get your belongings." Mr. Ricks' eyes darted about worriedly.

I backtracked and grabbed my stuff, giving José a nervous glance and not receiving any comfort from his rapid, fearful blinks. "'kay, see you tomorrow, Mr. Ricks."

He tilted his head and avoided my gaze. "Goodbye, Alejandro."

The woman in the gray suit moved in without hesitation, hovering around me like some kind of color-sapped bee. "Alejandro, my name is Suzie. We'd just like to speak to you for a moment, in the front office, if that's okay."

The cop may have distracted me at first, but when no one slapped on cuffs and the adrenaline began to wear off, I suddenly realized there was another dangerous force at work here—Suzie practically smelled of social worker.

Reacting on instinct, I threw up my defenses. "I gotta lot of homework, lady. I can't stay too late."

The cop crossed his arms, a silent witness to her annoyingly calm voice.

"Well, let's just settle in the office and see if we can't clear things up."

We entered the conference room together, and I sat stiffly in a little chair, reminding myself over and over again that I just had to keep my mouth shut. The school psychologist was also there, but I decided to ignore her since we'd never actually met. I was a little screwed up, I knew, but not bad enough to need her services.

She seemed satisfied with my choice as she folded her hands over her skirt and relaxed in her chair. She was obviously only there to observe…what could very well be my destruction.

Before Ms. Suzie Social Worker could even get out a word, the nurse bustled into the room in her gigantic flower muumuu and white overcoat.

"Let me see da burn, hun," she said in her thick Nigerian accent.

"It's nothing." I tucked my arm behind my back. "I spilled soup. Chicken soup."

The cop and the social worker exchanged glances. The kind of knowing glance that said, *oh boy, do we ever know he's lying.*

God damn it.

How could I possibly have been so stupid as to slip up in front of Ms. Elridge? It had to be because I was hung over. I refused to believe that after fifteen years of managing my life perfectly fine, I'd let one lousy teacher get the better of me for no apparent reason.

The social worker rifled through some papers in a manila folder. "You and your mother live with a man named Hector Ramirez, correct?"

"So what?" I shot back.

"Did someone at home cause those burns?"

I felt my nostrils flare, so I shook my head violently to cover it up. "Nope. No. It was an accident. Why're you asking about Hector? Ms. Elridge said something? She's fu—…she's nuts. She's just pissed 'cause I'm wearing flip-flops…and talking about this girl's virginity in class…" And Jesus Christ, what had happened to keeping my mouth shut?

Suzie reached out to squeeze my hand. I let her keep her fingers there for a second—only because I was in shock—before pulling away. "Alejandro, you can tell us the truth. If someone is hurting you, you should not have to put up with it. You don't deserve to be treated that way."

Who was this lady? How did she know what I did and didn't deserve? In all fairness, I was the one who'd stolen the weed. He'd had a right to beat the shit out of me...just why hadn't he done it in a way that left no visible marks?

"No, really, it was my fault. I was being stupid." That was true enough, and thank God I was getting a little shorter with my responses.

The nurse grabbed my arm, clucking softly. "Boy, I don tink dat's from soup."

Holy fuck, how did she know? The woman could barely speak English, but she knew what soup burns looked like? Or maybe she was bluffing...and I'd just fucking given myself away with my shocked expression.

I straightened my gaze into one of indifference, which rapidly changed back to annoyance the moment she whipped out a camera and snapped a picture.

"What the—"

"For da records." She cut me off. Then she grabbed me by my upper arm to steer me toward her office. I went willingly—figured I was safer with her than with a cop and a social worker.

"Dis is gonna hurt a little," she remarked, placing my wrist under a faucet.

The cold water burned, and I took the opportunity to shout, "Fuck!" since I knew it'd be excusable.

Afterwards, she very gently applied some lotion, which also hurt like hell, and wrapped my wrist loosely in gauze.

Damn gauze. If I'd had that in the first place, I probably wouldn't have been in this fucked-up situation.

I was about to beg the nurse to let me slip off to my locker, but Suzie appeared behind me, putting an arm on my shoulder and speaking in a maddeningly soft voice as she led me back to the conference room.

"Has anything like this happened before?"

My pulse picked up—she'd gone from the questioning phase to the assuming phase. Not a good sign.

"No. Nothing ever happens." I twisted away from her and sank back into a chair.

"Alejandro—"

"My name is Alex, lady."

I knew I wasn't supposed to call women "lady" in that tone of voice...especially not the women at school. But I was angry, and my tongue got the better of me. If the cops so much as breathed a *word* about this to my mom, she'd probably never speak to me again. She trusted me to keep her life free of things she couldn't handle.

"Alex, you know it's the school's job to report issues of abuse to DCFS...and it's our job to make sure you have a safe home environment."

"Yeah, well there's nothing wrong with my home environment. Now can I go? My mom's gonna be worried if I don't get home." I wasn't sure when I'd last seen my mom truly worried about me, but that was what these people would want to hear.

Suzie sat back, crossing her thick legs and exchanging another look with the silent cop.

"Alej...Alex, if your home is unsafe, we can't let you go back at the moment. Now, we've been unable to reach your mother, and DCFS has to investigate before we can release you."

My jaw dropped. "Release me? Are you fucking kidding me?" Again, no one made a comment on my cursing...and if I hadn't been so overwhelmed, I would have realized what a bad sign that was.

"Well, do you have any other numbers where we could contact her?"

I tried to decide what the better plan of action was— providing a way to get in contact with my mom, or making it as difficult as possible to reach her.

"A working cell number, perhaps? The one listed on your emergency card seems to be out of service."

Then I remembered I really didn't have a way of reaching my mom, even if I'd wanted to. "Nope. She didn't pay for minutes this month."

"Well, could we possibly contact her at work?"

"She lost her last job."

"Could she be at a friend's house?"

"No idea."

Suzie exhaled slowly. Did she think I was being an ass on purpose? I wasn't, really, but I didn't mind the side effect.

"Alex, we do need to speak to her and Hector before we—"

I stood abruptly. I didn't want her to finish the sentence. This whole...*interrogation*...needed to be over. It needed to be over *now*.

Out of the corner of my eye, I saw the cop make a move for the door, like he was going to block me by force if he had to.

"Lady, I have to go home. There's nothing wrong in my house, I swear."

"This isn't the first time teachers have been concerned about your well-being, Alex." She gazed at me steadily, and for just a split second I got the feeling she might know more about my life than I was willing to admit...even to myself. "Nothing final is happening right now. Like I said, DCFS needs to investigate. Legally, we can't send you home right now."

Legally...can't...send home.

My brain processed the words in slow motion. They weren't going to let me go home. Not today, not tonight...maybe not ever.

I'd seen this happen before. Everyone around here had. But that was for kids whose parents were fucking crack addicts, for kids who went to school with their hair matted and their clothes stinking and torn...or for little girls who got molested. Not for me. Not for one little screw-up.

I glanced up at the large clock on the wall. The red second hand ticked, and then a bell sounded. End of the school day. End of the week, for that matter. Time to go home and recharge...maybe get into a little trouble here and there...have a little fun.

I remembered Blanca's note then. What would she say if I didn't go home this afternoon? I figured she was waiting for me, by my locker maybe, or outside the school. She'd want to know why I'd been marched out of class, escorted by a cop.

Maybe getting in trouble with the law could buy me a little street cred? She'd probably find me even sexier now. She seemed like that kind of girl.

And shit, I could handle her. Use her for a little while, then dump her. That should bump me up the social ladder, and buy me some more time to...to...

To what?

"Alex, do you understand?"

Suzie blinked at me. She didn't have dark, curly mascaraed lashes like Blanca or my mom. She had on very little makeup, in fact. Not that it looked terrible. I thought the girls around here wore too much makeup.

"Alex...you're going to have to come with me."

My eyes went back to the clock. The second hand was where I'd last seen it, so a minute must have gone by.

And I was still in the conference room. Still facing a short white woman who said I couldn't go back to my life right now.

"I...I need to go home."

"I'm sorry, Alex. We have to—"

Some part of me knew it was pointless, but I burst out of the office anyway. I wanted no part of what they were saying...well, of what Suzie was saying, since the other two fuckers were only watching. Watching me unravel.

I headed for my locker. In hindsight, I probably should have headed straight for the door, but certain habits were hard to break. I needed my science notebook for a homework assignment I probably wouldn't do, and I needed to get rid of the heavy social studies text currently in my bag. I always went to my locker after last period. To my locker, and then home.

After a few seconds, I noticed the cop trailing behind me. I sped up, cursing the fact that no one could run well in flip-flops.

I expected him to grab me, or order me to the floor or something, but he just followed from a few feet away. Maybe he was letting me waste my energy, since he knew full well I wouldn't be making it out of there.

I almost ran into José as he was packing up by his locker for the weekend. When he saw the cop on my tail, his eyes went wide—saucers of white in his round dark face. I knew his next move would be to cut and run.

"José," I shouted, and now the cop did reach out and grasp my shoulder.

José gave me a look like *holy shit, whatever you do, keep your mouth shut.*

"Tell my mom I didn't say nothing, okay? Tell her I didn't say nothing!"

That was all I could get out before the cop dragged me away.

Chapter 4: In an Instant

I waited in the office for almost an hour, while Suzie made *arrangements*. Then she and the cop put me in the backseat of her car. Once she'd pulled away from the school, she flipped on the child locks—as if there were any way I was suddenly going to open the door and roll out onto the 105 freeway.

"Where are you taking me?"

"To a group home." Suzie spoke softly again—white women didn't seem to raise their voices that much, but she was unusually quiet. "Just until we can contact your mother and find out what the situation is."

A group home? That sounded like some place the mentally retarded were sent, but I kept my mouth shut. Maybe I *was* retarded...I'd certainly managed to let things get out of hand pretty damn quickly.

I tried to fight off the dread by staring out the window, telling myself I should enjoy the rare chance to see the world outside my neighborhood. We sped on past billboards advertising casinos and a racetrack, and some gray industrial buildings heaving out plumes of black smoke. Nothing really glamorous—just more drab freeway, under dreary overcast skies.

We'd gone from one part of the ghetto to another. There were no 7-11s and no Starbucks when we took the exit…only one lone no-name gas station. And a good half of the billboards were in Spanish—a surefire sign of ghetto, if you asked me.

Suzie pulled up in front of a very ordinary house. It was bigger than most on the street, but I'd been expecting something more along the lines of Juvee, with a barbed wire fence, maybe—not a regular old home. A large white garage sat in front of the red brick building, which, though old, did not look like it was about to crumble. Maybe the neighborhood wasn't as ghetto as I'd thought.

The child lock clicked off, finally releasing me from my prison, but I didn't make a move until Suzie came around and got the door for me.

"Alex, I know this is a lot to take in. I promise you nothing final is happening right now."

"Better not be." I followed her toward the house. "How long I gotta be here?"

"This is just temporary." Her words might've been meant to reassure, but they sounded flat to my ears. "Hopefully, things can be settled soon."

Fat chance. I had the sickening sense in that moment that nothing would ever be settled again.

Still, I tried to push it aside. "Are you gonna talk to them? To Hector and my mom?"

"Well, perhaps, or perhaps another social worker will."

"And will the cops be there?"

"Most likely."

Oh, fuck. Hector would *kill* me for bringing the cops to his doorstep. Even if these people did decide I could go home, I probably wouldn't be able to. I might never have a home again.

A feeling hit me, and for a moment I didn't recognize it. I rarely felt anything this strong. But as I stood in front of the strange house filled with God-only-knew-what-kind of people, my throat tightened and my chest caved in on my heart and my neck no longer seemed strong enough to keep my ready-to-blow head attached to my body.

My whole life had changed in an instant. All because of a stupid pair of shoes. All because my damn feet wouldn't stop growing.

That feeling—it was complete fucking *terror*.

My flip-flops rooted themselves to the driveway, and I didn't budge another inch.

"Alex? Let me take you inside and introduce you to Ms. Loretta. She and her sister Ms. Cecily run this foster home together."

"No." I hitched my bag up on my shoulder, fingers locking around the strap, like holding onto that bit of my old reality could keep me grounded. "I don't want to meet any Ms. Loretta. I want to go home, right now."

"I can't take you home until we—"

"I said I want to go home *right now*!"

Jesus, I sounded like a two-year-old having a temper tantrum. My mind was spinning, and I'd started to sweat. What was I supposed to do in a place like this? Was I a *foster kid* now?

"Alex." Suzie placed an arm on my shoulder.

"Get the fuck off me, lady!"

I jerked away from her and went into a crouch stance, eyes darting around wildly in search of the best route of escape.

"Young man, you best close your mouth right now, 'cause you not gonna be usin' that kind of language in this house!"

A very tall and heavy black lady in a long red wrap dress stood at the front door, both hands on her hips and a glare on her face that froze me in my tracks.

"Now you bring yourself on in here, and don't you let me hear that foul mouth again."

"Alex, this is Ms. Loretta," Suzie said gently, and suddenly I didn't want her to go anywhere. Ms. Loretta looked a lot scarier than a chubby white woman in a gray suit. "Now, let's get you settled in."

Ms. Loretta was still staring me down, so I very meekly followed Suzie inside.

"Alex doesn't have a change of clothing. If he ends up having to stay the night, do you have something in his size?" Suzie asked her.

"Oh, yes, we got. Don't you worry, Ms. Suzie. He'll be fine, won't he."

Another glare had me nodding fearfully.

"All right." Suzie stretched out her arm for a moment, like she wanted to squeeze my shoulder again, but then thought better of it. She tucked her hands at her sides and just gave me a smile. "Alex, would you like to talk some more about the DCFS process right now, or would you prefer some time to rest?"

I said nothing.

After a moment of staring, Suzie sighed. "I think we can talk some more later, and I'll let Ms. Loretta take it from here." She walked away and closed the door behind her, leaving me alone in the foyer with Ms. Loretta.

The giant of a woman sized me up with a long, hard look, her expression daring me to back-talk her, or make some sort of complaint about where I'd found myself. I scanned my surroundings warily. A clean but bizarrely decorated kitchen lay just beyond the hallway, covered in wallpaper of golds and yellows and reds. That was really all I could make out from where I stood, except for Ms. Loretta herself.

I tried to look at her without actually making eye contact, still afraid to be caught by her stare. She was a lot like her kitchen—large and gaudy, with gold hoop earrings standing out against her dark skin and bright dress.

"Lights out at 9:30," she announced without further introduction. "Since we don't know how long you gonna be with us, I won't assign you chores, but dinner's at 7 o'clock, and you'll be expected to clean your own dishes."

The back door of the house swung open.

"Wipe your feet!" Ms. Loretta yelled, and a few seconds later a boy appeared.

He was about my height, and probably around my age, with short, dark curly hair and light brown skin. Of mixed-race, obviously…and a good mixture at that.

"A new kid?" he asked, eyeing me carefully.

"This is Alex." Ms. Loretta said. "He might only be here for the night. Take him outta my hair…I gotta start on dinner."

The boy cocked his head toward the back of the house, and I followed, still clutching my backpack strap with both hands against my shoulder.

"I'm Brandon. Dwayne's out back, Ryan and Andrew are at after-school care…you wanna drop your stuff upstairs first?"

I shrugged.

"Well you're talkative." He rolled his eyes.

I was no blabbermouth, but here in this foreign setting, I'd apparently lost my voice entirely.

He led me through a family room that lived up to more of Ms. Loretta's taste in bright colors, then up to a large bedroom filled with bunk beds and tiny desks. The walls were bare and the sheets a dingy gray…but the place was fairly clean, and I had to admit it was a step up from my usual sleeping space.

Brandon pointed to an empty bed, and I finally parted with my bag there. I wouldn't have, if I'd had anything valuable in it—I wasn't stupid enough to leave my stuff unattended like that.

Something shifted under a mass of blankets beside me, and I jumped back, hitting my bare ankle against the bed frame.

Brandon snickered. "That's Seb. He's a retard."

A retard named Seb? Shit, maybe I *was* in that kind of group home. Or maybe Brandon and this guy had some sort of issue with each other. I tried to get a better look at the sleeping figure, but I could only see a bit of ash-blond hair peeking out over the sheets, and the boy didn't say anything. Not much to go on.

"You gonna come out back or what?" Brandon huffed impatiently.

"Mhm." At least I made a sound that time as I turned and left the room.

Out in the small backyard, I came upon another tenant—Dwayne, Brandon had said—tossing a basketball into a leaning hoop.

Dwayne was black. Black black. Not that it was a problem for me—I probably had less of a beef with black people than most of my friends, 'cause of the time I'd spent in the projects. You either got along with your neighbors there, or you invited a shitload of drama into your life.

"New kid," Brandon said to him.

Dwayne gave me the once over as he continued to dribble the ball. He was tall and muscular, with the cut off sleeves of his t-shirt nicely displaying his biceps. "He here to stay?"

"Dunno." Brandon shrugged.

"I fuckin' hate new kids."

I'd never been one to take insults lying down, and as confused as I still was, I knew that moment was Do or Die Time. If, God forbid, I actually *did* have to stay there, I really needed to get my act together and shake off this lost little boy thing I had going on.

"Fuck no I ain't stayin'," I told Dwayne, glaring. "Who wants to stay in a shithole like this?"

"Like you ain't from a shithole. If you wasn't, you wouldn't be here."

"I'm here 'cause a bitch teacher couldn't mind her own fucking business. There's nothing wrong with my home, so I'll be outta here in no time."

Dwayne passed the ball to Brandon, who made a run for the basket and dunked it neatly. His shirt rode up a little, and I would have liked to take some time to appreciate that, but I couldn't really shift my attention from the current showdown.

"Then what's that bandage on your arm for, new kid? You tried to slit your wrists 'cause mommy and daddy don't love you enough?"

I took two steps forward and drew my arm back to punch, but suddenly found myself restrained.

Brandon had snuck around behind me, and he now had both my arms locked in his. My back pressed up against his wide chest as he pulled me away. "Easy, new kid. There are worse places than this, and you gonna find yourself there if you piss off Ms. Loretta."

I threw him off and stepped away from both boys. "My *name* is Alex."

"All right, *Alex*." Dwayne sneered, white teeth glowing against dark lips. "You play basketball? Or just soccer? 'Cause we don't have no soccer ball."

"Shit, I don't wanna play nothing right now." I crossed my arms. "I just want to get the hell out of here."

"Good luck with that." Dwayne shrugged, retrieving the ball and returning to his dribbling.

Brandon laughed beside my ear. "Wow, you makin' friends fast."

"And why would I want to make friends with you?"

"You never know how long you gonna be here…and like I said, there are worse places."

A little of the fury Dwayne had worked up began to deflate. Brandon didn't seem like such a bad guy, really. He was still grinning at me, and he had dimples. Small, round dimples in perfect caramel skin.

I mentally recited the alphabet once and uncrossed my arms.

"Yeah. So what's your story, then? Why you here?"

Brandon sat down on the steps by the backdoor. "My mom smokes crack. She's gonna go to rehab, though, so I can go back and live with her. What about you?"

I bit my lip. I wanted to tell him the truth all of the sudden, because I could tell he'd been honest with me, but I knew it wasn't safe.

"A mix up. A teacher reported this burn I got by accident."

Brandon nodded slowly. "So can't they just talk to your parents and clear things up?"

"Mom's out of town for the weekend. She'll be back soon."

"Oh. So then maybe you're not staying."

"Nope. I'm not."

"Good for you." Brandon stood and dusted himself off. "Andrew and Ryan are gonna be home soon, and I'm supposed to make sure they do their homework."

He didn't say goodbye as he turned to leave, and for some reason I decided that meant I should go with him. Another even larger woman, also in colorful clothing, was standing in the kitchen now, along with two younger black boys who looked like they were still in elementary school.

"And that's Alex. Hopefully just a temporary," Ms. Loretta said to the new woman.

"I'm Ms. Cecily, Alex." She stuck out a fleshy hand for me to shake, and I took it, mostly because Brandon was watching and I no longer wanted to seem like such a dick in front of him. "Brandon, take Ryan and Andrew upstairs and get them started on their homework."

The boys followed Brandon, and I trailed a little further behind, wondering why nobody was telling me what I was supposed to be doing. Maybe that was a good sign, though. Hopefully it meant I wasn't going to be worked into their little system.

Upstairs, I plopped back on a bed...*my* bed, I supposed, and watched Brandon settle one boy into a desk in a room across the hall. He returned with the other kid and took the boy's folder out of his backpack, then thumbed through the papers before setting it down. "Get to work," he ordered.

The boy glanced over his shoulder at me, baring crooked teeth. "New kid?"

"I'm not one of you," I spat, more severely than I'd intended. It was just that it was like the fifth time I'd been called that in a thirty-minute time period. I wasn't new, and I wasn't a kid. I was just…fucked.

"Leave him alone, Ryan. He's grumpy," Brandon said.

A squeak and a rustle reminded me that the Seb character was still behind me. I whirled around to see if I'd get a better look at him this time, but he remained covered all the way up to his hairline.

"I'm not grumpy. I'm just not gonna be staying here. I'm sorry for you all if you got problems, but I don't."

Brandon rolled his eyes. "Dinner's at seven. See ya." He strode out of the room, and I immediately wanted to kick myself. Driving away my first potential ally in this damn place was probably not the smartest thing to do.

Ryan started writing on a worksheet, ignoring me, so I lay back on the bed and stared up at the ceiling. Despite all my talk, I knew it was only that—talk. It would take a day or so until they reached my mom, if she'd only planned on a short trip. She'd deny Hector had done anything wrong, of course, but they'd probably want to talk to him anyway. And Hector wasn't really the talking sort.

Maybe he'd skip town?

That thought instantly chased most of the bad ones away, and I seized the opportunity to close my eyes and grab a few moments of rest.

Chapter 5: Bad. Very Bad.

"Dinner!" a woman's voice boomed. A loud, brassy woman's voice. Not my mother's.

Opening my eyes slowly, I took in the shadows that hung over wooden bunk beds, each perfectly made, and empty. This was not my furniture, and not my room.

The sheets I lay on smelled faintly of lilac. Not my bed.

I bolted upright as I finally remembered where I was. But in the dim light and without anyone around me, the whole thing seemed totally surreal. I was tempted to close my eyes again and let it all be a dream.

"You'd best be gettin' yourself down here if you plan on eating, 'cause you ain't gettin' nothing later!"

I picked up the edges of the pillow and curled them around my head, even if it wouldn't be enough to shut out that kind of a voice.

Footsteps pounded on the stairs, and a moment later Brandon appeared in the doorway. "Don't tell me you can sleep through Ms. Loretta's yelling…'cause if you can, I'm fucking jealous."

"What the fuck," I grumbled. "What time is it?"

"Dinner time."

"I don't fucking care." Why should I play house with these people?

"She wasn't kidding about no food later. The fridge and the cabinets have locks." Brandon smirked at me, one dimple showing in the hallway light.

Well, maybe one meal wouldn't hurt.

Dwayne, Ms. Cecily, Ms. Loretta and the younger boys were already seated around plates of chicken thighs and green beans. The table had a red cloth over it and it was fully set, with real silverware and glasses.

I stood back for a moment to take in the scene. I couldn't remember the last time I'd sat at a table for a meal—at home we ate in front of the TV, and our food tended to come out of a box. Definitely no fine china for us.

"Have a seat, Alex," Ms. Cecily said. She was a lot less brisk than her sister, but I still hesitated, feeling like an intruder in their foreign family ritual.

The food smelled good, though, and my stomach flipped, reminding me I'd had nothing all day but a bottle of water and some aspirin. I eventually slid into a chair next to Brandon and picked up a fork so I could nervously shove the green beans about.

"Those are for eating," Ms. Loretta said. "We don't waste food in this house."

I looked up at her round face just in time to see the last member of the household enter the room.

Seb the retard came in carrying a pitcher of water. His thin figure, strangely pale for the neighborhood, surprised me...though he had a kind of brownish undertone to his skin, so I didn't think he was straight-up White. Definitely not with eyes like those—huge and almond-shaped, and so dark they looked black.

Ms. Loretta caught my staring. "You haven't met Sebastian?"

"Seb was sleeping," Brandon answered for me. "As usual."

Seb—or Sebastian—poured water in everyone's glasses, then sat down and silently began eating.

"Did you finish all your homework?" Ms. Cecily asked, of no one in particular.

"Yup." Ryan slurped in a green bean through crooked teeth. "Me and Andrew finished everything, and Brandon checked it."

"And you, Dwayne?"

Dwayne mumbled something with a piece of chicken in his mouth, and Ms. Loretta slapped his wrist. "Finish chewing first."

He swallowed. "Yeah, I'm done."

"What about that paper that's due Monday? Have you started?"

"Um…" Dwayne rubbed the back of his head. "I was gonna start tomorrow."

"And if I hear that excuse one more time, no TV until it's done."

The taller of the two boys—Andrew, if I remembered right—snickered. "Good, 'cause Dwayne never lets me watch what I want."

Brandon served himself a second helping of green beans. "Too much TV will rot your brain, boy!" he said, and I got the distinct impression he was mimicking Ms. Loretta.

Ms. Loretta must have, also, because she gave him a glare. "Watch yourself, boy."

I finally raised my fork to my mouth and pushed in a bite of chicken. I felt like I'd stepped into some kind of wholesome family TV show: a meal of veggies and proteins, two parent-types, and their annoying but loving family.

It was freaking me out.

I was definitely the *which-one-of-these-things-does-not-belong*, with my complete silence. Well, me and Seb, 'cause he hadn't said a word to anyone, either. He just kept shoveling food into his mouth, black eyes lost and unfocused.

When we'd finished the meal, each one of us took our dishes to the sink, washed them, dried them, and then replaced them in tidy cabinets. Ms. Loretta watched me do mine with her hawk-eyes, like she was afraid I'd do it wrong without supervision. Maybe she thought I wouldn't know how, growing up in whatever shithole she'd imagined for me.

But unwashed dishes meant roaches, so I'd done a fair share of cleaning in my day.

Ms. Loretta nodded approvingly as I set my fork back in the drawer. "Suzie said she'd be by early to talk to you. You have a little over an hour to read and shower, then it's lights out. Don't be keeping my boys up—they have chores tomorrow."

She and Ms. Cecily headed off to watch TV in the living room, their wide backsides taking up the entire length of a ridiculously orange couch.

I followed the train of boys up the stairs, wondering if I should try to slip away during the night and make my way back home. It'd probably cause more trouble in the long run, but if I could at least warn my mom of what was going on, maybe she and Hector would have a chance to get their stories straight.

Then again, if I caught Hector at a bad time, he might just beat me senseless and worry about the consequences later.

"You wanna shower?" Brandon stood in front of a closet full of black metal crates stuffed with clothes. He tossed me a wrinkled t-shirt and a pair of faded gym shorts from some school I'd never heard of. "The boys go first, but they shower fast, 'cause they usually hate it."

Despite myself, I almost cracked a smile. I remembered that phase. "Uh, yeah, I guess."

Dwayne grabbed a book and climbed onto the bunk above Seb, who had somehow already managed to return to his cocoon of blankets. I sat on my bed and waited for further instructions

"You need shoes for tomorrow?" Brandon asked.

"Yeah. Sure." If I did have to bolt, shoes would be a plus.

"What size?"

"Uh...like ten and a half."

More like nine and a half, but I wasn't going to make the mistake of outgrowing another pair anytime soon.

"Well, these are a ten." A pair of scuffed-up, ratty-ass black Keds sailed across the room and landed by my feet.

Fucking perfect.

"You don't have anything less...fucked up?" I picked up the shoes by their laces, noting a sour odor.

"Hey, beggars and choosers, and all that shit." Brandon laughed. I let him mock me without a fight, mainly because when he laughed it showed off his dimples. The skin in those dimples seemed a little paler than the rest of his face...like dollops of cream against some cinnamon.

Time to distract myself.

"So...uh...do they come up and check on you or some shit? Or do they mostly leave you alone?" I directed the question to Brandon, since he was really the only one talking to me.

"If you do what they tell you to, they mostly let you be."

"How long you been here?"

"Just six months. Dwayne's been here the longest—almost a year now."

Six months to a year? Jesus, I hoped that wasn't going to be my fate.

"And what's wrong with him?" I jerked my head over toward the mound of covers that was Seb. "I haven't heard him say a word since I got here."

Dwayne rolled his eyes at me from his higher perch, turning a page in his book. "Seb's retarded."

I glanced back at Brandon for a better explanation, and he arched his brows at me with a smirk. "I wasn't kidding before. He really is. He don't talk at all. They said there's something wrong with his vocal chords or something, but he don't write or do sign language, so he's gotta be retarded."

"Oh."

I wondered if he were deaf, too, because he didn't stir at the conversation.

Scampering sounds followed by much more solid footsteps announced the younger boys and Ms. Cecily in the hallway. All three took a left into the room across the way.

"Showers're free," Brandon said, and a towel hit me square in the face. "Best hurry up before lights out."

"Are you gonna go fir—" I peeled off the towel to find Brandon undressing.

Oh, Jesus.

My fingers locked into fists as I looked away and concentrated on the strands of Seb's strange blond hair. "Uh, you first?"

"There's more than one shower." Brandon's laughter dragged my eyes back to him, but thankfully he now had his towel securely around his waist.

Only that left his entire torso exposed. His trim, caramel-colored torso.

I had a feeling I was going to need a lot more than the alphabet to get through this.

"Will y'all shut up now? I'm trying to read this shit for a book report," Dwayne growled.

Unfazed, Brandon sauntered out of the room. I took three deep breaths, went through the alphabet backwards, and followed.

At the end of the hallway was a large green-wallpapered bathroom—yet more evidence of the sisters' tacky taste—complete with a double sink and two tiny shower stalls that looked like they'd been ripped out of a school locker room. They had plastic on the sides but only that cheap-ass white curtain on the front. Brandon ducked into one with his towel still attached, then tossed it over the bar once he'd pulled the curtain shut.

Water splattered to life and I shuffled over to the sink to stare in the mirror. My face was a wreck, lids drooping with some unseen weight and circles of shadowy gray haunting my eyes. I couldn't be sure how much of it was the hangover and how much of it was a reaction to being ripped from my life, but I certainly hoped I'd look better in the morning.

Except, come morning, I'd still be trapped here…and if there was one thing I knew for certain, it was that I didn't belong. I didn't belong at family dinners, or with bantering boys in bunk beds. My reflection didn't belong in this large bathroom with its god-awful green walls and ugly showers.

These people…*no eran mi gente.*

I had a lot more despair to dive into, but something else in the room's reflection suddenly caught my eye: that cheap plastic curtain. As was always the case with those things, it didn't quite make it all the way to the wall, leaving a tiny sliver of the shower's inside visible.

Mid-inhale, my breath caught in my throat.

Brandon was under the stream of water, his back toward the opening, rubbing foamy shampoo into his hair. Cascades of liquid traveled down his shoulder blades, taking the suds with them—white on brown-sugar skin. Some of the droplets continued over the curve of a firm ass, while others disappeared into his crack.

He shifted a little, and I could just make out a mass of dark pubes at his groin.

Holy fuck.

I dove into the empty shower stall, trying not to moan at the nearly-painful erection I'd magically sprouted. I peeled off my clothes and kicked them out, then turned the stream of water on cold.

There was way too much temptation in this place. It wasn't like Brandon was the only one—Dwayne was no ugly fucker, either—and they were all far too close for comfort. Sharing a bedroom, a bathroom, practically showering together...I'd be lucky if I survived the weekend without making a complete fool of myself.

But as Brandon had said, beggars can't be choosers, and all that shit. I was already as hard as I ever got, and it seemed a shame to waste it. My hand slipped down to my dick, and I summoned Brandon's image back to my mind. Glistening-wet skin, sliding soap suds, dark curly pubes...best material I'd had in ages.

I began to stroke myself, quick-and-dirty, because I wasn't sure how much time I'd have. I half-registered that the shower beside me had gone off, and that Brandon had left. Released from some of my fear of discovery, I stroked even faster, letting out only the smallest of sounds that I hoped would be carried away with the pounding of the shower water and the creaking of the pipes.

A slightly louder gasp escaped me as I came, jetting out streams against the shower wall.

"Fuckin' a!"

The curtain abruptly flew back, and Brandon and Dwayne stood in front of me, slamming fists on each other's backs as they struggled to hold in their laughter.

"Jackin' off in the showers on his first night!" Dwayne hooted.

I shoved my body into the corner, attempting to keep the last shreds of my dignity from washing down the drain. "Close the fucking curtain you fucking dicks!"

"If you shout, Ms. Loretta will come in. That'd be fucking *perfect*," Brandon chimed, dimples glowing.

Fucking dimples.

They pulled the curtain shut and left the room chuckling, but I stayed cowering in the corner, waiting for the waves of shock and humiliation to stop traveling my skin. Two minutes passed before I could peel myself from the sticky wall and gingerly step back into the water to rinse myself off. I was still shaky, but common sense had started to filter back in—what I'd done wasn't that out of the norm. I was a teenage guy; it was what we were *supposed* to do. No one had any reason to believe I was...*different* yet, right?

Creaks and moans from the old wood flooring told me someone else was approaching. Panicked again, I hurriedly stopped the shower and snatched the towel to cover myself up. It was only then that I realized I'd forgotten to take the gauze off my wrist, and it was now thoroughly soaked.

"Alex?" Ms. Loretta boomed. "Is there a problem? You been in there way too long, boy. We don't take showers like that in this house."

I sank my forehead against the wall.

This was bad. Very bad.

~*~

I awoke to an empty room again the next morning. Or, almost empty. I could hear activity downstairs, but not a sound near me. Seb nearly scared the shit out of me—for the second time—when I finally got up. He rose from his bed like some kind of robot, instantly homing in on the sheets I'd left in a tangled mess. Within a few seconds he had them smoothed out and the pillow fluffed, so the bed fit in perfectly with the others in the room.

I made a mental note to fix my own bed from now on. I wasn't sure how I felt about having a retarded servant, even if he didn't seem to mind.

Then I made a second mental note, reminding myself there wasn't going to be a "from now on." Thinking that was like giving up…and I wasn't prepared to go down without a fight.

"Alex? Ms. Suzie's here to see you!" Ms. Loretta shouted from below. I could almost feel the walls vibrating with her call.

I glanced down at the gym shorts I wore. They were a little too tight, and not something I'd be caught dead in ordinarily.

"Hey…" I turned to Seb, since he was the only one around. "Can I get some clothes to wear?"

Seb cocked his head, giving me a strange look with his almond eyes.

I wondered if he even knew what I was saying.

"I'm gonna take that as a yes," I said slowly, walking toward the closet while Seb's eyes followed me. But before I could get there, Brandon buzzed through the hallway and shoved a bundle of clothes into my arms.

"Hurry it up. Suzie don't have all day."

I met Suzie downstairs on the orange couch, wearing a D.A.R.E. t-shirt with a hole at the shoulder, school-uniform navy pants, and the disgusting Keds. I looked like a fucking loser.

"So can I go home now?"

Suzie frowned. "Alex, do you have any idea where your mother and Hector could have gone? We still haven't been able to reach them."

I sank down into an upholstered chair. "I dunno. Vegas, maybe."

"Do they often leave you alone like this without any way to reach them?"

"I'm fifteen, la—Ms. Suzie. I can take care of myself."

I noticed her chewed, unpolished nails tapping away on a file folder with my name on it.

"I'm sure you can, but you shouldn't have to."

Rolling my eyes, I leaned over to see if I could figure out what she had in that folder. "So, what now? I keep waiting here until they come back?"

Suzie nodded. "We have a hearing this morning to establish temporary custody since we can't yet determine the situation at home."

"Temporary custody?" I recoiled at the words, and at the thought. "Like, I belong to these people now? What the hell! You said nothing final was happening!"

"*Temporary,*" Suzie repeated. "Just so that you can stay with Ms. Loretta and Ms. Cecily while we wait for your family to speak to us."

"But what if you talk to them and you...you don't believe that nothing happened? Do I have to stay here forever? I mean, do I get any say in this at all?" My voice rose in pitch, and I cut off the stream of questions before I ended up in a squeak.

"*If* we determine there's a problem at home, it doesn't mean you'll never be with your family again. DCFS is not in the business of ripping apart families. We'll work with them, through counseling and other services, to try to make sure you have a safe home to return to."

I rubbed at my eyes, feeling a fierce headache coming on. "So...just because you and a teacher are too stupid to believe me when I say *nothing happened*, you're going to keep me with a bunch of strangers, make my mom jump through hoops to get me back, and get Hector fucking pissed at me."

I didn't look at Suzie, but I could hear her flustered sigh. I caused adults to make that sound a lot, it seemed. "If it's our mistake, you'll go home, Alex. I've told you that."

This whole thing was a mistake.

"But what if you don't *believe* it's a mistake...what then? What about school and stuff?"

"Well, you'd be enrolled at the school here so you don't miss anything while we work with your family."

That's *all* I fucking needed—to be the new kid at some school I had no clue how to get around in—and not just in the literal sense.

"I don't want to go to a different school."

Suzie squirmed forward on the couch cushion, making a move to stand. "I hope it doesn't come to that. I'm just explaining all the possibilities to you." She rose and started to place her file back into her bag.

"What's that?" I tried to latch onto the folder, but she pulled it away.

"Just some notes...and your school records."

"My school records? Like my grades and sh— and stuff?"

She stopped her movements and looked directly at me, her eyes suddenly calm and studying. "Reports from the school nurses for the past several years."

Oh, shit.

"I'm...I'm a boy," I blurted out. "I get into fights with other kids and stuff...boys get hurt sometimes. It's totally normal."

"I never said it wasn't." She straightened her suit jacket—a dull brown one, this time—and gave me a sad look. "But if you ever want to talk about what's in here...or this"—she reached out to gently lift my wrist—"there are people who care."

I jerked my arm back and glared. "I have nothing to talk about. And I'm not staying in no house full of reject kids, or going to no new school."

Another exasperated sigh came from Suzie's lips. "We'll see, Alex."

And I saw—for the briefest of moments before I wrapped myself back in denial—

I was screwed.

Chapter 6: Don't You Even Care

When the water ran in that old house, every pipe seemed to moan. I didn't know which noise was worse—that, or the barking sounds from Ms. Loretta. From what I gathered as I drifted in and out of sleep on Sunday morning, the "chores" she spoke of were a daily ritual, and everyone else was hard at work while I hid in my bed.

Well, *hid* wasn't the right word. I chose to consider it my own form of resistance.

I finally wandered downstairs around noon, and only because my stomach wasn't on board with my plan to avoid everyone until it was time to say *adiós*. I slipped past Ms. Cecily reading to the younger boys in the living room and found Seb sweeping the kitchen floor, using long, practiced strokes.

"Hey, jack-off." Brandon trampled in behind me and grabbed a cup to fill. His t-shirt was stained with sweat, and he smelled of freshly cut grass. The scent instantly reminded me of the neighbor we'd had for a few months back when I was in middle school— a twenty-something-year-old gardener with the most amazing body. He'd taken me to work with him in the beautiful homes of Brentwood one day, but I was pretty much useless after he'd removed his shirt to mop the sweat from his brow.

And oh, crap. Brandon was still talking.

"You missed breakfast, but we'll have lunch in a little while. Were you trying to sleep all day or something?"

I couldn't imagine why he thought I'd prefer spending time with him and the others to being alone in the room...especially when they'd picked such a great nickname for me.

Seb had evidently finished gathering all the crumbs into a corner. He ducked behind my legs without warning, almost hitting me, and retrieved a dustpan from under the sink to complete the job.

"He's good at simple tasks," Brandon informed me as I moved out of the way. "When he showed up three months ago, me and Dwayne's chores got cut down by a third. If you stick around, we'll have even less to do."

"I ain't staying."

I really needed to say that as often as I could, because somewhere deep down I was starting to doubt it.

"I hope he ain't." Dwayne came in from the dining room to toss out a wad of paper towels. "Or he's gonna scrub the shower every time he uses it."

My cheeks burned, but hopefully my complexion covered it. "Yeah, well, I'm *sorry*...don't usually have to take care of myself, 'cause I got plenty of girls at home...but they not exactly in supply out here, is they."

Dwayne rolled his eyes and made a jerk-off motion with his hand.

"Fuck you," I snapped in response, growing more pissed when Dwayne's only reaction was to laugh.

"Watch that Ms. Loretta don't hear you," Brandon said, breezing out of the kitchen.

Obviously, coming down had been a mistake. I headed back for the temporary peace of the room and nearly collided with the soft white bulk of Suzie as she strode past, with Ms. Loretta directly behind her.

"Oh, Alex, good. I'm glad you're up."

Shit! She was back! And so soon…that *had* to mean she'd come to bring me home.

"Just a sec!" I darted past her and onto the stairs. "Let me get all my stuff! I'll be ready to leave in like one minute!"

"Alex, why don't we—"

I didn't let her finish her sentence. Instead, I galloped up to the room and began violently tearing off the disgusting hand-me-downs. Then I put on my own clothes—right down to the dirty boxers and cheap flip-flops—and barreled back down the stairs.

"I'm ready. Let's go!"

I came to a stop at the entrance to the living room, where Ms. Loretta and Suzie sat, mouths slightly open. Their sudden silence hung in the room, and their eyes slid back and forth warily.

Neither of them was smiling…and they both should've been happy to see me going home, right?

"Let's go?" I repeated, but my voice had lost most of its earlier energy.

"Alex, come have a seat for a moment." Suzie patted the orange cushion by her side. Ms. Loretta rose and shuffled off to the kitchen, declaring she needed to put on some water for tea.

"I'm ready to go," I said again.

"I know you are." Suzie had her super-soft *I care about you* voice on in full swing. "But I'm afraid that can't happen just yet."

"Why not? What now?"

"Well, neither Hector nor your mother has contacted us."

I exhaled, instantly relieved. If they hadn't talked to anyone yet, nothing final could be happening. Maybe Hector had won some money or something, and they were treating themselves to a few extra days in Vegas.

"All right." I shrugged. "They'll be back soon, though."

Suzie's hands twitched in her lap. She was wearing another gray suit, but this one had a skirt instead of pants. Her legs were crossed, and her pantyhose had a run—one tiny little hole, about an inch or so above her knee, with a long thin trail leading down to her calf and exposing her milk-white skin.

I wasn't sure why I noticed all those details at the moment, unless it was because I was trying not to read the expression on her face.

"There's something else, Alex. There's evidence they've received some of our notices, and that someone has been by the house."

"So then they are back!" I tried to stand, but Suzie's hand on my knee stopped me.

"Neighbors told the police someone was home last night, and they put some personal belongings in a truck and left."

"Personal belongings?"

"Suitcases, and some bags of clothes."

Please, my heart thumped to the beat of my useless prayer. *Please no.*

"Could they be going on another trip? Staying with a friend, perhaps?"

"I…I don't know."

"Is there a reason they wouldn't be willing to speak to us?"

"I don't know."

There was a reason they wouldn't be willing to speak to the *police*, of course. A pretty good one—Hector was a criminal…and not even legal.

"Alex…"

"I don't know! I don't fucking know!" I pounded my fists on the couch cushion, heat rising in my face. "I just…I want to go home."

Tears of shock were welling inside me, so I closed my eyes and kept my hands clenched at my sides, successfully fighting them off. I couldn't let anyone see me that weak.

Suzie squeezed down on my knee. "For now, I think it'd be best to stay with Ms. Loretta. When we do get in contact with your mother, we'll reevaluate things from there."

"Stay here? Go to school here and everything?" My voice was a strained whisper.

"Ms. Loretta and Ms. Cecily are some of the best foster parents I know. You're lucky they have the space right now…and it really can be a good experience, even if you go home next week."

Lucky. I'd never felt so far from lucky in my life.

"If you have a key, we can escort you to your house later to pick up some of your personal belongings— clothes, or books…"

"Whatever." I drew myself away from the pressure of Suzie's hand. Too numb to fight, I resorted to the old trusty don't-give-a-shit attitude. "Go ahead and screw up my life." And under my breath, I muttered, "Fucking bitch," just for good measure.

~*~

A sickly-thin gray street cat dashed across the road when we reached my neighborhood, just barely making it to the other side in one piece. I was pretty sure I'd seen that cat before.

In fact, I'd seen it all before. I'd seen the homeless man curled up in the green flannel blanket under the freeway bridge, one arm slung protectively over a plastic bag that contained all his worldly belongings. I'd seen those same wrinkled old *señoras* digging in the gas station trashcans and pulling out plastic bottles for the measly five-cent return rate. And I'd seen that ice-cream truck with the dent in its side, playing its obnoxious song over and over again as it rolled through the streets.

Everything was exactly as I'd left it.

Only I was different. I was the sell-out, being "escorted" to my own home by a cop and a social worker. God, I could only pray no one I knew would catch sight of me and set their tongue to *chismes*.

There goes Alex, hauled off by the police. And he thought he was so smart...

I pulled up the hood of the Army sweatshirt Ms. Cecily had loaned me, hoping it'd hide my face as we climbed the steps to the front porch. The house was the same, too, although it was strangely quiet. Without Hector's drunken breathing or my mom's telenovelas filling the air, it didn't feel like my home. Even when I was there alone, I'd flick on the TV or put on some music to keep from getting too lost in my thoughts.

A fly buzzed by the kitchen and landed on an unopened can of refried beans. I took that as a good sign. After all, if they still had belongings there, they had to be coming back.

Which reminded me, I should've been looking for clues.

I headed down the hallway toward Hector's room, only to be stopped by the cop's arm on my shoulder. I threw him off but turned to see what the hell he wanted and realized it was the same jackass who'd grabbed me at school just a few days ago.

It seemed like ages since then, though.

"No wandering around the house," he said.

"Alex, why don't you show me your room?" Suzie walked around him and blocked my path down the hallway.

I peered over her shoulder, just barely making out the edge of my mom's closet door. Were her nice clothes still in there? Then she'd definitely be back.

"You can only take your personal belongings." Suzie shifted to cut off my view entirely.

"I just want to see if—"

"Alex." She put her hand out slowly, palm facing me, and said my name like someone would say the word *stop*.

"Man, fuck you," I grunted, then stomped back toward my room.

Suzie followed and stood by the door to watch. Thank God she didn't try to say anything else to me. At the moment, the only thing that would have come out of my mouth would've been a stream of curses—and I had a feeling if I *did* do that, she'd just sigh and give me those pitying eyes, which would only make things worse.

With a swift jerk, I yanked at my top dresser drawer. It caught on the left edge, as usual, so I had to jiggle it to get at the t-shirts stored inside, folded neatly the way Mimi had taught me.

I pushed them out of the way and dug down until my hands closed around the carton of cigarettes and the lighter I'd stashed there. The box was half empty—I wasn't really a heavy smoker, but I'd let Diego bum quite a few off me at the party.

Diego. What would cool, confident Diego do in a situation like this? Take orders from some *gringa* and two old black ladies? Probably not. He'd go to his other family, and they'd take care of him.

But me...even if I gave them my loyalty...they wouldn't take care of me, if they knew.

Suzie had her back to me. She was scanning the hallway, most likely taking note of the grimy walls and warped flooring. Judging me and mine for what our home was like, looking down on us with her superior white-lady attitude. And actually, the place would have been even more of a wreck if Blanca and me hadn't straightened up the morning after the party. Only a few bottle caps and a little bit of ash remained.

She pulled out a notebook to scribble something down, and I took the opportunity to tuck the lighter into the cigarette carton and then stuff the whole thing into the waistband of my boxers.

A small act of rebellion, but anything I could do to maintain my sanity seemed worth it.

Suzie walked in just as I'd added my final pair of shorts to the duffel bag. "We will keep trying to find them. You know I'd like nothing better than to see your family put back together."

I didn't even look at her as I slung the bag over my shoulder and left, slamming the door behind me.

~*~

The bare, sterile look of the room at Ms. Loretta's suddenly made me furious when I returned. I took my bag and dumped all my belongings on the floor, then kicked them about, deliberately upsetting the tidiness.

I thought of throwing more of a fit as I crashed face-first into the bed, but that wasn't really my style. It would've been a relief, though—to tear things apart, or pick up a chair and smash it to pieces. To scream at the top of my lungs, maybe throw a few punches—not that I'd ever hit a woman.

Brandon and Dwayne, on the other hand…if they came in right now and so much as *looked* at me the wrong way…

But it was Ms. Loretta who barged in first, her wide shadow looming over my head. "Sit up, Alex."

I resisted until I swore I could feel her gaze burning a hole through my head.

"This is a list of responsibilities." She handed me a piece of paper. "I expect our rules to be followed, and I expect general politeness. You'll help out with the chores, you'll do your homework, and you'll go to school. Break the rules, and you're out. I have young boys here and they can't be having no bad influences."

I drew my brows together and stared at her. Was she serious with this bullshit?

"You'll set the table for dinner on Friday, and you'll take a turn on dusting, sweeping, mopping and cutting the grass. You can figure out when with Brandon and Dwayne. Laundry days are Tuesday and Saturday. We use the laundromat down the street, and we all wash and fold or we don't get no clean clothes."

Air brushed against my tongue, and I realized my mouth had fallen open as she continued to bombard me.

"Twice a week you'll help Andrew and Ryan with their homework. Ms. Cecily and me check it before it goes to school, so you'd best be doing a good job."

The paper in my hand slipped from my fingers, and I watched it fall in gentle arcs to the floor. "Are you fucking kidding me? I could've just lost my mom, my home, my whole life...and you're giving me a list of fucking *chores*? Don't you even care?"

Ms. Loretta headed for the door. "Don't I?" She glanced over her shoulder at the threshold to pin me with another ruthless stare. "Clean up this mess...and that best be the very last time I hear foul language coming out of your mouth."

I geared up for an angry retort, but she whirled around one last time and leveled me with a look. I blinked twice, somehow strangled into silence. She nodded, then left.

I swore that woman was a fucking witch.

Brandon replaced her a little while later, strolling into the room with arms folded in smug victory. "Told you."

His dimples were starting to get on my nerves, since they seemed to go hand in hand with that high-and-mighty smirk.

"Fuck off."

"Hey, at least you get a few days off before you have to go to school. Fucking lucky."

Lucky again. Did these people even know the meaning of the word?

"Can you please just fuck off? I don't feel like talking right now."

Jesus. Now I was resorting to asking *please*.

"Can't." He leaned against the plain wooden dresser, one hip jutting out, allowing his t-shirt to pull a little tighter against his abs. And damn it, I wasn't thinking about his body again when my life had taken a turn for complete shit. "This is my room. Dwayne's coming up in a sec anyways. He never finished that paper."

Fuck.

I got up from the bed to grab my jacket—at least it was good to have some of my own things around again—and left the room without another word.

And definitely without another glance at Brandon's abs.

"Just where do you think you're going, young man?" Ms. Cecily caught me at the foot of the stairs.

"I need some air." I kept on my path for the back door. Ms. Cecily didn't freak me out the way her sister did. She was softer, somehow—and not just because she was quite a few pounds heavier.

"You can go out to the backyard." She followed after me. "But only until lights out. And you should know, child—you only get one shot at this."

I stopped, but didn't turn around. "One shot at what?"

"At staying here, with us. If you plannin' to run away...well, we not gonna have a place for you here anymore if you do."

What had Brandon said to me when we'd first met? That there were worse places than this? I hadn't given his words any thought at the time, and not just because I was distracted by the rise and fall of his chest against my back. But now I did pause to wonder...if I ran away and got caught, would I end up in some sort of foster care jail?

"I'm not running away. I just really...I need to be by myself, okay?"

Her heavy footsteps stopped echoing mine after that.

Out in the backyard, I took a long, deep breath and attempted to calm myself enough to think. The night sky above me was the same hazy purple it was at home—nice to see that hadn't changed—but somehow the air smelled different. I ducked behind a metal shed for some form of privacy and sank to the dirt and grass below.

Now I was trapped. *Really* trapped. And I just kept getting caught up on the fact that the tiniest little thing…a measly *shoe*…had set this all in motion.

Not that rehashing my screw-ups over said shoe was going to help any. I needed to focus…come up with some sort of plan.

Maybe a cigarette would help.

I drew out the carton and lit one up, trying to ignore how badly my fingers were trembling. The first deep inhale and the familiar scent actually did help keep me from spiraling into a pool of self-pity.

Now then…what next? Try to find my mom? Get hold of a phone and see if José had any idea where she was? Though if what Suzie said was true, she *knew* I was out here…which meant she'd…

No, Hector was controlling her, the way he always did. My mom knew I could take care of myself, and she had to have a reason for what she was doing.

I could've tried looking for Mimi. She'd turned twenty-one back in August—not that they'd ever release me into her custody. Not without a pretty big miracle, anyway.

One tiny crunch of a twig was the only warning I got that someone was near me, and by then it was too late. I jumped backwards and smashed the cigarette into the ground, my heart hammering in my chest.

Seb stared at me, his head tilted slightly to the side.

"Are you gonna fucking tell on me?" I shouted the moment I'd regained my wits. "That why you followed me back here, retard?"

He continued staring.

"Well? What, you never seen no one smoke before?"

SARA ALVA

I knew he'd already caught me, so I picked up the cigarette and waved it in front of me. "Get a good look, retard, then go run and tell your two mommies."

Shit, maybe my next decision had just been made for me. They didn't seem like the types who would tolerate sneaking around with cigarettes.

I waited, glaring fiercely, until my brain finally caught up with my mouth. "Fuck...you're not gonna tell, are you. You can't even talk."

He blinked.

"Well...sorry I yelled." Heat crept up my skin, more out of shame than anything else. I'd just screamed my head off at a poor handicapped kid who hadn't done a damn thing to me...and that certainly wasn't the best way to make sure I stayed out of immediate trouble. "You just startled me."

No response. Well, of course there was no response.

"Um, are you gonna go back in? Or...you wanna...?" I patted the ground by my side. I wasn't ready to head back into the lion's den—I needed some time to let the air carry away the smell of smoke.

He hesitated a moment longer before joining me behind the shed. In a smooth, graceful movement, he folded his body so he was sitting cross-legged beside me.

I waved my hand around, hoping to encourage a breeze to help remove the scent. "So...Seb...what's your deal? Why you here?"

He glanced at me, and an eyebrow twitched. I giggled. Shit, that wasn't very masculine, but I suddenly felt like I was in this unstable place between complete misery and hysterical laughing...and asking a retarded mute to tell me his story deserved at least a giggle.

Besides, it wasn't like he could go and spill to anyone about my girlish laughter.

"Sorry. Guess you can't answer that one."

He dug his long, pale fingers into the dirt and drew up some soil, then let it drift back to the ground.

66

"You really retarded?"

I didn't get a response to that question, either—not even a nod. I supposed I should take that as a yes.

I leaned my head back on the shed. "Shit. I really don't want to be here...no offense or nothing. I just...have my own life, you know?"

He sifted through some more dirt. It left his pale skin coated with a dusky brown layer—a much more familiar color in my eyes.

"I mean, this is fine for those little kids, and for people like you...but I don't need no one to take care of me. Just because I'm not eighteen some damn law says I can't be on my own? Those people who wrote that law don't know nothing 'bout my life. I been taking care of myself for years now."

Seb folded his hands in his lap and turned toward me. His huge black eyes stared directly into mine...and it was fucking unnerving. I couldn't say why, but for just a second I felt like he was trying to call me out—like he didn't buy what I was saying.

But that was a stupid thought. He probably didn't understand a word that came out of my mouth. Including the curse words, which meant I could cuss to my heart's content around him and not be afraid of Ms. Loretta's wrath.

"Hey, you want a cigarette?" I held the carton out to him, and it finally drew his gaze away from my face.

He didn't make a move, though, so I pulled one out and gently placed it in his dirty fingers. They curled around the cigarette carefully, like they were holding a foreign object for the first time.

"All right, now I just gotta light it up..."

I flicked the lighter on near his hand, and he jerked back, dropping the cigarette on the ground.

Shit, not only was I trying to corrupt the kid with cigarettes, but I was scaring him with fire.

"Sorry. Here, let me light it up." I picked it back up and lit it myself, then grabbed his hand again and arranged his fingers in the right holding pattern.

His skin was oddly smooth...or maybe that was from the thin coating of dirt still on it.

He lifted the cigarette to his face, sniffed once, then deposited it cherry-first into the ground, smashing out the embers.

"What the hell? Why the fuck did you do that? If you didn't want it I woulda smoked it. This one box is all I got!"

Interestingly, Seb didn't flinch at my outburst. So fire freaked him out, but not yelling.

"Hey, kid...you deaf?"

He stood and offered me his hand.

I glanced up, confused, until the back door squeaked open, followed by Ms. Loretta's holler. "Lights out!"

Shit. I quickly buried both cigarettes in the ground, then let Seb pull me up.

He was a lot stronger than he looked. Our chests almost collided, and standing close like that I could see he was actually an inch or so taller than me. Maybe I shouldn't have been calling him 'kid'.

"Fine. I'll go in tonight...but if this shit gets any worse...I'm outta here."

Almond eyes narrowed on me before we turned toward the house and headed inside.

Chapter 7: Not Me

"Move it."

Dwayne rushed past me in the hallway, shoving me against the wall. Why the hell was he in such a hurry?

If I went any slower, I'd be going backwards.

The younger boys were gone already—Ms. Cecily drove them to school before heading off to work—but Ms. Loretta was still there to watch my every move. She'd forced me up with everyone else to water some fucking plants and eat a bowl of cereal, and now we had to leave early so Seb could catch the short bus to his special school.

I dawdled for a few more minutes, holding on to the impossible hope that Suzie would show up and fix this mess for me. Or my mother, maybe. Where the hell was she?

"You best pick up your pace, Alex." Ms. Loretta crossed her arms, standing a few feet in front of me.

I choked back my immediate desire to counter with, *or what?*

She'd have an answer to that, and it'd probably involve scrubbing, sweeping, dusting or mopping. That was all I seemed to have done in the past couple of days while Suzie worked on enrolling me at the new school. I had a sneaking suspicion Ms. Loretta had become a foster mother for the free labor.

Swinging my backpack over my shoulder, I increased my speed only the tiniest bit. Couldn't let her have *that* much control over me.

Brandon and Dwayne were waiting for me outside the front door. I got a dirty look from Dwayne and a smug one from Brandon before we started off together, with Seb trailing a few steps behind.

My first real trip into the neighborhood, and it had to be to fucking *school*. Not that there was all that much to see in this part of LA, an area unimaginatively named Mid City. I guess the houses we passed were kind of cool, if you ignored the bars on the windows and the jalopies parked out front. No two were alike—and they looked old, like they had stories to tell. Once upon a time some of them might've even been classy, but they were jammed so close together you could practically flip pancakes in your neighbor's kitchen. And there was still trash in the streets—a stained mattress at the end of a cul-de-sac—and graffiti along the fences.

Different tags than I was used to, though. Different gangs in these parts. God, I hoped I stayed off their radar.

"So I figured I'd be taking you around, showing you where stuff is…" Brandon said as we approached the ugly brick building surrounded by chain-link and barbed wire, "but that was when I thought you was a sophomore. You not gonna be around the same parts as me and Dwayne. Gonna be spending most of your time in the little freshman wing."

Dwayne huffed a laugh. "Maybe he should go to school with Seb."

I stared at the cracks in the concrete walkway. "Maybe you should shut the fuck up."

"You one pissed-off dude," he responded, shaking his head and stepping a few feet ahead.

Damn it, how was it that I always ended up the loser in these situations? This was all wrong. I knew how to stand up for myself.

But the moment had passed, and I just gritted my teeth and climbed the brick steps to my doom.

As promised, Brandon and Dwayne peeled off their own separate ways the moment we set foot in the blue and beige school hallway. Seb stayed outside, waiting for his bus by a lonely sycamore tree, while I leaned against the wall near the front office.

For all that I was surrounded by hordes of students, I might as well have been out there alone at that tree. I didn't know any of the people who passed me, so all the faces merged together into a sea of brown and black. No José smiling up at me like I was his role model for cool, no Diego sauntering by to catch my wandering eye. Not even a Blanca to throw a lip-glossed kiss and let me know I was a desirable human being, even if the feeling wasn't mutual.

Here, I was no one.

"Alejandro Alvarez?" A woman with freckles and long curly hair emerged from the office and stuck out her hand for me to shake. I didn't take it. "I wanted to introduce myself. I'm Ms. Morrison, and I'll be your guidance counselor here."

I arched a brow at her. "So you know Suzie?"

"Your social worker spoke to me when you were enrolled. I just wanted to let you know if there's anything you need, you can come to my office, any hour of the day. The door is always open."

My eyes drifted to her left hand, where she held a printed piece of paper. "That my schedule?"

"Yes, I have your classes here."

"Then can I have it so I can go?"

She hesitated for a moment, trying to read me—probably wondering if she could push me enough that I'd crawl into her lap like some kind of pet.

Things might've been screwed up, but I still wasn't that kind of kid. In fact, I was pretty sure I'd forget her name by the end of the day.

I held out my hand and spoke slowly, like she was hard of hearing. "Can...I...please...go?"

She sighed and gave me the schedule. "Homeroom is in room 17."

"Yeah. Thanks."

I crumpled the paper and turned left toward the freshman wing. The school was a bit bigger than my last, but as Brandon had pointed out, I would be spending most of my time in semi-isolation. I supposed schools thought it was safer that way, so us freshmen could keep our innocence just a little bit longer.

Someone should have told them it was a lost cause.

The homeroom teacher looked me over with disinterest, smoothing her hair into her loose bun. "Alejandro Alvarez?"

"It's Alex."

"Fine, Alex. You may have a seat in the back."

She didn't give me a second glance after that, and for that matter, neither did anyone else. A few pairs of eyes slid over to me as I made my way to my chair, but then went right back to books, or to friends.

I slunk into my seat, spreading my hands out wide over the small desk and staring at them. My nails were clean—cleaner than normal—and less dirt seemed to have gathered in the creases around my knuckles. Maybe 'cause there was less soot in the air, away from the tracks that ran by my home.

Home. As unenthusiastic as I was about school, if I'd have been home, I'd have had people to reconnect with during this brief period. I'd have had gossip to catch up on, or rumors of my own to pass along. Here, I had nothing.

I waited for a while, with both dread and hope, for someone to turn to me. But I couldn't look like I was expecting it, so I studied my hands until I'd practically memorized every pore and hair on the skin. No hellos, no *ey cabrónes*, no flirting smiles—at least not that I could see while I avoided eye contact with these strangers. Every nameless, faceless person around me seemed content to let me keep my position as the outsider.

And I was fine with that. I really was. I didn't need them—or anyone, for that matter.

After about five minutes, I dug into my backpack and pulled out an old paperback—a required book at my old school. I didn't know if I'd need it here, but I was that fucking bored that I actually began reading.

Might as well have slapped a stamp on my forehead: I give up on being me.

~*~

Somehow, I got through the day, though not without a splitting headache. Most of the stuff I was studying was the same, but there were new assignments, new testing schedules, and new papers to write. It felt like more work than I was used to, but that might've been because it was the first time I was worried I'd actually have to *do* it.

My mom never really cared how I did in school. She hadn't minded when I was held back, and she didn't often make time for those parent-teacher conference things. The most I got was a sigh and an *ay, papi, you should study more.* Her main concern was that I actually *went* to school, 'cause cutting class too many times could've gotten her in trouble.

But now I felt like there were at least *three* freaking adults who were going to be breathing down my neck. I'd seen the sisters interrogating all the boys on their assignments. Even though I was the only one in ninth grade, I didn't think they'd buy the "nope, no homework today," that my mom always had. And then there was Suzie, who'd come to see me the night before, telling me in her sickeningly soft-sweet voice that even though circumstances were difficult, I shouldn't lose sight of the fact that an education was just *so* important.

What would be worse, pissing them all off, or actually doing the work?

There would have been an evil pleasure in getting them angry, sure, but it'd probably only make my situation worse. And it wasn't exactly like I had a life anymore, so what else was there to do *but* homework?

The internal debate raged on while Brandon and Dwayne traded their school-uniform navy pants and polos for jeans and t-shirts. I congratulated myself on keeping control of my thoughts as they changed, though I sort of slipped up afterward, staring out the window to watch them toss around the basketball in the backyard.

Brandon looked good sweaty. And if he got a little sweatier, he might even have to take off that shirt…

The small bodies of Andrew and Ryan suddenly burst into the room, chattering with the energy and excitement that only little kids still have.

"Ms. Loretta says it's your turn to help us with our homework."

I turned reluctantly from the window. "Are you fucking kidding me?"

Ryan's brows shot up to his clean-cut hairline. "Ooh, you said a bad word! I could tell on you."

I rolled my eyes. "Like you've never heard no one say that."

"Still a bad word," Andrew said, tugging his batman shirt down and puffing out his chest authoritatively. "And you could get in trouble."

When *couldn't* I get in trouble here?

"Fine. What do you have to do?"

"Our homework!" Ryan sang out. "We got to do our homework! We got to do our homework!" He danced around himself as he sang.

Kill me now.

I took them both downstairs to the dining room and dropped their backpacks on the table in front of them. "All right, then. Do it. I'll…come back to check on it in a while."

"But I need help!" Ryan protested before I could even take a step away, scrunching his nose and curling his lip to reveal his messed-up teeth. That kid really needed braces.

Andrew nodded solemnly. "Ryan always needs help."

I shook my head. "But you haven't even tried it yet. How can you know you need help?"

"Because I do," Ryan whined.

"Jesus, just take the homework out and f—…and *try* it."

Ryan huffed and finally dragged out his folder. "Okay, but I'm still gonna need help."

I took my break upstairs. Seb had slipped in at some point while I'd been with the boys, and he was already hidden in his blankets by the time I reentered the room.

Lucky kid.

I stared at the back of his head for a minute or two, wondering if I should follow his lead, or go out back and quit being such an antisocial freak.

"*Alex!* I need help!" Ryan screeched.

I rushed back down before Ms. Loretta could leave the meatloaf she was making and call me out for failing at my duties.

"What? What do you need help with?"

The scene I came upon stopped me in my tracks: three paper airplanes on the floor, and Andrew making a goal with his thumbs and index fingers as Ryan flicked a crumpled wad toward him.

"Aw, you've gotta be f—"

"Bad word!" Andrew warned.

I took a deep breath. "You've got to be kidding me. You haven't even picked up your pencil."

"Duh." Ryan rolled his eyes. "Because I need help."

Dwayne wandered past, the smell of his sweat thick in the air. I pretended to be hard at work studying the outside of Ryan's folder so I could ignore the fact he *had* actually stripped off his shirt. I wondered if Brandon had as well? Maybe if I could sneak back upstairs I could catch him out the window...

"Ya know," Dwayne said, "it's easier if you separate them. They never do their work when they together."

Andrew's eyes went wide. "But I need help, too. Who's he gonna help first? My show's on in thirty minutes, and I gotta be done to watch!"

"Maybe you shoulda thought of that before you started playing paper football," Dwayne responded.

The headache I'd had earlier was gearing up for a sequel. Actually, I felt like I'd been in various stages of headache for at least a week now.

"Can you just take one of 'em?" I muttered, face buried in my hands.

"Okay."

Dwayne's reply startled me enough that I looked up. Fuck, he had way too many muscles for a sixteen-year-old.

"Okay?"

He shrugged. "Sure. I can take Andrew up and help him since you probably too stupid to help him anyway. But what're you gonna do for me if I do?"

"Huh?" I blamed my less-than-brilliant response, as well as the fact that I'd ignored an insult, on the way the sweat coating his muscles gave them a brilliant sheen.

"I ain't gonna do it for nothin'. I'll take Andrew today if you mow the lawn for me this Sunday."

"Fuck no," was my immediate answer.

"Bad word!" Andrew trumpeted.

"Jesus, will you shut up!" Whirling around, I very nearly clamped a hand over his mouth. "Fine." I jerked his chair back violently, and was pleased to see him flail from my efforts. "Take him. I'll mow the f—...I'll mow the lawn. Whatever."

Dwayne dropped his hand on Andrew's shoulder to lead him away. "Nice doin' business with ya."

Ms. Cecily came in just as I opened Ryan's folder to get a look at whatever it was a first grader—or was he in second?—well, whatever it was a kid his age was supposed to have for homework.

"Afternoon, Alex. Is Andrew doing his work? You know that one likes to sneak away and turn on the TV before he's done."

"Mhm," I mumbled, digging for a pencil in Ryan's backpack and then shoving it into his hand. "Dwayne offered to take him."

"Did he now?" She laughed. God, I really was the butt of everyone's jokes here. "Well, you see that they finish up before Ms. Loretta has dinner ready. We havin' meatloaf tonight, my favorite."

I thought she'd had a few too many loaves of meat in her lifetime, but I just nodded so she'd leave us alone.

"Okay. So what all do you have to do?" I asked Ryan. He was doodling in the margins of a piece of paper he'd yanked out of his folder.

"Gotta write a paragraph about my family."

"So...do it."

"Yeah"—he stuck his tongue to the top of his crooked teeth and stared up thoughtfully—"but which family do I write about? My real one, or my foster family?"

Foster family. My skin prickled with immediate rejection. No way was I part of any foster *family.*

"Write about your real family, kid."

"Okay." He nodded, gripping his pencil. It didn't quite make it to the paper, though. "I have a brother. Do you have any brothers?"

"Nah."

"My brother's bigger than you."

"Good for him."

"He plays football."

"Will you please just write?"

"You don't play football? Dwayne and Brandon do."

"No, I don't. And I don't want to."

"My brother Jordan was gonna teach me how to play."

"Well maybe if you finish your homework you can go back to your real family and he'll do that, okay?"

Ryan bit his lip, his eyes fluttering down. "Nah. He won't."

"Great brother you have there," I muttered. Though I was really one to talk.

Ryan's pencil finally started to move across the paper, and I sighed in relief. Thank God he only had to write a paragraph.

"'kay, done!" He shot up from his chair. "I'm gonna go watch TV!"

At last. I picked up the paper and was shoving it into his folder when I remembered Ms. Loretta had said they'd check to make sure things were done right. That wasn't really a big deal, though. I could just fix any mistakes myself—it'd be easier than having to drag the brat back over here.

Pencil poised with the eraser tip down, I looked at what he'd written.

I have a brothr. His name is Jordan. He play futball and he wus guna teech me but he ded now cuz he wus shot.

Oh, fuck.

~*~

I couldn't get away for the cigarette I so desperately needed until after dinner. It was really fucking hard to get any time alone at this place.

I crawled behind the shed again, but this time I sat facing left so I'd be able to catch Seb if he tried to sneak up on me. Not that I'd minded him all that much. Of all the people I was trapped here with, he was pretty much the most tolerable. At least he kept his mouth shut.

One cigarette shrunk down to the butt, and I stamped it out. I'd told myself I was going to ration the pack—no more than three a week—but I really didn't have much resolve. The day had sucked beyond measure, from my complete lack of a life at school, to dissing a little kid's dead brother. Another cigarette was in order.

This time it was only a slight breeze that caused me to look behind me, where I saw Seb standing inches away.

Little fucker. How had he managed to get through the barely-one-foot clearance on the other side of the shed? And why?

I stood up and crossed my arms. "Really, man?"

His eyes bounced slightly, but his face remained completely expressionless. Maybe the retard had a sense of humor?

"I hope you didn't come for another cigarette, 'cause I ain't gonna waste any more on you."

More bouncing black eyes.

"Well, if you gonna stay, then sit down."

I did first, and he followed my lead. More comfortable leaning straight back against the shed, I rested my head and stared up at what would've been stars, if not for all the light pollution. "Shit, I've had a lousy day. Did you know that Ryan kid's brother was dead? Do you know what happened?"

Seb had started digging in the dirt again, tracing out spirals…and I really needed to learn to stop asking the kid questions.

"Well, I'll ask Brandon or something. I just wish I woulda known. I sorta said something stupid. I mean, he didn't say nothing about it…maybe he'll forget. Kids forget shit like that, right?"

He lifted a pinch of dirt and then opened his fingers, letting the breeze carry it away.

"I'm such a retard…uh, no offense or nothing." I sighed. "I guess I just forget that everyone has their own shit going on. Maybe I've had my head up my ass…but today at school was just such complete crap."

Shifting his weight, Seb turned to look at me. I took that as my pass to go ahead and complain some more.

"Do you know what I did during lunch? I ate alone. No one fucking said a word to me, so I finished in like five minutes and went and hid in the bathroom. Me, hiding in the bathroom! Can you fucking believe that shit? That ain't me. I don't hide in the bathroom unless I'm waiting to make a fucking deal or something!"

I clamped my mouth shut, embarrassed by my sudden outburst.

"This place…" I continued more calmly, "this is just not me. I don't belong."

Seb wiped his hands on his jeans, leaving behind smudges of dirt, then gingerly reached over to me. I held still until his fingers came to a stop millimeters above the gauze on my wrist.

"Oh, that?" I laughed bitterly. "Well, that's it. That's why I'm here."

Now that he'd drawn attention to the area, it started to itch. I scratched a bit through the fabric, but it didn't really offer that much relief, so I went ahead and unwrapped it. Seb appeared fascinated, and I let him brush his pinky along the outskirts of the wound. It was healing up now, but it still looked pretty nasty, with red and pink rivers of flesh running through it.

"It don't really hurt anymore…and it definitely wasn't worth all this shit. See, what happened was, this bitch teacher—"

One of Seb's fingers accidentally touched a part of the wound, and I inhaled sharply through the pain. "Hey, watch it."

He shoved his hands back into the dirt.

"Anyways, I was saying, this bitch…" but I faltered there, thrown off by Seb's wide, attentive eyes. I shook my head slowly. "Okay, so I guess she's not really a bitch. I mean, I don't think she liked me very much, but I wasn't exactly a good student. I guess she was just doing her job. She thought my mom's boyfriend did this to me."

Seb cocked his head, eyes narrowing. It was probably just my own thoughts getting in the way, but I really imagined that look said, *And did he?*

I bit my lip. "You sure you can't talk, right?"

No response.

Blowing out a breath, I finally gave in. "Yeah. Hector did it. He's done other shit, too…but it wasn't gonna go on forever. I had things under control."

Seb's eyes drifted to the ground. He scooped up a handful of dirt and deposited it in a neat little mound, then smoothed out the sides.

"So, whaddaya think, Seb—should I stick around? Or run away and try to find my mom?"

Busy making another mound, Seb glanced up for only a second, and I thought maybe the corner of his lip twitched before he was expressionless again.

And I still hadn't learned to stop asking him questions.

Without warning, he stood.

"It's lights out, huh," I said as I followed. "You got super hearing? Or you one of those genius retards who can't take care of himself but like always knows the time or something?"

His eyes bounced again.

"Well, anyways…thanks for letting me bitch for a while. Even if my problems ain't such a big deal, compared to others." I stuck out my hand and tousled his white-blond locks. "Too bad you can't actually understand me."

It wasn't really, though. I didn't want anyone in this house to have the satisfaction of knowing just how lost I was.

Chapter 8: Like You Wanna Kill Someone

Watching the tips of my black Keds, I shuffled along in the lunch line. Someone jostled me from behind—by accident, probably—and I pushed back, making sure to give the offender a look that said he'd better not mess with me again. Then I returned to staring at my feet, absentmindedly tugging down the sleeve of the thin sweater I wore to keep my wrist hidden. Ms. Cecily had replaced the gauze with a rectangular bandage, but it still seemed best to keep it out of sight. The fact that it was on my damn wrist really did make it look like I might've tried to off myself.

God, Hector was such a fucking asshole.

I snagged a shrink-wrapped plate of tater-tots to add to the apple and chocolate milk already on my tray. The condensation along the top of the plastic film was starting to drip down onto the fried potato bits, and I knew by the time I got to a seat my food would be all soggy and gross. Not that I really ate much at lunch. I'd just make up for it later, 'cause as much as I couldn't stand Ms. Loretta, she did cook some fucking good meals.

There was probably another reason I didn't have much of an appetite at lunchtime—that whole no-place-to-belong thing stood out here more than ever. Sometimes I skipped the meal altogether and went to sulk by the bathrooms, but today I spotted an empty table where I could keep to myself.

On my way, I passed a laughing group of girls who had their eye on a guy in an athlete's jacket a few seats down. I'd have liked to have my eye on him, too, if I weren't feeling so sorry for myself. And besides that, I didn't think I could get away with being both a loser transfer student *and* a creepy perv who stared at strangers. Without a social life to speak of, there really wasn't an excuse for me to look at or hang around any hot guys.

I sat with my back to the crowds and tried to block out the happy sounds. At this point, I didn't know what would be worse—recognition that I was a fucking loser, sitting all by myself, or no recognition at all.

"Hey." A soft thunk accompanied the tray that suddenly landed to my right.

I looked up to see a thin black girl with hair done in careful braids and tied off with white ribbons.

Was she talking to me?

"Uh, I said hey," she repeated, eying me like I was a complete retard. I wondered if I looked at Seb that way.

"Do I know you?" I returned the stare.

"I don't think you know anyone here."

Well, she certainly had me figured out. "So what?"

"So, is that what you want?"

"What do you care?"

She stuck her shapely legs into the bench and sat next to me. "Who says I do?"

"You're the one talking to me."

"I know. I must be crazy or something."

"Must be," I muttered, tearing the plastic wrap to get at my mushy tater-tots.

"You been here a while now, and I haven't seen you try to talk to anyone."

"Yeah, well I haven't seen no one try to talk to me, either. What's your point?"

"Maybe they would if you didn't walk around looking like you wanna kill someone."

I popped half a tater-tot into my mouth and turned to glare at her.

"Yeah, like that." She laughed. "That's the look."

All right, maybe she had me there.

I rolled my eyes, but grinned a little. She wasn't bad looking, really. Nice skin, pretty smile…I wondered if I should try to make something of this.

She probably took my half-smile as progress. "My name's Laloni."

"Alex." I gave her the cool Diego-style head nod.

"So, Alex, what's with the death stare?"

"I don't have a death stare." I rolled my eyes again.

"Don't you want to make new friends?"

"Not really. I was all right with the ones I had before I got here."

She nodded. "Fair answer."

"And what about you? Don't you have your own friends already?" I highly doubted a girl like her was unattached from a social crowd.

"Oh, I have plenty of friends…but I've been told I also have a thing for the charity cases."

"I didn't ask for no charity." I turned away, knowing my glare was back and not wanting to give her another thing to laugh at.

"'Course you didn't. I didn't say I liked the needy types."

I was out of things to say that made any sense. Could she really have picked me out of a crowd just to flirt with? I mean, I knew I was attractive enough, but this seemed a little out of the ordinary.

"Well, anyhow, I'm gonna go back over to my friends." She pointed to another table. "But maybe I'll see you around."

She left abruptly, and I watched her curvy rear as it swayed away. On second thought, she was more than just 'not bad looking.' Pretty, actually.

I ate one more soggy tater-tot before switching to the apple for a better texture. Chewing thoughtfully, I considered taking the opening Laloni had given me. I had to admit it was possible I could establish a new life for myself at this school…but did that mean I was giving up on my old one?

Shit, not my old one. My *real* one.

Still…being less of a loser at school wouldn't hurt. Maybe it'd make me feel more like myself, and help me get a grip on what it was I should be doing to make things right in my life again.

And Laloni was hot, which could only help my reputation. I'd also never been with a black girl before, though I didn't think my mother would've been too pleased.

If she only knew the half of it.

~*~

As it turned out, I didn't have to wait very long to meet up with Laloni again. I caught sight of her leaning against the light pole in front of the school that afternoon, one knee turned in like she was posing for a picture. A few guys passed by to talk to her, and she tilted her hips, swinging her braids around as she laughed at whatever it was they were saying. With that level of easy confidence, no doubt the girl knew she looked good.

Conflicting emotions rose in me immediately. Did I really want to start another pointless relationship? And even if I did, should I make contact again so soon? It might seem a bit desperate, and I'd kind of wanted to talk it over with Seb and a cigarette before taking any action.

Then I shook my head violently, trying to clear the cobwebs from my mind. Talk it over with a retarded mute?

That was the kind of behavior that was contributing to my loser image in the first place.

"Hey, Laloni." I called out to her, keeping my hands in my pockets and walking over slowly.

"Hey, Alex," she responded with a knowing smile. It kind of unnerved me, but I figured it was just because I was out of practice.

"So, uh...you a freshman?"

Brilliant conversation-starter. Of course she was a freshman, since we shared a lunch period.

"Mhm. I think I have English after you...saw you leaving the classroom late the other day."

"Oh." I shrugged. "Why rush out of class? Only losers do that."

She laughed. "Whatever you say, Alex."

I was striking out here, and I knew it. I didn't usually have to work this hard to get a girl interested. Maybe since I'd never really wanted a girl interested in the first place.

"So...uh...I just moved here. Neighborhood seems kinda lame. What do you guys do for fun around here?"

When she laughed, the ribbons on the ends of her braids danced back and forth. "Hang out with friends, mostly. What was so great about the neighborhood you came from? They had some kind of under-eighteen club or something?"

"Uh..." I kicked at a white scuff on my Keds. "No. We'd throw our own parties, I guess."

"And there's a rule that says you can't do that here?"

There was, actually. Ms. Loretta only allowed birthday parties, and mine wasn't for another few months.

"Oh, guess you'd need friends for that," she added, her face straight but her eyes mocking.

I cringed. Maybe she hadn't liked me at all. Maybe the whole reason she'd talked to me at lunch was for her own amusement.

Either way, it was seriously time to make my exit from this train-wreck of a conversation.

"I'm gonna go home now," I mumbled. No reason to wait around for Dwayne and Brandon, since they liked to loiter in the hallways after class. I didn't really see the appeal in that, but then again, I didn't see the appeal in going back to the house, either.

"I'll walk with you," Laloni said, and without hesitation fell into step beside me.

Now I was *really* confused. She was going to follow me home? I didn't even know Ms. Loretta's rules about having girls over. Didn't sound like something she'd go for.

"Uh, sure," I stammered, as if she needed my permission. We were already on our way, anyhow. "You don't got nothing better to do?"

She lifted one shoulder in a half-shrug. "Not today."

We crossed several squares of sidewalk before I could come up with something else to say. "So...you know of any parties happening around here?"

"If there are any, I'll be sure to let you know about 'em."

Finally, a fucking inkling of a chance with her. Though when I thought of having to go to a party, my guts rolled around in protest. I wished there was a way to be cool without having to plaster on a fake smile and act like you enjoyed drunken morons. Which reminded me...

"You guys drink and stuff?"

She shrugged again. "Depends on the party, I guess. But I don't do that shit."

I might've stopped walking for a second.

"What, that surprises you?" she asked, crossing her arms as her head darted from side to side.

"Sort of. Usually the girls that stay clear of that stuff are...losers...and you don't seem like that."

"Huh. That's funny. Because you *do* seem like a loser, and I'm gonna take a wild guess and say you don't stay clear of *that stuff.*"

I stuck my hands out defensively. "Whoa. What the hell. I wasn't trying to insult you."

She smiled brightly, braids bobbing. "Neither was I."

We'd almost reached the house, and I was torn between an overwhelming urge to be rid of her, and a desire to know just what it was she'd seen in me that had caused her to approach me in the first place.

"Look, I don't really get you," I said—one of the most honest things I'd told anyone in ages. "Why exactly are you hanging around me right now? Do you, uh…"

My question was cut off when caramel-colored arms suddenly encircled her from behind, then whirled her around to sweep her into a kiss.

"Heya, baby." When he was through sucking on her mouth, Brandon draped his arm over her shoulder. "I see you met the new kid."

And that would've been the perfect moment for an earthquake. Not a really horrific one, of course…but just enough to knock Brandon flat on his ass and give me a chance to get the fuck away from my total humiliation.

"Uh huh." Laloni's laughter cut sharply into my wounded pride. "He's been really shy so I thought I'd talk to him today."

"I ain't shy, bitch," I snapped.

Brandon stepped in front of her. "You better watch how you fucking talk to my girl."

She slapped his shoulder. "I told you not to call me that. I ain't no one's girl."

But Brandon kept glaring, and for once I actually felt like I needed to back down. Not 'cause I was scared of him, or anything…but I had a sister. I knew you weren't supposed to treat girls like that.

"Sorry, Laloni. I just didn't realize you…you knew about me already."

"You mean that you a foster kid?" she asked.

I gritted my teeth.

"It's okay. Obviously I don't have a problem with it. I put up with this asshole."

Brandon made a hurt face. Laloni laughed and kissed it off him.

I was getting sick to my stomach.

"All right, so maybe I shoulda told you I knew who you was...but then I woulda missed your really sad attempts to flirt with me," she finished with a giggle.

Pretty sure the wanting-to-kill-someone look was back, I decided to cut my losses and leave. Maybe I could curl up in a cocoon of blankets and spend the rest of the day in bed, like Seb. It definitely would've been an improvement.

"No, wait, Alex." Laloni's hand came down on my shoulder as I stepped away. "I'm only teasing. I just like to get to know Brandon's foster brothers...see if they gonna be a good influence or a bad influence on him."

"I don't have no brothers," I growled.

Her eyes fluttered up dramatically. "Whatever. You know what I mean."

I tried to keep walking, but Brandon's hand came down on my other shoulder. "You know, you don't always have to be such a dick to us. We really ain't as bad as you like to think."

He ended by giving me a little pat, and I glanced back at him. His dimples were showing again, and the smile seemed pretty genuine.

Why did he have to look so freaking good?

I let my own expression melt into something reflecting grudging acceptance, and he grinned even wider.

"So, Laloni..." I turned to face her again. "What'd you decide...'bout my influence?"

She smirked and intertwined her fingers with Brandon's. "Not sure yet. I'll let you know." Then she looked up at him and batted her lashes. "Walk me home?"

Her eyes got all soft when she asked, and his responded the same way. "Sure thing, babe."

"See ya tomorrow, Alex." She waved as they walked off.

I watched them leave, hands still locked together, and besides being thankful the encounter was over, another sensation hit me. That way Brandon was looking at her...puppy-dog love mixed with regular teenage lust...shit, what I wouldn't have given for him to look at *me* like that.

But I squashed the thought as soon as it popped up. Jealousy didn't suit me.

Oh well. At least I still had the shed, the cigarettes, and Seb.

~*~

"You coulda told me Brandon had a girlfriend," I said to Seb that evening.

Today he was refilling the little holes he'd previously made in the ground, smoothing out the dirt so it was nice and even again. He used the blank canvas to draw squiggles with his finger.

"Not that I really mind, or anything...it's just...well, for a minute I thought she was interested in me."

Seb's hand made little *pat-pat* noises as he flattened another lump of soil.

"She's all right, I guess. You ever met her? Probably not, huh. I bet Ms. Loretta don't let you guys have girls over."

I pulled a cigarette out of the pack, but didn't light it up.

"You ever had a girlfriend, Seb?"

He was ignoring me more than usual today. Just more of the same turn-for-shit my life had taken...I couldn't even keep a retard interested.

I leaned back all the way to the ground, cushioning my head with my arms so I could stare up at the hazy-pink full moon. "Well, I have. Had a few. Was probably about to have another one right before I left...this girl named Blanca."

A shudder ran through me. She'd been so grabby and forceful. Probably one of those clingy girls...

"Kinda glad I avoided that one." I snickered.

Seb looked over at me for some reason, and I automatically stumbled into an explanation. "Uh...'cause she was annoying."

He seemed to have just noticed I was lying down, and decided to do the same, scooting his body close to mine.

"Do you want to have a girlfriend?" I asked, glancing over and catching the reflection of the moon in his dark eyes.

He stared back, but of course, didn't say anything.

Such a shame he was retarded. Those wide almond eyes of his were actually pretty fucking amazing.

"I don't."

Had I just said that out loud? Jesus Christ.

"I mean, 'cause, uh, it's much better to be a free man, ya know?"

Seb turned away again, the corner of his lip twitching.

What the fuck was wrong with me? I was getting way too close to saying things that shouldn't be said. Even though Seb couldn't understand, it was a bad habit to get into.

Would I have screwed up like this back home, too?

An uncomfortable thought struck me. I tried not to let it take root in my mind, but the more I fought to push it away, the stronger it became.

I didn't have a social life here. I didn't have a reputation. I didn't have to be the same Alex I'd been before. It might be easier to keep my secret.

And that notion filled me with an overwhelming sense of...*relief.*

Chapter 9: Smarter

"I have your in-class essays graded."

Mr. Salazar, my new English teacher, swept through the rows and dropped the stupid things on desks as he went. I'd decided I hated him in the first five minutes I'd known him. He was one of those *educated* Latinos who wasn't gonna cut anyone any slack, 'cause if *he* could rise above, then all of us could.

Fucking prick.

English was always my worst class, and while some things in my new life had changed out of necessity, English was not one of them. So I knew what was coming before the paper landed in front of me.

Lots and lots of red circles and scribbles, with a nice big F at the top of the paper. And, oh, fuck. What was that he'd written in the margins? *See me after class.*

Not even a month in and I was already being ordered to see the teacher after class. Maybe new me wasn't so different from old me after all.

I waited until the room was empty to approach his desk.

"Ah, Alejandro." Mr. Salazar looked up. At least he could pronounce my name right. "I wanted to speak to you about the essay you wrote."

I frowned. "Yeah, well, I just got here. I wasn't ready to write it, teacher."

"It's Mr. Salazar, and I'm aware of that." He met my eyes in a way that told me he was aware of more than *just* that.

Did everyone at this school have to know I was a freaking foster kid?

"That's why I'd like to offer you the opportunity to do a make-up assignment."

Just what I wanted. *More* work.

"I'm kind of busy."

He didn't seem impressed with my excuse, and handed over a piece of paper with a prompt. "Due Tuesday."

When he turned back to his computer, I stomped out, crumpling my failed assignment and the make-up prompt into tight balls. I was so pissed I rounded a corner at full speed and wound up smacking straight into Laloni.

The papers scattered on the floor, and she bent to pick them up first. "Nice," she remarked, unfolding one enough to catch sight of the flaming red F.

"Man, shut up."

"You gonna do this make-up?"

I snatched both papers back. God, she was nosy. There were way too many women in my life right now. Even my mom and Mimi had seemed like overkill, once upon a time.

"Fuck no."

"I could help you with it, you know. English is my best subject. I help Brandon with his stuff, and he's a year ahead of me."

"Look, no offense, but school isn't really my thing."

She rolled her eyes. "'Course it's not."

"Hey." Brandon emerged from the crowd behind her, slipping a hand on her butt, which she immediately pushed off. "Second time I catch you two together...should I be worried?"

She huffed, but opened her mouth obediently for him to stick his tongue into it.

"I'm gonna go to class." Suddenly queasy, I left them making out, and doubted they even saw me go.

~*~

Suzie was sitting in the living room when I got home that afternoon. I didn't bother greeting her.

"Did you find my mom?"

When her eyes got sad, I had my answer. "No, Alex. Not yet."

I nodded. "All right, then. I'm gonna go up and do my homework."

She swiveled around to watch me walk down the hallway. "I was hoping we could chat for a little while. I'd like to see how things are going for you here."

I paused with one foot on the steps. "If you have something to tell me, you can go ahead and talk...but I have nothing to say to you."

When there was no response—other than a sigh—I continued up to the room.

I knew I was being a dick, but Suzie was really the only adult I could talk back to and get away with it. Had to take my wins where I could.

Seb was already upstairs, in bed. I sat across from him and watched him sleep for a little while, noting that his lashes were much darker than his hair. They matched the undertone in his complexion better, and those black-brown irises.

"Got my first F today...well, not my first ever, but my first here," I said quietly.

He didn't stir. I closed my eyes for a second, trying to reason with myself. Why was I talking to him when he was asleep? Then again, wasn't it just about the same as talking to him when he was awake?

The *thud-thud-thud* of the basketball on the uneven pavement of the patio punctuated my thoughts. I should've been out there, hanging with Dwayne and Brandon, not upstairs discussing my continuing progress toward becoming a high school dropout.

"Brandon's girlfriend offered to help me with this make-up assignment…but I dunno."

The front door swung open downstairs. Ms. Cecily was home from work, and the boys were back as well. "Ms. Suzie!" they cried, footsteps scampering into the living room.

I bet she loved that. Two sweet little boys, showing her affection and appreciation for what she did, instead of sulky teenagers giving her lip. And she probably deserved the thanks in their case. But in mine…

"Do…do you think if I were smarter, I wouldn't have ended up in this place? I mean, if I could learn to write stupid essays, I could probably talk better with adults…maybe lie better."

Seb's eyes shot open. Wide open, without a hint of drowsiness in their black depths.

"Hey!" I punched his shoulder, but only lightly. "You weren't asleep, you little sneak."

He stretched and sat up.

"So, help me out, dude. What should I do? Should I actually try to do that essay?"

His long arm reached toward me, and I noticed he was staring down at my wrist. Only a tiny amount of white peeked out from under the cuff of my sweater.

"It's getting much better."

I let him graze his fingertips over the spot.

"People've been through a lot worse." Hell, even I'd been through worse. "I really shoulda kept it together better than I did."

Maybe some self-improvement *was* in order.

Thwack! The basketball hit the siding of the house, fairly close to the window. I moved over so I could see what was going on back there and found Brandon staring up at me.

"Get your butt down here!" he called out. The *butt* instead of *ass* probably had to do with the fact that Andrew and Ryan were standing beside him. "We're gonna play Dwayne and the boys versus you and me."

"And I'll still wipe the floor with ya," Dwayne added.

I glanced at Seb. "Should I go?"

He just blinked.

"Yeah, all right," I yelled back. "Give me a sec to get out of my school clothes."

I changed quickly, before I could talk myself out of it, though I did hesitate when I realized I'd have to play in my Keds. I really needed to get some better sneakers…maybe Ms. Loretta would buy me some? I decided I'd ask about it later.

I was already out the door of the bedroom before I thought of Seb again. When I turned around, I saw he was still awake, and still watching me.

"Hey, if you're not sleeping, why do you stay up in here all day?"

No answer, of course.

I backtracked and stood over his bed. "Why don't you come outside? You could watch us play."

He didn't move, so I reached down and shook his pale wrist. "C'mon. Get some sun. You could really use it."

My hand slipped from his wrist to his fingers, and I locked on to give him a gentle tug. "Come on."

He finally threw off the covers and stood.

"Retard," I said affectionately, then ruffled his hair and shoved him toward the door.

I passed Suzie again on my way out, but she was talking to Ms. Cecily now so I decided to ignore her. Seb planted himself on the steps of the back porch while I continued down to the makeshift basketball court, where a second hoop had been rigged up to the fence beside the shed.

Dwayne was warming up with Andrew, giving him very strict instructions, but the younger Ryan was just bouncing around aimlessly on his own.

"Hey, Alex!" He ran up to me excitedly. "We gonna play blacks versus browns!"

Brandon rolled his eyes. "Well I guess I can't play, then."

"Huh?" Ryan looked over at him. "Whaddaya mean?"

"'Cause I'm both, dummy."

I could tell Ryan didn't get it. He grabbed Brandon's arm, then mine, and squished them together.

The skin-on-skin contact was a really nice sensation. Really nice. Maybe we could compare skin tones more often.

"You closer to Alex than you is to me," Ryan said.

"Yeah, Ry." Brandon pulled away, and I quickly refocused myself. "I'll explain it to ya later. For now, let's just play."

We walked over to the middle of the concrete, and Brandon clapped his hands in the air. "Let's go, guys."

Dwayne scowled at me. "Didn't think you'd come down."

Grinning, Brandon stuck an elbow in my side. "Told ya he would."

The ball bounced between them as they checked it, and Andrew and Ryan instantly went into hyper-drive, jumping around and waving their arms wildly. "Pass it, Dwayne, pass it!"

He did, but only when Brandon had him cornered. I went to try to intercept, but I was up against a little kid for crying out loud. What exactly was I supposed to do? Once Ryan had caught it, I didn't really feel right taking it away.

The ball sailed back to Dwayne, and he made a basket on the far end by the shed.

He turned around and did a little dance, mocking us. "Go ahead and add all the teammates you want, Brandon. Ain't gonna stop me."

Brandon narrowed his eyes. "Oh, it's on." Then he punched my shoulder. "We got this."

"But what do I do with the little kids?" I protested, both pleased with his vote of confidence and afraid of letting him down. "I can't knock 'em to the ground!"

"Play around 'em!" he shouted, and we were off chasing the ball again.

I tried to take Brandon's advice, but I was not and never will be much of a basketball player. The first time I had the opportunity to get the ball, I made a clumsy pass that Dwayne easily intercepted. The next time, it was freaking *Andrew* who managed to snag the ball from me, but I still blamed it on the fact that I couldn't play all-out against a little kid.

I found myself wishing Brandon had been my opponent instead, as that would've allowed for more accidental closeness. Not that Dwayne didn't do anything for me physically, but the truth was I was a lot more intimidated by him. That probably didn't help my game much, either.

Seb kept his eyes on us the whole time, white-blond hair glowing under the direct sunlight. I hoped he wouldn't get a sunburn...and I was sort of regretting asking him to come down, if all he was going to see was me making an ass of myself.

But at least he wouldn't show any disappointment on that expressionless face of his.

I had to put up with quite a bit of Dwayne's heckling before the game turned. Luckily, he was also at a disadvantage with the little boys thrown into the mix, and Brandon was an okay player. It was neck and neck right up until the end, when I finally got a chance to make a praiseworthy play. Brandon distracted Dwayne long enough for me to steal the ball, and I made a mad dash for the leaning hoop. Skirting around the speed bump that was a screeching Ryan, I managed to dunk it, probably only because of the fact the basket was, well, *leaning*.

"Yes!" Brandon shouted. He ran up to me, clapping one hand on my back and the other on my chest. "We killed it!"

Laughing, I thumped Brandon's shoulder in celebration. I wasn't sure if it was from Brandon's arms around me or just the general excitement of victory, but I knew at that moment I was the happiest I'd been in weeks.

I looked over to make sure Seb was watching me in my triumph.

He was.

~*~

"Okay, seriously?" Laloni gripped her eraser and began violently smudging out my sentence. "Basic subject-verb agreement."

I tilted my chair back, resting it on the bookshelf behind me. I'd have snapped at her for giving me attitude, but the school librarian had already shushed me several times. Personally, I didn't think the rules for being quiet in a library should've applied after school. If I was willing to give up my free time to be in a freaking library, I should've been able to speak as loud as I damn well pleased.

"Don't even know what you're talking about," I said through clenched teeth.

She heaved a sigh. "I'm talking about...I don't, you don't, but he or she *doesn't*."

I arched a brow at her.

"He *doesn't* support his argument, not he *don't* support it." She stabbed my paper with the eraser.

I knew that, vaguely—the same way I knew about double negatives—but I forgot sometimes.

"Whatever." I crossed my arms. "You talk like that too, you know."

"Sure, I talk like that…but I don't write like that. English *don't* work that way."

She grinned, and I eventually unfolded my arms. She was trying not to get too annoyed with me, I realized. And she *was* doing me a favor. I probably owed her a bit more effort.

"Fine." I picked up my pencil and rewrote the sentence. "It just gets hard keeping it straight."

Tapping her chin, she looked up thoughtfully. "Hmm. Think of it like…you're writing in a foreign language. You speak Spanish, but you wouldn't go around writing essays for class in Spanish, would you?"

"Actually"—I cringed—"my Spanish is not that great."

She laughed. "Of course it's not. What *are* you good at, Alex?"

Ouch. That kind of hurt. I dropped my pencil on the table and stared down at the blue carpet. "I was perfectly good at my old life before I had to deal with all this fucking bullshit."

A very unlady-like snort emerged from Laloni. "God, what is it with you people."

"Who're you calling *you people*?" I shot back.

The librarian looked up sharply. "Quiet, please."

Rolling her eyes, Laloni continued in a low voice. "I meant foster kids. I don't get why it is you're so pissed someone wants to take care of you…why you always want to go back."

"Um, because it was my *life*." Obviously.

"Your life, huh?" Laloni grinned evilly. "Well let's see. Where you from?"

Something about that look on her face made me feel like I was about to walk into a trap. "Watts."

"Watts." She nodded slowly. "The most ghetto part of the ghetto. What do you got back there that's so great? Why would anyone want to *stay* in Watts?"

At one time, the answer to that question would've been my family. But I couldn't say that anymore.

"I had my friends."

"Right. Really great friends that you've kept in touch with."

Fuck. Brandon had probably told her I never spoke to anyone. And I bet I could have, if I'd really wanted to. But I hadn't.

"Whatever." I hoped that brush-off would inspire her to drop the topic.

It didn't.

"What, you were in a gang there or something?"

I huffed. "No, but I had an in if I wanted it."

"And did you?"

Stalling, I watched two studious-looking kids with glasses gather up a pile of books from a nearby table and leave.

"Well, no. Not really. I dealt a little on the side, just to friends. And only weed."

Laloni shook her head. "*That's* what you want to go back to?"

I closed my eyes for a moment, battling the feeling of emptiness that had suddenly overwhelmed me.

"Hey." She tapped my hand with her pencil. "Sorry, I wasn't trying to attack you. And it's not just you. Brandon wants to go back, too."

I looked over and saw the fear in her eyes, and realized yet again the world didn't revolve around me.

"I thought he said his mom was gonna go to rehab so she'd be able to take care of him."

"Yeah." Laloni's tone sharpened with sarcasm. "Don't suppose he mentioned it'd be her fourth try."

"Oh." I rested my head in my hand, propping myself up with an elbow. "No, he didn't. Actually, I don't really know much about anyone in the house."

"Too busy being all sorry for yourself," she responded.

She really did walk the line between halfway decent girl and total bitch a little too frequently.

"Well, since you seem to know everything, why don't you fill me in?"

"Sure." She shrugged. "Whaddaya wanna know?"

"Uh…" I paused to think it over. "Well, what about Ryan? I know his brother was shot."

"Yup." She nodded. "It was a gang thing. His brother was the one who was really taking care of him before that, so afterwards…well, you know. Wound up in foster care."

"Oh." Poor kid. "And Andrew?"

"Basic neglect. No food, no clean clothes…his mom didn't even send him to school."

That seemed strange. I was pretty sure my mom had enjoyed the freedom she'd gotten when I was in school as a kid.

"Okay. Dwayne?"

She hesitated, narrowing her eyes. "If I tell you, you better not say nothing."

"I won't."

After taking a few more seconds to decide, she leaned closer to whisper in my ear. "Sexual abuse. Not him, though—an uncle who lived with him did something to his sister. But they removed every kid from the house, just in case."

Shit. I was sort of regretting asking for all this information. It'd be hard to see any of them as just annoying jerks ever again.

"You didn't ask about Ms. Loretta or Ms. Cecily," Laloni pointed out.

"Oh, yeah." I hadn't thought about them. What exactly did they get out of running a home for fucked-over boys?

"Well, Ms. Cecily is an old spinster, but Ms. Loretta was married and had a son."

"What happened to them?"

"Car accident. When the baby was like only a year old."

Jesus. What a house of misery. And yet…no one really seemed all that miserable, except for me. And Seb, maybe. I'd never really seen him looking happy.

"What about Seb?"

Laloni reached up to retie a bow in her hair. "Him I don't know much about, besides the fact that he's, you know, *special*...he's sixteen, and he can't talk. I bet he was abandoned. Lots of special needs kids are abandoned."

Abandoned. My chest tightened.

"So anyways, are we gonna give this another go?" She yawned, glancing over at the wall clock. "I really should get home soon."

I looked down at my essay and found the words swimming in front of my eyes.

Abandoned. Like me?

"Well?"

I blinked, and the world came back into focus. On the table was a relatively simple paper waiting to be written; next to me was a girl waiting to help.

"Yeah." I picked up my pencil. "Yeah. Why not."

Chapter 10: Quick Thinking

I faced Suzie in the living room, sitting cross-legged in the upholstered chair while she leaned back on the orange couch.

"It's really good to get a chance to talk to you this evening," she said.

I ducked my head so she couldn't see my flushing cheeks. All right, so I'd been a brat for a while, but I was ready to start getting over it.

"I spoke to some of the teachers at your school," she continued. "They said your grades are showing improvement."

"Yeah." Was there a little bit of pride in my voice? "I been staying after to get some help on stuff."

"That's really excellent, Alex."

It wasn't so excellent I needed the help in the first place, but I knew what she meant.

"And how are things going here, overall?"

"Um..." I picked at the dirt under my nails. "Pretty good, I guess. Ms. Loretta still gets mad when I don't dust good enough, but other than that...um, I guess we're all getting along."

Suzie smiled warmly. "That's what Ms. Loretta said. I heard even Sebastian's been doing better...getting out of the room more."

I hid my grin by scratching my chin with my shoulder.

"Well, is there anything you need? Anything I could help you with right now?"

Bypassing the crucial topic—for the time being—I went to the next most important thing. "Shoes."

"I'm sorry?" Suzie leaned forward, straightening a faded brown suit jacket.

Jesus, that woman needed some serious fashion help.

"New shoes." I gestured to the Keds I still wore. "Sneakers. A good pair of sneakers."

"Oh." She laughed her polite white-lady laugh. "Well, I'll see what I can do about that. Anything else?"

I wasn't sure why she was prodding me. I almost didn't want to say anything, because talking about it just pulled back the thin layer of insulation I'd built up to keep from thinking about it every second of every day. But Suzie continued to look at me expectantly, and I cracked.

"You haven't heard from my mom, have you."

"No." She shook her head, her voice growing softer. "You know I'd tell you as soon as I'd heard anything."

"Yeah." I pinched the bridge of my nose, then let my hand spread out to cover my eyes. "I know."

Little explosions of white dotted the black canvas of my closed lids. I watched them for a time, working up the composure to speak again.

"Maybe…maybe she just doesn't know where I am?"

"It's possible, I suppose. But it wouldn't be that hard to find out."

And even though Suzie's lips clamped shut after that, I heard what remained unspoken: It wouldn't have been that hard to find out, *if she'd wanted to*.

Abandoned.

"I'm sorry, Alex." Suzie's voice dropped near a whisper.

She always said that. She was *sorry*. Everyone was *sorry*...except for my mother.

"Okay." I hit my thighs, using the impact to jolt me from a gathering cloud of dark thoughts. "You probably gotta get going, right? It's late."

Suzie frowned, and I felt a tug of guilt. But whatever, this was more than she'd gotten out of me in ages. She should've been grateful.

"All right, Alex. I'll talk to you sometime next week."

"Yeah, bye."

I stayed there as she gathered up her belongings and left. She always spoke to me last, since I was probably her toughest nut to crack—although with what I knew now about everyone else in the house, I didn't really have a right to be.

But maybe they'd all been like me, once. Maybe it was a process.

Dwayne and Brandon scrambled into the living room as soon as she was gone. They jumped over the back of the couch and began an immediate scuffle for control of the remote.

"You had it yesterday!" Brandon protested, working to pry Dwayne's impressively strong fingers from the device.

Dwayne held on tighter. "I am sick and tired of watching that CW crap!"

"Give it to me or I'll tell Alex your favorite channel is the cooking channel!"

"I watched one show, one time, 'cause they was making ribs, so shut the f—...shut the you-know-what up!"

I should've laughed at that. Or at least smirked. Dwayne trying to censor his language while defending his honor was obviously a funny sight, but I couldn't get into the right mood. Not so soon after talking to Suzie.

They both turned to me, as if they'd suddenly realized I was in the room—probably because I usually wasn't.

"Maybe we should let Alex choose," Brandon said slowly, his eyes sliding over to Dwayne.

Fully prepared for one of Dwayne's snide remarks, I geared up to force out a retort, even though all I really wanted to do was hole up somewhere and not talk to anyone for as long as humanly possible.

"Fine."

The remote sailed over and landed in my lap.

Startled, I lifted it cautiously, like it might suddenly come to life and bite me. I looked up at them and caught the tail end of a silent expressions-only conversation that seemed to indicate they'd both agreed not to mess with me—at least for tonight.

Seriously?

They must've felt sorry for me, too. As much crap as they'd been through, at least their families hadn't just up and abandoned them.

They felt sorry for *me*. I knew something wasn't right with that picture.

"Nah." I stood and left the remote on the chair behind me. "Not up for TV tonight...but I'd pick whichever channel has the hottest chicks."

Three seconds after I left they both sprang up and dove for the control, beginning round two of their playful fight.

Needing time alone, I headed upstairs. Ms. Loretta was reading a bedtime story to the boys, and as I passed by to enter my room, she looked up briefly. Even in *her* eyes I saw pity.

That was very nearly the last straw.

It made me want to scream. Scream in her face, scream at Brandon and Dwayne, scream at Suzie...hell, scream at anyone in earshot. My life wasn't that bad! It hadn't been that bad, that is, up until the point I realized I was...*disposable*.

I collapsed onto my bed, my feet knocking against the duffel bag I'd stashed underneath it. I still kept most of my personal clothes in there. I wanted to have them all packed up so that when it was time to go, I could make a quick exit. But with each passing day, that possibility seemed less and less realistic, and the worst part...the worst part was...

A streetlamp flickered outside. I looked through the window and caught a glimpse of something in the backyard.

Seb.

Even in the dark, I could see his skin had started to take on a bronze hue, now that he had a bit more contact with the sun. The color looked good on him.

It wasn't really a night to be outside, though. It was foggy and unusually cool, and it might've even been drizzling.

Taking my jacket and a sweater for Seb, I headed back downstairs. I didn't even think about the cigarettes.

"Hey." I met him behind the shed. "Were you waiting for me out here? It's kinda cold."

It wasn't actually raining, but the mist hung so heavily in the air that I could feel the moisture against my skin.

I draped the sweater over his shoulders and sat next to him. "Suzie was here, you know. That's why I didn't come out earlier."

He reached down to pick a few pieces of grass that had sprouted in a previously empty patch of dirt, then looked up at me expectantly.

"She...she still hasn't heard anything from my mom."

And in my head I added: *she might never hear anything.*

"Guess this means I should go ahead and unpack my stuff, huh? Might be staying a while."

I was trying for a light-hearted attitude, but I was pretty sure I was failing. Seb looked almost concerned, and if my voice and facial expressions were making a retarded kid who didn't understand me *concerned*, there was probably an issue.

"I wish I'd thought to bring more important stuff from my house, ya know? Like, maybe pictures or something."

Not that there were all that many, but I'd had a few in my dresser. And I knew my mom kept hers in her nightstand drawer—some of Mimi as a baby, and several of the two of us together after I'd been born.

"All I have left of my home now is shorts and t-shirts…and a jacket or two. Just *things*." I sighed, trying to release the weariness that had snuck up behind my anger.

Seb tilted his body toward me and the sweater fell off his right shoulder.

As I fixed it for him, the show of control abandoned me. "Seb…do you think…" I had to stop and swallow the lump of emotion that got in the way. "Do you think she…she doesn't want me back?"

He moved again, making it hard to get the sweater to stay in place.

"Or m-maybe…maybe she knows where I am, and she thinks I'm…better off?"

Better off. That was it. That was what was worse than the thought of being abandoned by my mother—the fact that somewhere, deep down, I was starting to wonder if I might not be *better off*.

And in truth, I probably *was*…in more than one sense.

Seb was kneeling now, directly in front of me, his black eyes shining from the light of the nearby streetlamps and the aura of the fog. His hair shone, too—it was starting to look more golden than ashen. The sun really was doing wonders for him.

I bit my lip and looked away. "I wasn't really a good kid. Got in trouble…got bad grades…drank…did drugs…"

Jesus, why *would* she want me back?

"And, well…there's something else, too."

The fog was so dense now I could barely see a few feet in front of me. I figured that was why Seb's eyes wouldn't stop shining. And if mine were shining, too…well, then that explained it.

Maybe it was the eerie weather, or maybe it was just because I was so damn *tired* of thinking about all of this, but whatever the reason, I suddenly found myself wanting to get everything off my chest…so it could be swallowed up by the silence of the night, and by the silence that was Seb.

"Seb…do…do you know what a gay person is?"

I nearly stopped breathing as soon as the words were out, but when he didn't react I felt my heart rate slowly returning to normal.

"Do you think they're…messed up? Like, maybe something went wrong when they were inside their mothers. You know, the way it went wrong with you?"

Not that it mattered. Whatever happened had happened, and I didn't believe there was any real way to fix it.

Seb lowered his eyes.

"But your life's not that bad, huh?" I patted his shoulder. "I mean, you have a home, you have people who take care of you…I never really see anyone messing with you…three meals a day, a nice bed to sleep in…"

I trailed off, my voice growing hoarse. I might've been talking about Seb, but I was really thinking of myself.

"Maybe…" I whispered, "maybe I do belong here."

The tears were coming now, gathering up inside me and fighting what little self-control I had left for their chance to break free. And I was tempted to give in. What did it matter, if I revealed my weakness here? If I added a little more moisture to the night air?

But the battle stopped unexpectedly when Seb's hand closed around mine.

I looked over sharply, and he stared back, silent as always.

"Seb?"

He said nothing.

The tears very nearly sprang back into action, because in that moment, the touch of his skin on mine just felt so *good*. I knew he couldn't really understand what was going on—he must've seen I was upset, and was trying to comfort me the only way he could think of. Still, it almost seemed like...*acceptance*, something I'd never experienced before in my life.

I sniffed in a bit of pre-tears snot. "Thanks, Seb." He scooted around so he was beside me again, and I rested my head on his shoulder. "You know, you've been a really good friend."

It struck me then that this whole time I'd been taking him and the comfort he provided me for granted. And even if it was only for my benefit, I now felt the need to correct that.

"I mean it. So if you ever need anything...I'll be there for you, okay? I got your back."

My hand still in his, I stroked his fingers softly. A tiny, closed-lipped smile played briefly on his face in response, and all of a sudden, I had an almost uncontrollable urge to hug him.

But it would've been kind of pervy to just jump on him without warning, so I decided to ask first.

"Hey, Sebastian, did your mom ever hug you?"

It was the first time I'd ever used his full name, and I kind of liked the way it rolled off my tongue.

"Mine did, when I was little. And Mimi—my sister— she did for a while after that...but I guess at some point the hugs just stop. Probably 'cause it's not manly or something."

Seb's brows rose.

"But I think…I think hugs could be nice. Just a way to connect with people, ya know? A way to show you're a friend…a way to say thanks."

I squeezed his hand.

"Seb…would it be okay if I hugged you?"

No response.

I took a long, deep breath, then reached out to encircle him with my arms.

For several moments, it seemed as though life were moving in slow motion. Inch by inch, I tightened my grip until his chest settled against mine. My face pressed into the curve of his collarbone and the breath I let out was trapped there, forming a pocket of warm air. Lips parted, I drew it back in slowly, inhaling the rich, earthy fragrance of his skin. Did that scent come from all the time he'd spent beside me out here, digging in the dirt?

Well, whatever the reason, I thought he smelled fucking amazing.

I tried to get myself under control at that point. I really did. But even if Seb didn't have the mind of a sixteen-year-old, he definitely had the body of one. And I'd never had the chance to be this close to a boy before…I guess I just hadn't realized how strong hormonal instinct would be.

My hands began roaming the curves of his shoulder blades, then down his back. He was solid but lean, with compact muscles that moved gracefully under my touch.

And they were moving because as I caressed him, his hands were doing the same to me. Was he just copying me? God, it felt so good.

Closing my eyes, I shifted so that my cheek rested against his. My lips brushed the newly-bronzed skin just above his defined jaw line…and all I needed was a tiny bit more pressure for that casual touch to become a kiss.

But before I had the chance, Seb pushed me away—forcefully—and I crashed into the shed with a resounding *thump*.

The magical spell broken, I finally had a chance to realize what I'd been doing.

Jesus *Christ*.

I was frightened, confused, sick to my stomach, and yet still fighting an erection. And all those emotions were multiplied times a thousand one second later, when Brandon's face appeared in the fog.

"What the hell are you two doing back here?"

I instinctively twisted my body to hide the bulge at my crotch, but beyond that, I had no ability to form a clear thought.

"Alex? What the fuck?" Brandon stared at me, waiting for my explanation, eyes narrowing from surprise into suspicion.

I still couldn't speak. Never in my life had I felt so close to spontaneously bursting into tears. No witty retorts, no clever explanations came to me. I couldn't think of a damn thing to throw him off the scent.

Meanwhile, as I lay in a quivering pile of nerves, Seb stood. With what looked like deliberate showmanship, he extended his arm toward Brandon, hand closed in a fist. Then, one at a time, he uncurled his fingers to reveal a small, dirty cigarette butt. He flicked it between his index and middle finger and mimed bringing it to his lips.

"Are you fucking kidding me, Alex?" Brandon exclaimed. "You're teaching him how to *smoke?*"

My brain spluttered back to life. "Uh…he…he doesn't even like it, so you don't have to worry."

"Teaching a special kid how to smoke. God, could you sink any lower?"

I scrambled onto all fours, then pulled myself up the side of the shed, still keeping my body turned away. "Please don't tell Ms. Loretta…I'll…I'll mow the lawn for you tomorrow!"

"Whatever." Brandon rolled his eyes. "Get your asses inside. Ms. Loretta and Ms. Cecily had to go visit a sick friend, and they left me in charge."

"Yeah. Okay."

With one last disappointed shake of his head, Brandon turned and left.

For several seconds, I stood completely motionless, fingers clutching the shed for support. What the *fuck* had I been thinking? Everything…*everything* I'd been doing back there with Seb was wrong, on so many levels.

Why had I developed such a need to talk with a retarded mute in the first place? Not that *talk with* were the right words. And how could I possibly have gotten so carried away as to even *dream* of…

Seb grabbed my hand and tugged me.

Hesitantly, I met his eyes, afraid of what I might find…but all I saw was his same calm, expressionless stare.

At least he didn't seem angry with me. Maybe he'd pushed me off because he'd been frightened by the sound of footsteps…footsteps I hadn't heard at all. In any case, it'd been a lucky break for me.

"Hey," I whispered. "Thanks for that. Brandon wouldn't have understood…about the hug thing."

Seb blinked twice, then started walking for the back door.

I let my hand fall out of his and remained still a moment longer, using the time to catch my mental breath and regroup. That had been a close call. Way too fucking close. If it hadn't been for Seb's quick-thinking response, I would've been totally screwed.

I took two steps toward the house, and then froze again.

Wait...quick *thinking?*

Chapter 11: Up in Smoke

"Wake up!" A pillow hit me square in the face. "You've got some mowing to do."

I peeled my eyes open slowly to see Brandon's smug grin.

"And really, I think you might also need to mow for me next time, too."

"Whatever," I grunted. Wearily, I pieced together the fact that my colossal screw-up of the night before had not been a dream. Damn. "When am I *not* mowing the lawn."

"Dunno." Brandon jumped onto my bed, jabbing his knee into my stomach and pushing out my breath. "But we're *so* glad you joined us! Dwayne and me may never have to mow again."

He stuck his hand in my hair and tossed it around, ending with a noogie.

"Get the fuck off me!" I gasped.

"Make me." He pinned my shoulders to the bed, and for just a *split* second, I looked up at him with what had to be a dopey smile.

Then I started struggling appropriately, swinging a leg out to knock him off balance and eventually toppling him to the floor. A part of me wanted to continue the play-

116

wrestling for as long as possible, but if there was anything I'd learned from what'd happened, it was that I clearly couldn't be trusted.

Brandon left the room whistling, and I immediately rolled around to face Seb's bed.

He wasn't there.

Fuck. I needed to see him. There were…things I needed to figure out.

Then again, maybe what I really needed was to avoid him until I had this whole urge-to-feel-up-a-special-kid thing under control.

I got up and threw on some already-dirty jeans and a white muscle shirt, then headed down to the shed to get the mower. Still no sign of Seb.

Before I could rev up the engine, Ryan came toward me holding a tray in his hands. He was walking with exaggeratedly slow steps, his tongue hanging out of his mouth as he tried not to spill a drop of the very large glass of lemonade that balanced there.

"What's that for?" I asked, giving myself a silent reminder to watch my language. I was in enough trouble as it was.

"It's to drink," Ryan responded with an air of superiority, like he'd managed to figure out something I hadn't. "It's lemonade."

"I can see that." I rolled my eyes and took it from him, smirking when he let out a sigh of relief.

"It's from Ms. Loretta," he added. "She said she don't want to know why you always mowing the lawn so much, but she hopes it's out of the goodness of your heart."

Fuck.

"That it?"

"Yeah, she also said she hopes you not quite so good in the future."

SARA ALVA

I ground my teeth. It probably wasn't a good idea to push my luck with this particular payment for favors. At least not now that it was tainted by something I *desperately* had to keep secret. Ms. Loretta cared a whole lot about bad influences—especially on the little boys—and I figured in her mind, Seb probably counted as one of those.

Oh well. At least Brandon hadn't told.

"Tell her...thanks," I mumbled, bringing the glass to my lips. It was pretty sweet, but I liked it like that.

Ryan skipped away, and I turned back to the mower. God, I hoped the sound of that clattering engine would be able to drown out my thoughts. I really needed a vacation from myself.

As I began cutting the grass, my eyes wandered over to the steps of the back porch. The last time I'd been mowing, Seb had sat out there and watched. It'd been his new spot to spend the afternoons, after I'd dragged him out to see that basketball game. Second step down, all the way to the left, every day for the last couple of weeks. Seb was a creature of habit.

But today, he didn't appear. Was it possible he was avoiding me, too? Maybe I *had* freaked him out. What kind of pervert was I...taking advantage of sweet, trusting Seb? And maybe the whole smoking cover-story was actually the last thing he remembered doing back there with me...or maybe he'd been *telling* on me. I had no way of knowing.

The back door swung open, but it was only Andrew who emerged. He was carrying a box with a picture of a dinosaur skeleton on it and wearing his favorite Batman t-shirt. He wore that shirt as many times as he could get away with, which seemed strange for a boy who'd once barely owned a single outfit.

I was almost done with the backyard when Brandon came out. He gave me a cheery nod before plopping down beside Andrew.

"Whatcha up to?" he asked the boy.

"I'm building a dinosaur."

"Where'd you get that thing?"

Andrew looked up proudly. "My teacher gave it to me for behaving good."

"Oh, so you mean when you behave good, you get rewarded?" Brandon said a little too loudly, with a smirk in my direction. "And maybe when you behave bad, you get punished?"

I flipped him off when Andrew wasn't looking.

"Yup." Andrew nodded.

"What kind of dinosaur is it?"

"T-Rex. The coolest," Andrew replied. "Could you help me hold the pieces while I put on the glue?"

Brandon hesitated for only a second before shrugging. "Sure."

They continued to construct the model together while I passed them repeatedly in my left-to-right mowing pattern. I couldn't help being just a little bit moved by the sight. There were so many sides to Brandon—the smug, confident, maybe a little arrogant side; the playful, teasing side; even the loving, considerate side he showed with Laloni…and now the patient big brother side. He certainly got along with the little kids a lot better than I did.

Why did he have to be so perfect? God. It was probably his fault I was all over Seb. I knew I couldn't have him, so I just transferred my raging hormones over to the next available person.

Yeah, that sounded about right. I could buy that.

~*~

119

Fifteen minutes before lights out, I still sat in the living room—an unusual occurrence for me. Brandon had on some CW show while I was mostly watching the clock.

I didn't know where Seb was, and I'd only seen him in passing all day. I hadn't heard anyone go out back that evening, but then again, he could slip around like a ghost when he wanted to.

Not that it mattered where he was. I couldn't go out behind the shed anymore. That place was no longer safe…which meant I had nowhere to hide out here. I'd either have to become a full-fledged member of the household, or leave.

And by this time, I knew I wasn't going to leave. Not unless my mom showed up, anyway.

Brandon offered me the remote. "Think I'm gonna turn in. Might go in to school a little early tomorrow to hang out with Laloni."

I shook my head. "Yeah, that's okay. I'm not really watching."

He turned off the TV, and we headed upstairs. Andrew and Ryan were already tucked in, and Dwayne was reading in bed. Seb was nowhere to be found.

"Who's in the shower?" Brandon asked, dropping his jeans and pulling up his pajama pants. I watched, but not really with much interest. I was more concerned with keeping my peripheral vision on the window, waiting for a glimpse of anything blond.

"Seb," Dwayne answered.

Brandon and I both did double takes. "Seb never takes showers at night," Brandon protested.

"Well, he is tonight. Who knows what goes through that kid's head?"

Seriously.

I put on my own pajamas, trying to ignore the strange sadness that haunted me. Seb was changing. I was changing. We'd never have those innocent, peaceful moments behind the shed again, where I could talk through my problems, say things out loud I could never say before.

And it was my fault. I'd gone and taken the innocence out of the whole thing.

The lights went off at the appropriate time and we all settled into bed, but the shower was still running.

"Should I go get him?" Brandon asked. "Maybe he forgot what he's supposed to do in there."

Dwayne chuckled, but I didn't think it was very funny. He wasn't *that* retarded...right?

A little while later, the sound of rushing water stopped, and relief coursed through me.

That was, until Seb came into the room.

As soon as he walked in, he looked at me like he hadn't looked at me all day—with that long, deep, uninterrupted stare he had that was so intense, I usually had to break eye contact. Only this time, I didn't. He finished drying off and draped his towel on the hook behind the door.

Fuck. No clothes. Just a pair of too-loose boxers that fell below his hipbones.

Why today? Why'd he picked today, of all days, to decide to walk around mostly naked?

Because shit, he had a good body. Not that I'd really doubted it before, but seeing it brought a whole new level of appreciation into the game. Definitely no stunted development there.

"Go to bed, Seb," I whispered, because he was still staring. "It's already past lights out."

I wondered why he hadn't gotten yelled at...but on second thought, I supposed there were special exceptions for the...*disabled.*

He climbed into bed, still watching me, but there again he did something completely out of the ordinary. He didn't pull up the comforter and hide himself in his usual tunnel of blankets. Instead, he gripped the sheet lightly and left it lying halfway up his thigh. Then, with one last, long blink in my direction, he slowly turned around.

Jesus Christ, *why* didn't he have boxers that fit him properly? These were drooping so far down I could see crack, and the soft starting curve of two perfectly-formed butt cheeks.

I sucked in a gulp of air and held it. Held it for what felt like an eternity. Dwayne's little snores and Brandon's deep, even breaths became louder in the silence. Time ticked by, and I grew more confident that everyone was asleep.

But I wasn't even close. I was still staring at the exposed body lying right next to me. Almost reluctantly, I reached under my blankets to confirm what I already knew.

Yup, I was hard. And touching myself just made me harder.

I was now faced with a moral dilemma the likes of which I'd never had to deal with in my life. Was it wrong to be attracted—in a purely physical sense, of course—to someone who was mentally handicapped? Or was it only wrong if I acted on it?

Or was it only wrong if he *knew* I was acting on it?

My hands were shaking, but all the same I dug into my duffel bag and pulled out the first t-shirt I found. I didn't have anything great in there, so I didn't really care which one I selected. Careful not to make a sound, I pulled the t-shirt under my covers and lowered it to right below my waist.

Was I really going to do this in a room full of people?

I looked at Seb's back side, touched myself again, and wild shivers ran up my spine. Yes, apparently I was. And I knew I could be quiet enough, if I really set my mind to it.

After this, I promised myself, *no more perving on Seb*. I really needed to get a hobby.

My vision of him blurred as my eyes rolled back in my head, but it didn't matter. I'd already seen enough, and felt enough the night before. Seb was gorgeous and I was a horny teenager…and what he didn't know couldn't hurt him, right?

Short, hissing breaths escaped my teeth as I bit down on my lip. My blood warmed, and in the pursuit of release I forgot all the wrongness of what I was doing and dared to imagine Seb's smooth hand closing around me. Tentative fingers, tightening into a firmer grip, leading me closer and closer to the edge until…

Seb rolled over.

My hand froze around my dick and my breathing stopped.

Fuck, fuck, fuck. His eyes were open, and I felt like he was looking straight *into* me. Did he know what I was doing?

We just stared at each other for a few minutes, his lips parted slightly, my dick hard and aching.

Then he closed his eyes and stretched. And when he stretched, his boxers pulled down even more, so that I was given a view of his hips, his lower abs, and the thickening trail of fair hair that led to his pubes.

Shit.

For around five minutes I lay perfectly still. This was *such* a bad idea. I was pretty sure I was going to hell.

Not that that stopped me. When I was certain Seb had fallen back asleep, I went right on stroking myself, this time admiring his front half instead. The new image kept me from slipping back into the questionable fantasy of Seb touching me, and I worked methodically, my movements slight and more controlled. It wouldn't be the greatest release of my life, but it would still be a relief. Eyes glued to his happy trail, I drove the energy inside me to its peak.

Right before I came, Seb's eyes opened again…and it was too late to prevent the inevitable. Staring directly at his dark irises, I shot my load into the wadded up t-shirt, an uneven intake of breath the only sound to mark the occasion.

Yup. Hell for sure.

I didn't move a muscle, holding onto my belief that the blankets would shield me from being found out. Seb couldn't see where my hand was beneath the mound of covers. He *couldn't* know what I'd been up to.

Afraid that looking away would be like admitting guilt, I held his gaze. It was then that I realized there was no drowsiness in his eyes at all. He'd been awake the whole fucking time.

Shit. I felt like I needed to say something to play it cool, and I was about ready to blubber out a few lame excuses for my odd behavior, once the initial shock wore down.

But a moment later, I got a much bigger shock.

Seb smiled.

Not a little lip twitch, not a slight grin, but a full-on, teeth-bared, glowing-in-the-moonlight *smile*.

Then he pulled up his boxers, pulled up his comforter, and with a pleased-with-himself look that I could've sworn meant, *Well, goodnight, Alex*, rolled back over and went to sleep.

~*~

Brandon did go to school early the next morning, crashing about and waking me up before the alarm. I only opened my eyes for about a second, though, before chasing after my sleep again. I'd been dreaming, and whatever it was seemed a lot more pleasurable than sorting out the jumble of thoughts that loomed just at the edge of consciousness.

Unfortunately, the next time I decided to join the world of the living, I'd slept *past* the alarm. And by the time I tripped down the stairs, Dwayne was already waiting impatiently by the front door with Seb.

Seb.

As soon as I caught sight of the now-golden hair drifting over his downcast eyes, my heart sped up and my hands grew clammy. I suddenly had the feeling I'd been dreaming something exciting about *him*...and conveniently trying to avoid dealing with what had happened last night in the harsh light of day.

And what exactly *had* happened?

One thing was certain: I really, really needed to talk to him alone. Not like we'd talked before...that'd basically just been me talking to myself. Now I needed to talk *to him*...to get some kind of answers. Was he really the person we all thought he was? Was I completely insane to think he was aware of what was going on last night...and was maybe even *pleased* about it?

I knew I should've been frightened. If, by some chance, Seb *wasn't* special, it meant I'd laid bare nearly all of my secrets to someone who could judge me...or worse, reveal me. I should've been fucking scared shitless.

But I followed him and Dwayne out the door and realized...I wasn't. I was confused, sure, but underneath that...underneath that was something like a whole swarm of butterflies, turning my stomach into a playground for fluttering dips and twirls. Something that made me have to fight to keep my usual slow swagger instead of bounding down the street like a joyful lunatic.

It was hope.

Because if Seb wasn't really retarded, then maybe it was okay for me to like him. And maybe he might like me. Maybe we could like *each other*.

It was such a beautiful feeling, I could barely think straight.

Seb showed no signs of anything being different as we walked to school. He trudged a few feet behind Dwayne and me, mostly looking at the sidewalk. I bit my lip and held my tongue, reminding myself to play it cool. I couldn't talk to him with Dwayne around.

Not that Dwayne was talking. He didn't usually have much to say to me in the mornings. I was surprised he'd waited for me at all.

Some of my nervous energy found its way into my thoughts, and it suddenly occurred to me that Dwayne didn't speak to me because I tended to be wrapped in my own bitter silence. After all, he and Brandon always seemed to be pretty cool with each other.

And I'd probably been bitter long enough.

"Hey, man, Ryan told me you play football. You gonna play for the school?"

Dwayne gave me a suspicious look, like he wasn't sure why I'd opened my mouth if we weren't going to trade insults.

Then he shrugged. "Dunno. Maybe. Was gonna at my last school."

I wondered if Dwayne had really been *someone* at his last school. Seemed like a possibility, with his looks and athletic ability. Me, I'd pretty much been your average anybody…well known enough to avoid being hassled, unknown enough that I probably wasn't missed all that much now that I was gone.

Laloni was right. What the hell did I have to go back for? Dwayne'd most likely had more of an "old life" than I did, and he seemed happy enough in his new surroundings.

And back home, I'd never, ever had the chance to feel this completely crazy notion of *hope*. Hope that I just might be able to find someone to like me the way I'd never thought possible.

Hope made me act a little nutty, though. I stole a glance at Seb and the rush that followed had me babbling again.

"I think you should. Whaddaya have to lose? You make the team and you'll have a never-ending supply of girls from now until you graduate. Plus, you could get a scholarship or something. I bet you're good enough for that."

This time Dwayne looked at me like I'd grown a second head. "Jesus, did you take uppers this morning or something?"

I laughed, another uncharacteristic burst of energy making it a little too loud. "Nah, man. I was serious. Just trying to give some friendly advice."

He still had a disbelieving brow raised, but I did see a hint of a grin. "Sure, man. Keep taking the happy pills. Maybe you'll be a little more tolerable that way."

His comment didn't bother me. Not one bit. It was that damned hope again. I just smiled and let him chuckle a "see ya," before he took off down the concrete walkway into the school.

And at long last, I was alone...with Seb and the sycamore tree.

The scary side of hope suddenly reared its head, and those butterflies were doing more freefalling than they were flying...because whatever happened in the next few minutes could make or break all my insane dreams.

I really wanted to reach out and touch him—just his elbow, or something—but I couldn't with so many students around. Even talking to him was probably a little strange. People had to have known he was waiting out there for the bus that took him to Special School.

"Hey, Seb." I smiled at him.

He looked at me for a second, then back at the tree. Not a good start.

I tried again. "Seb?"

Still nothing.

"So, uh…" I kicked at a fallen leaf, my pounding heart betraying just how much I had riding on this moment. "I was thinking…you know how you sit out there and watch us play basketball sometimes?" He glanced over, and hope soared up from the pit of my stomach once more. "Well, I was thinking, maybe I could teach you how to play. I mean, I'm not very good…well, you've seen I'm not very good, but I could still help you with the basics. That might be fun, right?"

The short bus arrived. I looked into its windows and saw a boy with Down's syndrome sitting in the back, and a girl with an adult aide next to her in the front. The girl was drooling.

Hope was suddenly stomped on by the heavy foot of reality. I had to face the fact that everyone around Seb believed that he, like those students I saw, was *special*. Which meant this would never work.

Without any goodbye, Seb walked over and got on the bus. I sagged against the tree in my defeat and watched him take a seat on the side nearest me, toward the middle.

But then he lifted his hand and pressed it up against the glass. Waggling his thumb, he looked me straight in the eye and grinned.

Never before had a facial expression meant so much to me.

~*~

I couldn't stop thinking about Seb all day. I even formed a pretty elaborate daydream that I played in my head, over and over again. It started with the basic idea of Seb not being retarded—or at least, not enough to matter—then transitioned to us playing basketball together. Everyone else was out of the house for some (strange) reason, so we were completely alone. I'd begin by giving him a few pointers, bracing him from behind, taking every opportunity to feel his body against mine. Then, suddenly, we'd trip—not quite sure how; I hadn't worked out all the details—and I'd wind up on top of him. He'd look up at me with a dreamy, flushed smile, and I'd lean down to meet his lips in this incredible, time-stopping k—

"Why do I get the feeling you not hearing a word I'm saying."

Laloni shook her head—adorned with purple barrettes today—and I blinked several times until the library and the round table where we sat came back into view.

"I'd ask you what's wrong, but from the goofy smile you been wearing, I'm gonna guess it ain't something bad."

I scratched my head and grimaced. Was I that obvious?

"Sorry. I just, uh…didn't get all that much sleep last night. What'd you say again? I need another paragraph where?"

She giggled. "I bet it's a girl."

My cheeks instantly lit up. "Nah."

"It is, isn't it!" Laloni clapped her hands. "But it best not be me, 'cause you know I don't play like that."

I couldn't help laughing. "You think you're so hot any guy wouldn't be able to resist falling for you, huh?"

"Sort of." She shrugged, then burst into more giggles. "What, you saying I'm not?"

"I'm not saying nothing." I put my hands up defensively. "I'm staying far away from this. I say yes, I'm insulting Brandon's girl. I say no, then it's sorta like I'm flirting with you. Either way I'd be screwed."

"Huh, Alex." She punched me in the shoulder. "You not such a bad kid after all."

Grinning, I picked up my pencil to continue my work, just as an administrator's voice buzzed over the loudspeaker.

"Alejandro Alvarez, please report to the main office."

Laloni looked at me in surprise. "What do they want?"

I was just as stumped. "I dunno. I haven't done anything bad in a while." But a tiny seed of nervous fear took root all the same.

"Well, we'd better go see." She gathered up my papers and put them in my backpack—she was a bit of a mother hen like that—and we left the library together.

As soon as we stepped into the office, the looks of concern on the staff's faces had my fear jumping up several notches.

"Alejandro Alvarez?" the office manager asked.

"Yeah?"

"There's been an accident at the home where you're staying. If you'd like to wait for school police to take you…"

That was all I stuck around to hear. Laloni let out a frightened squeak, grabbed my hand, and we started running.

She might've been fit for a girl, but I could still run a lot faster than her. As soon as we hit the sidewalk, I let go of her hand and took off, leaving her in my dust.

She caught up to me, though, when I ground to a halt one street over and two blocks back from Ms. Loretta's place.

"Alex? What…what is…?" she gasped.

But she never finished the question, because even at that distance, we could both see the plume of thick gray smoke rising in the air.

Fire.

Chapter 12: Game Over

Laloni screamed.

As if a pistol had signaled the start of a race, the shriek immediately sent me sprinting.

"Oh my God, Alex!" She kept shrieking. "Wait for me! Wait for me, Alex!"

I didn't wait. I didn't have time to wait for her.

My home was on *fire*.

My *home?* Even tearing down the sidewalk, praying the ratty Keds would hold up to the beating, my brain locked onto the thought. Ms. Loretta's place was my home?

I'd never dreamed I'd think of it that way. It was supposed to be my prison—the place I wanted to escape, not the place I was running *to* like my life depended on it.

But I kept running, at full speed. I didn't have the mental strength to think logically about who would be home at this hour. In my mind, they were all there, all trapped by the flames that threatened to swallow them whole and leave only charred bones behind.

Crunch.

Glancing down, I found the remains of a broken beer bottle under my feet. For some reason, the sound injected me with a rush of angry fear, and I paused to scatter the shards forcefully before rounding the corner.

And then I was on the street, only a few blocks back, with no more time to waste. Panic stole my breath but I ran on, even faster than before, because I could see now just how bad it was.

Fire trucks. Police cars. An ambulance. Crowds of worried onlookers. Giant streams of water aimed at the blackened house. And lots and lots of smoke.

My lungs were already burning, and by the time I got near enough to make out the faces of the people watching, the smoke wasn't helping any. Still, I sucked in as much air as possible so I could shout for a path through the crowd. Not many people moved, and in the end I just went barreling straight into them.

"Stay back," a police officer ordered once I got near the front.

"Out of my fucking way!" I tried to push him aside, startled by the hysterical edge in my voice. "That's my house!"

"Son, you need to stay back."

"I'm not your fucking son!" This time I attempted to go around him. He grabbed me by both shoulders, squeezing hard, but I ducked and twisted—I had a lot of experience in that—and broke free.

I didn't get very far. I was looking around wildly to make sure no one was coming after me and wound up colliding with Suzie just a few steps away.

She held me by my shoulders, too, but it was a much gentler grip. "Alex! Alex, listen to me, everyone is okay."

"What?" I sagged a little under her touch.

"Everyone got out. Everyone is okay."

I glanced back at the house. Smoke, but little flame. The fire had happened a while ago…enough time ago that Suzie had had a chance to arrive, as well as the nosy neighbors from the entire block.

Why the fuck had I stayed after school?

"Everyone's okay?" I repeated, trying to ease my guilt.

"Yes, I promise."

Turning around, I scanned the front of the crowd. I found Ms. Loretta and Ms. Cecily first—Ms. Cecily was sobbing hysterically, her face buried in her sister's fleshy chest, while Ms. Loretta was stroking her hair and trying to comfort her. She was crying, too, but they were silent tears. Dwayne had an arm on her shoulder.

A few feet away, Ryan was holding onto Brandon's legs—really clutching them, like they might suddenly float away if he let go. Andrew stood in front of them, both arms wrapped around himself, body slumped with misery. Brandon reached down to rub his back, but he didn't seem comforted.

Laloni pushed her way onto the scene. She looked at the house and threw a hand over her mouth, the whites of her eyes large with disbelief. Then she ran up to Brandon and hugged him.

I passed my gaze over the crowd once more. Ms. Loretta, Ms. Cecily, Dwayne, Andrew, Ryan, Brandon...

"Seb!"

Diving into the mass of people, I slammed my body around with little care for who or what I was hitting. "Seb, where are you? Seb! Sebastian!"

"Alex!" Suzie chased after me. "Alex, calm down!"

"Where is he? Where's Seb? I don't see him!"

"Alex, stop!" Suzie maneuvered herself in front of me to halt my panicked charge. "Sebastian is okay, I promise."

My chest kept heaving, so I worked on catching my breath and bringing myself back to some level of sanity. "Where is he?"

"I already arranged for his transportation."

"Transportation to where?"

"A place to stay. I have to do that for all of you right now."

I swallowed hard, my throat coated with a mixture of smoky phlegm and the bile making its way up from my stomach. "We...we have to go?"

She didn't say anything, but she sighed, her eyes drifting down. I looked back at the house.

The brick front still stood, but through the now charcoal-colored window frames, I could see—most of it was destroyed.

"Why...why'd you send Seb away so fast?" I asked, fighting to keep my voice from trembling. "Won't we all be going to the same place? Why couldn't we all just go together?"

In my peripheral vision, I saw that Brandon and Laloni were near me now. Laloni was trying to hold Brandon's hand, but he shoved both of them in his pockets.

"It was Seb," Brandon said before Suzie could answer me.

I turned toward him. "What?"

"It was Seb. He started the fire."

It took me about two seconds to really process what he was saying...and then another two seconds for the meaning to burn through my system and build up a rage that demanded immediate release.

I sprang at him and took him down in the first move. With my grip on his shirt, I slammed his back into the soot-covered asphalt where we'd landed. "You fucking liar! You take that back!"

Shrieks surrounded me—onlookers and Laloni, probably, but I didn't let up. I lifted his chest a few inches off the ground and slammed him down again.

"What the fuck is your problem?" he choked out. He recovered from the initial stun and twisted his hands into the fabric of my shirt to try to throw me off. "You're fucking crazy!"

We rolled once but I came out on top, grinding my knee into his ribs to keep him down. I could feel he was trying to get a leg under me to kick me off, so I jerked to the side and shook his head against the asphalt once more in the hopes of disorienting him.

It worked, because he tried to shoot out to the left where I easily stopped him by connecting my other knee with his face.

"Alex, please stop!" Suzie shouted—the loudest I'd ever heard her voice. She grabbed one of my elbows, and Laloni grabbed the other. "Please, this isn't going to help anyone!"

"But he's lying." I shook Brandon one more time and then let them pull me off. "Seb's afraid of fire! He wouldn't do this!"

"He's retarded!" Brandon jumped up immediately, body tightened in a fighting stance. "How the fuck would you know what he would and wouldn't do? I *saw* him!"

Laloni ran to Brandon and threw her arms around him. She rubbed his chest soothingly and shot me a look like I was pure scum. "What the *hell*, Alex!"

I tried to match her anger, but found all the fury had escaped during the course of our fight. I was left with only broken, pathetic dreams, crumbling further with each agonizing second. "I don't think he…I mean, I'm not sure he's really…"

Brandon wiped a bit of spittle and blood from his lip with the back of his arm. He looked at the red streak it left behind and then fixed me with a glare. "It was probably your fucking lighter he did it with."

"You fucking asshole!" I lurched forward again, reignited, only to find my head trapped in Suzie's hands. She squeezed my cheeks slightly and leaned in so we were nose-to-nose.

When was the last time anyone had had the balls to cup my face like that? I couldn't remember. Mimi, maybe, when I was really little.

"Alex, you need to stop this *right now*. Even if Seb started the fire, we all know it was an accident."

I stared into her worried eyes. She was trying to be firm, but the little twitches of her gray irises told me she was unsure. I could've easily hurt her if I'd wanted to.

I didn't. I just needed to know what was going to happen to Seb. "But...but where did you send him off to? Is he gonna go to Juvee?"

She dropped her hands to my shoulders and each of her fingertips pressed against my shirt. No long nails like my mother, just stubby white fingers desperately trying to keep me from spiraling out of control again.

"Of course not. But Seb has special needs, and it's not easy to find a placement for him. I thought with all the commotion here, it'd be best for him to go somewhere safe right away."

"Where's safe?"

"He's going to a group facility. He'll be fine there, I promise."

Facility. Not a house or a home, but a facility. The word instantly brought to mind images of white walls and locked doors.

"What about the rest of us? Are...are we going there, too?"

"We're working on finding placements right now. Hopefully I'll hear within the hour."

A sudden absence of sound was followed by a shift in the mass of people around us, and I realized the hoses had stopped. Now that both the fire and the fight were over, the onlookers were drifting away. No more spectacles, just the fucked-up lives left behind. Not nearly as entertaining.

Suzie kept an arm on my shoulder as she walked me toward Ms. Loretta. I was only slightly aware that her thumb was making small circles against my back, probably in an attempt to calm me down. And strangely enough, I did feel calm...but it was an eerie calm. Something closer to giving up.

Ms. Loretta still held her sister tightly. Giant tears continued to travel down her cheeks, creating rivers that fell into the deep crease of her cleavage and eventually soaked into the front of her orange blouse.

Life liked to fuck her over, too, it seemed. The appropriate thing would've been for me to say something to console her, but I couldn't come up with anything that didn't sound empty and false. *Sorry* just didn't cut it. *Sorry for your loss* sounded too much like someone had died, and I doubted she'd want to be reminded of that feeling. And *sorry your home of many years just went up in a cloud of smoke* was probably a bit too graphic.

Better just to keep my mouth shut. Besides, even though I knew in my gut Seb hadn't started the fire, if my lighter had been used, it meant *I* could be the most guilty party. Maybe I didn't even have the *right* to say anything.

We watched the fire department load their hoses on their trucks, and I saw Suzie signal Laloni to keep Brandon back while she acted as a human barrier.

She really didn't need to bother. I was through with Brandon, and through with this entire life, it seemed.

Her phone rang and she answered, but I didn't listen to any of the conversation. Eventually she hung up and hunkered down near my ear to whisper, like she was trying to keep from waking a sleeping lion. "I'm going to go get the car. Would you like to come with me, or can I trust you to wait here?"

"I'll wait," I murmured, staring straight ahead, barely noticing when she left.

I didn't feel like moving, and neither did anyone else, apparently. We were all just...frozen. It wasn't safe to go inside the house, so each of us stood still, locked in our various poses of confusion and pain. I blinked and shifted my eyes each time, capturing the scene in mental snapshots with the sense this might be one of the last times I saw any of them again.

Ms. Loretta lifted her head, her face blank as the tears finally stopped flowing. Ms. Cecily had also turned to look up, though she hadn't stopped crying or clutching her sister for comfort. Ryan was now holding Andrew, and both boys were studying the house with desperate eyes, probably hoping there was some chance they could return to the protective structure. Dwayne was standing by a fire truck, his arms across his chest, his head bobbing up and down slowly like he was just accepting what had occurred.

I couldn't say any of them were like family...but they were....*something* to me.

Movement returned when Suzie pulled her beige Corolla in front of the ruined house and Ryan burst into tears.

"I don't wanna go!"

Ms. Cecily went to comfort him, finally dislodging herself from her sister. "When we get a new house you can come right back and stay with us, we promise."

I wondered where *they* were going to go...and whether they could have taken us with them, even if they'd wanted to.

Suzie got out and opened the passenger door. She put an arm around my shoulder and steered me toward it. "We need to get going now."

"Now?" Laloni whirled around and clung to Brandon. I'd forgotten she was even there. "But..."

Brandon pulled free and opened the back door to the car. "I'll call you later," he mumbled before slipping inside. Ryan and Andrew followed, but Dwayne remained by Ms. Loretta's side. Maybe he'd been chosen to stay; he'd been with them the longest, after all.

And how insane was it that I thought he was *lucky*? Lucky because the shit you know is always less frightening than the shit you've yet to experience. Not that life had been all shit with Ms. Loretta. There were those good meals, after all. Her chicken wasn't bad, and even the vegetables had a decent flavor. Of course, the meatloaf really was the best. My mom had never baked meatloaf. It wasn't really a dish of our people. I wasn't sure how it was even made, but somehow Ms. Loretta's turned out perfect every time.

I had only a passing notion that my thoughts were going off on strange tracks, as if my overwhelmed mind could no longer focus on anything of importance. There was no more anger, no sadness, no worry about the future, even. Just meatloaf.

Forcefully pushing aside the desire for one last bite of the dish, I sat in the front seat of the Corolla and mechanically buckled my seatbelt, then glanced in the rearview mirror to see the others do the same.

Ryan's tear-streaked little face should have made me feel some kind of emotion, but it didn't. Neither did Brandon's hardened one. But when my eyes drifted to Andrew, I caught a glimpse of something I instantly recognized.

His hands were clenched together, his eyes glued to the floor, brows wrinkled like he was in agony. And he probably was. Guilt could do that to a person. I looked back at Brandon and saw him shift his gaze to Andrew knowingly.

Of course. He was covering for the kid, like any good big brother would. Why not blame it on Seb? Seb was *special*, so no one could really be angry with him. He was the perfect fall guy.

That was the last clear thought I had before fixing my eyes on the little pine tree air freshener dangling from the mirror. I didn't trumpet the news when Suzie got back in and we started to drive off. What would've been the point? Seb was gone. The house was gone. My new life was gone.

Game over.

~*~

After dropping Andrew, Ryan, and Brandon off at an office building I assumed was filled with more stuffy white people in drab suits, we left for my new placement.

I didn't speak at all while we drove. Suzie talked a lot, her voice a drone that coated my already-sluggish mind with another blanket of numbness. I heard her say she was sorry, as usual, then speak a little about some lady named Eleanor, some man named Greg and their son who'd just graduated college. Then the words *grief counselor* passed through her lips a few times before it was back to *I'm so sorry* again.

I looked out the window, but I wasn't really looking. It was just a way to keep from seeing the pity in Suzie's eyes. I'd hated it when we'd first met, and now it was ten times worse because a part of me actually felt like I *should* be pitied—and that was a dangerous emotion to give in to. So I stared at the scenery, comfortably feeling next to nothing as we left the industrial buildings of Mid City and passed into the neatly tree-lined streets of West LA.

And I didn't feel anything as the flat roads with trendy businesses became rolling hills with fancy houses, or as we drove by the large ornate sign that read *Bel Air*. I didn't even bat an eyelash when Suzie pulled up in front of a white gate and rolled down her window to press a button on an intercom box.

"It's Suzie Gardell from DCFS here with Alex."

Suzie Gardell. I hadn't even known she had a last name.

The gate opened, revealing a long cul-de-sac driveway. She drove down and parked a few feet away from a house big enough to be a fucking mansion, then turned off the engine and moved to face me.

"Alex, I know this is…I know this is hard. And I'm so sorry you've had to go through all this…"

One of my last shreds of attention drifted off at yet another *sorry*.

"It's understandable that you're upset, but please don't take it out on Mr. and Mrs. Richards. They're very nice people and they're here to help you. I just ask that you try to be respectful."

I didn't respond.

The front door of the house opened and a thin redhead came out, followed by a taller gray-haired man. The guy put his hand on his wife's shoulder, and the two of them stood in front of their mansion like the poster couple for the American Dream.

"Let's go meet them, okay?" Suzie said.

I got out of the car robotically, reaching back to grab my school bag. *Just like the last time.* A bitter smile crossed my lips. That backpack was all I had left in the entire world.

"Alex, I'm Eleanor." The redhead stepped forward. I was surprised to see she was several inches shorter than me, dressed like a teenager in tight jean capris and a black tank top, though she was probably in her fifties. "I'm so sorry to hear about what happened to your home."

I remained silent. It might not have been polite, but I had a feeling Suzie's real fear was that I'd suddenly wrestle someone to the ground and start throwing punches.

Eleanor looked troubled by my lack of response, but Suzie nodded for her to continue.

"Well, this is my husband, Greg..."

The man stepped forward and offered me his hand. I'd never been into older guys, but I could tell he'd been hot when he was younger, with his strong jaw line and defined cheekbones. She probably had been, too. They were Mr. and Mrs. Perfect.

I didn't shake his hand.

After a few seconds of awkwardness, he tucked his arm back by his side.

"Alex has had a long day," Suzie said apologetically.

"Of course he has!" Eleanor exclaimed, though she didn't really raise her voice all that much. She was soft-spoken, like Suzie. "You must be tired, and hungry. Tell me, what would you like for dinner? We can get anything you like. Magda can make it, or we could order out..."

Meatloaf popped into my head, but I squashed the thought and let silence follow while Eleanor's eyes filled with more and more despair.

Eventually I turned to Suzie. She'd asked me to be respectful, and the truth was, I had no energy to fight. But I had no energy for anything else, either.

"I can't do this right now," I murmured to her.

She nodded immediately. "How about we let Alex settle into his room?"

"Right, yes, that's a good idea." Eleanor plastered on a nervous smile. "We have the room all set up...I do apologize, though, we were expecting someone...younger, so I decorated with a few of my son Dylan's old things. But if you don't like them you can always take them down."

She kept yammering about Dylan and law school as she led us inside. I noticed her husband peeling off immediately and making his way toward a spacious living room. It was open to the rest of the house, all clean and white, with some huge artsy photograph of train tracks hanging on the wall. A chandelier dangled from an enormously high ceiling.

This place was the total opposite of Ms. Loretta's...and in all that light, airy space, I felt completely lost.

I decided to focus on the floor, counting the steps it took to climb the spiral staircase. It wasn't until we reached the end of the hallway that I finally raised my eyes from the cream-colored carpet.

"This will be your room right here." Eleanor gestured, her freckles dark against her pale, anxious face.

I scanned the scene quickly. Baseball posters hung above large pieces of hardwood furniture, and in the center of the room was a queen-size bed covered by a blue Dodgers comforter. A teddy bear wearing a cap and holding a bat sat on the nightstand.

This was supposed to be *my* room? Craning my head, I caught a glimpse of a toy box in the corner. I had a feeling it was fully stocked.

"Is it all right?" Eleanor asked, hands twisting restlessly.

I just blinked. I had no more words. Was this how Seb felt when people spoke to him?

"I'm sure it's fine," Suzie answered for me, then put an arm on Eleanor's shoulder and started guiding her out of the room.

I listened to the soft clip-clop of Suzie's low heels and the clacking of Eleanor's flats as they descended the stairs. For about thirty seconds, I was immensely relieved to have them gone…until I discovered some of the numbness fading.

One huge room in a mansion, all to myself. It was like winning the fucking jackpot. And yet for some reason, I had the strangest childish urge to crawl into a corner—or maybe behind that large armoire—and pull my legs up to my chest to keep the bad feelings from getting in.

What the fuck was *I* doing *here?* Ten hours ago I'd woken up in a room full of boys, dreaming of one in particular. I'd been on the verge of a kind of happiness I'd never felt before.

Now, I was alone. I wouldn't hear Brandon and Dwayne thumping the basketball out in the backyard. I wouldn't catch Andrew and Ryan scrambling through the house.

And I wouldn't see Seb's amazing almond eyes peering at me from the bunk next to mine.

Before I actually *did* crawl into a corner, I hurriedly made my way to the bed, lifted the blankets and slipped underneath. Then I tucked the edges securely around myself and pulled the covers all the way up over my head.

Suzie returned a few minutes later. Through the comforter I could make out the dark outline of her body leaning heavily against the doorframe.

"Alex, I'll be back tomorrow. I know you're going to need some time, so we won't talk about school for the rest of this week. Please remember Eleanor and Greg are here to help. This won't be a permanent placement, but I just wanted you to stay somewhere safe and comfortable while we work things out."

I almost asked why I couldn't have stayed somewhere with Brandon and Dwayne, before I realized it was my own behavior that had probably caused her to separate us. I'd flown off the deep end and attacked someone, and my punishment was a private bedroom in a mansion in Bel Air that I really didn't want. Life was insane sometimes.

"Is there anything else I can do for you before I go?"

Her quiet sigh filled the silence.

"If you need to talk to me, or if you want to speak to a counselor before tomorrow, please ask Eleanor to call me…I'm so sorry about all this, Alex."

I stayed hidden for a few more seconds before throwing back the blankets and startling Suzie in her retreat. "Was he scared?"

"I'm sorry?" She turned around.

"Seb. Was he scared when you sent him away?"

She blinked several times. "I'm…I'm sure he was upset about what happened…about the fire…but no, he didn't seem scared at all."

Of course not. When did Seb ever show any emotion? Except for those few, brief, glorious smiles he'd given me.

My stomach hurt. No butterflies in there anymore. I had the feeling they'd all died and were now piled in a mass grave at the bottom of my gut, which would explain the knot in there.

"I'll see you tomorrow, Alex."

I yanked the blankets back over my head.

After Suzie left, I had a few moments of peace. I might have dozed off for a while, because I didn't hear Eleanor approaching the bed. She hovered a few feet away, her tiny body a blur of quivering black from my shrouded viewpoint.

"Would you like to have dinner, Alex? We've ordered pizza."

I said nothing.

"Would you prefer something different?"

I rolled over to face the wall.

"Some pasta, maybe? Magda made lasagna yesterday. I think there's leftovers."

How long would I have to wait before she got the picture?

"Well, if you get hungry later, please let me know. I can make you something anytime you'd like."

No locks on her cabinets, evidently.

She finally gave up, wisping out of the room like a frightened little gnat. I wondered what was so scary about my silence. Or maybe she was just frightened of *me*? I hadn't actually done anything to cause that—yet—but I obviously wasn't what she'd expected.

In any case, her feelings weren't my concern. More time passed in the blue darkness, and it started to grow warm under there from the heat of my breath. I made a little hole for my mouth and nose so I could get some fresh air, but didn't move very much.

The sun set outside, my blue surroundings gradually darkening until they were black. I listened carefully to the shuffling sounds as Eleanor and Greg—and I suppose Magda, whoever she was—puttered about the house. Eventually I heard closing doors and running sinks and then silence.

Too much silence.

When there was nothing but the faint chorus of crickets for what felt like ages, I ended up doing something I hadn't done since the fifth grade.

I cried myself to sleep.

PART TWO

Chapter 13: Like a Brother

Eleanor and Suzie were murmuring out in the hallway while I pretended to be asleep. I wondered if Suzie realized I could hear them. Maybe she wanted me to know just how *concerned* they all were for me.

"He barely eats," Eleanor whined. "He doesn't speak to me, he hardly leaves the room…he hasn't ever come down to join us at the table…"

"I know this is asking a lot for your first foster, but I really think he just needs some time to work through what's happened. It's a tremendous amount of change for a young boy."

"Maybe…maybe it's too much change. Maybe he'd be happier…somewhere else."

Bitter, near-silent laughter left my lips. The woman was ready to pawn me off already.

"I did want to speak with him about a possible placement that would allow him to go back to his school in Mid City…"

"Maybe I should take him to my therapist? I've nothing against the one you brought, but she didn't seem to get through to him. Dr. Eisenberg has a lot of experience with kids—he's even seen my Dylan. And Greg and I would be happy to cover the expense."

"We could consider that. Maybe give it another couple days. I can try to bring another counselor we work with—a male one. Maybe Alex will relate better to him."

I doubted it.

The conversation drifted downstairs, leaving me to the silence. I wasn't really that bothered by it anymore, though I found it easier to fall asleep during the day, when there was at least some noise to distract me from thinking.

Judging by the light streaming through the arched window, it was still before noon. I could expect a sandwich at my door in about an hour, so I decided to kill time by thumbing through a few of Dylan's old sports magazines. I'd never really been into professional athletes, but at least *some* of the guys within the pages had to be good looking. It felt like ages since I'd seen anyone who'd made my heart beat a little faster.

At the edge of my mind, thoughts of Seb tried to push their way to center stage, but I fought them back. No sense in torturing myself.

Eventually I found a few pages on surfers, and that kept me occupied for a while. But it was only a mild interest—certainly nothing I felt inspired to act on—so after a few minutes I tossed the magazines aside. I hadn't felt inspired by much since that last night with Seb.

Damn. Those memories were still lurking in my brain, just waiting to make me all depressed.

I got out of bed and headed over to the toy box, where I sifted through the mess of action figures and Legos. There was also a handheld videogame console in there, but I usually saved that for the nights I couldn't fall asleep. So my only options were the TV and computer outside the room, or one worn-out old baseball that sat in the corner of the chest.

I chose the baseball. The less I was forced to interact with Greg and Eleanor, the better.

Settling back on the bed, I tossed the ball up in the air a few times while a lawnmower started outside. An older Latino man was toiling away on Eleanor and Greg's yard, trimming the grass around the edge of their pool. I wondered if there was any chance he was from my neighborhood, and for a second I thought of calling out to ask before I realized how stupid that would be. There were thousands of Mexican gardeners in LA. What were the odds he lived near my home? And besides, what would I say to him even if he did?

There would be no one coming to my rescue...not that a sane person would need rescuing from where I was.

I lay down against my forearm, wrist up as I still gripped the baseball in my palm. The bandage was off now—my burn was about as healed as it was ever going to get. Dragging my other hand over the area, I felt the little hills and valleys of puckered flesh with my fingertips.

An image of pale, delicate fingers running over the spot where my dark ones now rested suddenly flashed in my mind, and a pang of loneliness hit me. As if the damn thing didn't remind me of enough, I now had to add Seb to the list. It had to remind me of his wide, wondering eyes each time he'd been distracted by it.

Before I could toss the memories aside, something about them gnawed at me, and I sat up slightly.

Had he just been distracted? If he was really a special kid, then sure; he saw something out of the ordinary and wanted a closer look. But if he wasn't...

I thought back to the conversations we'd had, and to the moments his attention had wandered. Was it random, or had it been his answer to my questions? Maybe it'd been his way of letting me know that I *did* belong in foster care...his way of reminding me what my life had really been like.

That patch of skin on my wrist was the only part of it I couldn't deny—the two-inch visible mark of a larger hidden truth.

My eyes burned, but I was determined not to cry again. I just kept stroking the scar, wishing it were Seb's touch along it and not my own.

God, I missed him. I missed all of them, really, but Seb most of all. And not just because of that slim hope of a relationship. He'd been a friend long before that thought had even crossed my mind.

Not that I deserved his friendship. What had I done for him? Taken advantage of his startlingly beautiful body while he tried to sleep? Promised him I'd be there for him if he ever needed me, and then let him get carted off to some sort of facility, away from everything and everyone he knew?

What the fuck kind of person was I? Seb was probably stuck in army-style barracks, and here I was in the lap of luxury, wallowing in a pool of my own pity.

Suddenly disgusted with myself, I launched the baseball across the room. It hit the wall with a satisfying thump, and I imagined Eleanor somewhere down below, letting out a frightened little squeak in response.

I was obviously a selfish asshole. A selfish asshole who needed to get over himself, and now was as good a time to start as any. Before I could talk myself out of it, I scrambled for the door, flung it open and took a giant step out.

Two seconds later, I was flat on my ass. Apparently my reflexes were a bit rusty from all the wallowing, and I'd failed to notice the box with the blue satin bow that lay in the hallway until I'd tripped over it.

I scooped it into my lap and read the small note attached.

Thought you might like these.
~Eleanor and Greg

The ribbon slipped off with a single yank and I uncovered a pair of bright white sneakers, adorned by a familiar check mark design.

Shit. Name brand and everything. Suzie must've told them they'd make me happy. And a couple weeks ago, they would have. Now...I was pretty sure only one thing would. Or one person.

I slipped the shoes on and laced them up, pleased to feel they were a little loose, then stood and jogged down the stairs.

Eleanor was in the kitchen, humming to herself as she stirred some honey into a glass mug of tea.

I cleared my throat. "Thanks."

"Oh!" She whirled around, her hand flying to her chest. "Oh, Alex! You startled me."

"Thanks," I repeated, pointing to my feet. "For the shoes."

"Oh, you're so welcome," she gushed, green eyes lighting up victoriously. "I hoped you'd like them...those were the kind Dylan used to wear."

"Yeah, they're...good."

"I'm so happy to see you out of the room," she went on. She must've been thrilled to finally be getting something out of me, and it looked like she wasn't going to let this opportunity go. "Oh, you must be hungry! Tell me, what can I make for you? Or maybe you'd like to go out? We could get frozen yogurt if you like, there's a Pinkberry's nearby..."

I put up both my hands to try to stop the onslaught. "I'm not hungry."

"Oh." She deflated instantly.

"Look, I just need to talk to Suzie."

"Oh...well, she was here earlier..."

I rolled my eyes. "I know that. And now I need to talk to her."

"I believe she said she'd be back early next week..."

I clenched my fists, biting back an angry retort. Eleanor was already jumpy around me, and if I was going to get her help, I probably needed to stay cool.

Keeping my voice low, I looked her straight in the eye. "I really need to talk to her now."

"Well…why don't we give her a call then?"

"I need to talk to her in person."

"Oh." She frowned. "I'm not sure…"

I took a deep breath and lowered my voice even more. "Please, Eleanor."

Bingo. Her resistance melted away and she placed her tea on the counter as she headed straight for the phone. She had a hushed conversation with Suzie in the living room and returned a few minutes later with a heroic smile.

"She's very busy with paperwork today, but she said we could stop by her office in an hour, okay?"

I gave her a grin, since I knew how happy it'd make her. "Yeah. Great."

~*~

Suzie didn't get a smile. We had business to attend to.

I was surprised to find she worked in a cubicle, with brown filing cabinets all around her. A picture of a hefty man and woman tacked against the blue wall was the only decoration I could see. Could've been her parents.

A last name and a family—guess she was a real person after all.

"Well, this is certainly a surprise," she said. "A good one, though. I wanted to ask if you'd prefer another placement in Mid City so you could continue going to the same school."

I frowned. "Is anyone else still going there? Anyone from Ms. Loretta's, I mean."

Suzie shook her head. "Not at the moment, no."

So everyone had lost. Ms. Loretta and Ms. Cecily had lost their home, the boys had lost their makeshift family, Laloni had lost Brandon, and I'd lost…

Time to get to work. "Look, I didn't come to talk about school. I really need to see Seb."

Her brows shot up, but she quickly brought them back down. "Oh. Well, we can arrange for a visit, maybe next weekend."

"No, listen. I need to see him now. Today."

She started to shake her head. "Alex, I don't really think—"

"No!" I slammed my hand on her desk for emphasis. But then I saw the hints of fear in her eyes, and I quickly dampened my frustration, deciding on a new play. Maybe that whole soft-spoken technique that had worked on Eleanor would work with all white ladies.

Suzie's hand was resting on her keyboard, and I reached over to place my own on top of it. "Suzie, it's been a while already. I didn't even get to say goodbye. He's been sent away to some strange place without anyone he knows. He might be scared or lonely and I promised him—*promised* him—I had his back. I can't let him go on thinking no one cares about him."

Her expression softened and I went in for the kill. "Please, Suzie. Please."

Still looking hesitant, she passed her gaze to a large clock on the wall. "Let me finish up a few things here…maybe you'd like to come back in an hour? I know Eleanor would enjoy taking you out to lunch."

I sat back in the chair. "I'll wait."

~*~

Thirty minutes later, we were on our way out to Pasadena. I wasn't happy the place was so far, and I was even less thrilled when Suzie pulled off the freeway to make a pit stop in Silverlake.

"I just need to run in and grab something," she said, parking by an apartment building with cheesy potted ferns lining its entranceway.

Again, I was surprised to find she didn't have a house, as I'd assumed all white people over the age of thirty did. This was just a regular old apartment complex, its front painted a pinkish color in a sad attempt to look like adobe. Balconies big enough for only one person jutted out awkwardly from each floor.

Now that I thought of it, I supposed social workers didn't make that much money. Seemed like a pretty thankless job, all in all.

I waited in the car, and Suzie was back down in a minute, grinning and tossing a briefcase in her backseat. "Might as well get some paperwork done while I'm there…kill two birds with one stone."

I wasn't sure why she was talking about killing birds, but her attitude seemed to have shifted away from the initial reluctance to take me. Now she was smiling brightly, practically bubbling with positive energy.

"Ready for our road trip, Alex?"

Damn. Looked like I was going to have to pay for my transportation in chitchat.

"Do you think you'd also like to visit with Dwayne and Brandon sometime?"

"Uh, sure," I mumbled. I doubted she'd turn around and take me back, so I didn't plan on being the greatest person to talk to.

She nodded happily. "And is everything okay at Eleanor and Greg's? I realize they don't have a lot of experience fostering, but everyone has to start somewhere."

At least there I had something to say. "They wanted a little kid. Why didn't you just give them Andrew or Ryan?"

Slight jowls formed on the sides of her face as she frowned. "We always try to do the best for everyone involved, Alex, but there aren't always perfect solutions. I wanted to keep the boys together, and Eleanor and Greg were only interested in housing one foster child at the moment."

I folded my arms against my chest. "You didn't even ask me if I wanted to stay with anyone. Bet you didn't ask Seb, either."

Her frown deepened. "Like I said, there aren't always perfect solutions."

"There aren't *no* perfect solutions when you're taking someone away from their family," I shot back. "I dunno why the hell you'd even try to do this job."

Her nostrils flared, but she didn't offer an explanation.

After that, her chipper attitude didn't reappear, and I was grateful. She let me put on the radio, and I used it to drown out my thoughts about what I was going to say or do when I actually got to see Seb. The only thing I wanted to focus on was looking into his eyes again, and maybe even getting a smile out of him. I was positive things would work out from there.

"We're just about here," Suzie remarked as the music gave way to an annoying car commercial.

"Really?" I sat up and looked around, finding nothing but grass-covered hillsides. That alone was pretty remarkable, since it was about the most nature-covered place I'd ever been.

"Mhm." She turned up a windy gravel road and parked in front of a small white building. Similar house-like structures dotted the hills directly beside and behind it, in addition to a full-sized basketball court and a soccer field. I could even make out a pool in the distance.

"*This* is it? This is the *facility*?"

She laughed. "What were you expecting, a sanitarium?"

"No, I thought it'd be like a hospital or an insane asylum."

She just laughed again. "I wouldn't do that to Sebastian."

We left the car and entered the building directly in front of us, which turned out to be some sort of office. A short black woman met us at the front desk and extended a notebook toward Suzie. She scribbled down our names while the woman peeled the backs off some bright yellow visitors stickers and handed them over.

"Just bringing Alex to visit a friend," Suzie told the woman, who smiled and waved us past.

We exited the back of the office, and Suzie paused for a moment, bringing her hand up to shield her eyes from the sun. "Now, let's see, if he's in his room, I think it's that building off to the left…"

I led the charge, somehow positive he would in fact be in his room. It wasn't really a giant leap of faith.

"Seb!" I burst into the little cabin. "Hey, it's me, Alex!"

The creak of bedsprings came from the end of the small hallway. I dashed into the room there and immediately spotted the lump under the blankets of the bottom bunk.

"Seb!" Unable to contain myself, I pulled back the covers rather than waiting for him to emerge. "Hey, man, I'm here."

His eyes met mine, and for an instant, his pupils widened into pools of pure black surprise. But just as quickly, the curtain of blankness snapped over them once again.

Suzie had entered the room.

"Still sleeping during the day, Seb? You know the other kids have been hoping you'd join them outside for soccer on Saturdays."

He didn't look at her, but he sat up slowly.

"Well, Alex wanted to check up on you. I'm sure the next time he comes he'd like to see you getting out more and enjoying everything this place has to offer."

The blanket fell from his chest, and I stood back a few inches, mostly to resist the overpowering urge to gather him in a hug. From that viewpoint, I could see the color in his skin had started to fade, leaving him pale again. He also seemed thinner, his collarbones jutting out and his eyes even more immense than usual in his drawn face.

"Shit," I murmured, resting my hand against his arm. "I don't think he's been eating right. Doesn't he look really skinny?"

Suzie nodded. "I've heard he's been having some difficulties adjusting…like you were at Eleanor's. Maybe you could encourage him to start eating a bit more?"

Guilt swirled in the acid of my own empty stomach. How could I have let Seb down like this? He looked terrible, he obviously wasn't fitting in here, and the whole time he'd been suffering I'd thought of no one but myself.

Forgetting Suzie was in the room, I put my other arm on his shoulder. "Hey, you okay?" I asked softly. He tilted his head down and some hair fell over his eyes. "And you need a haircut, huh."

A squeak startled me, and I drew back. It was Suzie's shoes on the tile floor. "You know what, I think I saw someone else I need to visit with." She patted her briefcase. "I'll be back shortly."

Thank God.

As soon as she was gone, I ran back to Seb and bent over to wrap him in my arms. "Shit, Seb. I missed you. I'm so sorry about this. I'm so sorry."

For three terrifying seconds, he remained stiff in my embrace. But then his arms slowly tightened around me and I practically collapsed into him, resting my head in the crook of his neck. He smelled different—sort of chemically, and not at all like the earthy scent he'd had before. But his skin felt the same against mine, soft and warm, and I turned to press my cheek into his for as long as I dared.

"I'm so sorry, man. They took me to some other house and I didn't know they'd let me come see you…but I shoulda tried harder. I'm so sorry."

I finally pulled back enough to look in his eyes. There was definitely *something* there, but not really anything I could read—especially when he immediately ducked away from my gaze.

"Look, I'm going to figure this out, okay? I'll have Suzie find us a place where we can stay together, or if that doesn't work, maybe…maybe I can come stay here."

I pushed some of the hair from his face.

"Okay, Seb? I promise. I'm gonna work this all out."

He glanced back up, and fuck if his eyes weren't full of doubt. In all those moments I'd longed to find emotion in their depths, this wasn't one I'd wanted to see.

"I'll be back for you. I promise." I swept his hair to the side one more time, and then, before I could really think about what I was doing, I pressed a kiss into his forehead.

My whole body hummed in response, filling up with energy like it was ready to explode with the declaration: *Yes, yes, yes! I want more of that!* I wanted to take him into my arms and kiss every inch of his smooth, pale skin, to pull off his shirt and slide my chest against his, to feel his heartbeat echoing mine…

My trembling hands trailed down his body and eventually grasped his cold fingers. I gave him the most encouraging smile I could manage while I worked on controlling the rest of my emotions. "I promise."

His hands fell out of mine and I finally stepped away. Only a few seconds later, Suzie reappeared.

She cleared her throat before speaking. "Alex, maybe you and Sebastian would like to go for a little walk around the grounds? I brought that paperwork to do, so I don't mind waiting."

Seb dove back into his bed and immediately yanked the covers over himself. I tried not to be discouraged by that, and instead took it to mean the faster we got back to Suzie's office, the faster I could get her to set things right.

"No. Let's go. Now."

~*~

Suzie shuffled the papers around on her desk when we returned, making the piles neater without actually putting anything away.

"So, Alex, have a seat," she said with a lighthearted flip of her hand. "Let's talk about school."

Her attitude seemed a bit off for someone who'd just been forced to drive nearly two hours round-trip for a five minute visit, but in any case, I was ready to take advantage of it.

"I want a placement where Seb can stay, too."

Suzie pursed her lips. "I don't have any openings like that at the moment."

"He didn't start the fire."

"No one is being charged—"

"I don't think he's really retarded."

"I never said he was, and I would never use that word. Seb has…special needs."

I inhaled deeply, counting to ten before I released. "Fine. Then I'll go stay at that camp…facility…whatever it is."

"I'm afraid it doesn't work like that. But we can make a schedule of monthly visits, if you like."

My restraint failed me. Really, it'd been remarkable I'd kept it for so much of the day. But now that I'd seen Seb again…seen how much he needed me…I had no time for this bullshit.

"No fucking way! Listen to me, lady. I'm not gonna stay nowhere without Seb, so if you even give a shit about us you'll go into your little files or computer system or whatever and figure something out!"

"Alex, please calm d—"

I picked up the stapler on her desk and hurled it into a nearby filing cabinet. The metal-on-metal clank echoed in the building and several people rushed over to see what the commotion was, including a security guard. I geared up for a fight.

"It's all right, it's all right," Suzie told everyone. "We're fine."

"You sure?" The guard asked, eyeing me suspiciously.

"It was an accident. Yes, we're okay. Thank you, though."

The crowd scattered and I sank shamefully into my seat.

"Alex, I want to be able to help you, but I just don't have any other options for Seb right now."

"I don't believe you," I muttered through clenched teeth. I wanted to cry, but I channeled the feeling into bitterness instead. "You fucking show up at my school and take my whole life away from me...then you give me a new one, and now you're gonna fuck that one up, too?"

Suzie didn't respond right away. She looked at me sadly, tapping one finger against the arm of her chair.

Finally she said, "I didn't realize how close you and Seb had gotten."

My turn for silence.

"Not that it's out of the ordinary. Many children who are placed together in foster care develop sibling bonds with each other."

My eyes narrowed. Where was she going with this?

"Is that how you'd say you feel toward Seb? Like a brother?"

Oh Jesus Christ. My heartbeat went into a wild mariachi rhythm, pounding into my throat and my ears. Was she *on* to me?

"Alex?"

Lie, I ordered myself. And that shouldn't have been very difficult. After all, I'd spent a good portion of my life lying. I'd lied to teachers, lied to friends, lied to Hector, lied to my mom...hell, I'd even lied to myself.

God, I was so fucking sick of it.

I opened my mouth with one more strict internal command for the simple response of *yes*, but instead found myself saying, "It...it was Hector."

"I'm sorry?" Suzie leaned forward.

"Hector. You were right. He did it. He burned my wrist."

Holy shit. Where was this coming from? Was I actually telling the *truth*?

"Oh, Alex," Suzie murmured.

"It was my fault. I stole his w—...I stole his stuff, 'cause I needed to sell it to buy some shoes. And he found out and lit them on fire and then burned me with his lighter."

"Alex, that is not your fau—"

"He's done other shit, too. In the fifth grade he broke my arm. I was trying to stand up for my sister when he was throwing her out of the house...shitload of good that did."

"You were just a little boy then, you couldn't have—"

Obviously, a mental dam in my brain had crumbled, as words continued to gush out. "My second year of fifth, he snapped my collarbone, but I pretended like it happened at the park by falling off the jungle gym."

Suzie came around her desk and perched in front of it, bending over so she could take my hand.

"The rest is mostly bruises, I guess. Those were easy to hide 'cause I always got into fights. He tried to stab me with a knife once, but he was so drunk he only scratched me."

I was surprised at how little emotion I experienced, saying all that out loud for the very first time. If anything, I felt relief...like I was releasing the asshole that was Hector from my life. I didn't owe him anything anymore. He might've put a roof over my head for six years, but where the fuck was that roof now?

Suzie's eyes were red. She stroked my hand with her thumb. "Thank you, Alex," she whispered. "Thank you for sharing that with me. It was incredibly brave of you."

I shook my head. "But you already knew, didn't you."

"That's not the point. It was your story to tell. And now that it's out, I hope you'll come to know...you didn't deserve any of that. None of it was your fault. You were—*are*—a child, and it's the adults in your life who've let you down."

The *adults*, plural. I had lots of excuses for my mom, and I knew I loved her, but deep down, beneath that...

"Can you answer my other question now?" Suzie interrupted in the nick of time.

"What?" I blinked at her, confused.

"About Seb. About how you feel toward him."

Fuck. After all that, she was still on about Seb? She had to have more than a hunch, then. What if she'd seen that stupid kiss?

And why hadn't that little twerp warned me she was nearby? Maybe he was off his game. I fucking was, obviously.

Suzie stood. She walked over to a filing cabinet and shuffled through the folders, then pulled out something and returned to her spot in front of me.

"I thought you could look over some of this reading material...see if it answers any questions you might be having."

She handed me a pamphlet, and the percussive beat of my heart came to an abrupt stop.

Lesbian, Gay, Bi, Transsexual and Questioning Youth

I read the title several times, and each terrifying pass of my eyes added more nails clawing at my painfully-still chest, willing me to scream or cry or run for my life.

This was it. I was exposed. Revealed. Naked.

As if to mock me, smiling faces of all racial groups stared up from the glossy paper, complete with a kid in a freaking wheelchair. How the fuck could they be so happy? Didn't they know what this meant? My deepest secret—

deeper than the drugs or the dealing or the fucked-up family—uncovered for the whole world to see.

"If you are having a…different kind of feeling for Seb, I want you to know, there's nothing wrong with you."

I couldn't breathe. My field of vision narrowed on the pamphlet, the bright colors swimming out from the sea of murky brown and gray around them.

"But remember that Seb is…is special. And the kinds of feelings you might be having, well, you know it's important to make certain they can be reciprocated—"

A thump in my heart so loud I was sure it could be heard several cubicles away brought me back to life. I leapt up and crushed the pamphlet with all the force I wanted to use on myself for my stupidity.

"Shut the fuck up! I don't need your damn advice! I already know what I am, but I'm not a fucking pervert! Seb is my friend, nothing more!"

I raised my fist in front of me and Suzie cowered back, her plump rear knocking a bottle of whiteout off the desk.

"A-alex," she stuttered.

"Fuck you, bitch. If Eleanor calls, tell her I'll be waiting outside."

By the time I burst out the front doors, my chest was rising and falling in strange, uneven jerks, like my body had forgotten how to breathe. It wasn't until a gust of wind came by that I realized it was because I was crying. A few tears had slipped down my face, their trails now cooled by the evening air. I rubbed them away with the fist that still held the pamphlet, my hand shaking wildly against my skin.

Who the fuck did she think she was? Guessing shit about my life and giving me fucking *reading material*, like a couple of paragraphs would fix all my problems. I uncurled the paper, still trembling, and glanced one last time at the posed multicolored happiness.

Then I tore the damn thing in half, straight through the face of some Latina lesbian. I doubled the remains over and ripped them again. And then again. Gripped by the need to destroy each and every smile, I kept working until only shreds were left, watching with satisfaction as the little rainbow pieces fluttered down to the dirty street below.

When it was all over, I was sure of one thing.

It was time to pack my bags and run.

Chapter 14: High School Dropout

Back at Eleanor and Greg's, I hurried into my room to take stock of my belongings. I didn't know if Suzie would tell them what she'd discovered, or if that would change things at all, but I still had a crushing sensation in my chest that told me I had to act fast.

The only things I owned were my backpack, the few notebooks and pencils inside, and the clothes I'd arrived in—not much to start a life on. I didn't really want to rip the Richards off, but a few pairs of underwear and some of Dylan's old t-shirts wouldn't be missed, so I rolled those up and stuffed them in my bag as well. And the shoes...those were mine, right? After all, a gift was a gift.

Eleanor's gentle knock interrupted me. "Alex? Would you like to come down for dinner? Magda made us some shepherd's pie before she left work yesterday."

I didn't know what that was, but the bigger issue was whether I wanted to break my grouchy streak by joining them. Would that tip them off that something was up, or set them more at ease?

"Alex?"

I finally let my stomach decide. Whatever shepherd's pie was, it was probably a decent meal, and I had no way of knowing when my next one of those would be.

"Yeah. Just a minute." I shoved my backpack under the bed.

Eleanor beamed at me when I opened the door. "Oh, and Suzie wanted you to have this." She handed me a DCFS business card with an extension number scribbled across the back. "In case you ever wanted to talk with her about anything."

I crushed it into my pocket, my skin flashing hot and then cold. "Sure. Whatever."

Still smiling, Eleanor gestured for me to follow her down the stairs. "Table's all set. Let's go eat!"

Greg was less enthusiastic about my appearance at dinner. He'd barely said two words to me since I'd arrived, and I had a feeling he'd been dragged into this whole fostering thing by his do-gooder wife.

"Did you hear the Bentley's are planning some sort of charity event? I forgot what it was for," he remarked to Eleanor over the dish of meat, veggies, and potatoes. I didn't see how that was pie, but it tasted good enough.

Eleanor was fixated on me, and she waved him off with a quick nod. "Alex and I are going to stop by the school on Monday to pick up his home study packet...unless you've decided to go back to Mid City? Suzie said you hadn't quite resolved that."

"Um..." I swallowed a lump of mashed potatoes. "We can go pick it up."

"All right. And did you finish the last week's packet? We're supposed to turn it in to that teacher...what was her name? Ms. Cranfield?"

She was pretty much talking to herself, so I just shrugged.

Greg made a harrumph sound. "You should finish it."

"Sure. I'll do it tonight." No sense in upsetting them now.

Practically swooning at my obedience, Eleanor stumbled to her feet. "I think we should have a special dessert. I'm going to go get that ice cream cake that's in the freezer."

She returned with a blue-frosted cake and a fancy silver serving knife. "I was saving this for tomorrow—oh, that's right! I haven't told you!"

I raised an eyebrow questioningly.

"Dylan is coming by! I'm sure he'll be excited to meet you. Maybe you boys could hang out…go to the movies or something. Won't that be nice?"

A large slice of cake was placed in front of me, and I stuck my fork in to take a bite before answering. I didn't feel bad for what I was about to do. They were nice people, but they already had their picture-perfect family to go with their picture-perfect house.

They didn't need me. And I didn't need them.

"Sure. Sounds great."

~*~

I stared at the green-glowing clock numbers that night, so anxious I had to keep reminding myself to blink. At around eleven, the sounds of an active household stopped and I was left with the crickets. I'd never appreciated their shrill song as much as I did then, and I listened to it for about an hour before the agony of waiting got to be too much.

Still fully dressed, I rose from my bed and quietly slung my backpack over my shoulder. I kept my shoes off so my footsteps would be softer as I tiptoed across the room. My door slid open with a tiny squeak, and I froze for a moment, counting ten seconds of complete silence before continuing down the hallway. Creeping along the wall, I hid in shadows until I reached the stairs.

Those I took like a tightrope, placing one foot directly in front of the other, straight down the middle. Even though the carpeted steps creaked a lot less than Ms. Loretta's wooden ones, I didn't want to take any chances. Avoiding the more trafficked spots meant only the whisper of my swishing jeans could be heard as I pressed forward.

At the landing, I sat down under the chandelier and pulled on my shoes. I secured the laces several times, determined not to let my footwear fuck up my escape this time. Once I was satisfied I'd be able to make a run for it if I had to, I stood and cautiously made my way toward the front door.

My fingers poised on the handle, I took a deep breath, waiting for any last minute doubts.

None came. This was almost too easy. I could've done this at any moment, here or at Ms. Loretta's, if I'd wanted to.

But I hadn't.

I hadn't because I'd had Seb. He'd given me a reason to stick around in that strange place. Somehow talking and sharing my secrets with him had made me feel like I wasn't so lost. But without him, I was just a pathetic little foster child, letting a system boss me around. No friends, no family. Alone, I was a *victim*.

I pushed back the deadbolt in a sudden rush and flung open the door. A gust of floral-scented wind hit my face, and the unfamiliar smell filled my nostrils, reminding me of how far I was from home. Not that we didn't have flowers in Watts, but there weren't as many, and there were other, less appealing smells that could sometimes overpower them.

But it didn't matter, because home was *home*. And the breeze along my skin meant I'd left my fancy prison behind, hoping for the chance things could return to normal—*my* normal—once again.

A twelve-foot high hedge woven around a fence and the mighty iron gate loomed in front of me, blocking my escape. That meant I was stuck with the hedge. Sure, I'd fuck it up a bit as I went, but it'd be nothing their gardener couldn't fix.

I shoved my foot in to get to the fence, grabbed some of the leafy clumps, and pulled myself up. The green bristles attacked my face as I jostled them, so I closed my eyes and shut my mouth, heading up through the foliage by feel alone. One branch snapped back and caught me in the cheek, but I didn't stop to check the wound. Grasping the top of the fence, I threw myself over and then dropped down the rest of the way. I hit the street with a thud and toppled back onto my ass, but I barely felt the impact. I was much too high off my accomplishment.

No more answering to strangers. No more letting Suzie dictate where I went and what I could do and who I could see. No more feeling small and insignificant.

I was my own man now.

After about thirty minutes, I found my way out of the maze of hills that was Bel Air. Lights and noise greeted me on Westwood Boulevard, and another swell of confidence hit me. I'd reached *city*—maybe not my city, but it meant I was that much closer.

I was right near a college—UCLA from the looks of bumper stickers on passing SUVs—and even though it was one in the morning, the place was alive. Girls in short shorts and tight tank tops traveled together in little packs, their high-pitched laughter filling the air. There were plenty of guys, too, looking casual in jeans and t-shirts, hands in pockets as they overlooked their domain.

Some of my teachers—the smarter ones—had tried to convince us that college was the place to be because it was *fun*. It sort of looked like they'd been telling the truth. I passed a line of people waiting for ice cream cookie sandwiches, the scent of alcohol floating all around them. A blonde with a bobbing ponytail was blasting a song on her cellphone, swaying drunkenly on the sidewalk to the delight of her friends. A few feet in front of her, a tiny Asian girl was busy sticking her tongue down the throat of a white guy about a foot taller than her. He hunched over awkwardly to meet her mouth, but didn't seem too disturbed.

Partying late into the night while still doing *the right thing* and going to college? Seemed like a pretty good deal, actually.

Not that I'd ever get the chance. Even if I'd wanted it. I'd already realized that consequence of running away, but I honestly hadn't given it much thought.

No more school. Not unless I got a fake ID and enrolled myself somewhere, and that was about as likely as me ever getting into college in the first place.

So I was a high school dropout. Kind of cliché…but I'd always had a sneaking suspicion that was where I was headed anyway.

The college activity died down as I headed south, the sounds of happy partygoers fading to just the murmur of excitement. Less people were on the streets, and I started to feel out of place walking around by myself. I quickly retreated to the shadows, ducking from one storefront to another, until I arrived at the next major crossroad.

And there, on Wilshire Boulevard, I found my people.

They were at the bus stop, many of them still dressed in their cleaning uniforms. Must've been the night shift for some of the huge office buildings I could make out down the street. They crowded around the metro sign, occasionally checking the time, occasionally yawning with spent, weary faces.

Maybe they weren't laughing and dancing in the street and having the time of their lives, but their presence put me more at ease than any college kid ever could. In the sea of brown, I could easily blend in, and chances were whatever buses they were waiting for could take me where I needed to go.

I approached an older woman who was clutching a worn gray purse to her chest.

"Excuse me, how much is the bus here?"

"One feefty," she replied in a thick accent.

"Can I borrow that? I'm trying to get home."

She immediately turned away from me and dug her way deeper into the crowd, holding onto her purse for dear life.

Damn. Now why hadn't I thought to steal the measly bus fare in advance? It certainly wasn't grand theft, and it would've been easier than hitchhiking.

I weighed my options, glancing at the map on the little glass enclosure by the bench. A highlighted route headed straight to South LA caught my eye, and I made my decision. I couldn't let this good an opportunity go by.

After backtracking a few blocks to the ice cream shop, I set my sights on the little Asian girl. She was holding hands with the guy now, resting her head against his arm. I pulled my nervously clenched fists out of my pockets and put on my most innocent expression, walking straight for them.

"Excuse me, but do you maybe have a dollar fifty? I'm trying to get bus fare to go home."

The girl automatically backed up against her towering boyfriend, like I might try to snatch the money by force. But then she took a second look at me, probably to guess my age, and her expression softened.

"Why're you out so late?" she asked.

"My friends brought me here for a party, but I didn't like it and I want to go home."

I was glad to see my lying abilities were still intact after my fuck ups with Suzie. Maybe I just needed to keep my mind focused—by keeping thoughts of mysterious blond boys out of it.

She looked up at her boyfriend, craning her neck to catch his eye. "You have any cash, Brent?"

Brent gave her a smile, but me a suspicious glare. Still, the wallet appeared and he fished out a couple dollars so he could look honorable in front of his girl.

I'd been counting on that.

Cash in hand, I thanked them quickly and dashed away, adrenaline pumping from my victory. I'd only been on the streets for an hour, and so far, things were going exactly my way.

My lucky streak continued as I approached the bus stop and saw the line headed for Huntington Park already there. I easily caught up to it in my new sneakers and found a seat all the way in the back.

Now all I had to do was enjoy the ride, and hope the rest of my night would go as smoothly.

~*~

I got off at Compton and Gage, where the sense of *belonging* immediately flooded me. A cheerful yellow rooster glowed from above a fried chicken joint, wings spread wide as if in welcome. And even though it was closed, the *Pizza Loca* I passed smelled of familiar greasy goodness, making my mouth water.

But I had to push those feelings aside, because this was *not* my home, and it was dangerous to get too comfortable. Even a change of a few blocks could have meant new gangs to deal with, and I was a good six miles away. Since no one here would know me, it was likely they'd consider me an enemy first and ask questions later.

I started heading down Compton Avenue, stopping at each side street to peer into the darkness. All I saw were tiny, rundown houses with windows barred and doors double-bolted, bravely defending their occupants from the crime that surrounded them. By the time I hit Florence, I felt like I'd gone too far, so I turned around and tried going north instead.

Ten blocks later, on 62nd street, I saw someone who I thought might be able to help. She was sitting next to a bush on the side of the road, wearing a mini-skirt, black hose, and ankle-high boots. Large, squishy-looking breasts—the kind that came from being sort of fat—popped out the top of her low-cut t-shirt.

I headed over at a swift pace, keeping a wary eye out for any trouble.

"Isn't you a little young, sweetheart?" she asked when I came to a stop in front of her. Then she stood and dusted off her ass. "But hell, if you gonna pay, I can still help you out."

She had a cold sore on her lip, coated with a blob of makeup, and my stomach turned. "I don't want…I mean, I'm not here to…"

"I don't take no little boys to the prom," she said impatiently, her hands on her hips. "What *do* you want?"

"I'm…I'm looking for Mimi. A friend said she…works around here."

"Mimi? Boy, you don't need her. If you got the cash, I'm sure I can—"

"No, no, no." I shook my head, jerking back as though she'd tried to touch me. "Mimi's my sister. She's about…five-five, brown hair, pretty skinny, the last time I saw her…"

The screech of wheels on asphalt had me ducking for cover behind the bushes, and a black car with tinted windows pulled up beside us. Heavy bass pounded out through the speakers, making the ground shake.

A man rolled down the window, a cigarette poised at his lips. "There a problem?"

"Nah. He just wanna know where Mimi at," the girl answered.

"Get moving," the guy growled at me.

I wanted to tell him to fuck himself, but thank God common sense got a hold of my mouth before I did. His car squealed away again in a cloud of smoke, and I pulled my backpack tighter against my shoulder, preparing to take off.

"Try 71st," the girl shouted after me.

"71st? I was already by there."

She shrugged. "Try it again. You maybe gotta look a little harder. There been police around here lately and we been trying to stay out of sight."

I nodded. "Yeah, thanks."

It was nearing three a.m., and I was starting to think it'd been dumb not to have headed straight home, and maybe crashed at José's or Diego's. But that was probably the first place they'd have looked for me, and I was *not* going to go through all this trouble just to be sucked back into the system after a single night of freedom.

I didn't put much faith in the girl's word, but all the same I turned right when I reached 71st and headed down the street, my eyes darting about for any signs of life. After this, I'd have no other choice but to walk the forty blocks down to Watts, and that thought had my feet already dragging in protest.

I saw nothing. Just more little homes, several of them converted into apartments so they could squeeze in as many people as possible. All the lights were off. The place was dead to anyone but the roaches scuttling through the garbage on the street, or the rats that were clever enough to remain hidden.

"Alejandro?"

The hair on the back of my neck stood on end, and I turned slowly to face the oncoming footsteps.

"Alex? What the hell are you doing out here?"

Then I ran. I ran straight for her, keeping the tears from my eyes by laughing like a lunatic instead. "Mimi!" I buried my head in her shoulder.

Mimi was still for a few seconds before she brought her hand up to stroke my hair. "Alex, what the hell?"

"I came to find you."

"But...why?"

My breath started to catch in my throat. If I wasn't careful, tears would soon follow. "They took me away from Mom."

"Who did?"

"The cops and social services."

"Shit. For real?"

I stepped back to avoid the temptation to cry in her arms. She was even thinner than I remembered, her hair in greasy curls and her eyebrows penciled in with dark makeup. She wore a spaghetti-string tank top that hung off her bony shoulders, and a skirt I could barely make out below it.

"So what're you doing here in the middle of the night?" she pressed.

"I ran away."

"Jesus, Alex." She shook her head. "Why?"

"It's a long story." The day with all its insanity was finally catching up to me, and my eyelids were the first to signal defeat. They drooped down halfway and refused to reopen fully. "Can't we go to your place to talk?"

Her gaze drifted left, then right. "I'm working, Alex. I can't go."

"But I'm tired."

She tousled my hair. "Same old whiny Alex."

I was too weak to protest.

Mimi dug into her bra and produced a key. I tried not to think about it resting against her breast while she worked as she handed it over.

"6724 Makee Avenue, number two. It's the unit on the right. Go get some sleep and we can talk in the morning."

I smiled. A home. A bed. I had *family* again.

"And don't scare Star when you go in."

"Star?" I crinkled my nose.

She sighed. "I know. Angel didn't like Estrella. Said it sounded too ethnic or whatever."

I shook my head, closing my hand around the key and squeezing it tightly enough to leave an imprint. "Okay, then. See you in the morning."

I'd already turned away when I heard her respond softly, "See you in the morning, *hermanito.*"

~*~

6724 Makee Avenue was worlds away from the mansions of Bel Air. But it was a hundred times more familiar, and I kept grinning like a fool as I approached the door, floating on the cloud of everything-is-working-out happiness.

Reality sank in after I took a step inside and turned on the lights.

The place was a dump. Even worse than my house had ever been. There was trash on the floor, and no one had taken the garbage out in a while because it stunk, with fruit flies dancing above it. The cabinets were old and broken, and the sink was piled with dishes.

I tripped over a stuffed animal in the hallway. My ankle connected with a stained couch, and I hopped around clumsily as I tried to muffle the cries of pain.

But I wasn't quiet enough. The hall light flicked on, and a pint-sized girl in a long-sleeve pink shirt and Barbie underwear appeared in front of me. "Who are you?" she asked.

Crouching down to her level, I smiled and tried to appear non-threatening. It must've been scary to wake up and find a strange guy in her place, especially since she was home alone. "I'm Alex. I'm your *tío*. Your mommy is my sister."

"Really? I didn't know you were my tío."

"I am," I responded, hoping I sounded authoritative and not creepy. "Your name is Star, and I haven't seen you since you were like two years old."

"I don't remember stuff from when I was a baby." She rolled her eyes at me. "No one does. Don't you know that?"

She was Mimi's kid, all right.

"Yeah, I know." I laughed. "But you can get to know me now. Your mom's... working...so she said I could stay here to sleep for a little while."

"Do you have any snacks?"

I shook my head. "It's the middle of the night. You're not supposed to have snacks in the middle of the night."

She sighed. "Okay. Let's go to bed."

Without hesitation, she grabbed my hand and began pulling me down the hall. I tried not to think about why a five-year-old would be this undisturbed by a stranger breaking into her home that she actually invited him to her bedroom.

As it turned out, there was no bed in the closet-sized room, just a mattress on the floor, covered with a mess of blankets.

"You can sleep with me," she announced. "Tuck us in?"

She threw her body onto the mattress while I hung back. I didn't really want to sleep with her, but the couch outside looked disgusting, covered with ash and cigarette-burned fabric, and I was sure the other room was the one Mimi shared with Angel.

Whoever that fucker was.

"Okay. But you go right to sleep, all right? I'm really tired."

She nodded solemnly.

There was only one beat-up pillow, so I let her settle on it first before I kicked off my shoes and took a tiny corner for myself. Then I pulled the blankets over her, happy that though old, they at least seemed clean.

She yawned as she burrowed in against me, her miniature mouth stretching into a perfect circle. "I always wanted a tío."

"That's good, kid." I patted her head awkwardly, and silky soft curls shifted under my fingertips.

Her drooping lids popped open a few times, like she was checking to make sure I was still there. But eventually she gave in, drifting off to sleep with her lips parted slightly and a bit of drool making its way onto the pillow.

Tiny fingernails—painted pink—rested on my arm. I gently moved them to the side so I could scoot back in an attempt to make myself comfortable on the thin cushion.

Reality was a bitch. The excitement of being home was steadily seeping away. Seeing Mimi again meant more to me than I'd probably admit, but I couldn't deny the fact I'd traded my bedroom in a mansion for a mattress on the floor of a dingy apartment. I couldn't hide from the truth of what my sister did for a living. And I couldn't forget that my life had dead-ended. Without a high school degree, I'd be destined for a career in manual labor—or dealing.

Star squirmed, making a cute little noise, and I glanced over at her.

178

She was a really pretty kid, with Mimi's straight nose and a fair complexion. Still so innocent, she looked perfectly happy sleeping on the dirty floor. What kind of life would she have, I wondered?

No father, a mother who...did what she did, and an uncle who was a high school dropout. Did she even stand a chance?

I slid my finger into her little hand, and she squeezed down.

"Don't be like us," I whispered in her ear.

Chapter 15: Rescue

"Tío!" Tiny hands shook me awake. "Tío, I'm itchy!"

I blinked wearily, fighting off sleep as I attempted to focus on the room.

"What?"

"I'm itchy," Star repeated. She was standing above me, still clad in the Barbie underwear, her leg directly in front of my face. "See? I got bumps."

My eyes adjusted. "Shit," I mumbled.

Her thigh was covered with tiny raised spots—some old and scratched into scabs, others fresh. I quickly looked over my own body and found five bumps along my left arm.

"Fucking bedbugs."

Star didn't jump on me for my cussing. I had a feeling she heard that kind of language a lot.

"Bugs in my bed?" she asked, tiny nose curling up. "Ew!"

"Yeah. Ew," I agreed, untangling myself from the sheets. "You got any cream to put on the itchy bumps?"

She shook her head. "Mommy washed the sheets and she said that would make me stop being itchy."

I rolled my eyes. "We'll have to tell her the bugs are in the mattress."

She really should've known that, but I supposed she had a lot on her mind.

I brought Star with me to the bathroom and did a search of the medicine cabinet. There was actually a decent amount of first-aid stuff, but no anti-itch cream. Eventually I wet a wad of toilet paper and dabbed it along her legs.

"Now, don't touch the bumps. Just blow on them."

"Blow on them?"

"Yeah, like this." I made my lips into an *O* and gently released a breath against her skin.

"Oh!" she nodded. "That feels cold." Then she eagerly pulled off her shirt. "I have some bumps here, too."

I blushed. She was only five years old, and there was certainly nothing womanly going on yet, but I still felt strange about her being mostly naked with me in the little bathroom.

In a few seconds I got over it, though. I wet her down some more, blowing on spots here and there. I could see all of her shoulder blades and even parts of her vertebrae as I worked on her back, and I hoped to God it was just because she was a picky eater.

"I'm hungry, Tío," she announced.

"Yeah." I helped her back into her shirt. "Let's go get something to eat."

The kitchen was just as gross in the daylight as it had been at night. It really didn't seem like Mimi. She'd always kept her room tidy, always cleaned the table after we ate. I wondered how she could have changed this much in five years. Maybe it was the Angel guy who caused the mess…or maybe she was just so tired after working nights that she didn't have the energy to keep a clean home.

"Why don't we fix things up a little before we eat?" I asked Star. "That'll make your mommy happy, right?"

She considered for a moment, tapping her fingers on her lips. "Okay. Let's help Mommy."

I tied off the trash and threw it outside, then sat Star on the counter next to the sink. "I'll wash and you dry." I handed her some paper towels.

She nodded, arms outstretched for her first plate. "This is fun!"

I couldn't remember if I'd ever thought doing the dishes was fun, but I wasn't going to argue.

There were some roaches nibbling on leftover bits of food, but they were the small kind and I washed them down the garbage disposal, hoping that would chop them to pieces. I scrubbed all the dishes thoroughly and let Star place them back on the cabinet shelves.

"All done!" she announced as the last mug was put away. "Now can we eat?"

"Sure." I dried my hands on my pants. "What do you want?"

"Cereal!" She slid down from her perch and grabbed a spoon that had been lying on the other side of the counter. "I want cereal!"

The spoon was too large for her little mouth. And it was burnt. And right behind its former resting place, there was a butane lighter.

"Wait, Star, don't use that spoon. Let's use one we just washed."

"Oh, yeah." She giggled. "This is Angel's spoon."

My heart sank.

I took a box of frosted flakes from a cabinet and poured it into some clean bowls, but when I opened the fridge, I found it nearly empty. Only a few slices of cheese, some bread, and a tomato graced the shelves.

"Sorry, kid. There's no milk."

Star stuck out her bottom lip in a pout. "But I want cereal."

I scratched my head. "Well, you can eat it dry, I guess."

"Can we go to the store and buy milk?"

"I don't have any money."

She hopped around excitedly. "Ooh, I know where Mommy keeps the money!"

Before I could stop her, she scampered down the hallway and disappeared into the other bedroom. A few seconds later, she returned with a sock stuffed full of cash.

"See? Now we have money to buy it."

Some invisible hand reached into my chest, squeezing down on my lungs and making it hard to draw in a breath.

"Uh, yeah. Okay. But let me have that." I could barely bring myself to pick out the ten-dollar bill, and I gripped it with just the tips of my fingers, like I might catch a disease by touching it. "You'd better go get dressed."

"Yay!" Star jumped up and down again as she headed toward her room. "I love you, Tío!"

I was going to have to tell Mimi that girl was way too free with her affection.

Star reappeared wearing the same pink shirt, a purple tutu, and white shoes with heels that were too big on her. "I'm ready! And see, I can put my clothes all by myself."

"Can you walk in those?" I pointed to her feet.

"Mommy said I could wear *tacones*." She faced me stubbornly. "They look pretty."

"Sure, they *look* pretty, but what if you were being chased by a...tiger? Could you run in them?"

With one hand on her hip, Star gave me a withering gaze that was just like Mimi's. "There are no tigers here, silly. They live at the zoo."

We both erupted in giggles.

It felt really good to laugh. I needed to do a little more of that, and a little less thinking about all the negative shit around me.

There was a knock at the front of the house, and Star climbed onto a chair so she could look out the peephole.

"Mommy!" She flung open the door and launched herself into Mimi's arms. "Mommy, I have a tío!"

183

"Yes, you do." Mimi scooped Star up and propped her on her hip. "You met him before, but you don't remember."

"That's 'cause I was a baby, Mommy. No one remembers stuff from when they was a baby."

"And you still a baby!" Mimi bopped her gently on the nose. She seemed really happy holding her daughter, but there were dark circles under her eyes, and wrinkles and creases on her face I hadn't ever seen before.

"Me and Tío are going to the store to buy milk," Star said.

"Is that so." Mimi looked over at me.

I pointed to Star. "It was her idea."

Rolling her eyes, Mimi set her daughter down on a chair at the kitchen table. "Have a Pop-Tart, baby." She grabbed a packet out of a cabinet with a broken door. "Your tío and me have to talk about some stuff right now."

The moment of truth. My hands grew slick with cold sweat as I sat beside Mimi on her wrecked couch.

"So? What's the long story? Only make it short, 'cause I'm tired."

There wasn't time to fuck around, but I still found myself grasping for words. Mimi kept looking at me expectantly, her lips unevenly smeared with the remains of some shimmering red gloss.

She'd always been hot, even though I'd never wanted to think of my sister that way. But I'd known it, and she'd known it. And the guys had known it, which was how she'd ended up with a kid when she was just a kid herself. But she really didn't look as pretty anymore. Was she just getting old? Was it because she was so thin that her face didn't have the same glow?

"Well?"

"Star's bed has bedbugs," I said abruptly. "I got bit a few times, and she has bumps all over her."

"Fuck," Mimi muttered, shaking her head. "I thought maybe it was just fleas—Angel has a couple pit bulls he brings around here sometimes—so I washed all her sheets and her clothes."

"Nope. It's bedbugs. Don't you remember—we had them that one summer, when we were still living in the projects?"

"Yeah." She pulled a napkin off the table beside her and wiped the lipstick from her mouth. "Fuck. I'll have to throw out the mattress. I don't know where I can get another one."

I felt guilty about weighing Mimi down with crappy news, but I knew she wouldn't want Star to suffer. And for some reason, I wasn't quite ready to share my story—maybe because I was afraid of what a bad reaction would mean for my future.

"So…this is Angel's place?"

Mimi gave me a wary look. "Angel takes care of the rent and I…pay him back."

"And does he live here?"

She shrugged. "He stays here sometimes. He was here yesterday. I know we left a mess…" She glanced around the kitchen, her brow furrowing.

"Star and I cleaned up."

"Oh. Thanks." Her eyes sank closed, and she rested her head next to a dark brown stain on the back of the couch. I couldn't really tell what color the fabric had been originally.

"What's that burned spoon on the counter over there?"

"Angel used it yesterday."

"Used it for what?"

Her lids snapped back open, and she narrowed her eyes with that same look Star had given me earlier. "You know for what. For crack."

I picked at one of the tiny welts on my arm. "And do you use it?"

"No. Not like Angel does."

185

"So you do sometimes, then."

"Jesus Christ, Alex. Is that why you fucking came here? To get all up in my business and judge me?"

"No, no." I shook my head quickly, spreading my fingers wide to signal I was dropping the subject. "Sorry. I came because…I really need your help."

"Okay." She sighed. "So then tell me what happened. Even though I don't know how I'm gonna be able to help."

I started at the beginning, with Hector and the shoes. Her expression grew really hard at that part, and she snatched my wrist to examine the scars while she muttered under her breath, "*Hijo de puta.*" Then I told her how I'd been taken away, straight from school, and all about Ms. Loretta's. I left out the parts with Seb, though, skipping to the fire and ending up with my escape from Greg and Eleanor's house.

When I was done, Mimi waited a full five seconds before smacking me on my head.

"Are you fucking crazy?" she cried. "Why would you leave a fucking mansion?"

"It's not like they was gonna adopt me!" I shouted back. "They didn't even want me! They wanted a little kid!"

"Go get your shit!" She stood and marched into the kitchen, where she grabbed some keys out of a drawer. "I'm gonna take you back there right now, and you just better pray they forgive you!"

"What the fuck, Mimi. I came to you for help! I'm not going back!"

Star had finished her Pop-Tarts, and she glanced up at us worriedly as she licked the crumbs from her fingers. "Is Tío in trouble?"

"Go get dressed, baby. I'm gonna leave you with the neighbor 'cause I gotta go somewhere. And yes, Tío is in trouble."

"But I am dressed!" Star protested.

"Mimi, listen to me—"

"*No te creo*," Mimi went on, pulling at her hair violently as she stuffed it into a ponytail. "I don't believe you. You have a fucking chance to get out of here, and you run away. Jesus Christ, Alex."

"Mimi!"

She finally stopped her angry movements, placing her hands on her hips as she stared me down. "What? What is it?"

"I wasn't finished," I ground out, teeth clenched. "Will you please sit down and let me finish?"

She kept glaring for a few seconds before she flopped back on the couch. "Fine. Finish. But you best make it good."

"Can we go to the store and get milk now?" Star interrupted. "I'm still hungry."

"Go play in your room, baby," Mimi ordered. I supposed it said something for her parenting skills that Star immediately obeyed.

"Okay, listen. When I was at the first house—the group home—I had this friend. And they thought he was the one who started the fire, even though he wasn't. So he got sent away to this, uh…facility, and he can't stand it there. He needs my help to get out."

Mimi rubbed her eyes. "So you ran away for a friend."

"Yes. I promised him I'd always have his back. And I'm gonna keep my word."

"That is the stupidest thing I've ever heard."

God, I was so sick of relying on other people to get what I wanted. I couldn't wait till I'd figured out how to take care of shit all on my own…but in this case, I really did need her help.

"Mimi, I *owe* him."

"Well, you wanna know what I think? I think you should never owe shit to no one."

I slammed my fist into the couch, and a puff of dust arose from the impact. "He's my best friend, and it's not like I've had a fucking shitload of those! You know things haven't been easy for me since you fucking left!"

"I didn't leave because I wanted to, asshole!"

"But you did!" My voice cracked, and heat gathered in my face. Weak, pitiful tears would be next if I couldn't get a handle on myself. "You left, and Hector kept beating up on me, and there was no one there!"

Mimi didn't deserve this. I knew she didn't. It wasn't her fault.

"Alejandro, I didn't want to leave you alone." Her tone softened. Old Mimi might've cried with me, but this one kept her emotions in check, her expression oddly calm. "I had to do what I had to do."

I wiped my face with the back of my arm, catching any moisture before it could escape. "He's the first person I've been able to count on in a really long time, okay? And I'm not gonna let him down." A small part of me knew I was building Seb up to be more than he was—or maybe ever could be—but I couldn't stop. "So either help me, or get the fuck out of the way, 'cause I'm gonna get him out."

Moments of silence ticked by while Mimi studied her nails. They were painted pink, like Star's.

Then she sighed. "I dunno, Alex. What all do you need?"

Hope burst forth in my chest. I scooted forward on the couch, trying to contain my excitement and probably failing. "I have a plan. But this place is really far away, so I need a car...and a few other things."

Mimi crossed her arms. "I hope you know what the fuck you're doing."

~*~

We parked Mimi's beat-up Camaro—or *Angel's* beat-up Camaro—in the same spot I'd been in with Suzie. It was already eleven in the morning, because Mimi had insisted on showering before we went to the store to get the supplies. I could only pray the Richards hadn't discovered my absence yet—after all, I could've still been sleeping. And if they had, well, hopefully Suzie wouldn't realize I had the means to get all the way out here again.

I tugged on the sweater I'd used since Ms. Loretta's, then secured a baseball cap on my head. "Okay. I'm ready. Remember, we gotta make this fast."

Mimi scowled. "If you get me arrested, I swear I'll fucking kill you."

A different lady—an older Latina one—was sitting at the front desk. I walked up to her casually, letting Mimi do the talking.

"We're here to see a friend," Mimi said in her most adult voice. I reminded myself that she *was* an adult now—almost twenty-two.

"Who are you here to visit?" the lady asked.

Shit. No one had asked Suzie any questions, and I wasn't really prepared for an in-depth interrogation.

"Sebastian," I answered, since I'd never told Mimi that detail. And all of a sudden, I realized I didn't even know Seb's last name. *Fuck.*

"Oh, yes." The lady smiled. "That's nice."

I guessed Seb was a pretty memorable kid. I'd certainly never be able to forget him.

The lady wrote down *Sebastian Smith* in her sign-in book, under the Resident's Name column, then turned it over to Mimi.

"Names and ID, please."

ID? Jesus fucking Christ. Suzie must've been able to skip all this since they knew she was a social worker. What the hell were we going to do now?

"I f-forgot mine," I stuttered.

The lady seemed undisturbed. "Just hers is okay."

Great. Not that Mimi was going to want to give her name and ID when we were about to arrange a fucking prison break.

Mimi smiled a very warm smile, reaching into her oversized purse without a hint of concern. "Here you are." She handed over a card. While the woman examined it, she took up the pen and wrote on the visitor's line: *Elena and José Marquez.*

"All right." The lady passed back the ID, and I caught a quick glimpse of Mimi's picture on it—next to the name *Elena Marquez*, of course. "You just need your visitor's stickers"—she peeled off the backs and gave them to us— "and do you know what building he's in?"

"I know," I said quickly, already walking away. "Thanks!"

I didn't breathe again until we were outside in the sunlight. "Holy shit, Mimi," I gasped. "I was scared there for a minute."

Mimi smirked. "I'm always prepared, *hermanito*."

"That was a really good fake."

"It better be, for what I paid." She huffed. Then she took a look around. "Jesus, Alex. I thought he was going to be in some detention hall or something. This place looks really nice."

"He hates it here," I said defensively.

She rolled her eyes. "You two sound fucking perfect for each other. You hate mansions, and he hates beautiful countryside."

I ignored her. She didn't know what she was talking about—she was just trying to get a rise out of me. And I had other, more important shit to worry about. "Let's go."

We reached Seb's cabin, and by the time I got to his room at the end of the hallway, he was sitting straight up in the bed.

He must've heard me coming, but maybe he had to see me to believe it, because the moment I stepped into sight his eyes grew wider than ever before, and his mouth fell open to accompany them in shock. *You came back for me!*

I didn't care that Mimi was in the room. Nothing in the world could have stopped me from running to him and pulling him into a tight embrace. "I told you I would!" I laughed in his ear. "Didn't you believe me?"

"Alex," Mimi said testily, her eyes trained on the door. "C'mon, move it. You can do this shit later."

I knelt down in front of Seb. "Listen, I got a plan to get you out of here...but it's gonna involve breaking some rules. You okay with that?"

He nodded.

I'd already turned around to get the stuff we needed from Mimi's purse before the importance of that moment sunk in.

He'd fucking *nodded*.

"You and me," I said as I ripped open a plastic bag containing a brunette wig, "we're gonna have a talk when we get out of here about what you can and can't understand, you got it?"

No response.

I settled the wig over Seb's blond hair, tucking the loose strands away so that none could be seen. Then I took the second baseball cap we'd bought and stuck it on top.

"What do you think?" I asked Mimi.

"I think he looks like a white kid in a wig."

I rolled my eyes. "Gimme your makeup."

She handed over a bottle of cream foundation, and I worked quickly to smear it on Seb's face and neck. It was sort of fun, actually, getting to touch his skin like that. His complexion gradually darkened, and I finished by putting a bit of it on his hands. Then I gave him my sweater, complete with the visitor's sticker still attached.

He wasn't a perfect replica of me, but it'd have to do.

"Now, you gotta walk out the door really fast," I told him. "Don't stop at the front desk. Let Mimi do the signing out or whatever if she has to. And keep your head down."

That last part should've been easy enough for him, but the rest of it had me worried. I was counting on the fact that he could understand and follow my directions, and that was actually a pretty big risk to take.

But I had to believe he could handle it. I *had* to.

"All right. Go ahead, Mimi. And if that lady asks, tell her the reason we left so soon is 'cause he was sleeping, okay?"

Mimi nodded impatiently. "I know. I got it, Alex."

Seb stood and walked to Mimi's side, and I couldn't resist giving him one last hug. "Mimi's gonna drive to the bottom of the hill and I'll meet you there, okay?" I adjusted the sweater, smoothing it out on his shoulders. "Listen to what she tells you, all right?"

No nod this time, but maybe that was because he was nervous.

"And Mimi," I whispered, even though he'd obviously hear me, "just so you know…Seb don't talk."

"What?" She stared at me.

"He can't talk. He's like…mute or whatever."

"Oh, Jesus Christ," Mimi muttered. "Can we please just get out of here?"

I pushed them out the door. My hand might've lingered a little too long on Seb's back, but I was pretty sure Mimi didn't notice.

Once they were gone, I started taking really deep breaths to calm myself. Filled with both excitement and dread, my body shook in weird, jittery spasms. I wanted to pace or do jumping jacks or something to pass the time, but I couldn't risk wasting any energy I might need later.

It took an eternity for each minute to go by. Eventually I felt I'd waited long enough, and I stepped out the door with a purposeful stride, psyching myself up for success.

I'm gonna walk right out of here, and no one's gonna stop me.

When there was no activity at the front desk—and no sign of Seb or Mimi—my heart leapt. I didn't stop and instead plowed right past toward the door, almost at a run.

"Excuse me." A voice froze me in my tracks. "Didn't you already leave with your sister?"

I only turned around halfway. "Forgot my hat," I said, touching the cap.

"Oh," the lady responded. She blinked a few times, then seemed to shrug off whatever concern she'd had.

I forced my ready-to-explode body to go three more normal steps, open the front door, and slowly close it behind me.

Then I took off.

I ran down that hill so fast my shoes skidded across the ground, spewing bits of rock and dirt in all directions. About twelve feet from the bottom, I slipped on some wet grass, but decided to use the momentum to my advantage, tumbling over headfirst as I tightened myself into a ball.

It got me down there faster, anyhow.

The Camaro was waiting for me by the roadside, and Mimi and Seb burst out before I could gather my scrambled brains enough to stand.

"Alejandro! Jesus, are you okay?" Mimi cried.

"I'm okay." I laughed, struggling to my feet. "I'm okay." Then I grabbed Seb, lifting him off the ground with a crushing hug. "We're okay!"

Seb smiled—his *real* smile—and his hands tightened around my shoulders. I could just feel the happiness coursing through his fingertips and straight into my body.

"We made it, Seb! We made it!"

Mimi opened the car door, looking at us like we were both insane. "Will you two *idiotas* please get your asses inside so we can leave?"

"Oh, right." I grinned at Seb, and he grinned back. "Let's get the hell out of here."

Chapter 16: Vermin

Mimi and I sat at the kitchen table, waiting for Seb to emerge from the shower. I could tell he hadn't liked the feel of makeup on his skin because he'd been smudging it all over my sweater during the ride back.

"I don't get it." Mimi swirled a spoon around in some black coffee. "How do you even know he's all there?"

I sighed. "I just know, okay? Just because he can't talk don't mean he's retarded."

"But what all did he do for you that you felt you owed him this much?"

Shit. I'd never be able to explain that one.

"You wouldn't understand."

Mimi snorted. "That I believe."

To cover my annoyance, I took a sip of my coffee, then grimaced. Mimi had run out of sugar.

"So now what're you gonna do? What're your plans?"

"Well…" I gulped down more coffee and instantly regretted it. "I was hoping we could stay here. Find some work, help you out. That kinda stuff."

"Stay here, huh." Mimi pursed her lips. "Well, I dunno. I'd have to talk to Angel. And what kinda work is it you think you're gonna get?"

"I dunno. Anything. I could help look after Star, too, if you want. Like, I could help her with her homework, or pick her up from school or something."

"Star don't go to school yet."

"Really?" I squinted, double-checking dates in my head. "Isn't she five? That's when you go to kindergarten, right?"

"I'm waiting till next year," Mimi responded. "Saving up more money so I can buy her nice clothes and stuff. You know how the kids at school can be."

"Oh."

I put another mental check in the disadvantage column for Star.

The bathroom door opened, and Seb appeared in a cloud of steam. I was really disappointed to see he'd put back on his dirty clothes.

"Hello," Mimi said, her voice too loud and her face too animated. "Do you want coffee? Coffee?" She proceeded to point to her mug in an exaggerated fashion. "You want?"

"He's mute, Mimi, not deaf."

"Shit." She slumped against the chair, her shoulders sagging and her legs spilling open. "How'm I supposed to know?"

"And I don't think he'd like this coffee. It's fucking awful."

Mimi glared. "Thanks, Alex. Thanks for coming by to tell me what's wrong with my coffee."

"Mommy!" Star pranced in a moment later. "I'm scared to play Barbies on my bed because the bugs'll get me!" Stopping short in front of Seb, she stared up at him curiously. "Who is he?"

Mimi slouched down even further. "I don't know. Ask your tío."

I pushed back my chair and stood to take Star by the hand. "I know what job I can do right now, Mi."

"What's that," she mumbled.

"I'll take care of Star's room and her bed while you go to sleep."

She glanced up. "Really? 'Cause I'm so fucking tired."

"I know you are. So go to sleep. There were little boys in that group home so I kinda know how to look after kids now…you can trust me with Star."

That was stretching the truth, but it seemed like a harmless enough lie.

"Yeah. Yeah, okay." She smiled at me—a soft, familiar smile. I was grateful to see it again. "Thanks." Then she repeated it louder for Seb. "Thanks."

Trudging footsteps took her to her room. I stared at the closed door for a few seconds, that invisible hand pressing down on my chest, but Star soon jolted me back to reality.

"Tío, who *is* he?" She yanked on my arm.

"This is Seb. Seb, this is Star."

Seb blinked at her, and she blinked back.

"He's not my tío," she declared. "He's not the same color."

"No, he's not." I laughed, patting her head. "He's my friend."

"Oh." She waved her tiny hand in front of him. "Hi, Tío's friend!"

Seb blinked again.

Star frowned. "Why don't he say hi?"

I crouched down to talk to her. "He can't, because…his throat don't work right. But he can still hear you, okay?"

"*Ohh.*" Star's eyes widened with understanding, her long, full lashes almost reaching her brow bone. "Oh. Maybe he needs medicine."

"Maybe." I looked up at Seb, who remained expressionless, and my heart pounded unsteadily. *If only it were that easy.*

Since arriving at Mimi's apartment, he'd been pretty withdrawn. I hadn't caught so much as a smirk, but I really thought it was because all the changes were so overwhelming. Once everything calmed down again, I was sure my Seb would reappear.

Or I hoped to God he would.

"So we're gonna take care of your room now," I said to Star. "Get all those nasty bugs out of it, okay?"

"Yay!" She clapped her hands, twirling around in her tutu. "Let's kill the bugs!"

I got a trash bag and instructed Seb to pick up all the clothes he could find in Star's room. I remembered Brandon had said he was good at simple tasks, and he didn't let me down. In no time he had the bag full—well, half full—with all of Star's clothing.

I scanned the room for any other bug hiding-places. Most of her toys were scattered in the living room, but she had a few Barbies in a nightstand under the window, and I examined them carefully. When I didn't see any signs of insect life, I tossed them aside and went to tackle the bed.

"Pull off all the blankets," I told Star, who'd been hanging back. "We gotta throw out the mattress."

"Throw out my bed?" she protested, voice rising to a squeak. "But where will I sleep? You can't throw out my bed!"

I sighed. "We have to. It's got bugs living inside it. You don't want them making you all itchy anymore, do you?"

"My bed." Her eyes watered. "I want my bed."

I found myself stupidly wishing Seb could jump in and handle this for me. But he stood motionless, like a tree trunk, bag of clothing in hand as he waited for his next direction.

"Um..." I stared up at the cracked ceiling. Maybe I *should've* spent more time with the little boys so I'd have a better idea of how to deal with situations like this. "Well...we're...we're gonna sleep on the floor in the blankets, like...like they were sleeping bags. We're gonna pretend we're camping."

Star sniffed. "Camping?"

"Yeah, you know. When you go camping, you sleep in sleeping bags on the ground. That's what we're gonna do. Me and you and Seb. We'll have a campout."

"And you eat marshmallows," Star added, rubbing her eyes. "I saw it on a movie."

"Yeah. Yeah, we'll get some of those next time we go to the store, okay?"

The marshmallows clearly won her over. I'd have to remember that for next time. "Okay! I'll get my blankets so you don't throw those out."

She went to retrieve her comforter and sheets, and I took the clothing from Seb. "Help me carry this out." I set the bag aside and pointed to the mattress.

He grabbed one end, and we turned it on its side so we could walk it out of the house. We threw it on the curb, because there was nowhere else I could think of to put it. I knew some other poor fool would probably end up taking it home, but I couldn't be concerned with the whole world right now. Just my own.

A lump of blankets with Star underneath walked through the hallway and met us in the living room when we returned. "Now what, Tío?"

"Now we wash everything to make sure the bugs are all gone."

"At the laundromat?"

"Yeah."

"Yeah!" The blankets exploded into the air and landed at my feet. "Lemme get my *tacones* and my Barbies!"

That seemed like an odd list of requirements for a laundromat, but maybe that was what she brought when she went with Mimi.

I picked up the covers and stuck them in another plastic bag, then handed it to Seb for him to carry. When I went to get the one with the clothing from Star's room, I found her stuffing Barbie dolls into a plastic purse, white

198

heels on her feet, a purple scarf around her neck and bright pink gloss on her lips.

"Ready!" She swung her purse over her shoulder and placed her hands on her hips, making a pose like a miniature runway model.

Who knew going to the laundromat could be such a glamorous event.

~*~

I watched the laundry flop around and around in the dryer, mesmerized by the movement and by the steady hum. Seb and Star were on the hard blue plastic chairs by the glass storefront, where the Barbies were chatting up a storm.

"No!" Star whined, her glossed lip sticking out and reflecting the sunlight as it streamed in the window. "That's not how she goes. Don't you know?"

Seb had one of the Barbies in his hand, but he was holding it upside down.

"Like this." Star snatched it away and gave it back with the feet pointing down. "So she can walk."

Panic tried to chip away at confidence that was already wearing thin. *He's just playing with her. He's not really retarded.*

Right?

"Do you want to make a cake?" Star's Barbie asked Seb's.

"Yes, I want to make a cake. Yummy!" she replied for him. "Now we make a cake. So stick the arms out…"

She continued to direct him, but I couldn't watch anymore.

What was wrong with me? I was still supposed to be celebrating our successful escape, not feeling crushed by doubt. I had Seb back again. Seb who made butterflies dance in my stomach, Seb who held my hand when I was hurting and hugged me when I was lonely and let me see his gorgeous body when I…

I stopped myself there. It was too much, too fast. He'd been taken away before I'd even had the chance to figure out my feelings properly. Or to figure him out properly. I couldn't just leap ahead to happily ever after.

Maybe he was as *special* as everyone thought. And maybe he couldn't be what I wanted.

But—and I almost shouted this out loud to keep myself from spiraling into a pit of depression—that didn't matter. It didn't matter if he were special because he still deserved to be happy, and I knew I could give him that, just by being his friend. Even Suzie had admitted he'd been happier since I'd come into his life. He'd be better off with me than alone at that facility any day.

Star's giggle caught my attention, and I glanced back over at them. Now Seb was in the sunlight, his hair shining like a halo, his skin lost in the glare. He caught me observing him and turned his almond-eyed gaze on me with its full intensity.

And then he smiled.

God, he couldn't have been more beautiful than he was at that moment. An angel in a laundromat. I wasn't able to look back for too long, because it was—literally—staring directly into the sun.

I just needed to get him alone.

Yeah, that was it. I just needed to get him alone.

Bzzzt!

The ringer went off on the dryer.

Fighting back my arousal, I opened the machine door and started emptying out the clothes. "All right, you two. Time to fold. Put the Barbies away…unless they want to help."

"Tío!" Star laughed, scrambling to my side. "You're silly!"

"Yeah." I grinned as Seb sat on the bench and started folding pairs of really tiny pants. "I am."

We placed all the clean clothing in fresh plastic bags, because I was afraid the old ones might have bugs. I tried to remember what else my mother had done when we'd gotten bedbugs, but really the best solution she'd come up with had been to move out.

Except then we'd moved in with Hector, who was vermin on a whole other level.

Star skipped alongside Seb and me as we walked the couple blocks back to Mimi's apartment. Seb wasn't smiling anymore, but he seemed more at ease than he had earlier in the day. Hopefully spending time with Star would be good for him—it was hard to be scared when a five-year-old was dancing around you without a care in the world.

"I wanna do something nice for Mimi," I said to him, and realized it'd been ages since we'd talked like we used to. He probably needed that back, too, so he'd be more comfortable.

I knew I did.

"She really helped me out, y'know. I kinda want to make her dinner or something, but all she has is bread and cheese and a tomato. I guess maybe I could make sandwiches? But that's kinda lame, huh."

Seb tilted his head slightly. I took that as a yes.

"I have ten dollars from this morning, from when Star wanted milk. But I dunno if I should spend it. I know she's trying to save money."

And I didn't want her to work a single minute longer than she had to.

"Well, maybe I'll find some pasta in a cabinet. Spaghetti is easy enough to make."

We reached the apartment, and I was surprised to hear the TV blaring from inside—I'd figured Mimi would still be asleep. But after opening the door, I knew in one whiff it wasn't Mimi in the living room.

The smell of cigarette smoke and wet dog assaulted me, almost knocking me back a step. Even Seb put a hand to his face in discomfort.

Muddy paw prints led from the front door to the couch, where a sleeping pit-bull lay next to a man probably in his thirties. He had a cigarette in one hand and a can of beer in the other. Baggy jeans left his boxers exposed, and his wife-beater was stained with underarm filth. A ton of cigarette butts lay on the floor in front of him—he must've been chain smoking to get through that many so quickly.

"Angel!" Star ran around my legs and jumped into his lap. "Hi, Angel!"

"Hi, baby girl," he said, pulling her against his chest in a hug. "How's my princess today?"

My vision flashed red for a moment. *Don't call her that.*

"Good." Star wiggled around, kicking her legs up and down as she patted the dog on the head. "I have a tío."

"That's right." Angel looked up at me slowly, like he'd just realized Seb and I were standing inside the apartment. "You're the brother."

"Hey, man." I gave him a very slight nod as I walked past and put Star's clothes down on the table.

"Might have some work for you," he went on.

"Cool."

"And this is the white kid." Now he turned his gaze on Seb, and I had to dig my nails into my palm to keep from grabbing him and tucking him behind me protectively. "The white kid that don't talk."

"Yeah," I said for Seb.

"Huh." Angel inhaled from his cigarette. "Yeah. Could be useful. I'll think about it."

While I think about stabbing that cigarette into your eye.

"Did you bring me a present, Angel?" Star's legs were kicking even harder, causing her to bounce. "You said last time you were gonna bring me a present."

"Of course I did, baby girl. Right there." He pointed to a bag by the side of the couch. Star immediately hopped down to grab it, then climbed into his lap again. "What is it?"

Angel reached into the bag and pulled out a little tank top with purple sequins all over it.

"Ooh!" Star squealed, clapping her hands. "It's so pretty and it's shiny!"

"What else would I get a princess? Let's try it on and see if it fits." He put his hand under her shirt, sliding it against her skin as he removed the pink long-sleeve she'd been wearing.

I wanted to puke. Or scream for Mimi. Or commit murder. He hadn't actually done anything wrong, but seeing this man...this man who let my sister do what she did...seeing him touch her daughter in *any* way...

Fists clenched, I took a step forward. But then Seb jerked and dropped the bag he'd been carrying, knocking over a salt shaker, and I got distracted. By the time I turned around, Star had already slipped on the other shirt.

And she'd moved back enough for me to see the handle of a gun sticking out the top of Angel's baggy pants.

Fuck.

He picked Star up and set her on the ground, where she began twirling and admiring the glint off her sequins. Laughing, he finished a beer and lit up another cigarette.

"All right, baby girl," he said after a few puffs. "Go tell your mommy to get up and get dressed." He gave Star a pat on the butt as he sent her on her way.

Anger rising again, I snatched the bags of clothing. My sudden movement caused the dog to perk up, and he bared his teeth in a snarl.

"Don't mind Glock," Angel said when I froze. "He don't bite people."

"Right." I gave him a cold smile. "C'mon, Seb. Let's go put Star's stuff away."

Safely inside the tiny room, I backed myself up against the wall and inhaled deeply. The air was a little less smoky in there, but really, it was being away from Angel that allowed me to breathe again.

"That guy is a fucking asshole," I told Seb, who was staring at the spot where the infested mattress had been. Maybe he felt like he needed a place to hole up right now, too. But there wasn't a bed for us to hide in anymore, and we didn't really have the time.

"We'd better not leave Star out there alone for long."

After setting up the blankets on the floor, I brought Seb back out to the living room with me. Mimi appeared a second later, wearing a cheap skin-tight dress that stopped somewhere just south of her hips and a huge oversized sweat-jacket that hung down to her knees. She zipped it up when she saw me.

"Hey, Sexy," Angel greeted her. She walked past and he pulled her into his lap for a hug, the same way he'd done with Star. Only with her, he added a sloppy, open-mouthed kiss.

I didn't know how much more of this I could stand.

"Yo, brother." Angel waved his cigarette to get my attention. "Go grab me that spoon on the counter." With his other hand, he pulled a tiny plastic bag and a straight pipe out of his pocket.

Before I could react, Mimi tucked her hand into the top of his shirt. "No, Angel. Not in front of the baby. Please."

He stared at her for a moment, then glanced over at Star. She was sitting cross-legged on the other end of the couch and petting the dog. "Fine. We'll take it with. C'mon."

I couldn't explain why my brain was about to short-circuit with fury. It wasn't like I'd never been around people smoking crack. Hell, plenty of Hector's friends had, and he'd joined in on occasion. But this was different. It was different because Mimi was my sister and I *knew* she didn't want this.

And Star was only five years old. Five fucking years old.

Angel stood, an empty beer can sliding to the floor as he went. Mimi was forced to stand at the same time, since she'd been on his lap.

"Now? Where're we going?" she asked.

"Need you to do me a favor. A quick one. You got the kid to watch Star, anyways."

I couldn't stop myself this time. I grabbed Mimi by her wrist and began pulling her down the hallway with me.

"Alex! What're you—"

"What the fuck, Mimi." I yanked her close so I could speak directly in her ear. "What the *fuck*. This guy is shit!"

She pushed me off, drawing a finger up to my face. "You keep your mouth shut." Her teeth were clenched as she spoke in a low growl. "You hear me? Keep your damn mouth shut."

Angel approached and Mimi whirled around. "Alex fixed up Star's bedroom. She had bedbugs."

"Nasty fuckers," Angel responded. "But let's go."

"Bye Mommy!" Star crowded in around our legs.

Mimi stooped down to hug her. "Bye, baby. Be good for Tío."

When she straightened up, she surprised me by giving me a quick hug, too. "I usually have the neighbor Betty look in on Star at night…I'll tell her you're gonna be around though, okay? You can make some sandwiches for dinner. Or look in the freezer—there might be a pizza."

"Right." I nodded numbly. "Okay."

Angel, Mimi, and the dog filed out, leaving me standing in the hallway and staring after them stupidly. My guts were twisted and I was sweating and the stench of animal and smoke and body odor was really close to making me have to vomit.

And in that moment I understood—this was why Mimi had never wanted me around her after she'd left.

"Tío?" Star looked up at me expectantly. "Can we have marshmallows for our camping now?"

I didn't move, but Seb put his arm on Star's back and started to guide her toward the kitchen. I'd almost forgotten he was even there. A few moments later, plastic food wrappers began crinkling, and I followed wearily to find Seb making cheese sandwiches.

Some of the darkness lifted from my mind. Sandwiches might've been a *simple task*, but right then they meant all the world to me.

I walked up behind him and rested my head on his shoulder. "Thanks."

We were standing too close, I knew, but Star was only five years old and not really someone to worry about. And I needed to feel his warm body next to mine—to remind myself that someone was there for me, even if it was only with the occasional smile or hug.

Seb leaned back against me, and I rocked us gently, for just an instant.

Then I pulled away.

"Guess what," I said to Star. "We're gonna have a picnic. People have picnics when they go camping."

"Oh yeah!" She ran up and hugged my legs. "I saw that on a movie, too! I love you, Tío!"

One picnic and two hours of television later, Star's head dropped down against my arm. I felt like doing the same on Seb's, but decided to just be happy he was sitting close enough that our shoulders touched.

"We should get Star to bed," I murmured, turning so that my lips almost brushed his ear. "And I bet you're tired, too. We had a long day…and you usually sleep a whole lot more in a day, don't you."

His lips twitched.

Maybe we weren't quite alone, but with Star asleep, it was about as close as we were going to get. Eager not to waste the opportunity, I gently lifted the still-dozing Star and carried her to her room.

"Are we going camping now?" she mumbled sleepily.

"Yeah." I set her down on the comforter, then pulled the sheets over her. "So go to sleep."

Seb stood in the doorway as I tucked her in, but his eyes were unfocused, like he was looking really far away.

"I'm not sure where we can sleep," I whispered to him. "Yesterday I slept here with Star...I think there's like one more sheet that we washed, but no more pillows. I guess we can just use a wad of clothes or something."

Seb went to the closet and pulled out the fitted sheet from Star's bed.

"You do wanna go to sleep, huh." I tried not to let the disappointment show in my voice. "Well, all right. Let's set it up."

Our makeshift bed consisted of nothing more than the sheet and a throw blanket. I decided I'd let Seb have it and crawl in with Star, since there really wasn't enough space for two.

Unless those two were pretty damn close.

When I lay down, I faced him, and he faced me, like we'd done that last night at Ms. Loretta's. Only this time, I could tell he was really tired, because his eyelids dropped steadily until they were closed, his lashes twitching slightly before his lips parted and soft, sleeping breaths emerged.

I fell asleep focused on those lips, wondering what it would be like to feel them on my skin. But a little while later, the wailing call of police sirens woke me up. I looked over to see Seb's eyes wide with alarm, and immediately rushed to his side.

"Hey, it's okay. Don't worry about it. It happens here all the time—shit goes down in the ghetto, you know. But don't worry. They're not coming here. It's probably not even anything bad."

The first whisper of regret wormed its way into my thoughts. Why had I brought Seb to this hellhole? I'd told myself it was for his sake—so he could be happy—but was I really just being a selfish asshole again?

He rolled over, staying close to me so that we were nearly spooning. I slid my arm around his chest and held him tight. "You're okay. And look, Star's still fast asleep. She knows it's no big deal."

His muscles relaxed gradually under my touch, and he let out a sigh.

He was so warm, and his heartbeat so strong against the palm of my hand. I couldn't pull myself away. I didn't want to, either.

Besides, he needed my comfort. And I needed his. There was nothing wrong with comfort.

"Goodnight, Seb," I whispered. Resting my head against my other arm, I gently nuzzled his neck and settled in to sleep.

Chapter 17: Busted

"But I don't want Pop-Tarts!" Star pushed the silver packet away from her with a sudden burst of outrage. It slid all the way across the table and stopped in front of Seb, who stared down at it with his typical blank face.

"C'mon, Star." I yawned, stretching to the side and trying to work some of the kinks out of my back. Sleeping on the bare floor hadn't been very comfortable, even with Seb by my side. "They're really good. And they're the s'mores kind. That means they have marshmallows. Marshmallows for camping, remember?"

"Camping is for nighttime," Star responded, scorn written on every detail of her tiny face, from her wrinkled little nose to her pursed lips to her scowling eyes. "I *said* I wanted cereal, and you *said* we could buy milk the other day."

Seb dropped his head. If I didn't know any better, I would've thought he was trying to hide his laughter.

"But we don't want to waste your mommy's money. Besides, we should wait to see what other stuff we need to get at the store, instead of just going to buy milk."

Unconvinced, Star crossed her arms against her chest. She was still wearing the purple sequin tank top and the

209

Barbie underwear. Some of the sequin color had already started to wear away, leaving them a dull silver. "I want cereal."

It appeared we were deadlocked. By some small miracle, a key scratched at the door, and Mimi entered the apartment a second later.

And she entered it alone, thank God.

"Mommy!" All the sourness vanished from Star's face as she ran to her mother.

Mimi picked her up and cradled her in her arms, but Star's presence didn't have the same effect on her worn features. Her eyes were sunken into dark voids of smeared mascara, and she wore no lipstick.

"Hi, baby," she said quietly.

I left the kitchen to walk to her side. I didn't know if she'd still be angry with me about yesterday, but I could tell she was drained—even more drained than she'd been the last time—and I wanted to be of some help.

And I also wanted to do anything I could to keep from thinking about *why* she might be so sapped of life this morning.

"You want me to make you breakfast? I could go to the store, if you need me to."

She shook her head. "No, I'm not hungry. I'm just gonna take a shower."

Star wiggled in her arms. "Me too, Mommy. I wanna take a shower, too."

Mimi cringed, the wrinkles on her forehead and around her eyes making her look so much older. Then she sighed. "Okay, baby. We'll wash you up first."

They disappeared into the bathroom. I looked back over at the table to find Seb, but he wasn't sitting there anymore. Somehow he'd snuck around and was now standing behind me, studying me with his head tipped to the side.

"I don't know if I'll ever get used to this," I muttered, turning to him. "Watching her leave at night...seeing her come home like this in the morning…" I paused to push down the lump in my throat. "And what about Star? What about when she gets old enough to realize…"

Seb's gaze fell to the floor. If he understood what I was saying, then I was probably depressing him…but misery loves company, and I kept on going.

"And that asshole Angel…I bet you anything he smokes crack around Star when Mimi's not there. I mean, what if Star used that spoon one day? Or if he dropped some or something? She's so fucking tiny…I think it could kill her."

Seb stepped a little closer to me.

"And the gun…yeah, great fucking idea to have a gun in your pants and a kid on your lap."

I squeezed my hands into fists, my anger from the night before suddenly revived.

"You know what the worst part might be? Now I have to deal with another fucking asshole in my life that I can't do anything to stop. I thought I was *done* with that shit."

A blast of warmth hit my neck, and I realized Seb had come close enough that I was feeling the heat of his breath on my skin. I slowly released the tension in my clenched muscles.

"Shit. I almost took a swing at him. That wouldn'tve ended well. If you hadn't distracted me I'd…I might've…"

Our chests were touching now, his inhales and exhales mirroring mine. Something about the train of thought I'd been on bugged me, but I let it go, deciding to forget my troubles for the time being and enjoy the comfort available right in front of my face.

I lifted my arms and wrapped him in a hug, breathing in deeply through the filter of his blond hair. All the frustration inside me was immediately reduced to a tiny, smoldering ember. My body shot signals to my brain that filled up the available room in there, telling me *this* was what it craved. To continue running my hands over his shoulders and admiring the firm, lean muscles of his back.

To make *him* my whole world and leave the rest of this shit behind.

Being this close to him was like a drug...and I was quickly becoming addicted. It took a very strong effort for me to step away.

"You'll eat Pop-Tarts, right Seb?" I asked, running my hand down his arm as I drew out our physical connection for as long as possible. "I'll even warm them up for you."

He stared at me, and while his mouth didn't move, his eyes were smiling.

We split one pack so there'd be enough left for Mimi and Star—if she ever gave in—then sat down in the living room to watch some TV. Five minutes later the bathroom door opened and a dripping wet Star was pushed into the hallway, clutching a thin gray towel to her shivering body.

"Alex, get Star dressed, will you?" Mimi called, and the door shut again.

I stood up and walked toward her while she hopped in place, shaking off the excess water. "I'm all clean, Tío!"

Her arms flew up in the air with her declaration, causing the towel to slip to the floor.

"Oh, Jesus." I ducked my head into my hand to cover my eyes. "Didn't you say you could get dressed by yourself?"

She giggled. "Oh, yeah." After picking up the towel and wrapping it around her butt, she flounced into her room.

"She can," I assured Seb as I sat back beside him. "She did it yesterday. And I'm starting to get the feeling someone needs to teach her about being a little more private. Like how you shouldn't just go wandering around in your underwear—or naked, for that matter—when there are people in the house."

My own words touched on a memory, which grew more vivid as Seb turned to look into my eyes.

Wandering around in your underwear.

Yeah, little girls shouldn't be doing it. But when *he'd* done it…when he'd let his boxers slide down below his waist, let me see the dip of his hipbone and the curve of his ass…

Let me? I snapped myself out of the daydream. There was no final word on that.

"Um, Seb…" I bit down on my lip slowly, rolling the chunk of flesh between my teeth. "You know those last couple nights at Ms. Loretta's?"

Did he remember them the way I did? I waited to see if there'd be any spark of recognition in his eyes.

His brows rose slightly.

"Well…it's just…I've been meaning to ask you about…about the stuff I said behind the shed. Y'know, about…about me…being different…"

"Let's go outside and play!" Star rocketed into the room. She was back in the tutu, but she had black leggings on underneath this time and a yellow shirt with a sunflower on it.

"Star." I barely controlled the sigh of irritation. "I'm talking to my friend right now. Can't you go play by yourself?"

"I don't wanna play by myself," she explained matter-of-factly. In two quick tugs she had Seb up, and she began leading him to the back of the house.

I stayed on the couch, twisting my ankles in little circles and cracking my knuckles. Maybe Star's interruption had been well-timed. I wasn't sure I actually wanted the answers to my questions—or the *lack* of answers that would be just as devastating.

Maybe I needed to learn to live with the mystery.

When I joined them, Seb and Star were building mounds of dirt on the tiny plot of brick-enclosed yard. I kept the back door open and sat in the entranceway to watch, but didn't feel the need to help them out. This was one game I was sure Seb could handle on his own.

Star's little fingers, coated with dirt, patted a hill with a final clump of soil. She instructed Seb to break a twig off of a tree and stick it in the middle, then stood back to observe their masterpiece and select the next place to break ground.

After a few minutes, Mimi came to stand behind me in the doorway. She was wearing jeans and a t-shirt now, and her face was free of makeup. I felt much happier around her when she looked like that.

"Seb's good with Star." I smiled as the two of them worked to create a giant pile of earth. "I think she really likes him."

"Alex." Mimi sighed, taking a hand towel to her hair and rubbing at the wet curls. "This isn't going to work out."

"What?" I gripped the doorframe and pulled myself to my feet. "What're you talking about?"

"You. And him. Staying here. It's not gonna work out."

A chill traveled down my spine and along my skin, leaving little bumps and raised body hair in its wake. "Angel said no?"

"It's just not gonna work," she repeated. She wasn't making eye contact, though, and my suspicions had anger taking over the anxiety.

"You didn't even ask him, did you. What the fuck!"

"I don't need to ask him." Mimi flashed her glare straight at me now that I'd figured her out. "I'm telling you, it isn't going to work."

"Well, you're being stupid," I shot back. "You need my help around here. You're gonna need my help with Star."

"I don't *need* your help with nothing." She backtracked to the bathroom and tossed the towel onto the sink. "I know how to support my daughter just fine on my own. What I *can't* do is support her and you and the white boy that may or may not be retarded."

"I said I'd get a job." I threw up my hands, chasing after her. "I don't expect to live here for free."

"What job, huh? What're you gonna do? And what is that boy gonna do? Please. Tell me."

My mouth flapped open and closed a few times as I hunted for a response. "Uh...Angel said he might have some work for me. Maybe he wants me to like...deal for him or something? I could do that, if you want."

Her hand flew at me so fast I didn't have a chance to react, and I received the full force of the slap across the right side of my face.

Staggering back, I turned toward the wall to inspect the stinging spot with my fingertips. I couldn't be sure, but I thought her nails might've left a mark.

"No I don't *want* that," she spat. "*Cabrón.*"

My eyes filled with tears. Not from the pain, really, but from the whole fucked-up situation I'd put myself in. And put Seb in, for that matter.

I smothered the urge to cry and looked out back, watching Star hop from one pile of dirt to another. Her laughter made the pricks of pain along my cheek feel even sharper.

"Mimi, please..."

She clenched the hand she'd hit me with and crossed her arms. "No. I made up my mind."

"But..."

"Besides"—she glanced up sharply, then immediately looked away again—"you know this neighborhood ain't no place for fags."

My blood turned to ice.

"Wh-what? I'm...I'm not. I'm not."

Fuck. Fuck. Fuck.

Mimi shook her head. "I just wanna know one thing...were you born like this? Or was it like something that happened in that group home? 'Cause back in school, they always used to say fag was catching...especially for the boys..."

All sanity shattered, I drew back my fist and slammed it into the wall with every ounce of force in my body. "*Stop saying that word!*"

Bits of plaster dust exploded into the air. Right before I shut my eyes, I saw the scrape on one of my knuckles turn from white to red as blood began to seep out. I pushed my face against the damaged wall, wishing I could melt straight into the foundation of the ugly little apartment and escape this moment without ever looking back.

Mimi touched my shoulder. "I'm sorry."

I didn't turn around.

"I'm sorry, Alex. It don't change anything for me, you know. You're still my brother and I still love you."

Tears escaped my closed eyes and I pressed my face even harder into the darkness, making strange squiggles and dots appear on the backs of my lids.

"But you know I'm right. It's just not safe around here. Especially not for him. And if Angel ever found out…he's weird about that shit. He could hurt you and I'd never—"

Mention of Angel caused another rush of insane fury and I whirled, screaming in Mimi's face. "Angel! Jesus fucking Christ! Why are you with that asshole? Why? Why, after seeing Mom with Hector, would you fucking do that?"

She backed up, cowering on the opposite wall like she was afraid I might hit her this time. "Because, Alejandro," she whispered. "Star and me…we don't have nowhere else to go."

Her whole body sagged in on itself, sad brown eyes practically begging me for forgiveness. She looked so small and defeated, stripped of the hardness and reduced to the little girl she'd once been.

"Mimi, I'm s—"

"You need to go back to that place. That house with the pool and the gardener. Please, Alex."

"I can't." I switched positions so I could rest the back of my head and look out at the clouds dotting the sky. It was also a way to let the rest of the moisture soak back into my eyes before it had a chance to fall. "They probably wouldn't have me back. And even if they did, they'd take Seb away and I...I can't..."

Can't what? Can't live without him? Can't break free from this mysterious spell he'd put me under without uttering a single word?

"I just...can't."

Mimi fell in beside me, resting her head along my shoulder. "So where will you go, then?"

I shrugged, trying to sniff in the snot I could feel trailing down to my upper lip. "I don't know. To find Mom, maybe."

"Right. Like she's gonna help."

"She's Mom, Mimi. I can't give up on her."

Mimi pushed off the wall. "One day you're gonna understand, Alejandro. She's not a mom. She's just a lady who happened to have babies."

I really couldn't blame her for thinking that.

Voice thick with anger and unshed tears, I yelled for Seb. He stopped his antics with Star and turned to me.

"Let's get our stuff. We're leaving."

~*~

"Will you come back?" Star tugged on my pant leg, her lower lip sticking out only slightly. She seemed to be deciding whether or not she was supposed to be sad.

"Sure, I'll come back sometime. And now you know you have a tío." I reached over and picked her up for a hug. Her tiny arms encircled my neck, causing an unfamiliar stirring in my heart. For two odd, stressful days, I'd gotten to be an uncle—and I'd never dreamed that'd be something I'd actually find rewarding.

Mimi came to me next, squeezing me so hard our ribs ground against each other. I wanted to tell her to eat more, but the advice died before it left my lips. I wanted to tell her to do a lot of things…and to *not* do a lot of things, but I knew she was just going to keep on living what she knew.

"Are you sure I can't take you back?" she asked one last time.

I took a deep breath, drinking in Seb's form with my eyes and using it to remind myself of why I needed to stay strong.

"No, Mi. We're gonna make it on our own. We'll be fine."

Shaking her head with a sigh, she pulled something out of her pocket and thrust it at me. I looked down to find a wad of crumpled cash in my hand.

"What's this?"

"Should be about a hundred sixty, I think."

"No." I pushed the money back at her, but she dropped her hands and stepped away. "I can't take this, Mimi. You and Star need it."

"Don't worry about us, I got it all under control. I'm doing all right, really. I just know I gotta be careful and save." She leaned in to whisper in my ear. "And I keep some stuff away from Angel, you know. I'm not stupid."

"Yeah." I swallowed hard. "That's probably a good idea."

I folded up the bills and stuck some in my pockets. The rest went into my shoe. "Well, we're gonna get going now."

Star hugged Seb and then Mimi embraced me again, giving me a quick peck on the cheek. "Be safe, *hermanito*. And I hope he really is…okay."

I couldn't bring myself to respond, so I just nodded, hitching up my backpack and gesturing for Seb to follow as we headed down the street.

"Bye, Tío! Bye, Seb!" Star waved. "Bye-bye!" Her little hand kept flying back and forth until we rounded the corner and she was out of sight.

And then, at long last, Seb and I were alone.

This wasn't exactly ideal circumstances, though. Despite all my brave words, I knew our prospects for a comfortable life anywhere in the near future were growing slim.

"Shit, Seb," I muttered, trying and failing to keep the uncertainty from swallowing me whole. "I really thought we were gonna be able to stay there. I wouldn't have sprung you otherwise. I'm sorry."

I wasn't sure if he'd heard me, because he was busy staring at a man pushing a corn cart across the street. The man stopped honking his little horn and yelling out "*elotes!*" to stare right back at him.

"Seb, quit it. Don't look people in the eye."

I could've smacked myself for my stupidity. There was a good chance the cops would be looking for us, especially since we were heading to my old neighborhood. They'd have to be pretty fucking observant to pick my brown face out of a crowd, but a white kid with blond hair in South Central was an odd enough sight to attract attention. He'd be like a neon sign to anyone looking for us.

"I think it's time for the wig again." I pulled him into an alley and dug it out of the backpack. Then I secured it on his head with the baseball cap, letting my fingers trace the side of his face and his jaw as I examined my work.

"I like your blond hair, but you can pull off the brown, too," I told him. "Especially since your eye color is so dark."

He batted his lashes.

Chuckling, I just barely resisted the urge to caress his face again. There was a whole lot more shit to worry about, but Seb's almond eyes seemed to have some magical power that allowed me to postpone dealing with it for the time being.

"C'mon. We should get moving. Gotta find ourselves a place to stay before dark."

Chapter 18: Home Sweet Home

Two hours later, we trudged past the 105 freeway. There wasn't exactly a wrought iron sign announcing our location like there had been for Bel Air, but maybe the old bum crouching under the overpass served the same purpose. He was still right there in his flannel blanket, drinking out of a brown paper bag. It was almost as if he hadn't moved since the last time I'd seen him.

"This is it," I told Seb. "This is where I'm from. Not so glamorous, huh."

Like he was just waking up, Seb lifted his eyes from the sidewalk and blinked slowly into the sunlight. He'd been staring at the ground for most of our trip, ever since I'd snapped at him about making eye contact with strangers. But now he looked curious about his surroundings again, and he swiveled his head in all directions.

I'd always thought there wasn't much to see, but I could tell Seb was interested, especially by all the vendors on the street selling shaved ice and *fruta con limón y chile*. His eyes danced from one colorful cart to the next, taking in the reds and blues and greens that stood out against the black and white backdrop of the projects.

I thought about stopping to get him some, but I was too nervous to let anyone get a good look at my face.

Turning onto 111th street, we headed for a gray apartment building. I stood on an overturned trashcan to jump the fence that surrounded it, almost ripping the crotch of my pants in the process. Of course, Seb made the leap in a much more graceful fashion, landing on both feet with perfect balance.

I shook my head at him, then climbed the outside stairs of the building and pounded on the door to apartment number five. "Yo! José! You home, man?"

The door swung open a few seconds later, revealing a hallway and living room stuffed with furniture, covered in more cheap porcelain figurines than it seemed possible to collect in a lifetime.

"Alex? Holy shit!" He clasped my hand and pulled me forward so that our chests bumped. "Where the fuck you been, man?"

"Fuck." I shook my head. "It's so much shit, I wouldn't even know where to start. Can we come in?"

Thick brows drawn up in confusion, José passed his gaze back and forth between Seb and me. He'd lost weight, I realized, because his cheeks weren't as round anymore and his collarbone was starting to jut out from beneath his white t-shirt.

"Who's this fucker?" He pointed to Seb. "And why the fuck is he wearing a wig?"

"That's Seb." I pushed my way into the cluttered apartment without invitation. "He don't talk."

"Uh, okay." José trotted after me as I sank down at his kitchen table.

I shoved a family of porcelain elephants aside so I could rest my elbows on the tabletop. "Look, man, have you seen my mom at all? You have any idea where she might be at?"

"Nah." José pulled up a chair, knocking off a mangy white cat that was furiously scratching at fleas. "I ain't seen her or Hector in like forever. Heard they left town. We all figured they was running from something, 'cause they left in a hurry."

"Shit." *But you already knew that*, I reminded myself, trying to dull the sharp sting of his words.

It didn't really work.

"So what the fuck happened, man? Are you gonna tell me? Why'd the cops take you?"

I nudged the cat away from my leg before the little bloodsuckers it housed could decide to snack on me. "It wasn't really the cops. It was a social worker. They put me in fucking foster care."

José blew out a breath, making his cheeks puff up. He looked more like his old self that way. "Fuck, man. That fucking sucks."

"Yeah. But we split, me and Seb. That's why I'm trying to find my mom."

"Yeah, I dunno." José eyed Seb, who was standing perfectly still in the doorway, right where I'd left him. "Like I said, I haven't seen her."

"You think we could crash here tonight?" I asked hopefully, even though there was barely a square inch of free space in the porcelain hell, and I was sure I'd wake up with fleas. "Till I get an idea where she might be at?"

"Damn, man. I would, but you know how my mom is. She's been on this crazy religious kick lately, 'cause she thinks I'm hanging out with the wrong crowd or some shit." He gestured to a cabinet full of baby Jesus figurines. "And you know she always hated you."

"Yeah." Fuck. When would I catch a fucking break?

A fly buzzed past and José swatted it, sending it whirling into a roll of flypaper that hung from the ceiling. "And, well, she's gonna be home soon."

"Yeah."

"Hey, I might be going to this party Blanca's gonna have on Friday. If you're still in town, you should check it out."

My lips twisted into a bitter smile. "Nah, man. Can't really do that."

In the silence that followed, it suddenly occurred to me that our friendship was over. Maybe it had never been that deep to start with—maybe because I never really let myself get close to anyone. But now that we didn't go to the same school or the same parties or hang out around the same people...we had absolutely nothing in common.

Seb was my only friend.

"Well, we're gonna get outta here. I gotta find some place for us to stay. Anyways, if anyone comes around asking about us..."

"Don't worry, man. I never saw you."

I rose from the table and headed toward Seb. "Cool. See ya, man."

"See ya," he responded, one hand already poised to close the door. "And good luck with shit."

"Yeah. Thanks."

I didn't really have a plan when we left José's apartment. I just started walking, with Seb calmly following by my side, and somehow my feet took me straight to my own street. I pulled up in front of my house and stared at the dull beige exterior like I was studying the portal to another world. My life had taken so many strange turns since I'd last slept within those walls...it didn't really feel like *home* anymore.

And as hard as I tried, I couldn't quite bring to mind the memory of the last happy moments I'd spent there with my mother—not with any detail, anyhow. It was just a general blur of bleached blond hair and polished nails and smiles.

I was looking at the house, but not really seeing. So I didn't notice the shadow moving behind the cheap white blinds until Seb tapped me on my shoulder and pointed.

"Shit, Seb!" I smacked his arm. "There's someone home!" A flying leap took me over the fence, and I raced to the door to pound on it steadily. "Hello? Mamá? You home?"

But the stout woman in the greasy apron who answered was definitely not my mother.

"Jes?"

"Oh." I stumbled back a step, colliding with Seb. "Oh, I was looking…I'm here waiting for my mom, 'cause this is my house…well, it *was* my house, and I was waiting here to see if she—"

The lady shook her head. "I sorry. My English no so good."

"Oh." My shoulders slumped in defeat. "Well, that sucks… 'cause… uh…*mi español…no es tan bueno tampoco.*"

She smiled. "What you…need?"

I kicked at some dirt by my foot, staring down at my once-white sneakers. They were a definite gray, now. "Um…my mom lived here. *Mi mamá…vivía aquí.*"

"Ah." She moved forward to peer into my face. "Ah, *sí, sí. El niño de las fotos!*"

The boy from the photographs. What photographs?

"*Pasen, pasen.*" She eagerly waved Seb and me in.

"Oh, um, okay. *Gracias.*"

As soon as we were inside, my mouth fell open and shock clamped down on my muscles, leaving me paralyzed.

What the fuck had happened to my house?

Some of the ugly bits of broken wall had been patched and repainted, leaving no scars behind of the vicious blows that had caused them. The floor was still the same old chipped linoleum, but it was practically spotless. The table was the same, too, except it was covered with a lace tablecloth and several lace doilies. A large recliner had joined our old couch, and both were wrapped in white sheets with tiny green leaves, so that no one could see the rips and tears beneath.

And right by the front door, where my head had once banged pieces of drywall away, hung a painting of Jesus.

"Um…" I gulped in some warm air, tasting the meat and spices that were cooking on the stove. "My mom…have you…"

"*Vienen por sus cosas?*" She asked over her shoulder as she hurried to the kitchen and lowered the heat on the pan.

"No, I don't want any of the things…*estoy buscando a mi mamá.*"

She turned to me and wiped her hands on her apron. "*No sabes donde está tu mamá?*"

"No. I don't know where she is. We lived here…in this house…"

My voice trembled as I spoke, and I cut myself off mid-sentence to avoid further humiliation. There was no denying now that our journey to Watts had been completely pointless. My mother didn't live here anymore. She was long gone.

The woman came around the table to look at me, her eyes narrowed and her brows tightly knit as if she couldn't believe what she was hearing. She was a good five inches shorter than me, and her skin was darker than mine. Grayed hairs twisted in and around thick black ones in a loose bun at the back of her head.

"*Se fue sin decirte dónde?*"

"Yeah." I rubbed at my eyes, like that might suddenly make this alternate reality of my home fade away and leave the old one in its wake. "They just didn't say where they were gonna go."

"*Bueno…lo siento. Es que estamos rentando, y no me dijeron nada sobre la gente que vivía aquí antes.*"

Still rattled, it took me a few seconds to process that she was basically telling me she was just a renter and knew nothing.

"Oh. Yeah. Okay. We'll…we'll get out of your way, then."

She stopped me with a gentle hand on my forearm. "*Tienen hambre?* You have…hungry?"

225

Food was the last thing on my mind, but I glanced over at Seb and wondered if one Pop-Tart was enough of a meal for him to last the day on.

"*Porque tengo tamales que ya están hechos*," she continued. "You like? Tamales?"

Once, a very, very long time ago, my mother had made tamales. If I closed my eyes I could almost picture the afternoon—Mimi and I laughing and hovering around her hips, bits of gooey *masa* stuck to our hands and clothing. But it had only been that once, because after that she'd decided it was way too much trouble to go through when you could just buy them from the lady who sold them on the corner.

I wondered if Mimi ever made tamales with Star. Probably not.

"Um, yeah." I sighed. "We could eat, right Seb?"

No answer.

The lady smiled and pointed to the chairs at the table. Seb and I waited in silence as she pulled a couple of tamales out of the fridge and popped them in the microwave.

"*Mami, estamos aquí!*" A little boy's voice rang out. A few seconds later, a chubby kid wearing the navy pants and white polo uniform of the local elementary school stomped into the house, followed by a thinner girl with waist-length straight black hair.

"*Tienen hambre, mis amores?*" the woman asked her children as each one came and gave her a hug.

The girl peeked at me nervously, grabbing her hair and twisting it into a knot. She was dark, like her mother—a lot darker than Star—but she had the same kind of straight nose, strong cheekbones and full lashes that Star did. I wondered if Star would look like her when she got a little older.

She was much more timid than Star, though, because she pulled on her mother's apron until the woman bent over and listened to her whispering. When she was done,

226

she ran off down the hallway, and I didn't think she had any plans to come back.

The little boy, on the other hand, was completely undisturbed and immediately joined us at the table.

Another tamale was added to the microwave.

"*Mami, quiénes son?*" From his seat beside me, he peered up at his mother, waiting for an explanation as to why two strange people were in his house.

"Uh, hi," I answered before she had a chance. "I'm Alex, and this is Seb. I used to live here in this house."

"Oh." The boy nodded. "You lived in here when we wasn't."

"Yeah. I came back looking for my mom…but I guess no one knows where she is."

"*Qué dijo?*" The woman asked, and the boy translated what I had said for her. She shook her head, her forehead creasing into deep, dark lines, like she was angry.

But she wasn't angry at me, apparently, because the tamales were soon placed in front of us. I split mine in half, encouraging Seb to do the same so it would cool off.

"My mom makes very good tamales," the boy said, his plump stomach folding onto his lap as he scooted toward his plate.

"Yeah, I bet." I chuckled.

One bite later, I was forced to agree. The tamales were warm and fresh, and the shredded chicken inside was perfectly spiced. I couldn't remember the last time I'd tasted anything so good. The meatloaf at Ms. Loretta's maybe—but that was a totally different dish, and it was hard to compare.

"These are delicious. *Gracias*," I added, acknowledging the lady who was still leaning over the stove.

"*El dice que los tamales son deliciosos, y gracias*," the boy translated again.

I rolled my eyes.

"*De nada.*" She set some glasses of juice in front of our plates, right on the doilies. Then she pointed to Seb. "*El es muy tímido, no? Como mi hija.*"

"Shy? No…he's not shy. It's just that he can't talk…*es que no puede hablar.*"

"Ah." She nodded thoughtfully. "*Bueno, voy a traer las fotos.*" Wiping her hands on her apron again, she headed down the hallway and into my mother's room.

Or into *her* room.

A moment later, she returned with a stack of photographs. She passed them to me, pointing to a skinny boy at the top of a slide with his arms thrown in the air and a wide smile on his face.

"It is you, no?"

The hand I'd felt at Mimi's—the one that seemed to think I shouldn't be breathing—squeezed down on my chest again. It *was* me in the pictures, me and Mimi and my mother. We'd gone to a park with a disposable camera when I was in the third grade and snapped pictures until the whole roll of film was finished, for no reason other than the fact that we'd had the time and the camera on our hands.

These were the photographs I'd kept in my dresser.

Mimi was posing in most of them, on the balance beam, or just leaning against a tree—she was a show-off like that. At fourteen, she was fully developed and you could tell she was proud by the way she stuck out her chest in each picture. She didn't wear too much makeup back then, and her hair was loose and wild and untamed by gels and she looked absolutely beautiful.

There were only two pictures with my mother, since she'd been handling the camera most of the time. Her hair was already blond, and she was probably too made-up for an afternoon at the park with her kids. But she was beautiful, too, resting on the park bench and draping her arms around me. Beautiful and young and happy.

I didn't even look at myself in the pictures. I didn't want to think about the boy I'd been. Of what hopes I'd had for the future or what faith I'd had in my family. I didn't want to relive the disappointment.

"Uh…" I struggled to draw in a breath. "Was this it? Was there any more?"

"*Quiere saber si hay otras,*" the boy told his mother.

"*No.*" She shook her head slowly. "*No creo…*"

"Yeah," I interrupted. "In my mom's nightstand. The nightstand in the bigger room at the end of the hallway. There were pictures in there. That's where my mom kept them."

The boy translated, but she continued to shake her head. "*Sí había una mesita de noche y unas cositas adentro, pero ningunas fotos.*"

"She say there was a *mesita* and some things in there but no—" the boy began.

"I got it," I cut in. "No photos."

Seb had finished his tamale. I pushed the remainder of mine in front of him and he made quick work of that one, too. He must've been hungry.

"*Dime,*" the lady said, finally taking a seat in front of us. "*Cómo es que no sabes dónde está tu mamá? Dónde estás viviendo ahora? Con tu papá? O tu abuela?*"

"She say how you not know where your mamá is, and do you live with your daddy or your *abuela*…ehh…your granny," the boy rattled off. Apparently, he was used to being his mom's interpreter.

I shook my head. "No. I don't live with…" I just barely stopped myself before blabbing out anything stupid. What was I even doing here? "Look, uh, thanks for everything, but we gotta go." I stood and yanked back Seb's chair.

The lady came around the table and clasped one of my hands, smiling warmly. "*Gloria. Me llamo Gloria.*"

"Oh, right. Well, *gracias por todo*, Gloria. We really gotta go."

Grabbing Seb's t-shirt on the way, I darted past her and out of the house.

I sank down to the curb right in front of the fence. My hands went numb and the pictures slipped from my fingers, falling into a pile of wet leaves and fast food wrappers. "I'm sorry, Seb. It was stupid to come here."

He squatted beside me and plucked up the photographs, stopping at one of me on the swings. Then he ran his finger over the glossy surface and smiled.

Did he know how much those rare smiles of his did to improve my mood?

I pulled off his hat and wig combo and checked to make sure the streets were empty before nudging a sweaty lock of hair from his forehead. "Hard to believe, huh." I reluctantly glanced down at the young me. "I was such a scrawny fucker."

Seb turned to study me, like he was counting the differences.

Suddenly self-conscious under his gaze, I flushed. "Seb…I keep making all these mistakes. Even if you *could* understand me…even if you were…I dunno why you'd want to b—"

The rickety screen door of the house burst open, and the little boy's voice interrupted me. "My mom say do you wanna stay for dinner?"

For some strange reason, Seb was still smiling. Maybe he'd liked the warm, inviting atmosphere Gloria had magically created in my home. It gave *me* a sort of dizzying, this-does-not-belong feeling…but keeping Seb happy was my number one priority at the moment.

"Sure. Why not."

Chapter 19: The Job of Family

Frederico—the little boy—snatched a book from a neat stack under the coffee table and climbed up on the couch beside me. He motioned for his sister Luz to join him, but she hung back shyly in the kitchen, helping her mother clean up the remains of our taco dinner.

As adorable as Star had been, I sort of wished she'd been more like that—more like the kind of girl who hid from boys.

"I gotta read for my homework," Frederico told me, his double chin wobbling as he nodded in agreement to his own declaration.

I didn't really know why I was still there, now that our meal was finished. There was just nowhere else to go. And Seb was relaxed, pinching bits of the sheet that covered the couch and rolling it between his fingers. So I stayed, trapped in limbo—unable to move forward, and with nothing to go back to.

"Okay." I lowered the volume on the TV. "Go ahead."

The TV was new, too. Well, not new, but it wasn't ours. So wherever my mom and Hector had gone, they hadn't needed a couch or a table or my dresser, but they'd needed a TV.

"Can…N…a…n…*Nan*…see…the…bu…g… *bug*. Can Nan see the bug!"

Frederico pointed to the page he was on and looked up at me triumphantly. "It say, can Nan see the bug!"

I had a really strange, split-personality reaction, where half of me wanted to roll my eyes and turn the TV back up—the kind of thing I would have done with Andrew or Ryan at Ms. Loretta's. But so soon after my time spent with Star, a different instinct won out.

"Wow, that's really good. How old are you that you already know how to read so good?"

He stuck out six fingers proudly. "I have this many. It was just my happy birthday."

"You in kindergarten?"

"Yeah, but next year I have to go to first grade with my friends if I keep reading."

Kindergarten and he was already beginning to read. I wondered if Star knew how to read at all…if she even knew the alphabet…and then recalled I hadn't come across a single book in that apartment.

Would she catch up, when she eventually got to school? Or would she always be a struggling student, the way Mimi had been? Would she find other things to occupy her time, the way Mimi had? Would she be the third generation of unwed teenage mothers in our family?

I knew it wasn't Gloria's lovingly-made-from-scratch cooking that was making me nauseous. To distract myself, I pointed at Frederico's book.

"You read it good, but you see that squiggly thing at the end of the sentence?"

"Uh huh." He nodded. "But I forget it."

"It's a question mark. That means you gotta read it like a question. Like this: Can Nan see the bug?"

"Oh, yeah." Frederico pulled the book away from my finger and placed his own on the words again. "My teacher say me that…Can Nan see the bug?"

I patted him on the head and looked up to see Gloria standing in front of the kitchen. She smiled and mouthed *gracias*—I guess because she thought I was helping him with his homework.

And that didn't seem like such an awful payment for dinner. It was better than breaking into our limited cash supply, after all.

"All right, Freddy. Let's read the next one."

Five pages in to the incredibly boring tale of Nan and the bug, the front door of my house opened and an enormous man stepped in.

"Papá!" Frederico wiggled off the couch, his round little body barely reaching his father's thighs when they hugged. Luz and Gloria also left the kitchen to greet the man, and I heard Gloria whispering to him in rapid-fire Spanish. Too rapid for me to make out.

After finishing his conversation with his wife, he strode over purposefully. "Hello. I am Raúl."

Seb stopped playing with the sheet, his face blanking out as he scooted further into the corner of the couch.

Was he scared? If he were, I wouldn't really have blamed him. Raúl was a man who could knock either of us out with one blow.

He was wearing overalls, stained with paint and crusted with splotches of plaster, and he smelled of sweat and burnt wood. Little flecks of soot dotted the stubble on his face. I figured he was a construction worker, or maybe just a day laborer. Whatever he did, it must've contributed to those bulging muscles, covered by only a thin layer of fat.

"Hey." I stood, because from the lower stance he seemed like an absolute giant, and I was starting to feel a little intimidated.

He gripped my hand with strong, calloused fingers and shook it forcefully.

"I'm…I'm Alex."

I forgot to introduce Seb, but that was probably because he was still seated, eyes glued to a carpet stain. I was pretty sure Mimi had made that, with an overturned cup of hot chocolate.

"My wife she say you can stay for coffee," Raúl's voice boomed as he ran his gaze over me suspiciously. He had a very heavy accent, but he spoke English with authority, not with the timid uncertainty Gloria had.

"Oh…thanks, but we'll probably…"

"*Vengan, vengan*," Gloria interrupted, waving us back to the kitchen. "*Tengo café y un poco de pastel.*"

When I didn't move immediately, she came over and placed a mug in my hand. Seb stayed zoned out, so she left his on the kitchen table.

Raúl dropped his heavy form into the recliner that sat in the corner of the room.

"Papi, read a story?" Frederico asked, grabbing another book and crawling onto the armrest of his father's chair.

Nodding, Raúl cupped his son's head in one of his gigantic hands. "I will read a short one."

He called Luz over, and she skirted around me to join them.

The story Freddy had picked was *The Cat and the Hat*. I recognized the cover right away—at least I'd learned *that* in school—and couldn't imagine a sillier book for someone of Raúl's size to be reading.

After clearing his throat with a mighty rumble, he began to read. His rich voice filled our little living room, sounding far too noble for the ridiculous scriblings of Dr. Seuss.

Seb relaxed and returned to his earlier game of picking at the couch cover. Whatever had upset him had evidently passed—maybe because the big bear of a man who'd arrived on the scene actually seemed a lot like a teddy bear now, with his kids smiling up at him adoringly.

For some reason, though, this unexpected side of Raúl had my guts rolling. *Father* was a completely foreign concept to me, but I'd never let that bug me before. It wasn't like I was the only kid in the ghetto without one. José didn't have one. And neither did Star.

But Star would've liked the story. I should've read to her while I was there, instead of just letting her play around in the dirt.

Raúl pulled Luz into his lap, and she tucked her long hair over one shoulder before resting on his chest. Where had they gotten a chair big enough to fit both him and his kids? Something that size couldn'tve been easy to find.

I blinked twice before it hit me. The chair.

There'd never been a chair in that corner of the room before. No furniture at all, actually. But I'd been there. I'd been crumpled on the floor in that very same spot, crying those long, hiccup-y sobs that left tears and snot all over my face, cradling a broken arm against my chest. I'd been there watching my sister—my closest ally—pack up and leave, watching my mother cowering beside the leg of the sofa, weak and confused and totally incapable of lifting a hand to help either of us.

The memory strangled me.

Abandoning my coffee, I scrambled to my feet and raced to the kitchen. I leaned over the sink and gasped in short, shallow breaths, my chest contracting too quickly for me to really draw in the right amount of oxygen.

I'd only been ten years old, but even then I'd had some understanding of what was going to happen to my sister out there on the streets. How she'd be beaten down by loneliness, how she'd be desperate for money, how she'd do anything to get by. And I'd tried to stop it. I'd tried to stand up to Hector, told him to go to hell like the scum he was, even smashed a glass vase against his chest.

And all I'd gotten for it was a reminder that I was ten years old, powerless and breakable.

With a weak, shaking hand, I grabbed some paper towel and wiped the sweat from my face.

Why was this hitting me now? I'd lived in this house for years after that day, and I'd always managed to keep thoughts of it right where they belonged—buried under a thick blanket of that's-just-the-way-it-is.

"*No te sientes bien?*" Gloria ambushed me from behind. Her eyes were full of concern, and she placed her hand on my head like she was checking for a temperature. "You no feel good?"

I wanted to tell her I was fine, that we were ready to leave, but my mouth fell open and all I could do was suck in more air.

"You lie down," she said, taking my arm and leading me down the hall to my own room.

Seb followed us immediately, standing close by my side as she opened the door to reveal a space that was almost as bare as it'd been when I'd slept there. The biggest difference was that there were two beds again—like there'd been when Mimi and I shared the room—and my dresser was covered in stickers. Only a few toys lay neatly stacked on the floor, and the closet was mostly empty. These people were just as poor as we'd been.

"You lie down," Gloria repeated. "For to feel *mejor.*"

I nodded, and she apparently trusted me to follow through with her instructions because she turned around and left us.

"That's just the way it is," I whispered into the dark room once we were alone, but there was no more power in the words. That Band-Aid had been ripped clear off the wound. I knew it didn't *have* to be that way. I couldn't blame it on Watts, couldn't even blame it on being poor.

We just hadn't been the right people for the job of family.

Strong arms surrounded me, and Seb brought his hand up to my head, threading his fingers into my hair and pushing down so that I rested on his shoulder. I was so exhausted it took me several seconds to realize this was the first time he'd ever been the one to start a hug.

"Seb," I mumbled breathlessly. "Seb, I..."

He patted my head once and pulled away, just as thundering footsteps sounded in the hallway.

Raúl flicked on the lights in the bedroom and stood in the entranceway with his beefy arms folded across his chest.

"My wife," he said slowly, "she trusts. I tell her here, you not always can trust. But she trusts. She say you can stay one night."

"O-oh," I stuttered. I'd almost forgotten the sun had set outside, and we were still completely without a place to sleep. All my stupid self-pity was going to cost Seb in the end, if I couldn't get my act together. "Um, yeah, that'd be great. Thanks."

"You sleep here." Raúl pointed to the beds.

"Oh, no." I shook my head. "We can sleep in the living room, right Seb? I don't want to take the kids' beds."

I started toward the doorway, but Raúl held his ground, completely blocking the exit.

"The children sleep with us tonight, because there are strangers." His eyes narrowed on us.

"Right." I swallowed, trying to recoat my dry throat with saliva. "That's...that's a good idea. I mean, not because of us, because we're not...I mean, we wouldn't...but in general..."

He walked off.

I was finally able to draw in a deep enough breath to clear my head, and I gave Seb a weak smile. "Guess we solved that problem."

If only for the night.

I settled into one of the beds—probably *my* bed, because it creaked the same way—and Seb lay down on the other one. He fell asleep right away, smartly building up his energy for the next day of uncertainty.

Lucky him. I couldn't even bring myself to close my eyes.

The mattress wasn't the world's greatest, but it was a whole lot more comfortable than the floor, so that wasn't the issue. I just kept staring out the window into the purple sky, listening to the sounds of the city night—the same sounds I'd heard all my life. Cars revving and tires screeching. Loud stereos with pumped-up bass. Cats in heat. Dog fights. Sirens.

All so familiar, and yet so foreign now.

An ambulance roared past, and I pulled the blankets more securely over my body.

I wished Star could've been there, in a warm bed, instead of lying on the cold hardwood floor, alone.

~*~

"*Y a dónde van?*" Gloria asked for at least the third time over breakfast the next morning. She was back in the apron, because she was cooking again.

"Uh." I blinked, my eyes sore and my lids weary from lack of sleep. "I told you, we're going to that friend."

Frederico shoveled a spoonful of cereal into his mouth and started to translate through the crunch of flakes. "*Dice que—*"

"Hold it." I patted his hand. The friend story obviously wasn't working on Gloria—I needed to come up with something more elaborate. Nibbling at my tamale, I bought myself a little time. "Uh, I have a *tía* we can stay with...*tengo una tía y vamos a...a quedarnos con ella.*"

"*Dice que tiene una tía—*" Frederico began, then stopped, his round face puzzled. "Oh...never mind."

Luz giggled, hiding her face behind a sheet of hair.

"Freddy, you should be a translator when you grow up," I said.

He took another bite of cereal and shrugged. "What's that?"

Gloria came around the table and handed me a warm package of food wrapped in aluminum foil. *"Algunos tamales."*

"Oh, thanks." I stifled a yawn as I tucked them away in my backpack. "Well, I guess we should get going."

"Los niños también," she added, *"a la escuela."*

Luz and Frederico stood at the mention of school, grabbing their own bags from the backs of their chairs. Each of them received a hug, a kiss, and a plastic lunchbox from Gloria before we all headed out the door.

"Adiós," Gloria called. *"Que les vaya bien."*

I nodded, taking slow steps down the walkway as the train rattled by and dusty air swirled around us.

Que les vaya bien. Basically...*may you travel well.*

But travel where? And how? And do what once we got there?

I ran through things quickly in my head. We needed shelter, somewhere where the cops wouldn't be looking for us. Warmer clothes if we were going to be on the streets at night. Food. More money. Jobs.

The tamales I'd had for breakfast, delicious but full of lard, suddenly became lead weights in my stomach. I wrapped my arms around myself and breathed deeply to work through the queasiness.

"So, Seb, we should—"

"Goodbye!" Frederico shouted. He and Luz were turning to go in the opposite direction, toward the elementary school. Luz gave me a timid little wave, but Freddy's plump hand waggled energetically. "Bye-bye!"

I waved back, though I tried to keep my mind on our current problems. Should we go further east? Or west? Leave Los Angeles? Or maybe leave California all together?

But I knew nothing of the world outside this city. How would we get by?

Freddy was still waving. Little kids liked to wave forever, it seemed. I focused in on his hand, letting my other concerns be pushed to the background for a moment—probably because I had no answers. But as I continued to stare, it wasn't his little fingers I was thinking about.

It was Star's.

I turned back to Seb, wishing we were alone so I could lose myself in his arms again. "Star will never have this, will she?"

He blinked.

"The dinner at the table and the fresh tamales and the story reading and the whole...this whole *family* thing."

His eyes drifted to the ground. *No. Probably not.*

The oppressive hand returned, clenching my heart in its mighty grip. "She...she doesn't really have a chance, does she?"

I stopped walking and inhaled through my nose, willing my breakfast to stay exactly where it was.

"Mimi didn't have a chance. She didn't. It wasn't fair. I...I tried to help her, but I just couldn't *do* anything. And now Star...now... they...they don't have a chance..."

They didn't, unless something changed. And who would change it? Not Mimi—she didn't know how. Star was too young. And the only change Angel would make would be to influence Star, maybe make her into a little wh—

I dry-heaved once, then began emptying the contents of my stomach all over the sidewalk.

Seb's arms were at my shoulders immediately, holding me as I continued to retch. Brown and orange half-digested tamale bits splattered on the ground. When there was nothing left to throw up, I stayed hunched over, staring down at them with sick fascination until my eyes stung.

Seb eventually pulled me up, and I spit to rid my mouth of the vile taste. As my vision cleared, a blur of black and blue in the distance slowly morphed into a payphone.

"I...I think I need to make a phone call."

The fifty-cents left over from the UCLA couple—my only change—went into the phone. Still shaking from being sick—or from shock or from fear or from whatever insanity had possessed me—I pulled the crumpled business card from my pocket and smoothed it out so I could dial the number.

It rang twice.

"Suzie Gardell, Department of Children and Family Services."

I hung onto the receiver, closing my eyes and breathing heavily.

"Hello? Hello? Is someone on the line?" Papers rustled in the background.

"Suzie," I whispered.

The noise of movement stopped. "Yes? Who is this?"

"Suzie...it's me." My voice sounded awful. Wobbly and scratchy and tearful, even though I wasn't actually crying.

"Alex? Oh my goodness. Please, tell me where you are. Is Sebastian with you?"

There was panic in her tone, but I ignored it. "He's here."

"Thank God. Alex, please, you need to tell me—"

I cut her off. "I have to know something. When you first picked me up...when you said that DCFS doesn't rip apart families...that they work with them to make a safe environment...was that true?"

"Have you found your mother? Where? If you've found her we can do this the right way—"

"Answer me!" I slammed my fist into the numbers on the payphone, and a series of tones emerged.

"Okay, okay." Suzie's breaths were growing shorter. I could just imagine her lifting her hands and motioning for me—and for her—to calm down. "Yes, it's true. We don't

remove children from households unless we suspect
immediate danger…like we did with you. DCFS can
provide counseling…we can recommend therapies and
drug rehabs and shelters and employment offices. There
are a lot of services out there, a lot of places that can help,
if people know where to look."

"They don't." I snorted bitterly. "They don't know
where to look."

"Then let us help you, Alex. Please tell me where you
are. We'll come pick you up right away."

I kept my eyes closed, as if the darkness would protect
me from the reality of what I was doing. "Swear to me."

"Swear…what?"

"Swear to me you won't rip children out of their
mother's arms. Swear to me that you'll help them."

"I swear, Alex. I swear that everything we do is in the
best interest of the children and the family."

"Then I need you to write down an address."

Some papers shuffled and a desk chair creaked. "Okay,
I'm ready. Go ahead."

"6724 Makee Avenue, unit two."

"And that's where you'll be? You and Sebastian?"

My lids fluttered, trying to open, but I squeezed them
shut again. "No."

"Alex, I don't understand."

"Promise me, Suzie. Promise me you'll help her. Help
both of them. Promise me you won't take Star away from
her. It's not her fault. She didn't have a chance. Sh-she
didn't have anywhere to go…sh-she…she…"

"Who are you talking about? Your mother?"

I shook my head, even though Suzie couldn't see it.
"My sister. She has a daughter…she's…she's only five
years old…"

My face was wet. The tears had arrived.

"What's happened? Please, let me come pick you up
and we can talk about this."

"She's only five years old," I repeated. "And my sister...my sister is a...my sister is a..."

My throat closed and I choked on the taste of vomit. I felt myself slipping—slipping to the floor, slipping into complete despair...until Seb's hand closed around mine.

He squeezed my fingers, stroking my knuckles with his thumb. I finally opened my eyes and found him gazing at me with concern...but beneath that, I swore I could make out a flickering of...*understanding.*

I took a deep breath.

"My sister is a hooker. But she didn't have a choice. She got kicked out and she had a kid to support. She didn't know any other way."

"Alex—"

"You won't arrest her, will you?"

"I don't work for the police department. Of course I won't arrest her."

"She's a good mom. She loves Star. But they don't have enough money and Star is so skinny and...and...what if the cops got her? They'd take Star away anyways. And then Angel...that fucking piece of shit...he's a fucking pimp and he carries a gun around Star and he...he smokes crack in front of her, and I'm afraid...I'm afraid that...and I want Star to...I want her to have a fucking chance!"

Trembling, I crushed Seb's hand in mine. It had to hurt, but he didn't flinch.

"I know how hard this must be for you, Alex. I promise you I'll do everything I can to help. There are resources available for your sister...but now you need to tell me where you and Sebastian are. Please."

"No." I bit a dry patch on my lip until it bled, just so I could have something other than the aftertaste of vomit in my mouth. "We don't need you."

"Alex, think about what you're doing. How are you going to take care of Sebastian? This...what you've done...it could even be considered kidnapping."

I turned to Seb, resting the receiver against my chest. "Seb…do you want to go back with Suzie?"

He shook his head.

"Do you want to stay with me?"

He nodded.

Even in *this* moment, this moment of complete torture, he could make my heart sing.

I put the phone back up to my mouth. "Seb stays with me."

"Alex, please, you can't…you can't take advantage of him. Even if you have feelings for him, please, remember, if you acted on them…it would be like ra—"

"Don't worry," I interrupted. "I'm not. I'm not going to do anything I'm not supposed to, I promise. I'm just gonna take care of him. I'm just gonna be…his friend."

"Alex, you need to come—"

I hung up.

With my free arm, I rubbed my face clean, staring at the phone and taking shaky breaths.

It was done. I'd done it. I'd turned my sister in to the very people I was running from.

And now that it was done, I was left with a bottomless pit of doubts. I had to trust in Suzie. I had to trust that Star was young and flexible and could adjust…but if I were her age, would I have accepted strangers walking into my life, trying to change it with the promise of something better?

Probably not.

Would I if I knew what I did now?

I still wasn't sure.

Oh, God. Please forgive me. Please God fucking forgive me.

Folding over, I started to retch again, like I was trying to expel what I'd just done from my body. But there was nothing left in my stomach and I just ended up spewing bloody saliva onto the grass below.

Seb touched the back of my neck, his soft fingers grazing the skin, and I gradually straightened up.

"I'm okay." I wiped my mouth on my sleeve. "I'm okay. It's okay. We're gonna be okay."

If I said it enough times, maybe I'd believe it.

Seb nodded again.

"We...we should get outta here, though. I don't know if they can really trace calls or anything like that, but I bet they'll be looking around here."

I started to move away from the payphone, and suddenly realized Seb and I were still connected by our hands.

"Um..." I searched the streets warily, noting a few guys loitering on the corner a block away. "Seb, I know you don't mean anything by it...but people could get the wrong idea about this." I squeezed his hand. "And around here, it isn't really safe."

Very slowly, his fingers slipped away from mine, but not before I caught a hint of something sad in his dark eyes.

"You're right. Around here...sucks." Spying a bus stop a few feet ahead, I slapped his shoulder to push him forward. "We need to blow this joint."

For good.

PART THREE

Chapter 20: Heaven and Hell

"Do you smell that?"

I stepped off the bus and into the brilliant sunshine, right under a tall palm tree. Seb pulled up beside me and blinked once.

I wanted the nods back, but at least he seemed alert—which was more than I could say for myself. My jaw and ear were still sore from where they'd been smashed up against the bus window while I slept.

"Take a deep breath, like this." I coached him, inhaling dramatically. Wafts of incense floated past my nostrils, making them twitch, but the breeze also carried hints of fried foods, grilling meats, and salt.

"That's the ocean."

Seb raised his brows.

"You've seen it right? Just right down here I think, and we'll get to it."

I headed down a narrow Venice side street, shoving my hands into my pockets to keep from touching Seb. Odd, tall houses with multi-colored exteriors and windowed walls lined the passage, but as we got closer to the beach, the buildings got even stranger. One place looked like it'd been plucked straight out of an old horror movie, complete with gargoyles, goblins and several dragons.

I curled my nose at a particularly demonic-looking creature, edging toward the opposite side of the street. "People are fucking weird. Why would you want to look at that shit every day? Especially when you live close to something awesome like the ocean."

When I turned to see Seb's reaction—or to see *if* Seb had a reaction—I was greeted by the sight of his blond hair racing ahead to a crowded pedestrian walkway.

"Hey, wait up!"

He kept going, bypassing a group of girls with bug-eyed sunglasses and squeezing through two street vendor tables selling that strong incense.

"Seb, stop!"

Plowing straight ahead, he wandered into the middle of a bike path. An angry cyclist swerved around him in the nick of time. Two more whipped by to the right, jingling their bells and glaring.

I sprinted over and tugged his shirtsleeve until we'd made it safely across.

"Seb"—I shook my finger sternly—"you can't just go running off like that. You gotta stick close."

Not even slightly disturbed, he stepped forward, kicking a pile of sand. He crouched down to feel it, then scooped up a handful and let it sift through his fingers in a long, wispy trail.

"Like it, don't ya." I laughed at his bright-eyed grin. "Shoulda figured you would."

He straightened up and walked on more calmly, heading for the water.

Sun glinted off the gray-blue waves as they rolled in. The Pacific wasn't like the postcards of those beachy paradises—the ones with the coconut tree and the crystal-clear waters—but it was just as beautiful. Maybe even a bit more interesting for all the secrets it kept hidden in its dark depths...sort of like Seb's eyes.

A wave crashed near the shoreline and a bit of froth sprayed our faces.

Seb picked up a handful of wet sand to mold in his palm. I got the feeling that if I left him alone, he'd spend the rest of the day exploring all the textures the oceanfront had to offer. But just when I was about to settle down to watch him, he stepped forward, and the waves licked at the tips of his sneakers.

"Hold it!" I hooked my finger into his shirt collar so I could pull him back. "We can go swimming sometime, but not in our clothes."

He glanced down at his feet, then kicked off his shoes.

"What about your pants? You know you only have that one pair right now."

He leaned over to remove his socks and roll up his pant legs.

"Oh my God." I shook my head into my hand, chuckling. "Fine, but hold up. I'm not letting you go in there alone."

I transferred all our cash over to my pockets and tightened the straps on the backpack so it was as high as it would go. Once I had my shoes and socks off and my pants up to my knees, I walked after him clumsily.

"Jesus, I look like a fucking fool," I moaned, but I wasn't really upset. How could I be, with Seb's brilliant smile still in place, his long white toes already touching the water's edge?

"Is it cold?"

No answer, just a grin. I took a step forward.

"Holy fuck!" I yelped, skipping back to the warm sand. "It's fucking freezing!"

A family with a toddler a few feet away gave me a dirty look, and I shrugged at them.

In the meantime, Seb waded in up to his calves. He had his head thrown back, his eyes closed and his mouth open, like he was waiting to catch salty drops of water on his tongue.

Braving the cold again, I clenched my fists and went to stand by his side. He must've heard the splashing because he turned to me, his lids fluttering open.

Still smiling. If only I'd had a watch so I could've timed this—I was pretty sure it was the longest stretch of smiling he'd done since...ever.

"There's a lot more to see. I mean, it's a bit of a freak show, but it's entertaining." I gestured behind me with a head nod. "I was here once, with...with Mimi and this guy she was dating."

I tripped a little on her name, guilt and regret fighting to recapture my thoughts. I knew I'd lost her. But I'd lost her before that, really, and I'd survived.

A powerful wave lapped at my leg, shocking me again with its frigid temperature.

"Seb, really, this is too cold. My people are a tropical people. Let's go back."

He followed me out, squishing his feet into the sand with each step.

When we reached dry ground, he suddenly plummeted down, lying back against one arm as a pillow and burying his free hand in the sand.

"Comfy?" I sat cross-legged beside him. "Well, don't get too comfortable. I don't think you should lie out for too long without sun block. I knew this girl once—she wasn't even white, she was just like, fair-skinned, and she got this burn so bad she couldn't even put on clothes. Got a special note to wear a tank top to school and everything."

He closed his eyes.

"Seriously, Seb. I'll just get browner, but you...you'll probably turn into a lobster."

"Well, we have some sun block you can borrow, if you like."

Glancing to my right, I found a brunette in a sundress and a floppy hat eyeing me from just above the rims of her designer sunglasses. A similarly dressed blonde was at her side, giggling.

"Oh, uh…sure. Thanks."

"It's no problem. Glad to do my part to prevent skin cancer." She smiled, digging into a straw beach bag, and pulled out a bottle. "I'm Carrie, and this is my friend Jess. We cut class today."

"Yeah. Thanks." I grabbed the sun block and ignored the introduction, turning back to Seb. "Here. Put out your hand."

He didn't move.

"C'mon, man. I'm not gonna rub it on you myself."

But God how I wish I could.

"Seb…" I dangled the bottle over him. "If you don't put out your hand so I can give you some, I'm gonna squirt it all over your face."

The corner of his lip twitched.

"I know you can hear me. Seriously. I'm opening the bottle now. I'm about to squeeze it…"

With his eyes still closed, he finally dragged his fingers out of the sand and held his hand up for me.

"Thought so." I grinned smugly.

I put a little lotion in his palm and waited, but he didn't do anything with it.

"Seb, put it on. C'mon, don't act like a retard."

As soon as the stupid comment was out, my insides went cold. Why did I have to choose *those* words?

But to my relief, he obediently reached up and rubbed it on his nose and cheeks. That was good enough for me— at least those seemed like the most important parts to protect. Besides, the time it would take to cover every inch of his exposed skin might further involve me with the girls, and I was pretty sure they had other things on their minds than just sun block.

"Here ya go." I handed back their bottle.

The brunette blinked, darting her gaze to the side to avoid eye contact. "Sure. Um, well, hope you and your…uh, friend have fun."

She and the blonde gathered up their stuff and moved away.

The exchange left me confused at first, and then a little disturbed once understanding sunk in. Since I'd met Seb, it seemed like everyone around me was figuring me out. Was it the way I looked at him? The way I talked to him? It was as if he'd activated some sort of gay vibe gene that continually gave me away. I wasn't sure how I felt about that yet.

I lay back with Seb, squeezing handfuls of sand the way I wished I could squeeze his fingers. "It's nice here, huh. I'm thinking we should stay…at least for a while."

A breeze blew past, tossing back strands of his blond hair. They were almost the same color as the sun-drenched sand.

"I mean, while I figure everything out, we might as well be some place nice. It'll be like a vacation. I think we deserve that."

We lay together for some time, listening to the constant waves and the murmur of the crowd, until Seb's stomach growled. At first it was just a quiet rumbling, but a few seconds later, it became a roar.

"Damn." I punched his shoulder, and he rolled onto his side to grin at me. "You've been pretty hungry lately. Maybe you're still growing? I thought you'd been looking a little taller. You're gonna be way taller than me, you jerk."

He sat up, sand falling from his arms and the side of his shirt.

"You wanna grab a bite to eat? Y'know, they've got fruit here, too, I think. Like the kind they were selling in Watts."

He got to his feet.

"All right." I dusted the remainder of the sand from his shirt with quick, forceful pats—instead of the slow, soft strokes I wanted to use. "Let's go back up to all those street vendors."

On the crowded Venice boardwalk, we did find a stand selling fruit, though I was disappointed to learn that for the beautiful beach atmosphere we now had to pay three times as much money. But I'd already promised Seb, so I ordered a large full of pineapple, watermelon, and mango, splitting it between two cups. I got mine *con todo*—salt, lime, and *chile*, but for Seb I only got salt and lime.

We settled at a small round plastic table, sticky with leftover fruit juice. I grabbed a couple of napkins to clear off the mess, and while my back was turned, Seb stuck his fork into my cup.

He speared a piece of pineapple and examined it curiously.

"That red stuff is chili," I told him. "It's spicy. And I kinda got a lot, so I don't know if you'll like it."

Bringing the fork to his nose, he sniffed at the fruit.

"Try a bit first to see if you—"

He popped the whole thing in his mouth. Within seconds, his eyes went wide and it came right back out again, bouncing on the table top once before spinning off into the crowd and smacking a lady on her heel. She glanced around to try to find the offender, but the poor piece of pineapple was kicked away by the stampede before she could spot it.

Seb reached past my elbow to grab the other cup of fruit and began eating.

"You are being a total nut today, you know that?"

He smiled.

"Thanks."

I didn't elaborate. He couldn't possibly have understood that his silly behavior was taking me miles away from everything that had happened back in South Central. But I knew it wasn't just because we *were* miles away that I felt almost…at peace. Seb gave me something

252

to concentrate on—a reason to keep going. And I couldn't explain that to him. Even if he *did* understand, it was too much pressure to put on his slender shoulders.

"Let's walk for a bit," I suggested as a bearded man in a white turban rushed past on roller skates, playing an electric guitar. Seb was up and after him in a second.

At this rate, I'd be chasing him all day.

The roller-skating hippie wove around a mass of people gathered to watch some sort of street show, and I finally caught up to Seb—but only because he'd stopped to see what all the commotion was about. His legs were longer than mine, and I had a feeling he could outrun me easily if he tried.

"I think they're break dancers," I whispered in his ear, though I couldn't really see through the wall of people. "Who knew anyone still did that."

Seb pushed forward, sliding through the crowd to get a better view.

"Seb," I groaned, hitching up the backpack and going after him. Within seconds, though, my progress was blocked by a skinny white dude wearing impossibly tight pants, an impossibly tight t-shirt, and a shell necklace. I went to move around him but found my path *still* cut off, by a bigger white guy in a similar outfit. A woman with a stroller prevented me from backtracking, so I decided to go straight through the duo, even if I had to resort to a little shoving.

Except, there, once again, I was cut off—by two joined hands. The two white guys' hands. Two grown men, holding hands, in a crowd of people in the middle of the Venice boardwalk on a warm southern California day.

I froze, darting my eyes around to see if anyone else had noticed. Nobody had. Or else they didn't care, or were more interested in the people doing back flips and spinning on their heads to make a fuss.

A basket was passed around for money, causing the crowd to thin as people tried to skip out on the obligation. The movement finally allowed me to get close to Seb.

"Let's go. We're not gonna waste our money watching some guy do a flip, and I don't feel like getting heckled."

Seb bounced off eagerly, waiting for the next spectacle to catch his interest.

The handholding men also started to walk, a few feet in front of us, their fingers still entwined. I kept one eye on Seb to make sure he was near me, but the rest of my focus was on them. How long would they stay like that? Would anyone say anything? I knew not all places were like my home—not all places were *dangerous*—but I just hadn't been around anyone so open before. And in a crowd, no less.

No one bothered them. A few pairs of eyes seemed to linger on them longer than they should, but Venice had so many other sights to offer—bodybuilders in speedos at the outdoor gym, pianists on the sidewalk, tons of shops and street vendors, and a homeless man building a dragon made of sand, complete with burning incense in its smoking nostrils. I guess gays in public didn't really measure up to all that.

Seb darted off the path and into a shop selling figurines made of old car parts, and I rushed to follow. His delicate fingers floated over the shelves as he studied each creation.

Such nice fingers. The way they twitched when they fell back to his side almost made it seem like they were just…itching to be held.

Do it, a voice said.

But what about my promise to Suzie?

How is holding hands breaking that promise?

It wasn't, of course. It didn't have to mean anything. And Seb liked holding my hand. If I ever wanted to do it, Venice Beach seemed like the place.

He tilted his head to the side, observing a rusty metallic Wall-E. My pulse raced as I drew closer to him.

The Alex I'd once been would never have considered this. And not just because it wasn't safe. I'd had a reputation to maintain, and handholding didn't really fit in with the whole ready-to-kick-ass image.

But I wasn't that person anymore. I wasn't sure *who* I was now, but I wasn't him.

The backs of our hands touched, and I gradually slid my fingers around to lace them with his.

He didn't look over.

"Just so I can keep track of you," I said quietly. "This way, the next time you decide to run off, I'll be coming along for the ride."

He gently pulled me back into the sunshine, and a vein in my neck started to pulse. I kept my head still, but my eyes continued to scan our surroundings restlessly.

A family of Asian tourists stepped around us. A man walking a beagle passed to my right. A few children stopped to point at a nearby seagull stealing popcorn. None of them noticed our hands.

Slowly, I turned my focus away from the crowds and toward the feel of Seb's fingers wrapped neatly around mine. Touching him like this in broad daylight was completely…mind-blowing. In a way it was like the highs I used to get from drugs—it even had that slight undercurrent of guilt beneath the floating pleasure. Some small part of me must've felt I was crossing a line best left uncrossed, but the rest of my heart was completely sold.

Strange, how one tiny point of contact with Seb could make me so happy.

We continued down the sidewalk, stopping to browse the vendor tables so that Seb could see and feel everything. Occasionally he'd tear away from my hand, but after satisfying his curiosity he always returned and thrust his fingers back into mine. I thought maybe I saw a few pairs of eyes narrowing on us with disapproval, but I didn't know who the hell those people were, and I was pretty practiced at giving my own looks—looks that said *mess with me and you'll fucking regret it.* I hadn't had an opportunity to give those in a while, and I'd actually kind of missed it.

My own stomach was starting to demand something a little more substantial than fruit as we reached the end of Venice Beach, just at the point where the Santa Monica Ferris wheel could be seen in the distance.

Seb peeled off again and I followed him to a rickety table selling rocks and minerals, run by a redhead with matted dreads. She stood by patiently as Seb lifted and examined each stone.

"Seb," I said gently. "Don't pick stuff up. If you break it we'll get in trouble."

"Oh, no," the woman interrupted. "It's important for you to touch and feel the energy of the rocks. He can go right ahead."

I raised an eyebrow at the odd comment and looked her over. She had on layers of cloth dresses and an old-fashioned military jacket, and behind the table there was a large camping backpack with several blankets and a sleeping bag attached.

"Your boyfriend seems most interested in the turquoise," she pointed out as he lifted a blue stone. "Certain cultures consider it a stone of communication—it opens the channels so that love can flow more freely. It can do wonders for a relationship."

"He's not my boyfriend," I responded immediately, but there wasn't the right amount of defensiveness in my tone. Just longing, actually.

"You I picture more as a red jasper man."

And you I picture as a freak who's smoked one blunt too many.

I turned to Seb and whispered in his ear. "I'll buy you something when we have more money, okay? But we can't really waste what we have right now."

He put the stone down.

The lady didn't seem all that disappointed by the loss of her potential sale. "Come back some time—I'm pretty much always here. If I get a hold of any red jasper, I'll save it for you."

"Yeah, whatever." I put a hand on Seb's shoulder to lead him away, but stopped when an idea struck me. "Hey, are you homeless?"

She pushed a dreadlock off her shoulder. "I choose not to live by social norms in a four-walled structure at the moment. I commune much better with my inner spirit when I am free of those restraints."

"And when you're free of bills you can't pay," I added. She scowled.

"If you're here to pester me, you can beat it, kid. I might be homeless, but I have plenty of friends here and some of them would be willing to escort you away by force. Or I could just call the cops."

I grinned at how quickly her whole mystical mumbo-jumbo attitude had disappeared. "Nah. Actually, I just had some questions…like where do you stay around here?"

Her eyes narrowed on my backpack and wrinkled clothes. "You guys runaways or something?"

I didn't answer.

She sighed. "My suggestion for you would be to find some place away from the beach itself, and somewhere you can't be seen from the main road. Maybe a vacant storefront—there's a few of those up Lincoln. They usually have big planters and stuff you can set up behind. Stay out of the cops' way, 'cause you guys are minors and they'll probably pick you up in a heartbeat. Oh, and you'll need blankets. There's an army surplus store a couple blocks north. Get some of those green flannel ones."

I was still in the sunshine, and there was only a slight ocean breeze, so there was no explaining the chill her words gave me. In just a few short hours, Seb and I would be facing our first night out on the streets.

"Well…uh, where are you going to go?"

I hadn't meant to sound so pathetic, as though I was willing to follow this woman I'd just met like a lost little puppy. I just wanted a more concrete plan of action.

"Listen, hon, you should probably go home. He looks a little delicate and sleeping out here…isn't always as fun as it seems."

"We don't have a home."

She shook her head sadly. "I guess good luck, then. And hey, at least you have each other."

"Yeah." I nodded. And she was right. Things weren't that bad, because I still had Seb.

I grabbed his hand. "C'mon. Let's get going, maybe try to find a place like she said. And I'm gonna take you out for the best dinner a dollar can buy, just as soon as we find a McDonald's."

He smiled.

~*~

The sun set and a starless night replaced it, but we kept walking up Lincoln Boulevard. I wasn't really sure what I was looking for, but at least looking gave me something to do. Pretty soon, though, we'd have to set up camp, or risk drawing attention from the cops.

"How 'bout here?" I pointed to a strip mall with a *For Lease* sign. Three large columns held up a covered walkway, and some bushes also blocked the view. "Seems like we could hide around there and be out of sight."

He nodded and we jumped over the chain blocking the empty parking lot. I pulled out the blankets we'd bought to set on the ground behind a column. "All right then…let's get…uh, comfortable."

The makeshift beds didn't offer much promise of that, but Seb plopped straight into his, tucking the covers around himself.

I followed more slowly and leaned my head back against a concrete wall. "Tomorrow maybe we'll see about a hostel or something. Although that lady was right—we'll have a problem 'cause we look under eighteen. We should think about getting fake IDs."

Seb yawned.

"If you get cold or anything, you can get…closer."

I tried to scoot nearer to him and winced. "Damn, I really gotta take a piss. Shouldn't have had so many free refills." Standing, I peered around in search of a place to relieve myself. "Guess I'll go down an alley or something."

A sudden noise caught my attention, and I turned to see a group of girls in leotards exiting the building to my left. I'd thought it was just an office space, but now I could make out a small plastic banner on the side—*Diana's Dance Academy.*

"Hey." I tapped Seb's shoulder. "You wanna check out this place over here? Maybe they have a bathroom."

Seb got up, taking our blankets with him and shoving them into the backpack.

"Cool. Wasn't really tired, anyways. It's too early for bed."

We waited until the dancers had scattered and then snuck up to the studio. After climbing the stairs, I could see the space actually *was* an office building, converted into rooms for different dance classes. The first door was closed and locked, but the second had mirrors and a ballet bar. The third I stopped and stared at for a while, because while it had the mirrors and the ballet bar, it also had a deep couch with silk pillows along the back wall, and stripper poles dotting the floor. A lady in a crop top and leggings was gathering up CDs and resetting audio equipment in the corner.

"Huh," I whispered to Seb, "I never thought of strippers having to learn how to dance, but I guess it makes sense."

Someone left the ballet studio and closed the door firmly before exiting the building. I had a feeling that room was now locked.

Seb pointed to a restroom at the end of the hallway and we hurried in so I could finally empty my bladder. He sat up on the sink counter to wait, and for some reason I turned away from him shyly, trying to keep my body from his view.

"So, I got an idea." I started babbling to cover my nerves. "I mean, it's sorta a long shot...and maybe a little old school...but what if we like sneak back to that room and shove something in the door? Y'know, to stop it from locking. Then we can hide out in here and wait till everyone leaves...and we won't have to sleep outdoors."

I shook myself dry and zipped up. "You in?"

He reached over to grab a paper towel, then crumpled it into a ball.

"Perfect."

The woman wasn't in the room anymore when I returned, but the door was still open. As quickly as I could, I walked by and shoved the wad of paper towel into the lock. Then I scrambled back to the restroom.

"C'mon. Into the stall." I pulled Seb in and helped him step onto the toilet seat with me. "I'm not sure how long we should wait...maybe half an hour? Looked like all the classes were ending. I doubt they'd be starting any new ones this late."

We sat on the tank, though it was a tight squeeze. I had to put my arm around him to keep my balance.

"Sorry, I know it'll be boring waiting...and this isn't exactly comfortable. But we probably shouldn't talk too much, just in case anyone walks in and hears us."

One of Seb's brows popped up, and I burst into a fit of giggles that I muffled in his shoulder. "All right, all right." I fought off the laughter. "I'll shut up then."

The lights must've been on a motion sensor, because they went off after a few minutes. I really wished I could've passed the time by talking, because in the dark there was nothing to do but listen to the sounds of Seb's breathing and feel the motion of his chest rising and falling alongside mine.

Even in complete darkness he could turn me on.

I actually shook my head to wipe the thought from my mind. I'd promised Suzie, and I wasn't scum. I might've made a lot of shit decisions in my life, but nothing like that.

The tiny strip of light from under the bathroom door eventually winked off, and I couldn't hear any more sounds in the hallway. After waiting another five minutes, I signaled for Seb to follow, and we tiptoed out.

The building appeared empty. We returned to the stripper studio, where I paused to whisper a brief prayer before turning the door handle.

It opened.

"Fuck yeah! We did it!"

Hazy purple light shone in through a wall of windows and lit up Seb's smile.

"Get ready to sleep in style. Nice bed, silk pillows...we fucking hit the jackpot."

I climbed onto the couch and tucked a pillow behind my head. "Perfect."

The only negative I could think of was that it was a little cool in the room...which meant it was a lot cooler outside, where we'd been planning on sleeping. That wasn't a good thought, but at least we didn't have to worry about it for tonight.

Seb crawled up next to me, bringing the blankets and draping them over both our bodies.

"Oh...yeah. It's a little chilly. I guess that's a good idea."

But it wasn't, really. He curled in close, his thighs brushing against mine. And he was still smiling. Shadows and light crisscrossed his face, accenting the sharp angle of his cheekbones and the slant of his almond eyes.

I tried to scoot away, but I was already against the back of the couch. Seb pressed in closer anyhow, throwing an arm around me.

It seemed like the most comfortable way to sleep, so I did the same to him, resting my hand on his hipbone. But I knew it was a mistake as soon as my fingers landed on smooth skin—his shirt had ridden up and his pants were sagging.

Seb stuck out his tongue and wet his bottom lip. It did look a little dry, with a slight crack running through the pale pink flesh.

Fuck. It was also a bad idea to focus on his mouth.

"Hey, you know what?" I moved my hand up to his shoulder and gave him what I hoped was a friendly pat on the back. "I think…I think that besides the morning part, this has been the best day of my life. I probably should've come here right away, instead of dragging you through my past like that."

He took a deep breath and let it out. The warm air hit my lips.

"Well…um, goodnight, I guess. I wish we had an alarm or something to wake us up, but hopefully the light'll get us."

Lowering his lids only halfway, Seb pushed closer to me still. The hipbone I'd managed to drag my hand away from was now pressing into my upper thigh.

Blood rushed to my face and to somewhere further south. *Can't can't can't can't* rang out in my head like an alarm, but my body wasn't listening.

What was it I did to get myself out of these situations? *A…B…C…D…E…*Fuck, that was never going to work.

I wanted him. No two ways about it. Wanted him more than I'd ever wanted anyone in my life. I liked to pretend I was taking care of Seb for all the right reasons, but at the most basic level I was just a horny teenager, coming up with an excuse to be close to the person whose body I craved.

Maybe I *was* scum.

But why was he pressing in so close to me? Why was he still looking into my eyes so deeply from beneath his lashes? Why did he hold my hand and wrap his arms around me and act like he was happier with me than he'd ever been before?

I would never really know. All his secrets were locked inside with no way out...I'd never be able to tell how he felt.

How he felt.

A seed of an idea planted itself in my head. An idea that needed to be squashed, but the more Seb's lashes fluttered in front of me, the more it grew.

If I could just *feel* him...see if his body burned the same way mine did...if he had the same urgent need in his groin...

Suzie would kill me. *I* should kill me. But what if this put the question to rest, once and for all?

I closed my eyes. Not to stop myself, but to make the moment less real. My hand traveled his body slowly, from his shoulder back down to his hipbone.

Don't. You can't. You promised. He's just a kid. A special kid.

But he's smarter than he pretends to be. He understands the things I say to him. There's more to him than he lets on.

The debate with myself continued to rage as my fingers reached the waistband of his pants. I didn't even have to unbutton or unzip...there was enough space for my hand to slip right in there.

Mere inches separated me from an answer.

If I thought I'd go to hell for jacking off to the sight of his body, this would surely earn me a spot in its most fiery depths.

I slid my fingers further south, brushing against his lower abs and the fine hair of his happy trail, then under the band of his boxers and down, down, down, until I reached…something completely unfamiliar.

Seb was uncircumcised.

The surprise caused me to pull my hand away quickly, and my eyes flew open. This close to him, there was no way I could avoid seeing the look of pure confusion on his face.

Of course he was confused. The person he'd trusted to care for him had just fucking *molested* him.

I'd never lost an erection so fast, and the heat of arousal I'd felt earlier rushed to my eyes. I couldn't keep looking at Seb's face, so in a way I was almost thankful for the blur of tears.

"Sh-shit. Shit. Fuck."

I'd broken my promise to Suzie. Broken my promise to myself.

"Seb…I'm s-sorry. I'm sorry. I'm so sorry."

The tears spilled out, hot and fast. Seb shifted to grab both my shoulders, and now he looked even more confused, his brow knit together and his mouth pressed into a thin, hard line.

It all hit me then. With my defenses down, every little thing I'd managed to tuck away or deny in the past several months came crashing to the front of my mind like the ocean waves, one after another and with no end in sight.

I'd been abandoned. I'd caused a fire. I'd run away. I'd taken Seb from a safe place. I'd turned my sister in to Social Services. I was out on the streets with someone who was depending on me and I really had no fucking clue what the hell I was doing. I'd *touched* him.

And I was so fucking sorry.

"I'm s-sorry. I'm sorry."

Sorry. Sorry to Seb, Sorry to Suzie. Sorry to Mimi and to Star. Sorry to Greg and Eleanor and Ms. Loretta and Ms. Cecily and Brandon and Laloni and my mom and any other person I'd ever let down in my fucking excuse for a life.

Seb pulled me into his arms, and I was too far gone to resist. I crumpled against his chest, sobbing out some garbled form of "I'm sorry" over and over again. I cried harder than I'd cried in years. Maybe in five years. All sight disappeared behind the wall of water, all thoughts evaporated into a single word. *Sorry.*

His arms tightened around me and he rubbed my back in long, even strokes. At first that only made me cry more, but after a while my eyes were too swollen to release any more tears. I lay in a weak, quivering mess, letting Seb rock me as my breathing slowly returned to normal.

I wasn't sure how long we stayed like that. It could've been minutes or hours, but eventually the silence calmed me and the storm in my mind settled to only a few persistent gusts of guilt. I gathered my strength and sat up.

Seb touched my cheek, wiping away some leftover moisture.

"I'm sorry," I whispered again, my voice hoarse. "I…I can't say that enough. But I swear to you, Seb, I *swear*…I won't ever do anything like that again. From now on, I'm just gonna take care of you, okay? I'm just gonna be your friend and take care of you."

He shook his head.

"What?" I pulled away abruptly, rubbing my eyes to clear my vision.

He shook his head again.

"It's…it's not okay?"

His lips moved, at first opening and then forming a small *o*.

I sniffled. A second wave of confused tears was coming. "I don't understand."

He gripped my shoulders and pulled me close. His mouth moved again, but this time a puff of air emerged that sounded like "*nhhh.*"

"I don't…I don't understand."

His fingers dug into my shoulder blades. And there was a new expression on his face—one I'd never seen before.

His brows were lifted and his eyes were raised toward the ceiling.

What *was* that? Frustration? Exasperation?

"Seb, I don't under—"

Lips collided, teeth crashed, and he kissed me.

Chapter 21: Whole

It was a forceful, bruising kiss. A kiss that knocked the air from my lungs and scrambled my brains to within an inch of an omelet. A kiss to make a point. But as overwhelmed as I was, I still pulled back.

"Seb, you—"

Lips stopped me from speaking. Softer now, he let his tongue slide in and caress mine before slowly dragging it out. My body quivered like a released string and I had to fight for breath in the stunned silence that followed.

"You...you..."

He kissed me again. This time, I kept my mouth shut. Or open, actually, so he could suck on my bottom lip. His shirt brushed against mine as he pressed in closer, and the light rustle of fabric added itself to the very faint smacking sounds of his active lips on my still ones. Warmth from the kiss slowly spread through my mind, thawing out the shock and allowing me to make some sense of what was happening.

This was it. This was his answer. Whatever mental abilities he did or didn't possess, he'd made his own decision about our relationship. He couldn't tell me in words, couldn't explain exactly what was going on in his head. This was the only way he could make me understand.

And right now, he must've wanted me to understand my unformed prayers were being answered.

Thank you, God.

All the shitty experiences in my life suddenly seemed so much less significant…like drops of water in the Pacific Ocean compared to this. I might've even chosen to live it again—even if it'd been worse—just to get to this moment.

I finally kissed him back, really gently, because I was trembling and I didn't want to bang into his teeth. My eyes drifted closed as I sighed into his mouth, and with each soft exhale I released a little more of the dark thoughts I'd had about the fate of my soul.

Because I couldn't be going to hell. Not if someone like Seb could find me worthy.

"Seb, I want you to know I—"

His hands slid under my shirt and I lost my train of thought. Long, cold fingers ran up and down my back, making me shiver deeper into his embrace. Every place he touched me burned—first from the icy contact, and then from some internal heat sparked by the pressure on my skin. I drew closer to his mouth and kissed him harder, imagining what it would feel like for his graceful fingers to roam over my *entire* body.

But I slammed on the mental brakes after a second, keeping my own hands safely above the fabric of his shirt. I couldn't rush this. Not with him. Kisses were one thing, but there was a whole lot more we needed to figure out before we went any further. Besides, this was already amazing, and if these kisses were all there ever were, well…I could be okay with that.

Maybe.

On the other hand, I could just follow his lead. Let Seb show me where he wanted this to go. After all, I'd been making our decisions for a while now, without any of his input. This was the first time he'd chosen to assert himself, and it seemed like something I ought to encourage, not crush.

My fingers crept down, restlessly fumbling with the hem of his shirt...until he stripped it off himself to reveal pale skin glowing eerily in the light-polluted night.

He arched his back, stretching seductively, and my mouth went dry.

Jesus, did he know what he did to me? I was starting to suspect he did.

So many previously forbidden places were now within reach. His collarbone. The small of his back. The slope of his waist and the lean muscles on his stomach and chest.

My brakes failed.

I went for everything at once. The force of my advance knocked him to the ground, where I continued groping at any flesh within reach. His body eagerly pushed back against mine and our tongues clashed—and if that wasn't a sign of support for my actions, I didn't know what would be.

Air was barely meeting my lungs before I was panting it out again. I pinned him beneath me, pressing frantic kisses into his lips. I didn't even notice him sneaking off my shirt until the fabric was whipped past my face. Palm spread wide on my heaving chest, he tilted his head as though he were studying the differences in our skin tones. Then he shifted to look me in the eyes, dragging his hand straight down my body and over my crotch. I bucked from the pressure, more sensitive there than I'd ever been before.

Seb used the moment of distraction to undo the button on my pants.

When my dick gave me back control of my brain, I took a shaky breath and tried to reevaluate where things were going.

"Really?" I blinked to the spastic rhythm of my pulse.

Maybe if I'd been a saint, I could've pulled back at this point...but lord knew I was no fucking saint.

"You really want to…to…"

While I floundered in search of words, Seb hooked a finger into both my pants and boxers and yanked them down.

Holy *fuck*. Who was this kid?

Smiling mischievously, he walked his fingers across my chest and stomach, stopping right above the dark mass of my pubes. I held my breath, desperately trying to keep from forcing him further down. But he was just so *close*—close enough that I really didn't think it'd be such a crime if I accidentally twitched into his grip…

He pulled away. Latching onto a stripper pole, he shimmied upright. I suddenly had the crazy notion that he might break into a dance—not that that would be anything like him, but he wasn't exactly being *himself* at the moment.

Turned out he'd stood so he could take off his own pants. They fell to the floor with a soft *whoosh*, leaving him in those too-big boxers. Then he lowered himself back down and nestled against my side, tilting my face so he could fill my mouth with lips and tongue.

Everything was perfect—every brush of his skin against mine, every moment I caught that expression of lust in his eyes before my own rolled back in my head. Everything-I'd-always-wanted-but-was-afraid-to-ask-for. And yet, the first real dose of fear crept in among the crazy desires that had overtaken my body. Things were moving *really* fast. And even though I was planning to go as far as Seb wanted, I wasn't entirely sure *how* to do that.

I knew how to have sex on auto-pilot—with a girl—but this was something completely different…and not just for the obvious anatomy reasons. It was different in the way my insides boiled, making me feverish, in the way I was violently gasping for breath between kisses, in the way I was clawing at his firm body, feeling like I'd never be able to touch him enough to satisfy the hunger.

None of *that* had ever happened before.

"Sebastian, I—"

His tongue tangled with mine, still sweet from the syrupy cola.

"Seb—"

More tongue. Apparently, talking was not meant to be part of this process.

He wiggled out of his boxers. Long, lean muscles tensed against my thighs as he shifted closer, causing my hand to land on his perfect ass.

Fuck talking about it. Going on impulse, I gripped a cheek firmly and pulled him toward me.

The closeness allowed me to feel his dick against my skin, and I had to peek down. I knew it was hard now—as hard as mine—but I hadn't seen a lot of uncircumcised guys in real life. He seemed to notice my interest, and he stroked himself a few times, showing it off.

Now things were getting fucking *insane*. With my mouth hanging open, I almost drooled, and a little something else leaked out below.

Eager to get my own hands on him, I tried to take over, but he crawled out of reach. His mouth traveled from my lips to my chest, nipping and sucking at the skin as he continued to make his way down.

"Tea—" A shudder rocked my body. "Tease."

His eyes flashed in defiance, and I had only a split-second to grasp his intention before he'd reached crotch level and pulled my entire length into his mouth.

"Ffffuhh…" I couldn't even get out the *k*. And I'd had blowjobs before, but nothing, *nothing* like this. Never with such perfectly formed, strong lips moving up and down so smoothly, never with dark almond eyes staring at me so intensely I could actually feel the gaze searing my skin.

It was a miracle I didn't come in the first five seconds, and an even bigger miracle I was able to gather the ability to speak. "Wh-what…what about…you? Sh-shouldn't I…"

He eased off with one final lick. Then he abruptly flipped over, pulling me onto my side at the same time so he could rub his ass against my dick.

"Whoa…I dunno if we're ready for all tha—"

He turned back around in a heartbeat, and our lips connected again. I didn't have time to dwell on what he may or may not have been trying to do, because our bodies had had enough of the foreplay. Magnetic force drew us together and after the first taste of delicious all-over pressure, I climbed back on top of him, grinding into his hips, pushing for more heat and more friction with each thrust.

I tried to keep kissing him, but eventually the fire in my belly and groin was so intense my lips stopped performing and my mouth twisted into odd shapes. All I could do was pant for air and press harder and faster, fighting for a release that promised to be more spectacular than any I'd managed with some fantasy in my head. Because Seb was real and warm and *alive*, and he was moving at just the right speed, in just the right way, and I could smell his sweat and taste the salt on his skin…and I could just *feel* he wanted this as badly as I did.

With my senses so filled by him, it was only a minute before I shot out all over his stomach. He jerked under me a few thrusts later and did the same.

I tumbled back to the floor and lay beside him, staring up at the ceiling. Somehow, speaking didn't seem right for the moment, so only the sounds of the cars traveling Lincoln Boulevard accompanied us as the tide of heat slowly faded away.

And I didn't feel like talking, anyway, because talking would require thinking. For now I was happy just to believe in this miracle. Seb and I were *together*.

He nuzzled against my neck, his exhales keeping me from a chill despite the fact I was lying naked on a hardwood floor. After a while his breathing grew deeper and more regular, and I knew he'd fallen asleep. I crawled over to the couch to grab the blankets and returned to arrange our bedding around him. Then I wrapped him in my arms and gently kissed his parted lips.

I didn't want to sleep. I wanted to keep watching him all night, to catch every wiggle of his nose and every flutter of his lashes. To study the lines and curves of his body and memorize each birthmark and freckle. To lay my hand on his chest and feel his heartbeat march on, forever and ever.

And I wanted him to know he had changed my world.

As the last wisps of clear thought swirled through my mind, I wondered…*is this what love feels like?*

~*~

Thank God for rude LA drivers. Day had fully overtaken night when the honking woke me up.

Seb yawned and blinked sleepily. I was tempted to throw back the blankets so I could admire him naked in the light, but I settled for watching his lips curl into a soft smile.

"You're so fucking beautiful," I blurted out, and then cringed. All right, so I wasn't the most poetic person, but the meaning was still there.

I ran my hand through his silken hair, and he looked back at me with so much affection that all my sappy emotions from the night before came surging back. It was such a rush, I got light-headed, and thoughts trampled their way to my lips without much resistance.

"I think…I think I might be in love with you. Is that weird? Like too soon or something?"

His smile spread. Then he gently placed his palm against my chest and tapped once before he moved it to his own heart.

I love you too, Alex.

Grinning like a lunatic, I caught his hand and held it. "I know this is totally crazy…but…sometimes I feel like I can almost *hear* you."

He nodded thoughtfully. *Sometimes I feel like that, too.*

"Whoa." I'd never thought of his rare nods as *thoughtful* before. Without knowing why, I backed up a little.

His forehead creased. *What's wrong?*

I didn't say anything for a moment, as I studied the downward curve of his mouth and the questioning look in his eyes.

Something was *different* about him.

"You know…this guy I knew, he used to say he'd get flashbacks after he smoked some bad weed or something." I chuckled nervously. "Wonder if that's what's making me imagine things."

He rolled his eyes and shrugged, lips twisting to the side as his brows rose skeptically. *If you say so.*

That was it. His face.

All of it was alive, in a way I'd never witnessed before. New combinations of movements. New expressions. New reactions. New ways of showing understanding. *Understanding.*

Alex, what's wrong?

Little wrinkles formed on the side of his eyes. His pupils darted back and forth as he looked me over for any clue to explain my sudden silence.

I scrambled away, grabbing my pants and pulling them on to cover myself up.

Alex?

"Stop." I put a hand out to keep him from approaching with that puzzled expression. That expression that said *I'm a completely sane human being, and you're the one acting nuts right now.* My heartbeat went into overdrive and my body broke into a sweat.

Stop what? He threw up his arms.

"Just…just stop."

He kept coming anyway, so I snatched my t-shirt off the ground and went straight for the door. "I need to…get some air."

Then I ran.

I flew down the steps and out of the building, and didn't stop until I was safely tucked away in an alley, hidden behind a dumpster.

"What the fuck," I mumbled, resting my head in my hands. And really, what...the...*fuck*. As in what the fuck was wrong with me?

I was scared shitless, apparently. And of course I knew I wasn't actually *hearing* Seb, but I also knew that somehow, sometime during our night together, he'd changed.

Or maybe he hadn't changed at all. Maybe he'd just chosen to *reveal* what had been there all along...which meant he'd seen me at my absolute lowest, and had understood every second of it.

But as terrifying as that thought was, it didn't really explain my behavior...because he'd seen all that and still made it pretty clear he wanted to be with me. So why had a few twitches of his lips and creases in his face turned me into a cowardly freak? If some method of communication *had* been opened through the magical mixing of our come, you'd think I'd be fucking overjoyed, not crouching behind a dumpster in fear.

I tried to take a deep breath but stopped short, curling my nose at the scent of decaying roast beef tossed out by the nearby Arby's.

Time to run through the facts. I could finally believe, without a shadow of a doubt, that Seb wasn't retarded. I also knew he was gay or at least bi, and that he liked me. All really, really good facts.

So what exactly was my problem?

Fact number one, of course. Seb wasn't retarded.

That should've been the best news of all, especially when put with the other two bits of information, but it wasn't. That was what had me hiding in an alley that stunk of rotten food and urine.

Things were different now. Seb was no longer just a safe place for me to unload my problems. I couldn't use him as my own personal mood-stabilizer…he had free will and would have his own desires, his own wants—and they probably wouldn't always match with mine. He was capable of accepting me—or rejecting me—whenever he saw fit. He didn't belong to me.

He was a whole person now.

I sank back into scum-hood when I realized that made me a little depressed. I couldn't assume he'd always care for me the way he did today. He wasn't a witless kid who gave out his loyalty like a friendly dog. There were no guarantees on his love.

Hell, he might've already changed his mind about me. After all, I'd just run off and left him alone in the middle of an unfamiliar place.

Jesus *Christ*.

I sprang up and raced back to the dance studio, nearly slamming into the door when I caught sight of him crouching outside the abandoned strip mall next door.

"Oh God, Seb." I ran over and knelt in front of him, gripping his shoulders. "I'm so sorry. I'm a fucking idiot. That was so stupid, wasn't it? I mean, I *want* you to talk to me. I've just…never been this close to anyone before, you know? I've never *let* anyone get this close to me. But with you…it's okay…and I…I want to be with you…and I hope you'll want to be with me." Panic rose from my chest and strained my voice. "I know you don't have to stay with me, but I really do love you, and I think we could be…good together."

Seb watched me calmly while I babbled on, his face motionless.

"And I won't run off like that again, I promise. I'm so sorry. You must've been so scared…shit, I'm sorry."

Then he snorted and rolled his eyes. *I wasn't scared.*

My laugh was so loud it startled the crows picking at food wrappers on the sidewalk. I pulled him into my arms, weaving my fingers into his hair, and rested my chin on his shoulder.

The bubble of tension in my throat burst once Seb's grip tightened around me.

"Tell me where you want to go," I said as I finally pulled away. "I'll take you anywhere you want. Just name it."

His eyes drifted west.

"Okay, breakfast and then the beach. Sounds perfect."

He picked up the backpack he'd been smart enough to bring along—not that him being *smart enough* was a surprise anymore—and took my hand before we headed off down the boulevard.

Chapter 22: Round and Round

What is that? Seb pointed as we approached the beach, eyes wide and curious.

It still rattled me. Each time I looked at him I was half-expecting he'd stare back with his old vacant gaze...and that everything I thought I'd realized would be part of some orgasm-fueled dream.

Well? He flipped a palm out impatiently.

I glanced at the Ferris wheel towering over the water, and my head spun right along with it. Would he continue to surprise me? Was he even the same person I'd first fallen for? And why *had* I fallen for him anyway, when I didn't even know who he was?

He punched my shoulder and pointed again. *What is that place?*

"Oh...that's an amusement park on the boardwalk, I think. José's been there a few times. Said it was lame."

He frowned.

Shit. A frown. A full-on *you've-disappointed-me* frown. My heart thumped loudly in protest. Not even a whole day into knowing a *real Seb* existed, and I was already disappointing him.

"We can go, though. I mean, what does José know? He's a dumbass, really—he probably just said that 'cause he heard someone else say it…he was always a follower like that…"

Seb interrupted me with an amused arch of his brow.

"Right, so…we can go, is what I'm saying."

He latched on to my arm, tugging me toward the pier. *Then let's go now!*

The cheery blue *Santa Monica Yacht Harbor* sign greeted us as we traveled down a steep road, then out onto the wooden planks. We passed by a Bubba Gump Shrimp restaurant, not yet open for lunch but still sending warm fried seafood scent into the air. Kiosks and street artists lined the rest of the pier's length, and at the far end a few fishermen had poles dangling into the ocean—though I doubted they ate what they caught from the polluted waters. Seb dragged me forward until he found a weathered old Latino making detailed landscapes of LA with finger paints.

Seemingly careless streaks transformed into fantastic scenery as the man worked, but I couldn't give him my full attention. I had other concerns on my mind…like why I felt so nervous standing beside Seb. Was I too close? Or not close enough? Why did that matter all of a sudden?

While my mind wandered, Seb noticed the entrance to the amusement park and rushed straight in.

"Seb! Not this again!"

I raced after him, trying to keep back my panic by reminding myself he *wasn't* special and probably wouldn't get into too much trouble on his own. And maybe I didn't need to be with him every second of every day…maybe I was smothering him.

A hand caught my eye—Seb waving me over to a water gun carnival game. I nearly tripped on my feet as I rushed to him in relief.

Isn't this fun? The bell rang, and his eyes bounced in excitement when the guns shot narrow streams of water toward their targets.

A little girl with braided pigtails started shrieking by her father's side, her high-pitched squeal making me cringe. It didn't help her father much, either, as he lost several seconds aiming too high and had no chance of getting his toy airplane to the top first.

She kept screaming anyway. Maybe she was just testing out her lungs to see how loud she could be…I vaguely remembered being that way as a kid.

Shifting my gaze to Seb, I wondered how old he'd been when he'd discovered he couldn't throw back his head and howl into the wind.

He elbowed me and pointed. *Can we play?*

"Uh…" I glanced at the posted price—two dollars per game—and shook my head. "Everything costs here, ya know. Like each individual ride…and we don't have all that much money, so we should try and be careful."

A tiny frown flashed across his face before he nodded. *I understand.*

God, *two* frowns in less than an hour? My left eye started to twitch. It wasn't all that surprising, really. Instead of making the most of this time we had to spend together, I was acting like his parent. Always telling him what to do—when to put on sun block, where to go, how to spend our money…I was like the epic buzzkill of boyfriends.

"Sorry," I mumbled, but a new game had started and I didn't think he'd heard. Hovering a few inches away from his neck, I zeroed in on a trickle of sweat as it zigzagged toward his shirt collar. I wanted to brush it away, but some invisible barrier blocked me—or maybe it was just that there were a lot of kids around, and I was afraid if I started touching him, I wouldn't stop.

My left temple joined my twitching eye, and together they played havoc with my face. Good thing Seb wasn't looking.

I really needed to turn this situation around.

"But you know...this *is* a special occasion," I whispered in his ear. "It's sorta like our...first date."

Shit, should I have said that? Did he want to *date* me?

He didn't answer—though a dying voice of reason tried to tell me I hadn't actually asked a question—and I scrambled to dig out a couple of bucks. "Here. Have fun."

Thanking me with a bright smile, Seb took a seat on a stool. His eyes narrowed as he aimed his gun, and when the game began he already had the water stream trained exactly on the bull's-eye.

I wasn't really surprised when he blew the competition away. "Let me guess...you're like a super hero. You couldn't talk, so you sharpened your other senses. Although talking isn't a sense, is it?"

He grinned.

The game operator was less impressed and tossed him an ugly pink stuffed dog for his efforts. Seb held it up to me proudly, until the girl with the pigtails started to sniffle.

"Papá, yo quería un peluche!"

Her father pulled her down from the stool next to him. *"Ya no tenemos más dinero."*

Before she could start crying, Seb walked over and handed her the dog. She gleefully hugged it to her chest as her father thanked us in both Spanish and English, several times.

"You speak Spanish?" I asked after they'd dissolved into the crowd.

He shook his head.

"You just...understand things, huh. You've always understood."

He smirked and linked his hand with mine, pulling me toward the Ferris wheel. *Come on. Let's go on the rides.*

A jolt of victory shot up my fingertips. He'd taken my hand, all on his own. And not as a little boy seeking my comfort...as a guy who *liked* me. My heart soared from the depths of my doubt into a dizzying high, like I was already spinning around on one of those carnival rides.

He kept holding my hand as we purchased some overpriced ride tickets and headed toward the park's main attraction. But once we reached the line for the Ferris wheel, he abruptly pulled away and turned his back on me.

I should've known every good high would have its low.

Was he tired of gripping my admittedly clammy fingers? Was he trying not to attract attention? Or just getting a better view of the ocean?

And why was every moment with him suddenly such agony?

The pimple-faced guy on the platform shifted his gaze away as we boarded the little yellow carriage together. Ignoring his obvious trying-not-to-stare look, I sat across from Seb, and we continued to wait in silence as we slowly rose off the ground.

I figured I should say something, but after running through a few opening lines, everything I had to offer sounded pathetic. And *pathetic* was exactly the right word for it. I'd had his naked body in my arms less than twelve hours ago, and now I could barely string two words together.

I just had no idea how to act around him anymore, and the uncertainty was killing me.

"So, uh…"

We climbed above the heads of the waiting crowd, and in one fluid movement, Seb leapt over to my side and kissed me.

My hands locked onto his shoulders, clutching tightly to help my mind process that this was real. I hoped the bitter aftertaste of my McDonald's coffee wasn't as strong in his mouth as it was in mine.

No complaints from Seb—just a long, tongue-twisting kiss that first sent me reeling and then actually managed to calm the whirlpool of nerves in my gut.

"You know what…maybe we should stay on here for the rest of the day." Confidence rising again, I stroked his hair and gently drew him in for another kiss. "I like the privacy."

He ran his hand down my back, ending with a quick pinch of my ass before pointing to a security camera.

I laughed. "Well, I think as long as we don't get naked up here, they can't throw us out or anything."

Seb nodded, and then reached out and tugged off my shirt.

"Hey!"

What? He batted his lashes, gesturing to the crowd below. *It's a beach. Lots of guys have their shirts off.*

Well, he had me there. His hands roamed my chest as he crawled into my lap.

"You're a little crazy, you know?" I mumbled in between kisses.

Seb's response was to rock forward against my crotch, instantly shutting me up.

He kept rocking, first every few seconds, then constantly. I almost, *almost* gave in and started trying to get off, but a squawking seagull brought me back to reality.

"Hold it." I pecked him lightly and pulled away. "We probably shouldn't do that here. You know this thing is gonna be back at the bottom again in a minute."

Pouting, he stuck out his lower lip. *But…*

"Besides"—I shifted him to the bench—"I kinda think maybe we should just…talk for a little bit."

He lifted a brow and crossed his arms. *Seriously?*

I supposed it was a strange request from a teenage boy who had the willing object of his sexual dreams right in front of him. But I'd never had a relationship based on love before—only convenience—and I had no idea if I was doing things right.

"Well, you pretty much know everything there is about me…and I know nothing about you. That's not fair."

The Ferris wheel jerked and began to spin faster now that the whole thing was loaded. We passed the waiting people again and I kept quiet until only the tops of their heads were in sight.

Well? Seb sat back, looking amused, his arms still crossed. *What do you want to know?*

"Um…" A million questions swirled around in my mind, but the first thing that came to my lips was a statement. "You're not…special."

He didn't shake his head, but his eyes said it all. *No.*

There was a lot more I needed to know in relation to that, but I decided to start at the beginning. "So…have you ever been able to talk?"

No.

"Then you were born this way?"

A nod.

"Isn't there anything you can do to fix it? Like, a surgery or something?"

He shrugged.

"Yeah." I sighed. "I bet that would cost a lot of money, anyways, and us foster kids ain't exactly rolling in the dough."

Grinning, his hand wandered onto my thigh, where he started to stroke me softly.

I was too weak to push him away, but I tried to keep my mind on track. "Okay. So you can't talk…but that doesn't mean people have to think you're re—, um, special. I mean, there are other things you coulda done…like learn sign language or something. Or how 'bout writing? You could write stuff to people so they know what you're thinking."

His cheeks reddened slightly. I'd never seen him blush before.

"You can write, can't you?"

He brought his thumb and index finger together on his right hand. *A little bit.*

"Didn't they teach writing in your special school?"

He bit his lip, gazing out at the ocean. Sunlight glinted off the waves and the reflection sparkled in his dark eyes.

Then he sighed and nodded. *They did.*

"So how come you can't write?"

All he could offer me was a shrug, but I read more into his embarrassed look. *Didn't think I needed it. Didn't pay attention.*

Shit. I could relate to that.

Except…

"But didn't you want to be able to talk to people? I mean, if there was ever a reason to pay attention in school…"

I cut myself off when I realized the answer to my own question. He *didn't* want to communicate with people. He hadn't even tried.

"Seb…why did you go on letting people think you were, uh, special like that?"

His hand crept from my thigh toward my crotch, and he left it there even as we spun past the ground again.

"Seb…"

The carousel rose and he was on me in a flash, tongue jutting straight into my mouth, teeth grazing my lips. Powerless against the attack, I surrendered within seconds. I edged him further into my lap, kissing him again and again with less grace and more urgency each time.

Although…I couldn't help wondering if Seb had just come up with a new and clever way to keep his secrets hidden.

The wheel spun even faster, air rushing past our skin and hair. Laughs and shouts from the people on the pier were swallowed up by the crashing waves, and everything in sight became a blur.

The zipper of my jeans dug into me painfully as Seb bounced in my lap. But I still kept pushing against him, not even caring that I was about to come in my one and only pair of pants.

The Ferris wheel slowed and came to a stop a quarter of the way from the ground. I was too far gone to do the same. We dropped a few feet lower, and I placed my hands on his hips to try and force just a little more pressure.

I didn't make it. Five carriages away from the loading dock, Seb finally removed himself. I had only a moment to adjust my protesting dick before we were ushered off.

Holding my shirt over my crotch, I pushed Seb back into the line. "Wait here. We're going again. Just let me run and grab some more ride tickets...and I gotta stop by the bathroom, too."

With a knowing smirk that made my skin flame, Seb did as I asked.

~*~

A pink and orange sunset touched the sky when we finally left the park with a funnel cake in tow. The horizon looked a little like the finger painting we'd seen earlier, with the sun's last colors blurred into smudges on the ocean's canvas.

"You got some sugar on your lips," I told Seb as we settled into the sand. His tongue darted out of his mouth to lick it off.

A little ways away, another young couple admiring the view started kissing, and I suddenly regretted not licking it off myself...though I wasn't sure where Seb would stand on PDA.

Eventually I drummed up the courage to rest my arm around him, mimicking the way the clean-cut guy was cuddling up with his girl. Maybe I could just follow that kid's lead for the rest of the evening—he seemed to have more of a clue than I did.

It could've been the Scrambler ride we'd taken two trips on, but my stomach was starting to roll with uneasiness again. The action part of our "first date" was over, and now I was stuck in this romantic setting with zero experience to fall back on.

The muscles in my arm tightened, and a little spasm caused me to knock into the back of Seb's head.

He looked over and grinned, patting my knee. *Relax.*

"Easy for you to say," I grumbled under my breath. "You've known the real me all along, but..."

I trailed off as Seb gazed steadily into my eyes. *Exactly.*

Exactly. He'd known the real me all along. I'd always been some nutty, uncensored version of myself around him, and he'd still fallen for me. So while Seb had changed for me...maybe he didn't actually need *me* to change at all.

It seemed kind of unlikely that anyone would want me in my raw form...but not more unlikely than this entire crazy week.

"Right." My face melted into a grudging smile. "Gotcha."

Seb squeezed my leg approvingly.

Relaxing was easier said than done, though. My body was restless, so I started digging around in the sand to pass the time. Seb did the same, and for a while we were quiet as we constructed a lumpy sandcastle city together.

As I put the finishing pat on one of my mounds, the girl from the model couple whispered something in her boyfriend's ear. Whatever she said made him laugh.

I turned my attention back to Seb. "Is there anything you miss about not being able to talk? Although I guess you can't really miss something you never had."

He shrugged.

"Like...you can't just share a joke with someone...you can't whisper to your friend in the movie theater...you can't tell someone off when you're mad..."

Another shrug. Then he tipped his head and scrunched his brows thoughtfully. *Well, maybe there's one thing.*

"Yeah? What?"

In the sand, he traced a small circle, then drew a stick directly beside it. He added a few more sticks and circles, including some with curvy tails.

Musical notes.

"Music? You miss music?"

He touched his throat.

I started to chuckle, squeezing him into a side-hug. "Don't worry. Just because a person can talk doesn't mean they can sing. I sure as hell can't."

He scowled and looked at me defiantly. *Yes you can.*

"No, I swear to God I can't. What, you want me to prove it?"

Yes.

I shook my head. "No, seriously, I can't."

Seb's fingers danced up and down my back, like he was playing the piano on my spine. He looked at me eagerly through his lashes. *Please?*

My cheeks grew warm. "I...I haven't sung since I was in the sixth grade choir...and I sucked then, too. I don't even know any songs."

More fluttering lashes. *Pretty please?*

"Oh, God." I dropped my head into my hand. "You're gonna regret this."

I really couldn't think of any songs. The radio was my only source for music, and I hadn't had access to one of those in ages. Searching for inspiration in the horizon, I eventually caught sight of a plane twinkling in the distance as it left the LAX airport.

"At least now you'll know this isn't one of the things you should miss." I lowered my voice to a half-whisper so the people around me couldn't hear. "Twinkle, twinkle, little star...how I wonder what you are. Up above the...uh, world so high, like a diamond in the sky. Twinkle, twinkle, little star, how I wonder what you are."

To further my embarrassment, Seb clapped when I was done.

"Shut up. I suck."

He shook his head. *I liked it.*

"Whatever."

No, really. He laced our fingers together and smiled gently. With his other hand, he touched my throat. *Sing another?*

"I don't know any others."

Come on.

Damn those dark lashes of his. He seemed to know just how to use them to make me putty in his hands.

"Fine. I do know one more. But this one requires audience participation." I took his hand and drew out his pointer finger, placing it in the sand.

"A...B...C...D...E...F...G..."

I sang slowly so I could make Seb trace the letters as I went. He gave me a really sour look but let me keep going, all the way to the end.

"Now that's a useful song, right?"

With a roll of his eyes, he freed his hand so he could dab the pastry crumbs off our plate. Then he pulled the backpack under his head like a pillow and lay down, his lids drifting closed.

The couple stood a few seconds later and the girl shook out their towel. Sand wound up spraying directly toward us and I glared at her, using my body to protect Seb's face. She sputtered out an apology, but I ignored her so I could focus on Seb—it looked like he'd fallen asleep. I just hoped her yacking wouldn't disturb him.

Positioning my back to keep any more flying sand from bothering him, I gazed at his still form. Affection and worry fought for control of my thoughts, and since he wasn't awake to comfort me, worry seemed to be winning out.

Maybe I could keep being myself around him, but the stakes really were higher than they'd been before. If I screwed this up, I'd lose *everything.*

He opened his eyes. Bright, alert eyes.

"Okay, enough with the fake sleeping!" I smacked his leg. "Seriously. There's a lot more you can do with life than just *pretend* to sleep through it."

Such as? He raised a brow expectantly.

"Such as…"

If I knew the answer to that one, I wouldn't have had this cold fear lurking beneath the surface of my happiness.

"Just gimme a sec. I'll think of something."

Chapter 23: *No Llores*

I couldn't come up with anything for the long-term, but I did decide we had to do some shopping.

The glaring fluorescent bulbs at the 99-cent store didn't cast the best light on Seb's skin. They made him look yellow, even though I was sure he was starting to pick up a tan again. Wandering down the aisles, he ran his hand over the merchandise and stopped every once in a while to hold up something he wanted to buy.

"Sorry, but I don't think pink marshmallows have any nutritional value." I took the bag from him and stuck it back on the shelf. "We need to get stuff we can eat for a meal...like granola, or something."

He sighed but nodded, adding a box of Nutrigrain bars to our basket.

"I mean, we can still hit up a McDonald's every now and then, but we kinda blew through a chunk of our cash today. The dollar menu is great and all but when you put in the drink and the fries and the tax, it starts to add up."

Money just kept on going out, but obviously none was coming in. And here I was about to spend more of it. But we *had* to eat, and this seemed like the cheapest option. Of course, there was one more way to go about it...

I glanced at the store employee manning the front door, then did a 360 to catch all the security cameras dangling from the ceiling.

Seb shook his head. *Don't.*

The odds didn't seem to be in my favor. "Yeah. I guess you're right. I mean, I was pretty decent at getting away with stuff back home…but those were little Mom and Pop shops. This place looks more—"

He stepped on my foot.

"Ow! Watch it, that hurt!"

Arms folded across his chest, he jerked his head left—to where a security guard was eyeing us from a few feet away.

"Oh, shit," I muttered. Teenagers with a backpack were probably always under suspicion. "I didn't see him. Hope he didn't hear us talking…not that we did anything wrong."

Seb tossed some pretzels at me.

"Sure. Yeah." I stuck them on top of our pile, even though I wasn't sure it was such a good idea to get something so salty—we'd just end up buying more drinks. "But, um, about that…security guard"—I dragged him further down the aisle—"how'd you notice him? How do you always notice things? Like when Ms. Loretta would be coming to yell lights out…or that time when Brandon showed up…"

He made his hand into the shape of a pistol and tucked it into his pants.

"Shit. And Angel's gun. You saw it first, huh. How do you do that?"

He shrugged.

"Do you think if I shut up more, I could be like you?"

The fake gun came back out of his waistband, and he used his barrel-finger to trace my jaw. *You're fine the way you are.*

I almost choked on the back of my tongue. Face-touching in public was…*literally* more in-your-face than the handholding we'd been playing around with. But really, I didn't feel as nervous or as uncomfortable as I would have thought.

Instead, I wanted to knock him back against the shelf full of snack cakes and kiss him until neither of us could breathe. Then I'd rip off his clothes and have my way with him on a bed of Twinkie boxes.

"M-maybe we should get a couple bottles of water on our way out."

Stocked with about eight dollars worth of food—and that important sun block—we rounded the corner to head back to the register. Seb gazed wistfully at some modeling clay and a fancy notebook as we passed through the school supply aisle, his fingers stopping on the items and forcing his feet to a standstill.

I shook my head.

"I have a notebook in my backpack you can have if you really want it. And there's always the wet sand to play with."

I was sure he was giving me a dirty look, but I didn't see it because something else caught my eye.

"Now here's something we can get for you." I grabbed a child's trace-the-alphabet booklet and stuck it in his face.

He pushed it away, glaring. *Why would I want that?*

"So you can learn how to write better."

And why should I? He huffed, a bit of hair blowing off his forehead.

"So you can…write me love letters." I gave him a cocky grin.

His lips tightened in a frown.

And then *pop!* my daydream of doing him against a fallen shelf burst back into my mind and completely overpowered me. Thankfully, I managed to show some restraint in the actual force of my advance as I leaned in and kissed him.

Kissed him right there in the middle of a West Los Angeles 99-cents store, with bright lights and cheesy elevator music and tons of shoppers. My hand latched onto his t-shirt and I dug in, drawing breath through my nose so I could keep our connection going for as long as possible.

I couldn't help it…not that I really wanted to. Because it'd finally struck me that each expression of his—including the frowns—just proved he was *real*.

The kiss dissolved into a final brush of our lips and I stayed close, basking in the warm glow of his eyes. I'd surprised him, I could tell, but he was happy.

He untangled his arm from where it'd slid around my waist and tapped his wrist.

"Huh?"

He tapped again. *The time.*

"Oh shit! We'd better move it. Shit, I hope that dance place is still open."

~*~

Of course, it wasn't.

"Fuck." I banged on the locked door. "Fuck. We shoulda come back here and waited a lot earlier. It's my fault. I'm sorry."

Seb rubbed my back soothingly. *It's okay.*

"I guess we'll have to go to plan B." Defeated, I led us over to the strip mall where we'd been the night before. "This fucking sucks."

Shaking his head and smiling, Seb took the bag from my back. *We'll make do.*

The blankets came out again, though neither of us was tired. I wanted to talk more, but Seb wasn't really paying attention to me. And if I couldn't see his eyes, I didn't think I'd be able to "hear" much from him.

He dug around in the backpack, laying my belongings out in neat piles in front of us.

T-shirts. Boxers. A few pairs of socks. The photos from my house. A notebook, a crumpled piece of paper, a stick of dried-up gum. Two pens, a pencil, and a smushed package of tamales.

"Oh, shit. I forgot about those. Think they're still good?"

Only one way to find out. He ripped back the foil and took a bite, then nodded. *They seem all right.*

I snagged a piece for myself. What was the worst that could happen? I'd already thrown them up once before and survived.

Good thing they were only cheese.

While we ate, Seb picked up the notebook and pencil. He opened to a blank page and began to doodle. At first, I couldn't make out anything in the mess of shapes and random lines—it just reminded me of the way he used to run his fingers around in the dirt. But eventually I saw something round emerge within the twisted scribbles: the Ferris wheel. As layers of details and shading were added, the scene expanded to include an abstract sketch of the whole pier.

"I didn't know you could draw."

He gave me an amused look. *There's a lot of things you don't know about me.*

"Well that I *did* know." I laughed. "How 'bout telling me some more stuff?"

Shrugging, he returned to his drawing.

But I wasn't going to let him get off so easily this time. With nothing else to do but sit holed up behind a bush all night, I was ready to get some answers.

"Listen, Seb, you're gonna have to explain some stuff."

He ignored me.

"Like…why have you been hiding all this time? I mean, why didn't you ever let anyone know that you were…in there?"

The pencil stopped moving across the paper. Brows raised slyly, he pointed at me. *Why do you hide who you are?*

"What? I don't hide."

He tipped his head. *Yes, you do.*

"No I don't."

Uh huh. His eyes narrowed skeptically. *So you're saying you share everything you are with everyone?*

I scowled. "Fine. So maybe I keep some stuff to myself. But we're talking about you here, not me. If you won't tell me why you decided to hide...then can you tell me why you decided to open up to me? I mean, why after all these years did you choose *me* to be yourself with?"

Again, he pointed at me and turned the question around. *Why did* you *decide to be yourself with* me?

My cheeks grew warm. How was I the one being interrogated here? "Um...because it felt...safe, I guess."

He nodded.

"So then...I make you feel safe?"

He took up the doodling again, his lips tugging into a grin.

Some moisture traveled to my eyes, making his drawing all blurry, but I covered it with laughter. "I make you feel safe. I think I really like that."

I leaned against the concrete wall, pulling Seb between my legs so he could rest on me. He flipped to a fresh page and kept drawing.

I watched each stroke, completely entranced by this new glimpse into his mind. Slanted, almond eyes appeared. Then he added sharp cheekbones and an angular jaw in an oval face, surrounded by long, dark hair.

"Who's that?"

He ran a finger over the drawing, smiling fondly.

"Your mom?"

His hair bounced as he nodded.

I tightened my arms around his chest and hugged him close. "You know, Laloni said something once...about uh, special needs kids. Do you think you not being able to talk is why she…abandoned you?"

He whirled around to face me, eyes boiling with fury. *She didn't abandon me!*

"Okay, okay." I scraped my back on the wall as I edged away. "Sorry. I just thought…" His eyes blazed even fiercer. "Never mind. So she didn't abandon you. What happened, then? How'd you end up in foster care? They took you from her?"

He turned away again and added a few more strands of hair to her picture, swirling them around her neck and shoulders. His Adam's apple bobbed up and down restlessly, and even though he didn't look at me, I could see the grief in his slumped shoulders.

She died.

"Shit. I'm sorry, Seb." I kissed his cheek. "I'm so sorry."

He started to draw spirals, the pencil spinning out in wider and wider circles and overlapping his mother's face.

"Were you really young when it happened?"

Yes.

"And then you went straight into foster care? Didn't have anyone else to take you in?"

He didn't answer.

"Seb? Did you go straight into foster care after she died?"

Still no response, but the spirals on his page grew darker as he crossed the same spaces over and over again.

"Were things always…okay for you after she died? I mean, like they were at Ms. Loretta's?"

A larger spiral took over all the smaller ones. His pencil moved faster and faster until the picture resembled a black hole.

I didn't know why I was pressing him when he was so clearly upset, but I didn't stop. Something had crawled into my stomach—besides the two-day-old tamales—and it lay there heavily, making me sick. "Seb"—my voice sunk to a whisper—"did anyone ever…hurt you?"

No answer. Then, with a *splat*, a pool of liquid appeared in the black hole. It seeped into the paper and smeared the lead into an even darker circle.

"Seb?"

Splat. Another tear fell. And then another.

I crawled around him and gently took the notebook and pencil from his hands. I'd already known, somehow, even before I'd asked. And I hadn't really wanted the answer.

As I gathered him into my arms, I tried not to think about all the horrible things that might happen to a little boy when no one could hear him scream.

"Shh, shh." I rocked him. "*No llores, mi amor. No llores.*"

I wasn't sure why I slipped into Spanish. It was just that the last time anyone had held me like this, I'd been really young, and those were the words I'd heard…from Mimi, or from my mother.

"You're safe now, remember? You're safe. I won't let anyone hurt you ever again."

He clutched my arms, his fingers digging into the flesh. Strange, squeaking breaths came from his throat as he cried.

Stranger still because I'd never heard him make a sound at all.

"Seb, please don't cry." My voice was strangled now, too. Maybe I wanted my ignorance back. What had happened to him? Who had done it?

I might never know. But I had my suspicions. I'd had them since the night before, I realized. Seb was *experienced*. And in a boy who'd spent his teenage years pretending to be special, that experience sent up red flags.

I tipped his head back to wipe his face clean. His eyes were red and just slightly puffy, the expression in their depths as naked and as vulnerable as I'd ever seen.

At least now I had an idea of why he'd put up this wall between himself and the rest of the world.

I couldn't take away his pain, but maybe I could replace it with another emotion. Maybe not tonight or tomorrow, but maybe, if we spent our lives together…maybe the happiness could outweigh the bad.

"I love you, Sebastian."

His lips found mine, melting into a soft kiss.

The rest of our lives. Making that kind of commitment to Seb was terrifying. I just wished I had some idea what that life together would look like…but I wasn't going to let uncertainty hold me back anymore.

The tears stopped. His chest fluttered against me, still heaving from the earlier sobs. I cupped his face and kissed him again, slowly and with just the tip of my tongue reaching in to meet his.

It was different from the other kisses we'd shared…and miles away from the wild lust of last night. I still felt the stirring in my pants from being this close to him, but I had no intention of acting on it.

Because tonight meant more than that. These kisses were a promise.

We loved each other, and I would keep him safe.

~*~

For all the warmth I'd felt the night before, I was surprised to wake up cold and hungry.

Seb lay curled against my shoulder. A little bit of tear-crust clung to his lashes, but beyond that, there wasn't any sign of how emotional he'd been the night before.

I didn't want to disturb him, so I lay still for as long as I possibly could. My neck ached, though, crushed up like it was against the lumpy backpack. Eventually I had to stretch it out.

He stirred at the slight movement, his face twisting into a grimace.

Ow. He rubbed his back. *That hurts.*

Taking over for him, I massaged deep into the muscle. "Yeah...and I'm freezing." I buried the tip of my nose in his neck to make my point.

He winced and pulled away.

"Sorry." I chuckled, until he slipped his ice-cold hand under my shirt and pinched a nipple. "Ooof! Okay! Okay!"

With a little grin of victory, Seb let me go.

"So...I know we should be saving money, but there's another thing we gotta buy."

What's that?

"A watch with an alarm." My back cracked as I sat up. "We are *not* missing out on that dance studio again. I guess I'm not quite built for life on the streets."

Seb nodded. *Good idea.*

"We should try and stay there from now on...or, you know, until we figure out something more permanent."

He sat up, too, giving my arms a few brisk rubs to warm them. *Okay.*

"You know what? I think we're getting the hang of this. We've got a place to stay, the beach to spend the days at, we've got...each other," I added shyly. "And, uh, ways to..." Seb started dropping little kisses along my cheekbones. "To, uh...pass the time..."

He landed on my lips.

And at that moment, I was pretty sure we had it made.

Chapter 24: Honeymoon's End

"Uh, maybe I made a mistake. Lemme double check…ten, eleven, twelve, thirteen, fourteen…and thirty-five cents."

Fuck. Where had it all gone?

I stared at the pile of crushed bills and change on the dance studio's floor, my heart sinking in fear that I carefully kept from my face.

Of course, I knew where it'd gone. To carnival games and rides, funnel cake and hotdogs and ice cream. To flannel blankets and watches and alarm clocks and McDonald's and junk from the 99-cent store.

Seb glanced over, unconcerned, and continued to trace letters in his booklet.

"We're…we're gonna have to figure this out."

He sighed and put the pencil down, then crawled over to embrace me. Damn it, he must've heard the worry in my voice.

His arms were golden now, the hair on them so fair it was almost invisible. I brushed my fingers through the soft strands, moving them against the grain. "This'll only last us a few more days. We blew almost all the money in a coupla weeks. I…I shoulda been more responsible."

It wasn't like I hadn't seen this coming. I'd known. I'd just put off dealing with it for as long as possible—or longer than I should've—because I was too busy enjoying myself with him. Too busy being selfish.

He shook his head and ran his knuckles over my cheek. *Quit blaming yourself. You're doing the best you can.*

"No, really." I freed myself from his comfort so I could try to think straight. "I have to take better care of us. We need to come up with a plan, right now, so we know what we're gonna do from here on out."

Okay then. He retrieved the booklet and pencil, but kept his attentive eyes on me. *So what's the plan?*

"Well…I need to get a job. Like at a fast-food place or something. Except they probably won't take me, because I'm too young…so I'll need a fake ID…which I can't get right now because we don't have enough money."

Seb looked puzzled. *Okay…*

"So, step one is to get more money…and to stop spending it so fast. You know, when I went to Venice with Mimi and that guy of hers, he was able to steal us all kinds of stuff. Kettle corn, cotton candy…even some sunglasses. I'm really not that bad at lifting stuff, and with you as a lookout…"

No. He shook his head firmly.

"But listen, with all those open air shops it'd be easier, and we could get some stuff to resell, or even just nab us some food…"

I said, no. He reached over and grabbed my wrists, locking them together like I was in handcuffs. *You could get caught.*

Dammit.

"We could be really careful."

He squeezed down harder, pressing into the bone.

"All right, all right, I get it. No stealing."

Satisfied, Seb returned to his tracing.

"I could sell flowers on the street."

I was joking, mostly. Plenty of my people did that…but I'd have to get the flowers from somewhere…and I never really saw kids doing it.

He arched a brow doubtfully.

"Yeah. I know. Out on the street like that…the cops might see me. And they're probably still looking for us, ya know."

He grinned. Seemed he liked being a fugitive with me.

I didn't blame him. Days at the beach and nights lounging on a couch, jerking each other off…I felt like I could live this way forever.

A little alarm went off in my head at the thought—reality trying to edge its way in. I fought it back by moving toward Seb and forcing him into a kiss.

He pretended to be irritated at the interruption, even though he kissed me back. I wished I could have more than just a taste of his lips right then, but the sun was already up, and it was almost time for us to hit the road.

"Okay, really, stop distracting me. I have to think."

Seb pushed me away, little bursts of air coming from his nose—his version of laughter.

"Well, look, I know you like staying here, but I'm just not sure how long we can pull it off. You're worried about us getting caught with the stealing…this is illegal, too."

He rolled his eyes.

Sighing, I pulled off my dirty t-shirt and put on a slightly less dirty one. We were long overdue for a trip to a laundromat—another thing that'd cost money. And now that I'd run through all the other options to earn any, only one way seemed to be left.

"Seb, remember how I told you I used to…uh, deal?"

He glanced up sharply.

"Well, maybe I didn't say it outright, but I'm sure I mentioned it in one of our conversations."

And your point is? He eyed me warily.

"So…the only way we stand a chance of getting money fast is doing that. I know some people I can talk to—this guy Diego, maybe. He might know of something I can do. I mean, it'd be small-time at first, but—"

A snapping sound interrupted me, and I looked over to see Seb's pencil lying in two pieces.

"Broke your pencil?" I gathered up the top half and brought it back to him, but he didn't take it from my hand. "We've got some pens, still...or I bet we could pick one up at a bank or something."

Strands of Seb's sun-bleached hair were draped over his forehead, so I couldn't see his eyes.

"Okay?"

No! He snatched the pencil from my palm and threw it across the room.

Icy fear flooded me, drowning my other concerns and pushing out goose bumps all over my skin. What the hell had just happened?

"Seb, what...what's wrong?" I crouched in front of him, hands hovering a few inches away because I was suddenly afraid to touch.

"Are y-you mad because of the money thing?" My voice shook.

Having him angry with me apparently reduced me to a trembling ball of nerves. No one else had ever had that effect before.

"'Cause I promise, I'm gonna work it out..."

Was he just calling my bluffs, now that he was no longer playing special?

He shook his head, then closed his hand into a fist and tapped at the vein that bulged in his arm.

"What?"

He glared.

"Drugs? You're upset that I'm talking about selling drugs?"

From the fire in his eyes, it almost looked like he was ready to take a swing at me. I rocked back on my feet to get away from him, unsure if I should feel relieved that I had gotten to the root of the problem...or worse. Did he look down on me for my past?

"I...I wouldn't use any, you know. I just wanted to get us some money so we can—"

No! He slammed his hand against a stripper pole. The metal vibrated from the impact. *No drugs.*

"Okay...I'm sorry...please don't be mad. I didn't realize that would bother you. I won't do it. I'm sorry."

His fury started to fade, but it wasn't enough for me. I still felt like I'd been through a blender and my heart had wound up on the outside, sliced through and through.

"Seb, I didn't mean to—"

He grabbed our backpack and shoved in the notebook, stomping to his feet. *It's time to go.*

"Oh. Y-yeah." I scrambled after him.

I wanted to know why he was so against the whole thing, but I was too afraid of another outburst to press him. Drugs *were* bad, after all. I knew that. Maybe Seb was just trying to make me a better person.

"Um, you wanna get some breakfast? Some Egg McMuffins? Or we could go down to the beach and get some funnel cake...or we could even go to Starbucks..."

He shook his head, rubbing his thumb against his other fingers. *We're having money problems, remember?*

"Oh. Right. I just thought..."

Thought what? That I'd buy his happiness?

Maybe I'd been doing that all along...maybe that's why I'd decided it was a good idea to spend most of our money on carnival rides and fair food. Because how happy would he be with me when we were forced to dumpster dive or beg for our meals?

Seb stopped walking in front of the Arby's on the corner. He unzipped the backpack and took out a couple of granola bars.

Here. As he passed one to me, his hand slid along mine, giving it a gentle squeeze.

I looked up to see his smile back in its rightful place, and I stared at it for a few seconds, using it as a temporary bandage for my battered heart.

"Thanks. And I am gonna think of something. Something not illegal. I promise."

I know. He grinned and ripped open his bar to take a bite.

He had more faith in me than I did.

A rustling down the alley drew my attention to a homeless man in tattered sweats who was digging through the garbage. He yanked out a couple crushed bottles and shoved them into his duffle bag.

"Oh…well, there's that."

Words from the past echoed in my mind. *Pick up cans with the immigrant children.*

"I mean, it won't be big money, but it's something, right?"

Seb blinked. *Huh?*

Guess he couldn't read *my* thoughts. "Collecting recyclables. A lot of homeless people do it. You can look through trash cans…like at gas stations and convenience stores, especially…then you take the stuff in to get the redemption value."

He nodded. *Oh, okay.*

"It would take a little investment, though. We'd need to get some big bags, 'cause there's not much room in the backpack, and we can't really carry it all in our hands. Guess we could stop at the grocery store…"

Seb's grin spread and he yanked at my hand. *Let's do it.*

It wasn't much, but at least we had a plan.

~*~

"Fuck, we are awesome at this!" I jogged over to Seb to show him my latest score. A family of five had stopped to get gas, and they'd turned out to be thirsty people. I hadn't even needed to dig for it—they'd simply handed over a bag of coke bottles once they saw me rummaging around.

Seb nodded, opening his tote full of cans so I could see he'd also added to the pile.

"Maybe 'cause we're young and so good-looking." I smirked. "Hell, if I'd known it was gonna be this easy, I'd have tried this ages ago."

And how different my life might've been...but I didn't dwell on that thought for long.

Is this enough? Seb shook his bag, testing the weight as he looked at me questioningly.

"Nah. I mean, it's a good start, but I think we need to get a whole lot. We should keep working till we have a few bags full and then see about finding a redemption place."

Seb turned and glanced back up Lincoln Boulevard. We'd already gone three or four miles from our home base, and he was probably worried about getting so far away that we were late making it back.

"Well, new stuff is thrown away all the time, so we could backtrack...or we could just stick around here and wait for people to drive up...or we *could* go check out some of the apartment building dumpsters."

Seb's eyes twinkled, and I knew which one he was ready for. The adventure.

We headed down an alley and stopped in front of a building with a low brick wall enclosing its parking lot. Seb made a foothold with his hands and I climbed over first, then crouched at the top to pull him up.

The green dumpster sat in the shadows, beneath the first story of apartments.

"Well, I guess let's have at it."

We jumped down and approached it slowly. Crap, was that scurrying sounds coming from inside? I started to reconsider our decision—this wasn't going to be very glamorous.

Seb propped open the cover, and a rancid sweet-and-rot scent confronted us.

"Yuck. We are so gonna need a shower after this."

He was already up to his elbows in garbage bags before I realized that would be an issue. We didn't exactly have access to any showering facilities.

"Or I guess we could just wash off in the ocean or something...but damn we need some swimsuits...or at least some more pants."

Fuck. Why did everything have to involve money?

Got some! Seb lifted out two large empty bottles of Gatorade and pumped his arms victoriously.

"Yeah, good work." I shoved them into my bag of plastics.

Well don't just stand there. Seb waved me toward the piles of garbage. *Start looking.*

I put aside my concerns for cleanliness and dug in. Ripping open bag after bag, I sifted through the mess of banana peels and coffee grinds and soggy paper towels for those few precious cans and bottles. But when I got to a bag full of dirty diapers, I had to take a break.

"Oh, Jesus." I stumbled back and knocked my legs against the hood of a car. "That is fucking disgusting."

The car proceeded to come to life, wailing and honking and blinking its lights like a demon possessed.

"Fuck." I grumbled, turning to face the annoyance. "Shut the fuck up you stupid alarm."

Seb kept digging for a few seconds, but then abruptly froze.

"Hey! You! What you do there?" An old man with wild white hair came barreling down the steps from the apartments, shaking his fist. "I call police!"

"Shit!" I bolted over to Seb and grabbed a handful of his t-shirt. "Let's get outta here!"

We both turned and clumsily jogged away from the enraged man, our full bags banging at our sides.

"Why you come to mess our garbage?" He pursued us, spittle forming on the edge of his lips as he yelled. "I am apartment manager! I call police!"

"We're leaving, you crazy old freak!" I frantically tied off our bags of loot and tossed them over the brick wall.

I didn't want to go first and leave Seb cornered by this guy. He was obviously a nut, chasing after us like this when we were a quarter of his age and easily could've beaten him to a pulp if we'd tried.

I gave Seb a foothold and he scrambled up to the top of the wall, then reached down for me.

Fuck, he really was taller than me. I stood on my toes but still couldn't get a good grip on his fingers. He had to bend down further, straddling the wall and leaning over toward me so I could finally grasp his hand.

The man was still yelling, but he'd slipped into some other language. Russian, maybe. He'd also taken out a cell phone, and I didn't really doubt that he was calling for the cops.

"Pull!" I screamed at Seb, and he did. Pulled too hard, though, because instead of regaining our balance at the top, we toppled straight over the other side and landed in a bed of plastic bottles and crushed cans.

"Ow." I coughed and rolled over. Seb was lying on his back a few inches away and I quickly crawled to him, holding myself up over his body. "Shit, are you okay? Does anything feel broken?"

He had a smudge of dirt on his cheek, and he reeked like the garbage we'd been knee-deep in just a few moments ago.

Squinting up at me, his lips stretched into a lopsided grin. *That was sorta fun.*

I smacked his chest and then kissed him, holding my breath so I didn't have to inhale our scent.

When the need for air finally forced us apart, I stood and dusted myself off. "Come on. Let's get our stuff and go…those cops might be on their way."

~*~

We held off on the bathing we so desperately needed in order to take our findings to the nearest recycling center. Thankfully it was back in the direction we'd come from, but it still took us over an hour and a half to walk out to the facility. Sweaty and surrounded in clouds of our own toxic fumes, we trudged in through the open gates.

"Damn, I'm exhausted," I muttered. This really didn't measure up to riding on the Ferris wheel all day long, or sharing foot-long hot dogs with our toes stuck in the sand.

Seb didn't reply, but I knew he was thinking the same thing.

I wasn't sure what I'd been expecting to find—maybe some sort of clean, white building where I could see bottles and cans carried away on a conveyer belt and stomped flat by a big machine. It was probably that word *facility* that did it...guess I needed to find a dictionary to look up its real meaning.

The money-making part of the recycling center was outdoors, on a floor of dirt and asphalt. A tin roof covered the scales, and the payout shack had a wooden storefront that had been spray-painted a hideous green.

And just like us, the place smelled awful.

Homeless, hippies and the poor huddled around blue bins, unloading bags and shopping carts full of recyclables. Most of the people were of the black and brown variety, but I was surprised to see a few white and Asian faces mixed into the crowd.

Following their lead, I dumped out everything we'd found and frowned when it seemed so small inside the big bins.

"Kinda thought we had more than that," I mumbled to Seb.

"It always seems like that," chimed in a guy in a torn Lakers jacket. "But we keep on breakin' our backs anyhow."

I gave him a hollow, half-hearted chuckle as Seb and I got in line for the weighing station.

A man with rubber gloves took our bins and hefted them up on the scale. I didn't bother looking at the numbers. Everyone before and after us had a lot more to recycle, and none of them looked like they were enjoying a very rich life.

He handed us a receipt and waved us on to the cashier across the way.

"Here you are," the older woman said cheerily from behind her barred window. The winds picked up, wafting more garbage-smell and dirt into the air than I could handle breathing. "Six dollars and forty-one cents."

I coughed into my elbow, trying not to suck in more polluted air.

Six dollars and forty-one cents. For a day's worth of hard labor.

It wasn't enough. It wasn't nearly enough.

I crouched down to shove the money into my shoe. While my head was lowered I summoned every bit of strength and concentration I possessed, so that by the time I rocketed back up, there was an unshakeable smile on my face.

"Hey, that's not too bad, huh. Maybe we should treat ourselves to a dollar sundae later."

Seb smiled back.

And now it was all on me.

Chapter 25: Broken

We trudged back toward home as the sun closed on yet another day. I'd already started to come up with a plan, but I still had a lot of details to work out. Details I didn't like.

I was going to have to leave Seb alone. I'd make up an excuse…maybe tell him I'd be scouring another area for recyclables. Now that we'd seen how easy the whole process was, I figured he could do it by himself. We'd just set a time to meet up later, by the empty strip mall, and he wouldn't have to know where I'd actually be spending the day.

Which would be back in the ghetto I'd just run from.

I knew damn well six dollars a day wasn't going to support us for long. What if one of us got sick? What if the dance studio closed, and we were out on the street in the wintertime? What if I got carried away and let Seb's magical almond eyes coax me into buying yet another thing we didn't really need?

I'd gotten us into this situation, and it was my responsibility to take care of us. And that meant going home and figuring out a way into the old business. I'd burned my bridge with Angel, but there still was Diego and all his connections to explore. There had to be *something* I could do.

It wasn't an easy decision to make. I didn't want to lie to Seb, or betray his trust. And I really, really didn't want to leave him alone. But I *had* to do it. Had to do whatever it took so we could survive.

Just like Mimi had.

Fuck.

Seb's fingers wiggled against mine right as a stabbing pain hit me between the eyes.

Thankful for the distraction, I looked up and noticed we'd drifted a few blocks west of the studio. The persistent roar of the surf could be heard close by.

"Hey, where are you taking us? It's a little late for the beach."

Seb shook his head and kept on going, crossing Ocean Avenue and zipping down the ramp that led to the sand. He hopped around on one foot and yanked off a shoe before I could stop him.

"You don't think we're actually going in, do you? 'Cause we're not."

He sniffed at me dramatically and then pinched his nose. *But you stink.*

"Look"—I chuckled through a fake-glare—"as much as I'd love to swim naked with you in the ocean…wait, no, that's a lie. More like float naked with you in a hot tub…but in any case, we can't just go in without suits, and we can't go in our clothes. Maybe after we save up a little we can buy trunks, but for now let's just make do with some soap and a sink." I pointed to the public bathrooms a few feet away.

Seb heaved a disappointed sigh. *Oh, fine.*

The restroom was yet another place that stunk on our tour of unpleasant Santa Monica smells. After peeling off our shirts, we soaked wads of paper towel and added in few pumps of soap. Then we scrubbed ourselves as best we could, drenching the concrete floor and our pants in the process.

A man walked in to use the urinals, and he gave us a *what-the-fuck-are-you-doing* look. I just kept washing off my underarms, smiling at him coolly in the mirror.

He left in a hurry and I burst out laughing.

"Imagine if we'd been rinsing *everything* down. That woulda given him something to fucking stare at."

Seb lifted an eyebrow with a devilish grin, then gathered some more sopping towels and ducked into a bathroom stall.

Was that an invitation? I tried to follow, but the door was locked.

Damn. He really was a tease.

Retreating to my own stall, I did my best to freshen up down below. I finished before Seb, and after emptying my bladder, I put on a different t-shirt from our backpack supply and waited out by the sinks.

Seemed like he had some other business to attend to, so I decided to use the time to lay down more details of my plan.

Now where had I left off? There was the excuse to get away, the meet-up spot, the decision to find Diego…and then that sudden realization…

I stomped on the thought to shut it down. I didn't have time for guilt trips.

A click echoed in the room, and the door to Seb's stall creaked open an inch. I waited a few seconds, but he didn't come out.

This time it *had* to be an invitation.

Oddly nervous, I opened the door and rushed to close it behind me.

Seb was naked. His pants and boxers lay neatly at his feet, and his arms were folded as he leaned back against the concrete wall in a casual pose of seduction.

You'd think I'd have known better than to try to talk when Seb had that look in his eye, but I didn't.

"In a men's bathroom? Not that I don't wanna, but isn't that a little…sleazy?"

Seb tipped his head thoughtfully. *Well, okay, if you say so.* He bent down to grab his pants, then began slowly dragging them up his legs.

"Wait a sec, I didn't say I wouldn't…"

The pants plummeted back to the ground, and Seb gave me his knowing smile.

"You…you…" I muttered with mock-irritation as I drew closer. But then I reached his lips and I dove into them, ignoring the faint taste of soap that still clung to his skin.

His hands crept under my shirt and nails pressed into my back. Not too hard, though—just enough to make my pulse jump and my dick stand at complete attention.

Seb went in for the kill immediately. He was probably more aware of our limited time than I was—more aware of everything else, for that matter. When Seb touched me like this, I could barely tell what planet I was on.

Friction-warmed hands with those long, delicate fingers closed around me. As he stroked, the soapy scent from our freshly washed bodies filled the air. It was a welcome change of odors and I laughed against his lips, feeling the sound vibrate in his teeth.

A few strokes later, I shuddered and collapsed back against the metal siding of the stall. Seb ripped some pieces of toilet paper to clean us off, then gently tucked me back into my pants and swept in to kiss me again.

God, I loved him so fucking much. It might not have been the classiest place for that to hit me, but when he kissed me I knew I'd do anything I had to for him. *Anything.* Even through my post-orgasm haze, my plan to solve our money crisis cemented itself into a reality.

Seb reached down and began to pull up his pants.

"What? Hold it."

He stopped and blinked curiously.

"You didn't get all naked in here just to turn me on, did ya? I mean, don't you want…"

Grinning, he walked his fingers up my chest and tapped my chin. *Why? Are you offering?*

Of course I was fucking offering. I'd much rather drag out our sketchy men's room hook-up than dwell on what tomorrow was going to bring.

I pushed him back against the wall with more force than I'd intended. He almost tripped with his pants still around his ankles, but I didn't let my screw-up distract me. I went with the flow instead, kissing him hard and wrapping my hand tightly around him at the same time.

A rush of air left his mouth, and I was sure if he could've, he would've moaned.

"You're always trying to take control with this," I mumbled as I kissed down his neck, the tendons twitching under my lips. "But you know what? I can take control, too."

Then I froze. Jesus *Christ* I was a fucking moron. What if someone else had been in control of him before, leaving him no choice but to go along with it? What if Seb took control now because he *needed* to feel that power?

Seb caught my chin in his hand and looked into my eyes.

"I…I mean…I mean, I want to…if you want to…"

Maybe he *could* read my mind, just a little bit. His brows drew together in worry, laced with sadness.

It's okay. He brushed his fingers along my jaw and drew me in for a quick peck. Then he tapped his chest and mine. *I love you. I know what you meant.*

Light-headed, I licked my lips and nodded. "So do you want—"

His laughter was a burst of warm air on my face. *Yes!*

The relief was welcome, but a streak of guilt was left swirling in my stomach. Maybe I felt I still had some stupidity to make up for, or maybe it was regret for the things I had yet to do…but for whatever reason, I decided to push myself further than I had before to bring him pleasure.

I dropped to my knees.

Alex? He grinned down at me, eyes alit with cautious excitement. *You don't have to…*

"I want to."

Before he had any more chance to argue, I placed my lips right on his tip.

He writhed and there was a thump—his head hitting the wall.

I widened my mouth and took him in deeper, drawing in long breaths through my nose in an attempt to steady my frantic heartbeat. Seb threaded his fingers into my hair. I was afraid he might push me more than my gag reflex could handle, but he didn't. He just let his hand follow the motion of my head as I moved in and out.

I had no training, and I couldn't rely on sounds of satisfaction to help guide me. So the only thing I could do was keep my eyes wide open and focused on him. On the way his taut stomach quivered with shaky breaths. On the way his chest rose and fell unevenly. On the way his shoulders rolled back against the wall and his chin jutted up toward a flickering fluorescent light. On the way his eyes squeezed shut and he caught his lower lip between his teeth, bit down, released it, then caught it all over again.

I did that to him. And though I never wanted to take away any of Seb's power, it was nice to feel some of my own.

His hands tugged at my hair. He was trying to pull me off.

I didn't let him. I waited until his head jerked into the wall once more and his mouth opened, as if to let out a loud cry. But all he let out was a burst of come down my throat.

I ducked my head so he couldn't see my grimace—it wasn't the best thing I'd ever tasted. Still, it wasn't going to make me puke, and I swallowed quickly so I could look back up at him with a smile of pride.

One more weak spurt hit me smack in the lips.

My triumph faded into a startled blink. Shoulders trembling with silent laughter, Seb pulled me up and quickly wiped everything away. But from the flush in his cheeks and from the way he yanked me into a heated kiss, it seemed I hadn't done too bad for my first try. And I'd be even better the next time.

I wrapped my arms around him and slid them down until both palms landed on his ass. "Hey…you wanna go again?"

His eyes said yes, but he shook his head. *It's getting late.*

I groaned. "Fuck. You're right."

So we'll just have to postpone this until later. He yanked up his pants, smirking.

Right. Later. Because we had all the time in the world. How could I forget?

Seb finished dressing and we stumbled out into the darkness like we were both still a little love-drunk. The time really had gotten away from us during our sexual detour, so I took us down an alley instead of walking out to the main road to make up for it.

"Oh, um, about tomorrow," I began anxiously, keeping up a quick pace.

I didn't want to bring down my high…but I figured it would be a good idea to set my plan in motion while Seb was still feeling all warm and satisfied.

"Let's split up."

His eyes snapped to mine. *Really? Why?*

"I figure we can cover more ground that way. You should work the same parts we did today, then bring the stuff over to that center and get whatever money you can. I was thinking I'll go a little further east. Santa Monica is full of hippies and they like to recycle…but there are other parts of West LA where the people don't care as much. I bet I'll have even better luck finding stuff there."

He crinkled his forehead as he frowned. *So why don't we just go together?*

"Look, don't take this the wrong way"—I forced a little laugh— "but you sorta distract me. I think we'll get more work done on our own. And we don't have to work that hard every day…maybe just a few days a week. Just until we save up enough money for me to get a fake ID, remember?"

His eyes were still troubled. *I guess.*

Shit, I hated myself so much. But if I didn't do it, he'd suffer. This way, I was the only one who had to live with the pain.

"I know. It's gonna suck being away from you…but you know I'll always be back, right? I made that promise to you once before, and I kept it, didn't I?"

Grudgingly, his lips pressed into a smile. *Yes.*

"Well, there ya go. I'm a man of my word."

I stopped walking to push Seb against a brick wall— unfortunately next to a dumpster—so I could kiss him firmly.

"Hope you're a man with money, you little poof."

The unexpected voice with its lilting accent had me flattening out against the brick and covering Seb with my body.

"Leave us alone, you fucker," I shot back without thinking, but I knew I wouldn't be able to get off any more cocky remarks once the man crept out of the shadows.

He was tall and gangly, with dirt caked into the crevices of his tan skin. Black stubble dotted his drawn face, and in his right hand he held a switchblade.

"Let's have it."

I remained still. For all my belief in being a badass, I had no idea what to do now. The only time I'd ever faced off against a knife, Hector had been drunk.

And I'd been alone.

But Seb was beside me now, and with my arm flung protectively across his chest I could feel his breaths becoming shorter and shorter. He was scared to death.

"Now," the man said. There was only a weak streetlamp to see by, and I couldn't find any compassion in his sunken eyes.

"We...we don't have any. We're homeless," I whispered gruffly. In a few seconds I was afraid my throat would close off completely, and I'd be left with silence, like Seb.

The man came closer.

Seb reached around and clasped my hand, drawing my gaze away from the knife for a terrifying second. *Give it to him*, he pleaded.

I shook my head, shock and fear clouding my thoughts. *But we need it!*

The knife hopped from the man's right hand to his left, but that didn't help prepare me for the punch that landed squarely in my stomach.

I crumpled to the floor, no air left in my chest for me to scream with.

Alex!

The despair in Seb's eyes as he dropped down beside me was like a second punch. But it was nothing compared to the horror that seized my body when a boot connected with his face. He stumbled back against the dumpster and then slid down to the floor, where he curled into a ball and lay motionless.

"NO!" My voice was back, fueled by rage for the man and for my own fucking uselessness. Another kick landed in my ribs. And then another and another, but I didn't feel them anymore. I struggled to get into the backpack, unzipping it with desperate force and spilling my photographs into the stream of dirty run-off that trickled through the alley. My hand closed on the money— everything we had to our names besides the six bucks in my shoe—and I thrust out the wad without looking. "Take it! Take it! Get the fuck away!"

The cash was ripped from my fingers and the man fled, his footsteps fading into the night.

"Seb!" I pulled myself over to him, angry tears blurring my vision. "Seb, are you okay? P-please, open your eyes. Please, Seb. Please."

I lifted his head into my lap and cradled it, stroking his hair clumsily as my hand shook. "Seb? Please. I need you. I need you to open your eyes."

A trickle of red seeped out the side of his mouth.

"No…no. No don't. Don't do that."

He was ashen beneath his tan, and the bright streak stood out sharply against his pale skin.

"No, no, please open your eyes. Please open your eyes, *amor*, I need you."

His lids fluttered.

"C'mon. That's it. You're okay. You're okay."

I wasn't sure who I was trying to convince, but I kept repeating it over and over, like a prayer.

"You're okay, Seb. You're okay."

Finally, his eyes opened all the way, and he stared out into the dark sky.

"Thank you," I whispered. To him and to God. Still frantic, I checked him over for injuries. His lip was split, but beyond that I couldn't see any other damage.

"Where does it hurt? What should I do—should I go get ice? Should we go to a hospital?"

He didn't respond. He just kept staring up at the sky. He blinked normally and breathed normally, but behind his eyes, there was nothing.

"Seb? What should I do?"

No answer.

"Seb?"

Panic like I'd never felt before tore at me. It ripped into my heart and stripped all sanity from my mind. My breathing became panting, each inhale more of a struggle than the last. I knew I was hyperventilating, but I had no way of stopping it.

Was it the kick to the mouth, or something else? He looked like he had when I'd first met him…empty. Vacant. Where was *my* Seb?

"Seb? Seb! What should I do?"

He turned his head away. And in that unfocused stare, I saw the truth.

Oh, God. He was gone. I'd lost him. Because I'd…I'd broken my fucking promise. The most important promise I'd ever made.

You're safe now, remember? You're safe. I won't let anyone hurt you ever again.

I'd failed him. I'd failed a lot of people in my life, but this…this was the worst of all.

"Seb." I clenched his shirt until my knuckles were white. "I'm sorry. I'm sorry. I'm so sorry. Please, tell me what to do. Please."

Still nothing.

I gasped for air as the world started to go black around the edges, and the sudden rush of oxygen pushed me into hysteria.

"Tell me what to do! Please tell me what to do! I can't…I don't know what…I…I need you…and I… I can't fucking do this on my own!"

My last words were a high-pitched scream, and they echoed in the dark alley.

Can't fucking do this on my own.

I grew quiet. Tears continued to fall, but they were silent now. And a strange calm settled over me, blanketing my fear and letting all my other wild emotions rest beneath that one final realization.

I really couldn't do this on my own.

When the tears dried up, I looked down at Seb through the daze and gently stroked his cheek. "It's okay, *amor*. It's okay. Don't worry. I…I know what we have to do."

Chapter 26: Sixteen

The bus dropped us off a few blocks away. I held Seb's hand as we walked, but it just hung there limply, like he couldn't even feel my fingers desperately clutching his.

My chest ached. Nasty bruises had to be budding on the skin, in those pinks and reds that would gradually blossom into purples and blues. Nothing I hadn't seen before...and it wasn't that pain that made it so hard to breathe. It wasn't those wounds that left my skin so raw even the gentle night wind was too much to bear. The daze was wearing off now, and each layer that drifted away left me more exposed to the truth.

We'd reached the end.

Out by the potted ferns, the finality of my decision delivered a sudden blow. My legs turned to rubber and I stumbled toward the apartments, then sank down against the fake-adobe wall.

Seb remained standing, his still face alternately shadowed and lit by a blinking streetlamp. I clasped a piece of his pant leg and rubbed the fabric between my fingers until I felt strong enough to speak.

"I screwed up. I screwed up so fucking badly."

323

I wasn't expecting a response, and I didn't get one. We were right back at the beginning, to all those evenings I'd used his presence as an excuse to talk out loud to myself. And just like then, I found myself *needing* to continue.

"You got hurt, and it was all my fault. You have every right not to trust me now. I'm so sorry. I'd do anything to change it."

Seb folded his legs and sat beside me, but he didn't look over. His eyes were fixed on a blade of grass.

"But that's not even why we're here."

I would've thought the tears had all dried up by now, but I could feel them burning behind my eyes, making my face hot and my world blurred.

"It's because...I lied to you."

He twisted the piece of grass and tore it off, not a muscle moving in his face.

I beat back the tears by ripping some grass of my own. It left a bald patch in the ground, and that last bit of control over my environment led me to keep going—to wrench fistfuls of green until I'd cleared an entire circle around me.

I wanted to strip my mind that way, but I could only forget for a second.

"Seb, the money from the cans was never going to be enough. We needed more and I...I was going to do something else. Something I'd regret. Something I swore I wouldn't."

I watched him carefully, hoping for a spark of anger. I never thought I'd *want* to see that, but at the moment I'd have given anything for him to lash out at me in a rage—smack me, beat my chest, kick me in the groin...*anything*.

He didn't move.

"You must be so sick of hearing me say I'm sorry."

I took his hand again, holding the dead weight in my lap and running my thumb over his fingers. He'd missed some scraps of dirt under his nails when we'd washed up earlier, and I carefully picked them out.

"But I want you to know…this doesn't mean I'm giving up on us. I…I can go back to school, or get my GED or whatever, and then I can get a real job, and I can rent us an apartment and we can live together…"

Crazy dreams. I wondered how I still had the power to dream after all this.

"I mean, if you want. Because I do. Even if you never talk to me again. And not 'cause I'm expecting…anything. I…I just—"

A twenty-something-year-old striding up the walkway in stiletto heels caused me to snap my mouth shut, and I was grateful. There was no point in dragging out my misery. It was all over now, and the sooner I accepted that, the sooner I could…

Could what? Move on? Heal?

Somehow I doubted that would ever happen.

I rose to follow the girl toward the building's entrance, and she absentmindedly held the door open. By the time I was done scanning the apartment list, Seb was right behind me.

I glanced back one more time, searching his face for a shred of hope. I found nothing.

"Let's go, Seb. It's time."

Suzie answered the door dressed in head-to-toe pink. Pink sweatpants and a pink hoodie. The outfit even *said* the word pink on it, right down her thick thigh. I was so surprised to see her wrapped in a bright color that I just stood there for several seconds with my mouth hanging open.

She was as stunned as I was, and only managed to reach out to me halfway. "Alex? Sebastian? Oh my God, Alex."

And then I launched myself straight at her, a few more tears unleashing themselves into her unsuspecting arms.

"I'm sorry, Suzie. I'm so sorry. I'm so sorry."

Recuperating quickly, she brought a hand up to press my face into her soft chest. It made me feel like a little boy again, but I had no intention of pulling away. She was all I had to cling to.

My backpack slid from my shoulders as she led us into the foyer and shut the door. She gently took it from me.

"Oh, Alex. I know you never meant to hurt anyone. I know you were just trying to be close to your friend. It's okay. It's okay."

"Seb…he…he…and I…" My words dissolved into whimpers.

"Just take deep breaths." Suzie urged. "Just take deep breaths and try to calm down."

Seb wandered past us into the small apartment. He sat up on a stool at the kitchen bar for a while, but when I kept crying he eventually moved to the beige couch, where he curled into a tight ball.

"Suzie…I'm so sorry. I tried. I really tried."

"Did something happen?" Her always-calm voice was right beside my ear, but for once, I didn't mind it. "Are you both okay?"

"I'm…he's…I don't know."

I wanted to tell her everything. From the very beginning. But the words just weren't lining up in the right order. When the sniffling finally stopped, I pried myself loose from her pink-clad arms. "Check Seb."

Suzie's eyes widened. "Sebastian?" She hurried to his side. "What am I checking for?"

Seb lay staring at her coffee table, which was littered with papers and books. Her whole living room seemed to consist of those piles—some scholarly, and some less so, like the one topped by a novel cover with a man baring his chest to the wind.

"Alex? He looks like he has a split lip. Did he get hit by something?"

"We got mugged back in Santa Monica. This fucker…he took all our money."

"And he hit Sebastian?" She dashed to the kitchen and opened a freezer stocked full of diet meals to grab an icepack. She returned to Seb and put the ice in his hand, but when he didn't move, she forced his arm up to his mouth. "Hold it here, Sebastian, okay? Hold it right here. You understand? Just like this."

Satisfied he'd gotten the picture, she turned her attention to me. "Are you hurt anywhere?"

"No."

Lies, my old friends. But I'd already cried my eyes out on her shoulder, and the need to be held and soothed like some helpless little kid seemed to be fulfilled for now. Hopefully forever. Seb was going to be taken care of, and that's all that really mattered.

"Don't you need to call the police or something? Report me?" From somewhere in the depths of my weary heart, another more familiar emotion started to gain strength. "Haul me away for kidnapping and endangering a minor…some shit like that."

Suzie walked back over to me. I thought she might try to hug me again, but she was smarter than that.

"Yes, if you were attacked and mugged then I need to call the police. But Alex…I'm not upset with you. You made the right decision coming back. You couldn't have lived out there on your own."

"Yes, I could have!" I snapped. And not purely out of anger.

Suzie took a cautionary step back.

"I could have," I repeated more calmly. I didn't really want to fight, as comfortable as the anger was in the middle of all the chaos. "I know how to get by. I know how to live one way…it's just…that's not the life I want for Seb."

Suzie nodded solemnly.

"It's not the life I want for me, either."

That surprised me. That I'd said it…and that I meant it.

I looked over at Seb. Curled up like that, he seemed so small and helpless. He was all I had left in the world, but even if he could never be a part of my life the way he'd once been...I knew there were some things I'd never go back to.

I owed him that much.

He shifted, closing his eyes and dropping the ice to the ground as he settled in to sleep. I walked around to the back of the couch and rested my arms there so I could keep watching over him.

"I wanted to be the one," I whispered. Mostly to myself, but Suzie heard. "I wanted to be the one to take care of him...but I just couldn't. I couldn't give him what he deserved." My throat closed again and I used bitterness to fight through the tears. "Because I'm just a stupid fucking kid."

Suzie shook her head. Her forehead was all wrinkled and her lips were twitching, and it took me a second to realize she was holding back tears of her own. "No, you're not, Alex. You're not stupid. That's actually a very mature thing for a fifteen-year-old to admit. There are adults who still struggle to understand it."

I cut off my instinct to argue back. Suzie probably knew what she was talking about, with her line of work.

My eyes drifted past her and landed on a large calendar tacked to the wall. A little old-fashioned, but it matched what I expected of her more than the romance novels and the pink clothing. Dates were circled in red, and some notes were scrawled inside the boxes in sloppy cursive.

It seemed like ages since I'd last thought about what day it was.

"Sixteen," I mumbled.

"I'm sorry?"

"I'm sixteen. My birthday was a few days ago. I forgot."

One tear escaped the edge of Suzie's lashes, but she quickly rubbed it away. "Well, happy birthday, Alex."

A weak half-smile touched the corner of my mouth, before a sudden swell of exhaustion wiped it away. We hadn't slept much in the last week. I'd been able to hold back the crash with coffee and pure love-adrenaline, but now that all that had been drained, my body was nearing a complete shut-down.

Suzie made a phone call in another room while I climbed over the back of the couch and sat beside Seb. She joined us after a minute, lowering herself into a recliner and leaning toward me like she was waiting to hear more.

I carefully moved Seb's head onto my thigh and wove my fingers into the golden strands. "So...what's going to happen now? Will I have to go to Juvee or something?"

Suzie smiled gently. "I think we can avoid that. I'm not saying there won't be consequences, but you did make the right decision coming back, and I'm sure that will be taken into consideration."

I nodded and tucked a lock of Seb's hair behind his ear. "Suzie...I know I don't have any right to ask this...but...if there's any way we could be near each other when we get placed...or just be able to see each other..."

"I'll work on that, Alex. I really will."

For some reason, I believed her.

"And are Mimi and Star okay?"

"They have a caseworker assigned to them. I hope that will give them the support they need."

I rested my eyes, continuing to shuffle through Seb's hair. The repetitive motion must've soothed me—I wouldn't have thought I could discuss my betrayal so easily.

"Mimi must hate me."

Suzie sighed. "One day, she may thank you. Or her daughter might. What you did shows how much you really care about them."

Showed that to Suzie and those like her, maybe. But it would look different from Mimi's perspective. "Is that why you do this job? So that one day, people might thank you?"

Suzie chuckled sadly. "I don't know. I don't think so."

"So then *why*?"

She ran her hands over her pink sweatpants. "I do it because…someone has to."

Someone had to. Someone had to be there to look after Seb and all the other Sebs in the world. Or else they'd wind up right where we'd been…out on the streets, willing to do dangerous things to get by. Some of them still would, even with Suzie's help.

But Seb and I wouldn't be among them.

"You care very much for Sebastian, I can tell," Suzie remarked, watching my hands caress his scalp.

"I love him." I traced his cheekbone, fingers barely grazing the skin so I wouldn't disturb him. Then I looked Suzie straight in the eye and added, "Not like a brother."

She nodded, a few rapid blinks the only thing giving away her concern.

"He's not special like that, I swear. Do you believe me?"

"I believe you probably know him better than I do."

That sounded like a no. It didn't really bother me, though. Seb was gone and there was no point in tearing my hair out trying to show her something that didn't exist anymore. Just a few hours without him, and I missed him so much it felt as though I'd been hollowed out, like a lonely old abandoned building, too trashed for even junkies to live in.

Would he ever come back? Was there anything I could say or do to get him to forgive me? *I'm sorry* clearly wasn't good enough anymore. Was he even gone by choice? Or was it whatever trauma he'd lived through as a kid that had stolen him away again?

"Suzie…" I dropped my hand on his shoulder because it was starting to shake. "Was Seb…abused? Like…physically or…or, um, sexually?"

Suzie closed her eyes for a moment and then shook her head. "I can't discuss Seb's case with you. I'm sorry."

I nodded. "Yeah. It's okay. I think I already know, anyway. I was just wondering about what made him decide to hide all this time. Maybe it was 'cause of that…or maybe it has to do with him losing his mom when he was so young."

"His mother?" Suzie edged forward in the recliner, her brow furrowing.

"Yeah. You know. Her dying must've been really awful. I could tell he loved her a lot."

"Alex, what do you know about Sebastian's mother?"

I dragged my attention away from Seb to focus on Suzie. Her eyes were narrowed…almost suspiciously.

Had I said something wrong?

"Um, not much. Just what he told me. That she died when he was little…and that she didn't abandon him."

"*How* did Seb tell you this?"

Oh, fuck. Right. And just what was I supposed to say—he drew a picture and I decided I was psychic?

"Uh…"

"Alex"—Suzie reached over to touch my knee—"this is important. Please."

"Why?"

She bit her lip. Whatever it was, she didn't want to tell me. "When Seb was found," she began hesitantly, "the person he was with…was not a blood relative."

When he was *found.* A horrible image of him chained up in a dank cellar sprang into my mind, and I gritted my teeth to fight back the nausea.

"And because he couldn't speak, we weren't able to find out anything about his family. We don't even know his real last name. If his mother passed away, that could explain why no one ever reported him missing…and he could have other relatives out there who don't know what happened to him."

My pulse fluttered. Seb might have *family*. Family who wanted him.

"So it's very important that you're honest with me, Alex. How did Seb tell you about his mother?"

I let her words sink in to my hollowed-self while I considered how best to be *honest*. Because the truth was, he hadn't said a damn thing. But did I actually believe in what Seb and I had shared...enough to report it to Suzie?

Thinking back to every moment we'd spent together...everything I'd read from the twists of his beautiful lips and the gleam in his eyes had felt so *real*. There'd been no room for doubt then, when we'd been so close I knew the exact rhythm of his heartbeat and pace of his soft breaths.

And even though that was gone now, the memories still refilled some of my emptiness, with a sad sort of love.

Yes, I believed it.

I turned back to Suzie. "He...wrote it."

Her eyes shot wide. "Sebastian can write?"

"Sure." I shrugged. "I mean, only a little. And not 'cause he's slow...just 'cause he didn't really pay attention in school. But he knows his letters."

"Alex, Sebastian has never..." She stopped herself, though I could tell she still didn't believe me. "Well, do you think you could get him to write some for me? Anything he could share...anything he remembers might be helpful."

"I...I don't know. He's really upset about everything that happened. About me letting him down like this—"

"You didn't let him down."

"But I—"

"You didn't let him down, Alex." Suzie's tone wasn't so gentle now. It was firm, and full of authority. "You didn't let anyone down. You brought him back to a place where he can be safe, and you did that because you love him."

And one day he might thank me for it? It was hard to see that future, right now.

I sighed. "Fine. I'll give it a go, but it's not gonna work." Nudging his shoulder gently, I tried to wake him. "Seb? Seb, can you get up?"

"Oh, no." Suzie reached out to stop me. "I didn't mean right this second. He must be so exhausted."

I lifted my hand, but while it hovered mid-air, a thought struck me. Or maybe it was a prayer.

I waved Suzie off. "He's awake."

If there was anything I knew about Seb, it was this. And if I was right, then as slim as it was, there was another chance to hope.

"I don't think—" Her protest died on her lips, because he sat straight up and looked at me.

It was still an *old Seb* look...but it wasn't the lost one. It was the one he'd used to stare right into me, like he could see me better than anyone ever had. The one he'd used before I even knew I loved him. The one that had somehow captured my heart and *made* me love him.

Dark almond eyes with unwavering focus, gazing straight into my soul.

"Seb?" I breathed, laying a single, trembling finger on his upturned wrist. *Please, tell me you heard what we were saying. How I did this because I love you. Tell me you understand.*

I didn't say anything else. There were no more words. I just stared back, willing him to *feel* all that he meant to me. All that he'd done to change me...for the better. How I'd never forgive myself for what had happened, but how I'd do anything I could just to make his life a better one. Even if it meant turning us in like this...even if it meant losing him.

He brought a hand to my face and brushed away a tear I didn't even know had fallen. I held my breath, too afraid to move or even blink.

Out of the corner of my eye, I caught Suzie's lips parting and forming a small, surprised *o*. Was she beginning to believe?

He let his slender fingers rest on my cheek for a moment before lowering his head.

And when he lifted it up again, his mask shattered.

Suzie gasped.

His eyes sparked to life first, brows scrunching and lids half-lowering as his face twisted in pain. *I'm sorry, Alex. I'm sorry.*

The explosion of joy in my chest couldn't be contained. I let out a yell so loud that Suzie jerked back and bumped her head on her chair. "Seb! God, Seb. I…I thought I lost you!" A new wave of tears flooded my already-sore eyes.

He was shaking all over, like he was just now letting the fear and the pain travel through his body.

"I was so scared, Seb—"

He gripped my shoulders and nodded, a fat tear rolling down his cheek. *Me too, Alex. I was scared, too.*

Scared and lost in his old-Seb world…but somehow he'd found the courage to come back to me. Did I deserve a miracle like that?

With a strength that still surprised me for his slender frame, he pulled me into his arms.

"I'm so sorry, God I'm so sor—"

He put a finger to my lips. *Shh.* With his other hand, he rubbed my chest, then his.

I let out a whoop of laughter, my eyes crinkling and forcing out a few more streaks of tears. He backed up to grin at me, and with the space between us, I suddenly remembered Suzie was in the room.

Her mouth was unhinged. "Oh, Sebastian," she murmured. "All this time…"

He peeked over at her. For a moment he seemed to be debating whether to play dumb again, but then he just gave an apologetic shrug. *Yeah. Well, here I am.*

I wanted to scream "I told you so!" and jump up and down and point with those game-show-host arms used to unveil a grand prize…but then I remembered this moment wasn't supposed to be about me.

"Listen, Seb." I cleaned my face with my shirtsleeve. God, I hoped I'd cried enough today that I never had to do it again. "You heard Suzie needs to know some stuff about your mom."

His eyes darkened and he frowned. *What could I possibly say that would be important?*

"I dunno. Anything you remember, I guess. Anything that could help them find some relatives. There might be people out there who want you, like an aunt or an uncle or something."

He shook his head, flustered. *How?*

"Just...write a few words or something."

Now he glared.

"Why don't you start with a picture, like you did the other night...and then see what comes to you."

He sighed, but eventually stretched out his hand to Suzie.

"What?" She looked at me. "What does he want?"

"He needs something to write with. Hold on, we've got stuff in the backpack."

I grabbed the notebook and pen and placed them in Seb's hands, letting him flip to a fresh page so Suzie could get a quick glimpse of all the other things he'd drawn.

On a clean canvas, he began to sketch, the lines shaky and unsure. It wasn't as good as he'd done before, but the angular cheekbones were still there, along with the almond eyes and the long, dark hair.

"That's her," I told Suzie. "That's his mom."

Suzie's eyes never left Seb's hand. "And what happened to her, Sebastian? Can you write that for me?"

He looked back at me hesitantly.

"You can do it."

Jaw clenching so tightly I could see the bones shifting under his skin, he brought his pen to the paper. Even his ears wiggled slightly as he worked.

Very slowly, he wrote:

She did

"She died," I blurted out, with way too much excitement, considering the subject matter. "That means she died."

Suzie nodded, still gaping. I didn't think she'd closed her mouth for more than a second since Seb had revealed himself. "R-right. What about…her name? Can you tell me her name?"

He gave us a rueful smile, and with less insecurity in his grip, he scrawled: *MOM*.

I chuckled and rubbed his back. "Yeah, that's okay. You were little."

Suzie jumped in, too. "Of course. You're doing wonderfully, really. Now, um…what about…do you recall…how she passed away?"

She looked really nervous asking that. Her hands were so sweaty they'd left imprints on her pink pants.

Seb swallowed hard. The pen didn't move. He just glanced back at me once, and I knew.

"Drugs." Shit, I was such an idiot. "She died from drugs."

He wet his lower lip, wincing when he struck the place where it'd been split.

"Is that right? An overdose?" Suzie asked.

He nodded.

"I'm so sorry for your loss," she responded automatically, and in the same breath launched into her next thought. "Do you remember when she passed away?"

Inhaling slowly, Seb shook his head and started to add some shading around his mother's eyes and cheekbones.

"Do you remember anything else? How old you were maybe? Or even what time of year it was?" Suzie pressed.

Seb stopped drawing and considered for a moment. Then he wrote: *hot*.

"Your mom was hot?" I asked.

He rolled his eyes at me. *No, retard.*

"Oh…yeah. You mean it was hot out. It was summer."

He made a little checkmark on the paper, soft puffs of air coming from his nose. The idea that I could still make him laugh, even at a time like this, was so exhilarating I felt faint.

"Okay. Then let's say she passed away in the summer." Suzie didn't want to get off track. I could just imagine how many questions she had for him, now that she *knew*. I'd felt that way not too long ago. "Can you tell me about how long it was before…before DCFS took custody of you?"

She'd chosen her words carefully, but we knew exactly what she meant: how long before he'd been rescued from whatever nightmare had swallowed him up after his mother's death.

From the *t* in the word hot, Seb began to draw a circle. It went all the way around until it touched the same letter again.

A full circle. A year.

"You found Seb in the summertime?" I asked. "Maybe it was about a year, then."

Suzie rested her round face in her hands. "Uh"—she cleared her throat with a watery cough—"yes."

Seb didn't respond. He was retracing his mother's face, fixing some of the wobbly lines.

"She *was* beautiful," I murmured, leaning in to press my cheek against him. Seb's nod moved my head with his, and I felt his jaw stretch wide in a yawn.

"Sebastian…this is…wonderful." Suzie's voice was still thick. "Thank you so much for trusting me and telling me this. You've given us a lot of information to work with. If you think of anything else, you'll let me know, won't you?"

Seb put down the pen, blinking sleepily.

With a shaky breath, Suzie stood. "The police will be here soon—not because you're in trouble, Alex," she added hastily, "but we do need to make a report, and we'll have to find you two a place to spend the night."

I tightened my arm around Seb. "Can't we just stay here?"

Suzie shook her head. "I'm sorry, Alex. Besides, I only have the one bedroom.

"That's okay. Seb and I can share the couch."

She chuckled. "I don't think so."

"What? Why not?"

"Because you're teenage boys, and from what I can tell, you're in a relationship."

"So?" I squared my jaw. "What the hell does that mean? We already sleep together. And we've already—"

"Alex"—Suzie held out a hand to stop me—"if I had kids of my own, they'd have the same rules. You're only sixteen. You have plenty of time to be together. It doesn't all have to happen so fast."

I kept scowling. "Fine. Whatever. But Seb and I *are* together, and no one's gonna make us slow down if we don't want to." I turned back to make sure Seb was on board with my declaration and found him admiring me with a smirk.

That was a yes, right?

"Just give me a moment to change," Suzie said, heading down the hallway. "I can trust you to wait right there?"

I rolled my eyes. I didn't have the energy to get off the couch, let alone make a run for it.

She vanished into her room, and a split second later, Seb closed in for a surprise kiss. Open-mouthed, and a little sloppy, but that might've been on purpose. At first his lips were cold from the ice but it wasn't long before they burned, pulling me deeper and deeper into a nothing-exists-outside-of-this kind of kiss. I snaked my arms up and down his back, a soft moan escaping my throat. We gasped for breath and dove back in again. Some blood mixed with our saliva—his blood—but the bitter taste of guilt washed away as we continued to plunge into each other, dissolving it into something warm and salty and *right*.

When my mouth felt bruised and raw from the friction, Seb finally pulled back, drawing out my bottom lip with one final suck. Then I turned and caught Suzie in a pantsuit out of the corner of my eye.

Her cheeks were as pink as her previous outfit. Mine probably turned a similar shade.

Well, at least she knew I meant what I'd said. No one was going to come between us, if I could help it.

Her phone rang. It had to be the cops, and whoever else she'd called, asking to be buzzed in.

I gripped Seb's hand.

Please, God. Let me be able to help it.

Chapter 27: Outgrown

"We're really happy to have a space for you," counselor Jessica said. She looked like a younger version of Suzie—Suzie in the sweats, because she was in a lavender tracksuit. Same mousy brown hair and rounder body, too, though Jessica was a lot peppier.

A couple of bedroom doors opened as she led me through the sprawling house. Floorboards creaked under my leaden feet and curious eyes peeked out to find the source of the noise, but I was too exhausted to pay much attention. This new place seemed a lot like Ms. Loretta's, except with cheerful camp-counselor style staff to keep me in line instead of those big old ladies.

I sort of missed them.

"Your room will be right down here," Jessica went on, gesturing to a small space with two desks, bunk beds and mirrored closet doors. "You'll be sharing with Carlos. He's a character, but very friendly, I promise."

The very friendly Carlos barely looked over from his top bunk, where he was busy typing away on a laptop. I couldn't have cared less. The roommate didn't matter. Neither did the room itself, or the house, or Jessica the peppy resident counselor. All that mattered was that I was only a mile away from Seb, at his facility's off-campus housing for "highly functioning youth."

I was surprised to hear that Suzie found me *highly functioning*, all things considered, but I wasn't going to argue.

"Maybe you two would like a moment to get acquainted?" Jessica suggested. "I'll be back in a few to check up on you before bed."

As soon as she and her cheerful smile headed off, I zeroed in on the bottom bunk. Leaving my new bag of clothing and the trusty backpack by the door, I crawled into the temporary haven.

I wrapped myself up in the blankets and ran my hand over the empty space beside me. That space was meant for Seb. I could still imagine the feel of his hair passing through my fingers, nearly two whole days since I'd last touched a shimmering strand. Two days since I'd last seen his face, troubled but trusting, as he'd been taken away.

And now another long night with that image seared on my brain stretched out before me.

I scrunched my eyes shut and gathered an armful of pillow, trying to ease the loneliness. *It has to be like this. He's just a mile away. The faster you go to sleep, the sooner you'll see him again.*

This arrangement Suzie had worked out was probably the best I could have hoped for, and yet my heart still ached like someone had torn a piece right out of it. Of course, it could've also been the bruises, but once my lies had been discovered the paramedic had assured me nothing was broken inside.

So it was just lovesickness, then. Lovesickness mixed with the horrible, very real fear that Seb might disappear again without my presence there to maintain him.

A thump startled me into opening my eyes—Carlos jumping down from his bunk. Then I saw Carlos himself, and my eyes opened a little wider.

He was a small kid, probably all of five-four. He had on tight pink shorts that I hadn't seen when he was under the covers, and the left side of his hair was streaked with purple. His nails were painted a silvery-gray and he wore a rainbow bracelet on his wrist.

I must've had my mouth open while I gaped at him, because suddenly he was flashing brown eyes on me in anger. "I hope you're not thinking about starting no trouble. 'Cause I can handle myself if it comes to that."

My brows drew up at the challenging note in his tone. It had to take guts to talk to me that way...not to mention dress like that in the first place. A kid like him would've been eaten alive at my old school.

"Take a picture. It'll last longer," he snapped, placing his hands on his narrow waist. "Then you can beat one off to it later."

I shook my head to cover a snort of laughter. "Sorry, man. Didn't mean to stare."

"Yeah, whatever," he muttered under his breath. Then he kicked at my backpack. "You gonna unpack? Or are you not staying long?"

"Not sure," I admitted. There were no guarantees on this placement, just like there hadn't been for any of the others. Just hope. Tired, battered, but amazingly still alive-and-kicking Hope.

I stood up to grab my bag, trying to think positively as I unzipped it. Maybe if I acted like this was permanent, I'd help make that happen. I found an empty drawer and clumsily flipped the backpack over to empty the contents.

A few photographs, creased and water-stained, slipped to the floor during the process.

Carlos bent to pick them up. "This your family?"

I snatched them out of his hands before he could get a good look. "Mhm."

"There are some empty frames in the den."

"Frames?"

"Yeah. Frames." He made a rectangle with his dainty fingers. "For putting pictures in. You know."

"I know what frames are," I grumbled, squaring the photographs into a neater pile. My mother stared up at me from the top of the stack, a bit of mud stuck on her face from her brush with dirty alley water.

I'd never thought about putting the photographs on display. Of course, I hadn't really had a place to display them before…but now that I did, I wasn't sure I wanted to be faced with them day after day, to be reminded of a past I no longer felt eager to claim.

I licked my finger and wiped off the smudge before gently tucking the pictures back in the drawer.

Counselor Jessica popped her head in the doorway. "Getting ready for bed, Alex? I know you've had a long day."

And it would be an even longer night.

~*~

A gentle tapping awoke me. "Alex? Are you up yet? It's nearly eleven-thirty."

I peeled back one lid at a time, re-accustoming myself to the new surroundings. Carlos was at a desk on his computer, still in the pink shorts and comfortably slouched over like he was settled in for a lazy Saturday. The little white buds in his ears explained why he hadn't noticed Jessica at the door—I could hear a faint strain of music coming from the earphones, so whatever he was listening to had to be on pretty freaking loud.

The knocks grew less gentle. "Alex? Your social worker called. She said you might be interested in heading up to Hill View to have lunch with your friend?"

I sprang out of the bed like I was on fire, startling Carlos into a duck-and-crouch move that left him in a little ball under the desk.

"Yes! Oof." I tripped over my shoes in the mad dash across the room. "Yeah, I do!"

I crashed into the wall and flung open the door at the same time, just as Jessica took a step back. "Oh, well, there's a shuttle leaving in a few minutes for afternoon activities. I just wanted to let you know."

"Yeah. Thanks. I'll be ready."

Running around—like a headless chicken—I threw on the first clothing I reached. Carlos crawled out from his hiding place, too busy eyeing me like the insane person I was to be embarrassed I'd scared him.

"Where does that shuttle thing pick people up?" I asked breathlessly, stopping for only a second to run my hand through my bed-hair.

He pointed down the hallway toward the front of the house. "Um, on the corner. To the left."

"Thanks, man!" Giddy and hyper-charged, I clapped him on the back a little too hard and raced out of the house.

The shuttle took me back to those grass-covered hills and dropped me off near the front building of the facility. I was a little reluctant to show my face in there again, but not enough to slow my frantic footsteps.

Nothing could keep me from Seb.

I signed in and received a special badge, since my group home was part of the "Hill View Family," then sprinted across the field toward the dream of being in Seb's arms. I pulled up short outside his bedroom, though, when I saw a woman crouching in front of him and speaking in a low, singsong tone.

"Sebastian, we'd really love for you to join us in the dining room for lunch today. All your friends are waiting for you there. And your roommate Harold…won't it be nice to eat lunch with him? Come on, sweetie. Come along now. That's it."

She stretched out an arm to take his hand.

"Quit it." I stormed into the room and pushed her arm out of the way. "Quit talking to him like he's a retard."

Besides, I was the only one who should be getting to hold his hand.

Seb's face lit up, and he smiled. A small, tight-lipped smile that was mostly in his eyes—but it was enough to quiet my fears.

He was still there.

I squeezed him in a hug. "Hope you didn't miss me too much."

The woman cleared her throat. "You must be Alex."

Reluctant to draw away from Seb, I only half-turned to her. She had an ID clipped to her pants, displaying a miniature replica of the syrupy smile and bobbed haircut she wore now. *Pam Garcia*, the tag read.

"Pam." I gave her a brief nod.

"Alex, I'd appreciate it if you wouldn't use the word 'retard'. There are many special needs kids here, and all of them deserve respect."

I floundered for a response. "I…I wasn't trying to…I mean, what I was saying is that Seb's not…" I eventually ground to a halt, deciding to cut my losses. Besides, she had a point. I was sure Seb had heard the word often enough in his lifetime. No need for me to add to the count. "Sorry. I just meant that…you shouldn't baby him like that. Right, Seb?" I elbowed him for support.

He blinked.

Shit.

"C'mon, Seb."

He blinked a few more times and lowered his eyes, that same light smile on his lips.

Who did he think he was fooling? I wanted to shake him. He hadn't gone completely blank, but he obviously wasn't ready to do much communicating. Didn't he know the genie couldn't be put back in the bottle? We all knew he was in there now. And I for one would never stop trying to get him to come out.

"He's nervous," I mumbled to Pam. "Could we maybe have a minute alone?"

"I don't think—" she began, then pursed her lips as she reconsidered. "Well, hold on a second. I actually do need to grab something."

She ran over to the window and propped it open so she could yell to a man who was kicking a soccer ball around with some younger kids. "Hey, Robert, come here for a minute?"

The Robert guy jogged over, and she leaned out the windowsill to whisper something in his ear. Then he went back to his soccer practice, though he kept one eye trained on Seb's bedroom.

Great. A fucking babysitter.

Pam left with a stern look in my direction that seemed to say, *I hope you'll be good.* Obviously, Suzie had filled her in about Seb and me.

I sighed and scooted closer to him, wishing his bed wasn't so visible from the window. "Hey, you all right? Everyone treat you okay before I got here? Sorry it took me a bit. I had to do a lot of explaining...and apologizing, y'know...to Eleanor and Greg, and I had to talk to this therapist lady...but Suzie really stuck up for me. So I'm not really in any serious trouble, and I'm getting to stay at that group home down the hill a little ways, and we'll be able to—"

A shout from outside interrupted us. One of the little kids had tripped and skinned her knee, and Robert rushed to provide aid.

Within a second, Seb was hovering over me, straddling my lap with a playful smirk on his face.

"Ugh." I flopped back on the bed as his hand began grazing my thigh. "Why don't you tell that lady the whole *keep-it-in-your-pants* look should be for you more than for me."

He swooped down and pecked my lips.

346

"I dunno how long that guy out there is gonna be distracted."

He kissed me again, forcing his tongue into my mouth.

"Besides... we should, um, talk or something... about...about you...and..."

It was hard to get my thoughts out through the persistent kisses.

"...and how come you didn't...you know..."

Seb kissed me one last time, hard, and then jumped off. I knew without asking that Pam was back.

"Now, let's see if we can't open the lines of communication a bit better!" she announced, striding into the room and triumphantly displaying a small white board and marker. "Here you are, Seb." She placed it in his hands. "What do you say, should we go get lunch at the dining hall? Maybe you could write a happy face for yes? We can work out a system."

She leaned over and stared, chewing on the corner of her lip, but Seb made no move to write anything.

"He's not a trained monkey about to perform a trick," I put in after a few moments. "Jesus. Why don't you give him some space?"

Pam narrowed her eyes on me. "Alex, your social worker suggested you might be able to help during this process, not hinder it."

"What? I didn't...I'm not—" I began, before again giving up. This lady obviously didn't like me, and I doubted there'd be much I could say to change her mind. "Look, could I maybe take him down to see my place? So he knows I'm nearby? It might make him more comfortable."

That wasn't my real motive, of course. With any luck, Carlos would've found a more exciting place to spend a Saturday, and I'd have the room to myself.

"That resident counselor lady will be there." I pressed on. "Jessica, right? So, uh...you know. All supervised and stuff."

Pam rested her hands on her hips. "I suppose that might be a good idea."

"Great!" I leapt up, pulling Seb by his shirtsleeve.

"Yes, it'll be a nice walk. I could use the fresh air," Pam responded cheerily.

If she didn't like me, I hoped she knew the feeling was mutual.

It only took about fifteen minutes to walk back, at a leisurely pace. Since Seb was as quiet as always, Pam quizzed me on the way down. Mostly about myself—what subjects I liked in school, and what hobbies I was into. She received short, one-word answers, and not just because I was annoyed with her presence. I really hadn't worked out my life yet…beyond the fact that it was going to involve Seb.

A few times, I thought I felt his fingers grazing mine, like he was expecting to hold my hand. I didn't reach for it, though. Even if Pam did know what was going on between us, there were more factors to take into consideration. Santa Monica and Suzie were one thing—in the first case no one knew us, and in the second, it was Suzie's *job* to help us, no matter what our sexual interests were. But if I was starting a normal, school-five-days-a-week kind of life again, things would be different. If I made the decision to step out of the closet with Seb, I might not even get the chance to figure out what kind of person I was going to be here. I'd be labeled and categorized automatically. I'd be *gay* Alex.

It was a lot to think about.

"Here it is." I pointed to the large one-story building for Seb. It was white like the little cottages at the main facility, but nothing really caused it to stand out from the other houses on the residential street. "Maybe you'll be able to move out to one of these group homes pretty soon, huh? I heard there's a couple around here."

Pam didn't say anything, but I saw the doubt in her eyes.

I led him inside and down the narrow hallway to the bedrooms. As I'd expected, the place seemed mostly empty…except for my room, of course.

Carlos was still at the desk, and still on his computer. He glanced up with mild interest as we entered, looking a little less flaming this afternoon in a pair of straight-leg jeans and a tight blue t-shirt.

I clenched my hands in frustration, though it didn't really matter since Pam the Watchdog was still with us.

"That's my roommate, Carlos, and that's my bunk—the bottom one. I always get stuck on the bottom."

Seb's eyes grew bright for a moment with silent laughter, and I rolled mine in response. Pam only saw my face, of course, and frowned. She paused in the doorway as Seb hunched over to sit on the edge of my mattress. I stayed standing.

Carlos took out his ear buds. "Are we getting another new person? I didn't think there were any more rooms."

"No," Pam answered. "Sebastian lives up on the grounds. He and Alex are friends, so they're just having a little visit."

I jerked a thumb at Carlos. "Seb, Carlos. Carlos, Seb." And then I held my breath and waited, hoping Seb would at least give him a nod of recognition.

He didn't.

Carlos raised one delicate brow—a plucked one, I realized. "Oh. He's, uh…oh."

Pam shot him a stern look, and he just shrugged.

I wasn't sure what to do. Did I need to start cheerleading for Seb to be more expressive? I considered it, for a moment—considered begging him to shake Carlos' hand, asking him *pretty please*, or encouraging him with a *you can do it!* But somehow that seemed a little too close to how Pam had spoken to him earlier…a little too much like he was a special kid who needed to be babied.

And my Seb wasn't a baby.

"So…uh…yeah, it's cool we're gonna be close like this. And Suzie said I'd be able to go up there all the time, to use the basketball court or the pool or whatever. We'll be able to, uh, hang out."

I continued to watch Seb closely. He stared back, and it took me a few moments to recognize *he* was also watching *me*. He was studying my behavior the same way I was studying his—noticing the little twitches as I drew my hand through my hair, picking up on the tone of my voice and the words I chose. Using those silent skills of observation that had led him to figure me out before I had figured out myself.

So what would he realize from his inspection?

That I was too nervous to sit next to him and be open about our relationship in front of a counselor and my obviously gay roommate. That I was one person when I was with him, and another when we were faced with a social situation. That I was still hiding who I really was.

Not exactly the best role model.

"Hungry yet, Sebastian?" Pamela stepped into the quiet. "We could go to the kitchen here and make some sandwiches, if you like. What do you say? You want to give the whiteboard another try?"

She'd brought it along, and again placed it in Seb's lap. He didn't even lift a hand to grasp it.

Crap.

"Do you?" I put in meekly. Even Carlos recognized how pathetic I sounded, and gave me a weird look.

Seb's dark eyes kept searing into me. I couldn't read much from the rest of his face, but there was a hint of something questioning in his steady gaze. *Well, Alex? What do you want?*

Not what did I want for lunch…but what did I want for *me*.

Decision time.

Old Alex should've been a more comfortable skin—something I could slip into with ease—but right now in this room it didn't feel that way. In fact, it was a little like those damn shoes that had changed my life. They'd been worn in all the right places, but I'd still outgrown them.

Gay Alex would probably face a lot of challenges, but so had old Alex. And while old Alex might've been content, he'd never been wildly happy. But what really sealed the deal was that I had one huge advantage over old Alex. I had Seb, and all the love Seb offered.

And love was something old Alex had never really gotten enough of.

My resolve strengthened by Seb's powerful eyes, I crossed the distance between us in two purposeful strides and sat next to him, lacing his fingers with mine. Then I shut out the rest of the room, so the only thing in my field of vision was his beautiful face.

"Seb, listen…you know I love our time together when we're alone. You *know* I love it."

His lips twitched in a quick smirk.

"But…I want you *here*…with me…all of the time. Even when there are other people around. 'Cause I'm just selfish like that."

I should've added that I'd like him to be more present when I *wasn't* around, too, but that selfishness I spoke of wasn't just a joke. I guess I did still want him to need me, in some way.

"Besides, you're an awesome person, and you really shouldn't deprive the world of you," I finished. And before I could overthink the move, I closed in for a very chaste but still square-on-the-lips kiss.

His brows lifted in surprise as I pulled away. *So that's how it's gonna be?*

"That's how it's gonna be. No more hiding."

For either of us.

He gave me a slow, dazed nod. *Okay then.*

"Yeah." I kissed him again. "It is okay."

351

Pamela let out a sigh, ending my Seb tunnel-vision. I thought she might've been angry about the kissing, but she was smiling. "I guess your social worker was right about you, Alex. Thank you."

Carlos was resting his small, pointy chin in his hands, leaning over on his desk and gawking at us. "Just my luck. I get a hot gay roommate, and he's already taken."

I caught my reflection in the closet door mirror as my skin went crimson. "You...you think I'm hot?"

Seb's hand tightened around mine and his eyes narrowed. *Watch it. You're mine.*

Carlos grinned. "Oh, and just so you know, you don't have to worry about any Jesus freaks in this house. Everyone's really cool."

Which meant of course I *would* have to worry at some point, but not even that undercurrent of reality could take away from the warmth in my heart as Seb's thumb traced my knuckles.

"All right then, boys, now I really am starving. Should we head to the kitchen?" Pamela asked.

Seb shook his head.

She smiled like he'd just popped a bottle of champagne after dropping rose petals at her feet. "No? Maybe back to the dining hall then? They do have a wider food selection."

He shook his head again.

Now her brows wrinkled in concern. "You're still not hungry? You barely even touched your dinner yesterday."

Seb started to shake his head yet again, but this time in a *that's not what I meant* kind of way. He picked up the whiteboard and worked diligently for a few seconds, holding it against his chest so not even I could see.

When he flipped it around, there was a picture of a big fat hamburger on it, complete with cheese and lettuce hanging out the sides and poppy seeds on the bun. And underneath that, spelled to perfection, he'd written:

McDonald's.

I almost let out a victorious cry, all charged up to celebrate Seb's accomplishment. But then I remembered I didn't want something like this to be an *accomplishment*. I wanted it to be a part of our everyday lives.

So I wrapped my arm around his shoulder and looked up at Pam. "Yup. What he said."

~*~

"I'm out for a bit, man. You go ahead." I tapped a chubby black-haired kid who was waiting on the sidelines. He might've been one of Seb's housemates, but I'd been too wrapped up in Seb to learn everyone's names these past few weeks.

The boy trotted off eagerly, joining the basketball game that was already underway. I wasn't really tired, but basketball still wasn't my sport. Besides, I'd thought of a better way to pass the warm spring afternoon.

Settling myself on a grassy hillside, I wrapped my arms around my knees and squinted into the sunlight. Any damage to my eyes was worth the view. Seb had taken his shirt off and thrown it carelessly on the court bench before jumping back into the game. Sweat trails danced further down his chest with each bounce of the ball, outlining his pecs and firm stomach. He faked left and then shot out to the right, springing to his toes to make the basket.

Of course, he'd needed only a basic introduction to the rules of basketball before he proved to be a natural. Far better than I was, anyway.

He grinned at me, all flushed and glossy with sweat, and I made sure to nod approvingly. It was hard to be jealous of his athletic abilities when I got to reap the benefits of that body.

Although, I could do with a little more reaping.

I was going to have to work on that—figuring out some time for us to be alone. Maybe they'd let us go on a picnic? We could find a spot of land, away from all these pesky prying eyes. Some place where I could hold him against my chest again, run my hands over his skin. Remind him of how much I loved him. Kiss him, maybe even…

Something large and gray suddenly blocked my view of Seb—Suzie, back in one of her old boring suits.

She just loved to piss on my parades.

"Hello, Alex. I was hoping I'd find you out here."

I shifted, hiding the signs of my growing appreciation for Seb on the basketball court—and Seb in my fantasies. "Hey. I hope you're not here to tell me I gotta move to a new placement or something."

"No, I'm not." She gave me an amused smile. "So you can relax."

"Shit." I puffed out a breath. "That's good. Hell, I wish I'd known all it took to get to stay here with Seb was running away. Pretty ironic, right? Wouldn't it have been easier just to skip that middle step and put me over here in the first place?"

Suzie shook her head and barely managed to stop her eyes from a roll. "Hill View is intended as a home for special needs and emotionally-challenged children. I can make recommendations, but I don't get to place people here at my will."

"Oh. Right. I guess I qualify as one of those troubled kids now."

She surprised me by dropping down to the ground, tucking her legs under her and smoothing her knee-length skirt so it covered as much as possible. "Somehow, I think you're less troubled than you used to be."

I grunted. "Then maybe you can tell me why you decided to blab me and Seb's personal business all over this place?"

"I did not *blab*, Alex. I told the people who would need to know about your relationship while you are under Hill View's care."

"But Pam and the rest of her goons…they never let us be alone. My place is like a mile away from his. And he still has to go to those special classes even though he's not *special* like that, so we can't even have school together…"

"Alex, you know Sebastian has a lot of catching up to do, education-wise. And he will need counseling and therapy, probably for many years."

"I know," I grumbled, coloring slightly at my bratty behavior. "It's just that—"

"And you remember the other thing I told you. The two of you are still young. You shouldn't force all the growing up to happen so fast—including those things that should be part of an adult relationship."

"Right. Because childhood has been such a blast, I'd just love to draw that out a little longer."

Suzie actually grinned. Seemed like my smartass comments weren't getting to her anymore. I guess she'd figured out they were just a part of my front.

She shielded her eyes to gaze out at the basketball court and neatly changed the subject. "Sebastian really seems to be enjoying himself. Did you teach him how to play?"

"Oh, uh, sorta. I bet he could teach me a thing or two now, though."

"He's a fast learner," she responded, and then burst into a sudden light-hearted chuckle. "I'm sorry." She sobered quickly. "It's just I never thought I'd get the chance to say that about Sebastian. All the therapists and psychologists and doctors who have seen him over the years…and you're the one who found him. You obviously have something special."

"Yeah. Special." I smirked, admiring the way his shoulder blades flexed as he blocked an opponent from getting close to the basket. "Then maybe we're both special."

Still caught up in Seb, I only half-saw Suzie fidgeting with her skirt hem and licking her lips. But I was starting to get the feeling she had something on her mind—some other reason for driving all the way out to Pasadena besides a casual check-up. Something that made her white cheeks a little rosy and her thin lips quirk in a smile. Good news, then.

News she just couldn't keep to herself.

"I've found them, Alex."

Chapter 28: You

The peaceful, sunny feeling in my heart abruptly vanished. I should've known my happiness was just like a handful of sand.

Confusion and fear moved in to fill the void. *I've found them.* I'd longed to hear those words once, but now…

"M-my mom? You found Hector and my mom?"

Suzie's smile dissolved. Her eyes went wide and her hand flew to her mouth. "Oh my God, Alex. I can't believe I said that. I'm so sorry. No, I haven't found them. I meant Sebastian's family. A grandmother and a cousin."

"Oh." *Idiot.* Of course. I blinked a few times, trying to fix the short-circuit in my brain as a hurricane of new emotions hit me. It was hard to pin anything down in the spinning chaos…but it would've been a lie to pretend relief wasn't a part of the picture.

And what did it say about me that I was actually *relieved* I wouldn't have to see my mother again?

"I'm so sorry." Suzie was grief-stricken, pale and practically shaking.

I blocked her out for a moment, more concerned with myself. Not because I was upset about the mix-up…but because I *wasn't*. And I didn't even feel guilty about it. "It's okay," I mumbled.

"No, Alex. That was so thoughtless of me and I—"

"Seriously. I think it might be okay," I repeated.

To prove my point, I took a breath and worked on untangling the knot in my mind. No, there was no guilt. There was a core of sadness, maybe just a touch of disappointment, and that relief I'd recognized earlier. But the truth was, I really felt okay with the idea of my mother never coming back for me. And it wasn't because I hated her, or thought she was worthless scum. I wasn't angry. I was just…ready to move on.

I thought of the photographs in the drawer, tucked away where I wouldn't have to see them. I might not've wanted to put them on display, but I'd never throw them out. Wherever I ended up in life, they'd end up, too. Maybe they'd always be in a dark drawer somewhere, but even if I never laid eyes on them again, they'd be a part of me. The part that said I'd had a mother…who'd tried and failed. That I'd had a sister who'd lost her way. That I'd had a childhood in the ghetto and it'd played its part in making me who I was today.

And then something else dawned on me. My mother had photographs, too.

"Alex?" Suzie's worried face brought me back to the brighter present—to the stiff green grass beneath my legs and the wide-open sky over my head.

"I'm okay. I think I just figured something out."

Suzie exhaled slowly, her hand twitching on her knee. "What's that?"

"I went back to my old house, with Seb, when we first ran away. There's a new family there."

She gave me a pained nod.

"And, well, my mom left all kinds of stuff that belonged to us. Furniture, clothes, the microwave…but she took the photos."

"Photos?"

"Yeah. All the pictures she had in her nightstand of me and Mimi. They weren't there anymore. I had a few in my dresser that were left behind, but she must've taken the rest. Maybe...maybe she took them because she really did love us. She just...didn't exactly know how to be a good mom."

Like Mimi. I was sort of grateful I wouldn't be having kids to carry on the family tradition of screwing the whole thing up.

"Anyways, I think...maybe that's why she left." I pushed on, my thoughts falling into place as I said them aloud. "She knew I'd be better off. And she knew if she'd stayed, I never would have stopped trying to get back. And I might have gotten my wish, eventually...and then my life would be...very different."

Suzie's nostrils flared and she swallowed slowly.

I went over my logic one more time, and it still seemed solid. "Well, that's what I've decided, anyways."

"That makes sense, Alex. That makes a lot of sense."

The sun was warm on my skin, bringing back some of my earlier calm. "Yeah. It does, huh." And maybe if I saw my mom again someday, I might even thank her...for letting me go.

A shadow fell over me, and I looked up to see Seb, wiping his face with his t-shirt. Tanned to a light gold, he had hints of freckles on his shoulders that glistened with sweat. If we'd had any place to be alone, I would have kissed each sparkling fleck and then his lips, even if they were a little dry and cracked from the heat.

Locking eyes with me, he smirked like he knew exactly what was on my mind. It also served as a pointed reminder that Suzie was beside me, and that I should keep my fantasies in check for a more convenient time.

He waved at her in greeting, and she waved back.

"You're looking well today," she began, but I interrupted.

"Seb, they found your family."

That was sort of rude of me—I should have let Suzie deliver the information herself. But I was too antsy to deal with her small talk, both because I needed to take Seb out behind a tree somewhere, and because now that the dust of not seeing my mother again had settled, my brain had finally caught up with the next reason to worry.

Seb's jaw fell open, and he squatted down beside us. *Really?*

"We've located your grandmother, Sebastian. And she'd very much like to meet you."

He blinked. Not exactly an enthusiastic response.

"Did you know you had a grandma?" I asked.

He shook his head.

"She didn't know she had a grandson, either," Suzie put in. Then she glanced over at me. "I suppose you don't mind me sharing information about your family in front of Alex, do you?"

Another firm headshake.

"Your mom was a runaway, though she ran when she was eighteen. So your grandmother never knew she was pregnant, or that she had you."

Now Seb nodded. Maybe he'd known his mother had issues with her family. And if that was the case, maybe this grandmother thing wasn't such good news after all.

Grasping a fistful of grass and soil, I stopped myself from going too far down that line of thinking…because a part of me was actually *hoping* that. The first night I'd heard Seb might have a family out there I'd been thrilled for him—but that was when I'd been in a completely selfless mode, trying to pretend my own desires didn't exist.

But they existed, all right. And now that everything finally felt right, with us here together in this safe, enclosed world, and Seb growing more confident being himself with each passing day…I just wasn't ready for things to change.

What if this family of his wanted to take him away immediately? What if they lived far away? Or didn't like Mexicans? Or didn't like *gay* Mexicans?

"She lives outside of San Diego. And this is very interesting—she was born with a unilateral vocal fold anomaly similar to the one that affects your speech, Sebastian," Suzie went on, totally unaware of my fears. "I think it'll be wonderful for you to meet her and see how she communicates."

Seb considered for a moment, tilting his head to the sunlight. Then he pointed at me and folded his arms decisively.

Suzie looked to me for a translation.

"He wants to know if I can come with him."

She laughed brightly. "Oh, I wouldn't dream of separating you against your will. Trust me."

~*~

Seb was tense. He'd started chewing his fingernails lately—a new nervous habit. I didn't like it, but I guessed it was progress when compared to the other ways he'd dealt with stress. And besides, that shrink he saw could handle the issue whenever she felt the moment was right.

I gently drew his hand away from his mouth so I could hold it. "Hey. Relax. It's gonna be okay. Suzie said she's dying to meet you. And what about her being like you, with that uni...unilateral thing? That's gonna be cool, right?"

Seb frowned.

I wondered if some of the same concerns I had were running through his mind. San Diego was a three-hour drive, and I wasn't eager for that kind of distance between us. Sometimes the mile we had to cross now seemed too much already. In the past month, I'd had to grudgingly relearn how to fall asleep without a warm body under my arm, my useless protests shot down by Suzie and my therapist. They just kept insisting our time apart would only help me appreciate our future "mature" relationship even more.

Thank God that magical age of adulthood was only two years away.

"She's gonna love you, Seb. No one who knows you could do anything different."

He smiled weakly, squeezing my hand. *Thanks.*

Of course, there was still that gay elephant in the room. But Seb hadn't brought it up, so I wasn't going to. And I knew Suzie had enough common sense to keep that from his grandmother. At least for now.

She glanced at us in her rearview mirror. She couldn't read Seb like I could, but the way I'd captured his hand and refused to let it go probably gave her a clue.

"We'll stay as long as you feel comfortable, Sebastian. I did get the background check and clearance for an overnight visit, if you wanted, but that won't happen today."

Seb's fingers tugged out of my grip with some force, and he reached for the whiteboard at his feet. Using the attached marker, he scrawled, *dus she wont?*

"She wants us to stay for an overnight visit?" I read aloud for Suzie. I added the *us* because I couldn't stand the thought of Seb being alone with some strange people, especially people who had caused his mother to run away.

Suzie nodded. "She does, eventually."

The dread in my heart began to solidify, and suddenly I was grabbing Seb's hand for my own comfort instead of his. She wanted him to stay the night. Which meant she probably wanted him to stay, *permanently.*

Seb wasn't in a mood to talk, so I concentrated on the orange and red mountains dotted with scraggly patches of green. That plant-life just kept fighting for its chance to exist, roots clinging to life around all the clay and rocks. I wanted to cling to Seb that way…but not at the cost of his happiness.

Eventually we drove into a community of small, older homes. Nothing very special, and I knew a poorer neighborhood when I saw one. Still, the houses were fairly well kept, and the families of various shades of brown scattered across yards and porches seemed at ease with their surroundings.

"Looks nice here," I whispered to Seb. He raised a doubtful brow. "I mean, not like fancy or anything…but nice and normal."

We both grinned. *Normal* wasn't really our normal. But it did hold promise.

Suzie pulled her Corolla into the driveway of a squat little bungalow and the engine went off, sputtering a few times before we were left in silence.

"Remember Sebastian, if this is too much for you at any time, I want you to let me or Alex know, okay? I don't want you to get overwhelmed."

She didn't want him to retreat in on himself, is what she meant. And maybe it was a risk to be bringing him here so soon after he'd settled into any sort of routine as a fully-functional person, but I didn't really think he'd disappear again. Not unless his grandmother turned around and smacked him or something.

I shuddered. Who was I supposed to tell if this was too much for *me*?

A woman emerged from the house. She stopped a few feet from the car and clasped her hands together as she waited for us to come out.

"That's your cousin, Diane," Suzie said. I'd seen a picture, but she looked a little older in person, even if she'd shoved her hair into pigtails.

My fingers clenched around Seb's one last time before I rapidly drew them away. There'd be no more handholding while we were here.

Suzie got out and greeted Diane as Seb and I followed more slowly.

"Don't be scared," I whispered, feeling his presence close behind me. Again, it was more for myself than for him.

Diane was a cheerful brunette, with an over-enthusiastic smile and a shine to her eyes that probably meant she'd be crying sometime soon. Her skin was beige and it was hard to pin down her ethnicity, but there were hints of something exotic in her mix.

"Hello, Alex, right?" She smiled at me first, since Seb was still hanging back. "Suzie told me what a good friend you've been to Sebastian." I shot a look at Suzie that she pretended not to notice. "I'm Sebastian's first cousin once removed...though I guess maybe I feel more like an aunt. I'm an only child, so I don't have any actual nieces or nephews..." she trailed off, either because she knew she was rambling, or because she was busy peeking over my shoulder to get a better view of Seb.

I turned to him. "Don't be so shy." Even as the words came out, my mind fought back. *Hide! Act cold and uninterested and then maybe we can go back to our regular messed-up lives!*

He stepped around me, and Diane held out her hand. "It's so nice to meet you, Sebastian."

Seb eyed her for a moment, and it occurred to me this might've been one of the few times anyone had greeted him like that—like he was fully self-aware instead of just *special*.

His gaze drifted to me—for reassurance, I guessed. I gave him a tight nod.

With a hesitant grip, he shook her hand.

The front door opened again and an older woman walked onto the porch. She was a little darker than Diane, with the same long, straight hair Seb had drawn for his mother, though this woman's was streaked with silver. She also had the same almond eyes, and the same sharp angles in her face.

Definitely a family resemblance.

She walked slowly, but not like she suffered from arthritis. More like someone who'd seen enough in her life to know you didn't let moments like this fly by. Regal to the last step, her small, sturdy body came to a stop in front of Seb, where she looked him over from head to toe.

Her black eyes became two reflective pools as they filled with emotion. *"My grandson,"* she rasped in a strange-sounding gulp of air.

"Holy shit," I mumbled, but thankfully it was under my breath. Then I added a little louder, "We didn't think you could talk."

His grandmother's hands started to fly about, and Diane jumped in a second later. "She prefers to sign now. I'm so very happy to meet you, Sebastian. I never imagined I'd get this chance. You look very much like Selena—your mother."

I saw the anxiety lift from Seb's features, his brows perking up with curiosity. There was no way to deny it now—this really was his family.

"Why don't we head inside?" Suzie suggested.

Obediently, we all filed in. A tray with iced tea and cookies was set out in the living room, where Seb and I stiffly took our seats.

I didn't find anything too unexpected inside the small house. The dark floors shone with a fresh layer of what smelled like orange oil, and a couple of paintings of Native American huts hung in frames on the wall. Nothing looked expensive, but all the furniture was real hardwood and it was old, the scratches of time carefully recoated with stain and finish. Some tarnished silver platters sat next to a row of books on a shelf, along with an old wooden crucifix propped up in the corner.

That last sight did cause some concern. I hadn't gone to church in almost ten years, so the God I called upon in moments of need didn't scare me. But the one usually tied to that crucifix made me uncomfortable, if only because the people I'd known who clung to it—like José's mother—would never have accepted me as I was.

And how would Seb be accepted here? I bit down on the inside of my cheek as fear started to grow.

"Would you like some iced tea?" Diane asked, pouring us all glasses before we could respond. "It's getting hot out there, isn't it?"

Seb's grandmother quietly walked over to her bookshelf and pulled down a large album. She handed it to Seb as she sat beside him.

Her hands danced again, and Diane translated. "I'd like for you to look through it and see pictures of Selena."

Seb's chest rose and fell a few times before he cracked open the spine. On the first page were a bunch of baby photographs, two tiny footprints, and a lock of brown hair. His fingers slid toward the hair, and when he touched it, he inhaled sharply.

Then he started flying through the pages, hunching over to study them and partially blocking my view. I caught sight of a beautiful, dark-haired child, occasionally surrounded by friends, including a skinny girl with pigtails and braces. The ages progressed, and I gathered that the gangly girl was Diane. The gorgeous one was Seb's mother, obviously, and when Seb arrived at one of her in her late teens, he reached under the plastic covering and yanked it out.

Cupping the photo in his palm, he bit his lip, probably to keep it from trembling.

"She was so beautiful," Diane murmured. "And such a good person." The tears I'd predicted were making an appearance, and she grabbed at a napkin to dab them away. "We were like sisters, growing up. I used to live here with her and Aunt Maria after my mom passed away."

Seb's grandmother—Maria—took her hand and smiled in comfort.

Seb flipped forward a couple more pages, keeping the photograph of his mother in his lap. He stopped again when he saw a few of her looking thin and frail, her long dark hair drowning out a weak smile.

Maria explained as Diane interpreted. "I didn't realize at first. I was a fool. I was too busy working and she wanted to be young and free and I'd always trusted her. I should have asked more questions, I should have figured out sooner—"

"No, no," Diane interrupted her own translation. "I'm the one who knew. I knew the kind of people she was hanging out with. I knew what they did...I just never thought that...that it'd take her *away* like that..."

"*You were a child*," Maria whispered in her breathy voice.

"Seb?" Suzie placed her iced tea on the coffee table and leaned toward him. "Are you all right?"

He was frozen, still staring at the photograph, but he broke from the moment and gave her a nod.

"Maybe we should save some of this discussion for another visit," Suzie began.

Now he shot me a pleading look, shaking his head. *No. I'm fine. Tell her I can handle this.*

"Um...I think he wants to know." I ventured into the conversation warily. I felt like an intruder, sitting there in front of the sculpted wood coffee table and the homemade cookies and the book full of some other family's memories.

Diane snatched another napkin. "We did what we could. I tried to talk to her, and things seemed better for a while. Maria spent every penny she had in savings to send her to that fancy rehab...but then she just ran away. And she was eighteen, so the cops wouldn't do anything."

Seb's fingers began to twitch, and I realized he'd left the whiteboard in the car. I scrambled up to retrieve it for him, eager for the chance to get away.

Because it was all starting to come together now. Drugs had robbed Selena of the nice, loving family in that little home. And then they'd robbed Seb of his family, too. And it was a tragedy, of course...but it seemed like it was no one's fault, and there was nothing really standing in the way of Suzie putting what was left of that family back together.

It wasn't jealousy, but there was something souring in my stomach.

I returned and handed the board to Seb, then watched over his shoulder as he wrote, *she wus a gud mom*. Before he could display it, I grabbed the marker and changed the *u* in *wus* into an *a*, just because it seemed like a word he'd need often. Unless Maria and Diane taught him some of that sign language. Maybe he wouldn't need me at all, then.

Seb flipped the board for them to see, and both women nodded, tears springing to their eyes. I didn't know how good she could've been, considering the way she'd left Seb…but I supposed we all told ourselves those little partial truths to make life easier.

Diane got up next, returning with a couple of yearbooks so we could go back to a happier period of time. She opened one to an elementary school picture of Selena—with a flashy side ponytail, and Seb cracked a smile. His finger moved down to trace her name: Selena *Woods*. Since there was no father in Seb's life, it might as well have been his last name, too.

Sebastian Woods. He wasn't a mystery child anymore.

When we'd been through what felt like a thousand pictures, we moved on to a brief tour of the house. There was a decent-sized backyard with an avocado tree and a chicken coop, a small kitchen tucked away in the far corner of the home, and two bedrooms. The second of those was a guest room, but I had a feeling it'd been set up for one guest in particular.

Seb took a step inside and craned his neck to look at it from every angle. It had been his mother's room, once. Now, the walls were a grayish-blue, bathed in direct sunlight from a large window, and the bed was covered with a handmade quilt. There was a desk in the corner with what looked like a brand new computer sitting on top, parts of it still in the packaging. New notebooks and pens lined the shelf, along with a framed portrait of Selena, young and smiling and happy.

The room was meant for Seb. The family was meant for Seb. And I was meant to…let him have it.

I didn't speak through the dinner of mashed potatoes and roast beef. Seb's grandmother didn't add much to the conversation, either, but that was probably because Diane basically never shut up. She wanted to tell us all about her father who cared for her but couldn't have raised a girl on his own, and Maria who was the second mother she'd been so lucky to have, and the little house she'd moved into down the road. And about how excited she was to have another cousin after all these years, and how she couldn't wait to show him around the neighborhood, to all those places she and Selena had liked to hang out at when they were kids.

Somewhere in the middle of a tale about a snake on Selena's favorite hiking trail, Seb yawned.

"He's tired," I announced, surprised by the volume of my voice. I hadn't meant to be that loud, or that excited. But Seb's yawn held the promise of leaving, and I couldn't wait to be alone with him again, to hold him and kiss him and slip back into the private little peace we'd found in each other's arms.

His grandmother bobbed her head in agreement.

"Maybe he could rest in the bedroom for a while?" Diane suggested.

Suzie nodded. "That sounds like a good idea. And Alex, maybe you might like to watch some TV in the living room? I do have some things I need to discuss with Maria and Diane."

Fuck.

Diane came with us and ushered Seb into the bedroom. "If there's anything you need, we put a bell by the nightstand." She flashed him that overly bright smile as she headed out, her hand on my shoulder to drag me along.

"No cable, I'm afraid," she chattered on, seating me on the couch and handing me a remote. "But you just make yourself at home."

And then she was off again, darting into the kitchen to get back to that *discussing* she and Suzie had to do.

I didn't even think about turning on the TV. Channeling all my energy into my hearing, I grasped wisps of conversation.

"I think a gradual transition would be best. From occasional visits to just weekends at first, to see how he adjusts."

"Of course. And we'd like to start as soon as possible."

"He still needs a lot of support. And right now, the psychiatrist is not recommending any sudden dramatic changes. The trauma he experienced as a child caused some deep psychological damage, and he really has only started to come out of it very recently—first with his friend Alex, and with everyone else, only for about a month."

There was a bit of whimpering—Diana, no doubt.

"We understand. We don't want to do anything to upset his recovery...but we do want him to find a home here."

Going into self-defense mode, my brain tried to shut out the rest. The words "custody" and "adoption" managed to sneak through anyhow, and I eventually sank my head to my knees, breathing short, strained breaths into the dark space between my legs.

It was Seb's happily ever after. The only problem was, I wasn't going to be a part of it.

And I shouldn't even try. I should let him go, like I'd been prepared to do before. Step out of the shadow of his life and back into my own. I shouldn't make his transition into his family any harder than it had to be. As my mother had done for me, I should cut ties and let him find a new happiness as a loved little boy, because sixteen wasn't too old to have a childhood, so long as I wasn't there trying to make us grow up even faster...

I jerked my head suddenly, though I didn't know why until my eyes locked onto Seb, who was standing in the hallway that led to his bedroom. I tried to wipe the despair from my face but it was a lost cause.

He signaled for me.

I shook my head.

He motioned for me again, this time with more force. *I said, come here.*

Feeling like a scolded child, I got up and followed.

He was sitting on the bed by the time I got in there, under the covers, and he patted the spot beside him.

"That's not such a good idea," I mumbled, looking at my shoes.

He rose quickly and shut the bedroom door. This time, he took me by the hand so he could force me onto the bed.

"Seb...we shouldn't do this."

He wrapped his arm around me to push my body onto the mattress.

"Seb..."

His fingers moved against my back, giving me a gentle rub.

"Seb, you don't understand. We can't do this. We can't do this here. You know there are people out there who don't like...people like us."

I closed my eyes so I didn't have to see the look in his.

"I've been thinking about this..." *And we should run away again. Escape somewhere new...join a group of generous hippies or live off the land...*

"I think...I think maybe we should cool it for a little while, you know? Because your grandma and your cousin, they really like you. I mean, they really, *really* like you. They want you in their lives and they've only known you for an afternoon. They're the kind of people who know you're their blood and are ready to give you anything you need to have a successful life. Do you know how *lucky* you are?"

A snort caused me to open my eyes. God, I did sort of sound like Suzie right now.

Seb drew closer, his warm breath on my lips.

"But you do get that not everyone can handle people like us, right? I mean…gay people. And I don't think this is something we should bring up right now, because you don't know how your grandmother will react…and you just can't risk this, Seb. You can't risk what you have here. You can't give this up. They're your *family*!"

Seb drew his hand back, and with a frightening burst of speed, jabbed a finger straight into my chest. The impact sent waves of pain shooting out from the small spot where he now touched me. There'd be a bruise there, soon. A tiny, round mark left on the shield of my heart.

Seb opened his mouth. "*You.*"

It was a harsh, scraping syllable. Hardly a beautiful sound by any stretch of the imagination. And barely louder than a whisper. But I'd heard it. I'd *heard* it!

He poked me again, gentler now, and though no more noise emerged, his lips moved slowly and deliberately so I could read every word.

You are my family.

"Oh, God, Seb." Before I could start weeping like a little schoolgirl, I drew him against me, seeking the heat of his mouth. He closed the distance between us and silenced my stupid fears with a steady, sweet kiss.

We're in this crazy life together.

I slipped my hands under his shirt, locking onto his back. Maybe he was my mountain, and maybe I was his. I wasn't going to question it anymore. I was going to hold on for all I was worth.

More kisses followed—his along my cheeks and temples, mine down his neck and into the dip of his collarbone. I even kissed his fingertips, one at a time, as his lids drooped and his legs tangled with mine. And when the warmth from his body and from the small, sun-struck room started to make me drowsy, I brushed his lips one last time and tried to draw away.

He didn't let me go, and my eyes slowly drifted closed.

~*~

I knew something was wrong before I woke up. Seb's body was rigid against mine, every muscle tightened and his neck straining like he was trying to lift his head off the pillow.

When I heard nothing for several seconds, I cracked open a lid and saw his grandmother staring at us from the doorway.

I instinctively jerked back, but found myself locked in place by Seb's unmoving arms. He was wide awake, and staring right back at her with a squared jaw and the fire of defiance in his eyes.

I'd never seen him look so confident before. Where had he gained all that strength? I'd never had that. I'd faked it, sure, but never really felt it. Maybe I could borrow a little of his strength now, to face whatever we had coming.

His grandmother continued to study us, her dark eyes wide and barely blinking. Seb gritted his teeth. I could almost imagine a telepathic conversation taking place between them as the seconds of silence ticked by.

Then, with that same slow beauty I'd seen earlier, her lips spread into a smile.

Seb's body collapsed back into the mattress. I felt his quickened heartbeat as my hand slipped over his chest and realized he hadn't been at all sure of this outcome. And maybe some of his strength had been a front, too, but that didn't make me any less proud.

His grandmother's expression changed then—into one that needed no words to be understood.

With an eyebrow raised and a finger pointed in gentle reprimand, she propped open the bedroom door as wide as it would go. *And you boys make sure it stays that way.*

I met her gaze sheepishly, and the warm smile returned before she walked away.

The moment she disappeared around the corner, Seb grabbed hold of me, crushing my chest in his powerful embrace. Little bursts of air tickled my skin as he laughed, kissed me, and laughed some more.

Eyes bright with happy tears, he wove our fingers together under the handmade quilt.

Welcome home, Alex.

ABOUT THE AUTHOR

Sara Alva is a former small-town girl currently living in big-city LA with a husband, two cats, and an avocado tree. She recently discovered— after a year in her house— that she also has a fig tree in her backyard, which might mean she needs to get out more. But sometimes the stories waiting to be told demand more attention, and when she puts fingers to keyboard, it's usually to write about journeys of self-discovery, heartache, personal growth, friendship and love. When she isn't writing, she's teaching or dancing.

For information, free reads and news on upcoming releases, visit http://SaraAlva.com/.

Other Works by Sara Alva
Social Skills
Pura Vida

CPSIA information can be obtained
at www.ICGtesting.com
Printed in the USA
LVHW091338180421
684838LV00008B/107